This book is dedicated to my mother. My mom has been listening to me tell her about all the strange and crazy stuff my imagination comes up with my whole life, and she has always been supportive and encouraging.
Mom, thank you for everything, and I love you.

WASTELAND PATROL

SERVICE TERM
BOOK 2

NICHOLAS TAYLOR

Wasteland Patrol

ISBN-13: 978-1-938387-14-2

www.NicholasTaylor.co

CONTENTS

ONE

I felt the sun baking my skin as I lounged in the beach chair. It was almost uncomfortably hot; another degree, and the burn would turn from pleasure to discomfort. A breeze picked up off the water, cooling me slightly. With my left hand, I reached out, wrapping my fingers around an ice-cold glass. Its coolness pulled heat from my hand as I raised the glass to my lips, the ice cubes clinking against the glass and each other. I didn't have a clue what the drink was. I'd told the system to bring me something refreshing, and it had done just that. Whatever it was, it had plenty of sugar in it, giving it what would normally be a sickeningly sweet taste; but with the heat and salty air of the sea, the cold and sweet were a perfect counterbalance. With my right hand, I gently squeezed Krista's. The sea air filled my nose as I breathed in and sighed contentedly.

"I'm not going back," I said matter-of-factly, referring to the leave we were on.

Krista chuckled. "Okay, me either… but you know they'll kick us out if we don't come back."

"Yes, and I'll stay right here on the beach."

"That too. This resort caters to HFDF, remember?" she said playfully.

I turned my head to look at her. Krista's brown hair danced in the breeze, her blue eyes hidden behind sunglasses. "You and the details. Shhh."

She laughed. "Is that an order?"

I thought for a moment. "Yes."

She laughed again. "I do think I could stay here forever."

"Now you're talking," I said, giving her hand another squeeze.

I knew I couldn't stay here forever. Not just for legal reasons, but because in about three days, I would go from the relaxing kind of bored to the annoying type of bored and swear off weekends like this again.

Before this leave, we'd been training on a dead world for over a month. It was cool, don't get me wrong, but it was nice not having to be buttoned down in my suit for fear of dying in the cold vacuum of space. While seeing more stars than I thought possible was something that would always stay with me and amaze me in an almost spiritual way, I was really enjoying Hunter's rays right now. I thought most of what we did was fun, but I always had the thought in the back of my mind that I needed to pay attention to what I was learning in case the day came when the bullets weren't fake and my team or I could get hurt or die.

Sitting here on the beach with Krista, I didn't have that concern. I wasn't worried about ever being in a combat situation that required sunbathing. The other nice part about not being in the cold depths of death was that I could actually see my girlfriend. I could hold her hand without a nano-material suit and look at her face instead of her helmet. Her skin was soft and smooth, and I was seeing her the way most people took for granted.

For us, our relationship was a combination of physical isolation from each other to being pressed together with nothing between us. This made Krista's and my relationship unique. Much of it was mental and emotional, like long-distance relationships, yet we saw each other daily and spent nearly all our time together. Being in the HFDF forced us to adapt to a different way of life.

Krista smiled again and looked out at the water. I did the same. We were right on Orion's equator. The ocean before us glittered with light. All around were people in black nano-material bathing suits. The hotel was right against the water, with plenty of stairs for easy access.

This hotel was one of the few places where HFDF members didn't have to wear their suits and be armed. In normal life, we wore our combat suits with a sidearm unless we were in our bunks or homes. We didn't really need to be combat-ready at all times; our planets and stations were safe from attack, but the constant readiness was a holdover from earlier days of the Human Federation when perceived safety outside of Earth's cradle wasn't so certain. Our suits and sidearms sent a clear message: We are always ready. Even in our down-time, we are prepared for anything. This was a point of pride, but sometimes I just wanted to sit on the beach without being covered from foot to chin in a skin-tight suit. There were only a handful of places where HFDF members could let down their hair, so to speak. Places like this resort. It was hard not to want to stay here forever.

We lounged for a bit longer until my Cerebral Central Processing Unit, or CCPU, pinged me that our shuttle to Orion City would leave in a couple of hours. We got up and started back to our room, which was on the second level. I let Krista walk up the stairs in front of me. I wasn't about to throw away one of the last chances I would get in months or years to stare at my girlfriend's ass in a bikini. And why would I? After all, Krista McLeod had a truly, wonderfully, spectacularly amazing ass, in my humble opinion.

On the note of clothing, for all the time HFDF members spent covered in our suits, you'd think we would be modest in the extreme, but we weren't—at least not around our own. The beach and resort were filled with people who kept their bodies in optimal shape, all wearing little black bathing suits that generally left little to the imagination. It was like a communal gift we all gave to each other. Like a 'here ya go, you earned this' for living in our suits.

Krista and I were nude every night when we slept, but in a tight bunk where you honestly didn't see much. Now she walked in front of me, only covered by a tasteful but very revealing bikini. All of a sudden, I was hit with thoughts of her soft skin and curves, along with the motion of her body. My heart fluttered just a bit. We walked into the room, Krista slowing at the base of the bed, looking around for her things. I came up to her, placing my hands on her hips, feeling her soft, warm skin, and kissed her shoulders. She faced me and wrapped her arms around my neck. I bent my head, kissing her. Her blue eyes sparkled.

"I know what you're thinking," she said with an expectant smile.

"I think I know what you're thinking too," I replied.

I smiled and kissed her again, feeling her lips mold to mine. I wrapped my arms around her waist, loving the feel of her silky skin against me. I sucked on her lower lip, enjoying the slight tension as she pressed into me a little more. Her lips parted, and I kissed her deeper; her tongue flicked out, teasing mine.

I chuckled. "We definitely have the same idea," I said huskily.

I kissed her, my lips parting hers, running my tongue along the roof of her mouth. A delightful sigh escaped her. My hand moved slowly up and down her back, and my heart raced, arousal building with each kiss. She kissed me back more deeply, her hands moving from my neck down my shoulders and arms. She stepped back and looked up at me, her gaze making my heart flip and seem to stop for a moment before it started beating again. Her hands touched my chest.

Her lips twitched into a lopsided smile. "I think we should make full use of this room before we don't have it anymore."

"Do you now?" I teased.

She nodded. I felt her hands on my hips, and she pushed. I sat back on the bed and moved up it as Krista climbed on top of me. I kissed her again, thoroughly looking forward to the last moments of our vacation. She straddled me, pressing her hips down on me. I groaned softly, my hand moving up her side to cup her breast. She moaned softly as I teased her nipple with my thumb. Her grin widened as she removed the top of her suit.

I wasn't sure there would ever be a moment in my life when I wouldn't love the sight of her taking off her top. There was something about it that always seemed to shoot to my core. My hands moved up and down her thighs. My fingers moved up her sides, and traced the curve of her breasts, enjoying how firm and soft they were under my touch. I kissed her again, hearing her sigh as my thumb gently rubbed her hard nipples, making her skin prickle with goosebumps.

I could feel myself getting hard quickly, and a zing of pleasure shot through me as her hips pressed down. The feeling intensified as she began to grind slowly.

"Fuck," I breathed between kisses.

She chuckled darkly, the sound seductive and full of lust. She let out soft moans as she moved against the bulge in my swim trunks. Her breath hitched.

"You know what I think I like most about these beds?" she asked breathily.

I felt her hand slide down my body to my crotch.

I moaned softly. "What do you like most about them?" I breathed.

She chuckled again. "The leverage," she purred.

I couldn't argue with that. I gave the command to my CCPU, and my trunks slid off, forming a small block at my side. At the same time, Krista's bottoms did the same, and suddenly there she was against me. My heart hammered as I kissed her deeply. She slid her slit up and down my shaft in the most heavenly way. I groaned and heard a satisfying moan from her as she moved. Her hips lifted, and then she slid down, her expression tightening in a mask of pleasure. Ecstasy surged through me as I sank into her; my thumb pressed at the top of her slit, feeling the tight bundle of nerves. I began to rub as she moved up and down, her hips rocking.

"Oh God, Alex," she whimpered.

I grinned, loving the sound of it. "Do you want me to do the thing?" I asked, my voice tight with pleasure, "so you can enjoy that leverage?"

Her head bobbed. "Y-yes," she said as she moved.

I never felt more sorry for pre-ageless people than I did during sex. Edging with a CCPU was so much more effective than it could ever be without one. Each of us could take ourselves right to the edge of oblivion and then dial down the sensitivity so we didn't go over that edge. Then do it all over again. You didn't even have to pay much attention to it; your CCPU could keep you riding that rollercoaster for as long as you wanted. We didn't do it often in our bunk, but on a normal bed?

My thumb swirled around her clit as she moved up and down on me. I felt my pleasure build rapidly as she pulsed around me, and I groaned, nearing release. As I got to the edge, the sensation nearly stopped. My heart still pounded, and I could still feel her move, but it was easy to control myself.

I grinned, my hand moving to her hips, guiding her. My other hand went to the back of her neck, pulling her face to mine for a kiss. A moment later, my sensation came roaring back, and I growled as her hips rocked.

We lost ourselves in it for a while until Krista clamped down around me, her body shuddering. She moaned deeply, and I watched the pleasure on her face as she went over the edge. My hips moved below her, pushing up inside her, letting her ride out her orgasm. As she finished, I told my CCPU to let me go all the way.

"Time to use that leverage, baby," I groaned.

"Yes, sir," she purred, leaning back.

As she did, exhilaration surged through me, and she began to move up and down, her body enveloping mine. I felt energy building inside me, getting more intense with each movement until pure euphoria washed over me as I released. I heard her moan and whimper as I throbbed inside her. Her walls clenched and pulsed around me, sending waves of bliss through me. She stopped moving, and we both panted. She lay down on top of me, her skin hot and sweaty against mine.

"Now that's how to end a vacation," I commented between breaths.

She laughed. "We need to take more vacations then."

Later, we grabbed our suits. It was time to go. Vacation, while not technically over until we reported back to the ship, was effectively over. I integrated with my suit, and it slid over my body, covering me like a second skin. In all fairness to the HFDF, the suits we were required to wear were some of the most comfortable things I'd ever worn in my life. I just didn't want to wear it because it was mandatory. I was sure when the day came that I left the HFDF, my first purchase would be a suit as close as possible to the one I had now.

The suits were one of the things that I hadn't expected to have such a profound impact on my life. With them, I could feel everything around me or toggle just the sensations I wanted. I could go into vacuum with them. They regulated my temperature, keeping me perfectly comfortable, made me stronger, and so on. They weren't very common planetside, but off-planet, suits like these were everywhere. Some people wore them under normal clothes, and in some places, they were the norm. While our suits were tailored to life in the HFDF, they were designed for every type of work and environment imaginable.

Once suited up, we checked our room for anything we might have left behind. Of course, there wasn't anything. We hadn't brought much to begin with—just sunglasses and the little blocks of nano-material that acted as bathing suits. Those were now molding to the thighs of our suits. We'd stow them back on the ship.

As we left the resort, a small bus waited outside. We got on, joining groups of civilians from other resorts. Krista and I sat in the back of the bus as it started to pull away. A little kid next to us eyed us with curiosity. While I was used to seeing HFDF members, most people weren't; we were one of the smaller branches of the government. His parents smiled politely and told him not to stare. The father gave us furtive looks. I knew those looks—I knew the conversation he was probably going to start. I sighed inwardly.

"So... how are things in the defense forces?" he asked.

Conversations like the one I was about to have were becoming more common. Our sergeant, John Monroe, told us that before Pike Prime, normal people didn't think much about the HFDF. They were thankful for us but didn't think about us. Why would they? The Human Federation was safe, and the HFDF could kick the asses of anything out there without issue, right? Everyone knew differently now. People recognized we were still top dogs, but we could take some hits, and that frightened many.

"Pretty good, just coming off some leave," I said.

He smiled as if that made him happy. Maybe it did. If we were on leave, everything must be right in the universe, right? Then he looked like he wanted to ask something but didn't want to be rude. That was fair enough.

"You want to ask about Pike Prime, don't you?" I said, trying to sound amused.

His face fell slightly. "Sorry."

"It's fine. Honestly, right now, I don't know much more than the news reports. I haven't checked in on it in a while," I said.

He nodded. "Did you?"

"Yes," was all I said.

The mother, who I assumed had been eavesdropping, turned to us. "Do you think there will be any other problems?" she asked apologetically.

This was also pretty normal. People wanted assurance, and even though I had no ability to know if there would be any other trouble, nor did I have decision-making power, I was closer to the situation than they were. Which, like it or not, gave me some perceived credibility.

I understood their concerns. They had one kid, and for all I knew, they had a ton more. They wanted to know if they and their family were safe from some of the meanest things the Human Federation Defense Forces had ever dealt with.

"I don't think we need to worry about the Venom anymore," I said.

They looked relieved to hear me say it. I wasn't saying anything the government hadn't already said; it was just that the news came from someone who had been there and was right next to them. That meant more.

"I don't see us getting into any conflicts anytime soon either," I continued. "Well, not unless we have to. I guess I should say I don't see the Hunter system getting into anything else. We still have troops on Pike Prime and a few on Erie Prime. We aren't spread thin, but if something comes up, they'll send other systems."

They perked up. "You're sure?" the woman asked.

"Pretty sure," I responded. "Again, Hunter has more than enough for defense, but if the HFDF needs to engage with anything else, there are lots of other systems that aren't currently engaged. As for the war on Pike Prime, it had been brewing for some time, and as for Erie Prime, they were looking for trouble and happened to have the poor luck to start it with us. If they'd attacked one of the hundreds of other species out there, they could have gotten themselves into a nice long, crippling war that could last decades or centuries. They might have won, or they might not have. As it was, they attacked someone too high up the food chain."

This seemed to satisfy them. There wasn't any other conversation for the rest of the way to the port. We checked in and boarded the shuttle to Orion City. Although we were heading to Orion Station, we were going to the Lift Terminal first. I'd found direct flights to the station, but there was only one a day that left in the morning. It would have saved us a couple of hours, but we would have just spent the afternoon sitting around on the ship. It was also four times the cost. Fuck that.

The PA boomed with an animated voice explaining the shuttle's safety features and what to do in case of an emergency. It skipped over the part that if something happened, it would probably take place just outside Orion's atmosphere and that when you fell and hit said atmosphere, you'd burn up and die. In the unlikely event that you didn't die in the fireball stage, you always had hitting the ground or ocean at terminal velocity to look forward to. But the seats floated, so no worries, right?

I was surprised as a quick CCPU search revealed most people in shuttle accidents typically survived the atmosphere, and it was the fall that killed them. It turned out the shuttles had a decent amount of shielding and traveled at a relatively low speed in space terms. Lucky me, my suit's space anchor would keep me alive if I made it clear of the shuttle. A CCPU search revealed the last shuttle accident in the Human Federation had occurred six years ago with zero loss of life. I didn't feel bad about ignoring the safety instructions.

I felt a small prickling sensation all over my body for a moment as the artificial gravity kicked in. The shuttle's system wasn't as good as a spaceship, but the sensation stopped almost immediately. Outside the window, the ground slowly started falling away. After a few minutes, the main engines started up, and the shuttle vibrated ever so slightly. The further up we got, the more the throttle was opened. The shuttle shook lightly. Again, it didn't have the most robust gravity control system, nor should it have. This thing was a puddle jumper and wasn't going to other planets or systems. I'd take a slight vibration over the hours of travel my parents endured when they were my age, flying on planes.

The shuttle rolled and headed toward Orion City. Part of me regretted the lack of direct flights, but I understood. Unless you were arriving or departing from Orion, there was no need to go to the station. While vast, it had limited space. Most people on this shuttle lived on Orion. Having to go to the station and pay docking fees just for people to return planetside would be a pain in the ass and a waste of money.

It took less than an hour to reach Orion City. The Lift terminal was part of the main port, and we exited and took a tram to our concourse.

"Dinner? I know it's early and all, but…" Krista asked.

"Yeah, we won't be on the station for a few more hours. Pho?" I suggested.

Her response was to make a beeline for the closest Pho restaurant. Like so many concourse restaurants, it didn't look out at the Lift but onto the busy hall in front of the restaurant. Krista and I ate, enjoying the hot soup and watching people move around like cattle. After dinner, we joined the herd and boarded the Lift.

No matter how many times I'd been on it, I loved watching Orion fall away as the sky turned from blue to stars and the inky blackness of space as we traveled up the elevator. The view of the planet below never failed to inspire awe. Nor did seeing the countless ships that were above the planet, from small shuttles to large mining and cargo vessels, created a scene of constant motion around the station. The station itself always amazed me; it was huge, with docks and ships jutting out from it like little hairs.

We were in luck. The Arbiter, the troop ship we lived on, was docked, so we didn't need to board another shuttle. It did take us four tram rides, though—first planet problems, I know.

It felt like coming home as I stepped onto the Arbiter. My steps felt light as we made our way to our squad's rooms. It didn't matter how nice of a place you'd been to; coming home always felt good. Most of our squad was in the room when we arrived. Some were talking at the table in the center, while others lounged in their bunks. Krista greeted people, and I pulled up a feed of everything we had for tomorrow. And with that, I was back at work.

Vacation was over.

TWO

My CCPU's alarm woke me at 0700. Krista shifted in my arms as her CCPU woke her up. I integrated with my suit, and it slid over my body. Once Krista was in hers, we rolled, and the screen to the bunk opened, letting us out. There was an art to rolling out of a bunk without looking like it was your first day in training; Krista and I had discovered there was a whole other layer to this when there were two of you. It was the difference between leaving your significant other's place the next morning and the walk of shame.

Around us, others in our squad were emerging from their bunks. This room and bunk had been my home since graduating from the HFDF training base on Arrow a little over a year ago. It would continue to be my home for the rest of my five-year term of service. I greeted the newest member of my fireteam, Melanie Clay. She was tall and thin, with long red hair. She'd replaced James Meyers, who'd been killed on Pike Prime. I liked Clay a lot. She was easy to be around and, more importantly, she was a good team member. James hadn't been either of those things, and I sometimes felt guilty for preferring Clay over my fallen teammate. Not so much that I was betraying him, but rather what it said about me.

Betts and Sweeting were out of their bunks now. I'd been with them and Krista since day one in the service. Sweeting was of average height, with dark skin and a bright smile that never really wavered. He was light-hearted and always kept the team in a good mood. Betts was a bit taller than Sweeting, with short tan hair and a short beard; Betts loved everything about the HFDF, and I had no doubt he'd be in it for decades, if not centuries, to come. We'd been in two wars together. With Clay, I'd fought on Pike Prime. The team had turned into a family for me. And at the center of it, Krista. Someone I hadn't thought was anything special when I'd met her, and now I wasn't sure I could live without her.

We left the room, getting out of the way for the other fireteam in our squad, led by Veronica Royle, a slender woman with long brown hair and piercing green eyes. We walked down the Arbiters' halls to the head, queuing up with other shipmates. When it was my turn, I entered the shower, a cylindrical room with automated water jets and fans for cleaning and drying you off. It was like a car wash for people.

After our showers, we walked down the passages of the ship to the mess hall. The passages were wide enough for several people to walk shoulder to shoulder. The floor, walls, and ceiling were the same flat gray color, with nano-material in a honeycomb pattern giving it texture. The lights ran along the corners. The floor, wall, and ceiling had seams showing the outline of handholds and defense systems that would appear if needed.

The mess was a large room with tables and benches running in rows. During breakfast, the others in my team talked and joked as I went over reports and informational updates. There were some cons to being a fireteam leader, but I liked the job for the most part. I worked closely with Royle in the other fireteam. She and I always had a running conversation thread and a private comm line. We had a briefing that morning for our new assignment. It was going to be a training exercise in space, but that was about all we knew at this point.

"Looks like it's with the whole platoon," I noted to Royle.

"Yeah, I saw that. I guess we better get there early so we aren't stuck behind the other squads."

"Agreed," I said. "You'd think in this day and age, people would just use their CCPUs for side conversations instead of whispering," I commented.

Royle smiled, "And could keep from stretching every five minutes with their arms in the air, blocking important parts of the screen."

"It's a talent for sure."

We prodded our teams to the briefing room without much effort. We were part of a spaceborne infantry company; but more importantly, in our platoon, we were an elite unit called Special Teams. We were the best in the platoon and had more training. Along with more training and harder assignments came more dedication to the job. We were pushed harder and had higher expectations in every way. It showed in how we acted and went about our day. We all knew that the rest of the platoon didn't truly see us as one of them. We were fine with that.

We knew every member of the platoon, along with what they were good at and what they struggled with, and the same info for their fireteams and squads as a whole. It was likely my team knew more about our other platoon mates than they knew themselves. We had to; if things went south, we were the ones that had to come in and pick up the pieces.

We tended to socialize more with the company's other special teams squads. Like us, they were part of a platoon but set apart from it in a small way.

We were seated in the front row of the briefing room well before the other squads arrived. None of them were late, mind you. Despite our opinions, I knew that every member of the platoon was competent and dedicated to their job... it's just we liked to show them how much *more* dedicated we were. The room had tiers of elevated seats looking down on a small presentation area with a large screen that currently showed the HFDF emblem—to the left of the screen sat the four other squad leaders and our Lieutenant.

We'd all given obligatory salutes to the group of leaders as we'd walked in, but I nodded a greeting to our squad leader, John Monroe, along with Lisa Middleton, the Lt., as I sat. Both nodded back, Middleton looking pleased as always that we were early and ready for the meeting. In our last deployment on Pike Prime, she'd commented on how much she depended on our squad. And over time, I could tell that she used our squad as motivation for the rest of the platoon. I wondered if the other Special Teams squads in the company were used the same way.

Middleton stood, and the room fell silent. The screen changed from the HFDF emblem to an agenda for the day. I was happy to see that the first item was updates on past conflicts.

"Good morning," she said.

"Good morning, ma'am," the room replied.

"We have a lot to cover this morning, so I will get right to it. First, we have updates on the conflicts our platoon has been involved in."

The screen showed stats from our first deployment on Erie Prime, where we were part of the invasion that was meant to knock the Erie into the Stone Age. From the info, I could see that it was going well.

"As you can see, the war on Erie Prime can hardly be called that anymore. Armies from all landing columns have met up and secured the planet. Career troops are in the process of removing infrastructure and technology from the planet. They are running on schedule as of now," Middleton said.

I could only imagine how many decades it would take the Erie to rebuild their civilization if they ever did.

"What little we have seen of the Erie shows that they are fighting among themselves as they had for centuries prior to coming together," Middleton added.

That was good news, in a way. I felt for the Erie. I really did. My time on Pike Prime had given me a taste of what it must be like for a race to have everything taken from them. That's what we'd done to the Erie. They'd attacked us, and we'd warned them not to do it again. They did it again. So we sent them to the Stone Age. It was unlikely they would ever attack us again if they recovered. I knew they were lucky. Had they attacked other races, they'd have been wiped out or entangled in wars that could last for decades, killing far more than our war ever could have. We'd seen lots of conflicts like that. Two races that were close enough to one another going at it. Sometimes it resolved itself as they ran out of resources and lives, but an alarmingly high amount of the time, they would turn to measures that killed off one or both planets, wiping out whole races or leaving the remnants of the races to wander the stars. Remnants that might take up residence on some world with a race that wasn't anywhere near them technologically.

Still, it had to suck for the Erie.

The screen changed again to info about Pike Prime and the Venom.

"We have contained the Venom on Pike Prime to a handful of underground colonies. Their initial colony is taking longer than originally anticipated," she said, talking about the colony that we had been in last.

The Venom had attacked Pike Prime several years back. The Venom were a race that had been taking out world after world for a while. The Human Federation, along with allies, had come to the decision to wipe them out before they could destroy all life other than their own in the galaxy. It hadn't been an easy war. And from the looks on the screen, it still wasn't.

"There have been three other colonies found north of the initial front since the one we'd helped contain prior to leaving the planet," Middleton said.

This got a few murmurs. I'd remember that day forever. We'd been about to leave the world when a Venom colony broke out near a Pike city. We'd dropped down from the ship to try and stem the flow of

Venom. I'd helped carry a wounded Pike from the area just before Fleet hit the Venom with orbital assets.

Of all the battles we'd been in, only two gave me nightmares. The day James Meyers died and the day we jumped back to the planet. The latter had been such a fast conflict, we'd done our jobs well, and no one got hurt. But I could see the Pike City in my mind's eye. Not like the ones we'd been in where the Venom had gutted everything down to the bones, but a living city. Pike moving around, the sky clear and bright. In my dreams, the city turned into a hollowed-out husk before my eyes, the Pike dropping to the ground and turning to bone. The air would fill with dust that covered everything. In the corners of the buildings, I would find the rotting bodies of humans. Sometimes ones I knew, and other times people I didn't know, or the bodies were so rotted that I couldn't make them out. All the while, I could hear the sound of Venom scuttling behind the walls and in holes in the ground.

In the dream, I'd see a Venom hole and walk into it. The tunnel snaked around until I came to a chamber. Lining the walls were baby Venom, snapping their jaws; little bits of flesh littered the area. A hand here, a head there, all the while, the snapping of their jaws got louder and louder.

I brought my attention back to the meeting. The Venom home system was on the screen. Two planets were listed: Venom Major and Minor. Middleton started talking, but I looked at the info on the screen instead of listening. We'd pushed the Venom back to their defense grids and were pounding the planets. We weren't going to get into a ground war there. Despite the fact that we were a better army, we couldn't take the losses that would be necessary for a campaign like that if we could kill every last Venom in a ground assault anyway. Instead, deep in the system, engineering teams were working on asteroids and comets. Soon they'd be sent at as high speeds as we could get them to the planets. The impacts would turn the crusts molten, sterilizing the planets and making them uninhabitable for a very long time.

There was a slight pause as she changed to the next agenda item.

We were to take part in a series of war games with several other ships in the Hunter Armada. We'd be doing this at the Hunter Space Warfare Training Grounds, along with troops that were stationed at various stations throughout the Orion constellation. Those troops, along with us, would be engaging in different games around boarding stations and holding them. For the crew of the Arbiter, we would also be doing drills on holding the ship from enemies boarding it, and in the case of Spaceborne, we'd be taking part in trying to board other ships.

"As you know, the Arbiter's combat battalion has infantry companies. The infantry will be helping out the stations that troops are being pulled from for the exercises. So the good news is that during the exercises, the Arbiter will be marked as un-deployable, so no getting called off if the shit hits the fan somewhere. But we will have some guests. The troops that are going to be taking part in the station exercise will be staying aboard. We will be setting up temporary bunks for them in the ship's holds," Middleton said.

She asked if there were any questions. Everyone looked at our squad, assuming that we'd be asking about some detail the other squads hadn't thought of. We didn't. It was a pretty straightforward meeting; they happen from time to time.

"If there are no questions, you are dismissed. First squad, stay behind," she said.

Some of the other squads smirked. They didn't like that we were the favorites, so to speak, but they loved that we pulled extra duty. As the others left, we stayed put. When they were gone, Middleton smiled at us, Monroe at her side.

"You didn't think you were going to be normal, did you?" she asked warmly.

"No, ma'am," we said.

"Good," she said, taking on a briefing tone. "We are going to be depending on you and the other Special Teams a lot over the next month. All of you have more than enough close-quarters experience after Pike Prime and Erie Prime. The others do not. We are not going to be putting you in the same roles as them, but rather as support. Educational support. You will be getting a lot of screwy missions to train and test the other troops. But you will also be working on taking other ships." She looked at us seriously. "This isn't something that you have had to think about, but I'm sure after what you have all seen, you know that sometimes we find someone that is on par with us. If the Arbiter finds itself having to engage an enemy ship more powerful than it and we cannot leave the area, our best weapon is boarding parties. And you'd be the first."

We understood the message. If we were first, that meant we'd be dealing with the worst part of a horrid situation. Thankfully, the chances of us ever having to board another ship were extremely low. But so was being killed in combat, and that had happened to our squad. We weren't going to take anything for granted. Before the meeting wrapped up, Royle and I had set up a meeting to strategize how we'd prepare our teams.

A few days later, I learned some of the extra tasks that my team and I were to do. Our infantry companies were leaving, but their rooms were not being occupied by the troops that were going to be calling the Arbiter home for the next month. One, personal belongings were still in the other companies' rooms, and two, there were way more people coming on the ship than leaving. More people than our MPs and logistics staff could handle. So that shouldn't be a problem, right? We have a ship full of troops that you can use. The rest of Spaceborne were catching up on that training. Me and mine, on the other hand, had spent hours with close combat training and had plenty of real-world experience. So we didn't need the extra training. Hence, here I was in the ship's hold.

At their core, troop transport ships are just cargo ships with a lot of crew. The bulk of the ship is storage. We have to bring all kinds of shit into combat with us, from extra drones, ammo, base components, and a glut of other stuff. All of that stuff was leaving for training. We weren't setting up a column on the training base; we were housing people.

I stepped out of the way of a logistics drone with a large pallet of bunks. I was pretty sure it would stop if I didn't move, but I was even more sure the logistics foremen would rip my ass for slowing the deck-hand drones down. So I moved. All around me was the openness that had just recently been full of cargo. From this perspective, I got an idea of just how big the Arbiter was. The empty hold was being filled with bunks a lot like the ones we slept in on deployments but in seemingly endless tight rows. Showers and bathroom units were being brought in, as well as tables for dining. For the most part, the newcomers would be kept separate from the rest of the crew.

My CCPU pinged me with a new assignment. I was to babysit some drones that were assembling the bunks. This was one of the few assignments my people were rated to do with the deckhand drones. We had to be able to set up shop planetside. So I went to an open patch of cargo space where drones began unloading bunks and stacking them up. They were all prefab, and the work was fast for the drones. I didn't have to do anything.

Troops had been trickling in all day. So far, no one had been an issue, and I wasn't sure anyone was going to be one, honestly. All of their commanding officers were with them, so it wasn't like anyone was going to get too out of line. I took a closer look at the bunks. They were stacked five high, with the sides facing the aisle. They each had enough storage for weapons and had a small cubby on the inside for a few personal effects like cards or a ball. They had a place for suits to go at the base of the bed like ours, and the same screen door for privacy. They didn't look too bad. That said, I was sure the troops coming here would think they were roughing it. All were from stations, places that weren't known for being hard to live in. Most of them were even stationed on satcities. The Service Term troops had mostly the same training we did but would never see combat unless attacked or if they had to board a ship. Even the chances of the latter were low, as the fleet almost always dealt with those missions.

I reminded myself that while the assignments they were on seemed easy to me, most of these people were career troops, with only a handful of groups being Service Term. I should try to get to know some of them. Talking with career troops hadn't disappointed me yet, and I was interested to hear what garrison duty was like on a satcity, or what other postings and positions they'd held over the years had been.

"Met a few nice ones today," Krista said at dinner.

"Oh yeah?" I asked.

She nodded. "Yeah, a couple I met said they have been in for thirty years."

"No shit?" Sweeting said. "How much of it has been garrison postings?"

"The last ten. Said that having kids isn't that bad on garrison duty."

"That makes sense. Being shipboard or deployment-based wouldn't work if you wanted to have kids," I said. "But a satcity has all you need. They aren't worried about reassignment?"

Betts rolled his eyes. "It's the HFDF we're talking about, Taylor. You say you want to start a family but don't want to leave the HFDF. They'll find a way to make it work."

"That's pretty much what they told me," Krista said. "Turns out most people don't want garrison duty. It's more hours than normal civilian jobs and pretty boring. Sounds like a lot of people who want to have families go for it."

"Makes sense, I guess. Glad they're nice," I said.

"You know who's a pain in the ass?" Clay said. "The Service Term troops. Cocky little assholes. I had several of them mouth off to me today. They seem to think they are better than us for some reason."

Sweeting snorted a laugh.

"I take it you didn't have too many problems?" I asked.

"No, sir. One of the careers asked what my close-quarters scores were, where I served, and what type of unit I was in."

"Garrison Service Term Troops are some of the lowest scoring. I bet that shut them up," Betts said.

Clay grinned.

"Thankfully, there are only two platoons of them. And in the middle of the Careers," I said.

"Pretty sure that's on purpose," Clay said.

Thankfully, after everyone was on board, the newcomers would mostly be the MPs' problem. As the team got back to eating, I pulled up the schedule. The Arbiter would be undocking tomorrow and starting a one-day trip to the training grounds... well, space. Once things got underway, the Service Term troops would be too busy to be a pain in the ass. Plus, I figured our team would probably be opposite them sometimes, and that would be fun.

———

I TOOK A LONG SIP OF A BEER. A VR ONE, AT LEAST. THE SETTING WE WERE in was that of an old pub. We were in a comfy booth with lots of room, the conversation around us just loud enough to almost not be background noise. The other patrons were fake, of course, so we could always adjust the sound if needed. I took another pull on the beer. It was dark brown with a rich taste.

Next to me were my friends Jon, then Liz and Monica. I didn't appreciate VR or the ability to transmit large amounts of data over light-years instantly until I joined the HFDF. Before, when I wanted to hang out with friends, we got together. But right now, we were all extremely far apart. Monica was on a satcity, Jon at a deep space shipyard, Liz in Orion City, and I was comfortably lying in a VR pod on the Arbiter, a little over one AU away from Hunter. We were also all in this cozy little pub.

"Any word on your new assignment?" I asked Liz.

"By the time you are wrapping up training, I should know. Working in research has been fun, for sure, but I'm looking forward to something more people-facing. How's your assignment?" Liz asked Jon.

"I love it. The shipyards are a-mazing! We just finished work on a new Super Carrier, the Helios. The whole thing can fit in the shipyard station and slides right out."

"Start to finish?" I asked. "I've seen those things. That's a lot of tonnage; there's nothing bigger in the HFDF fleet."

"From raw materials to finished ship with drones and everything. The only thing not aboard is food and a crew," Jon said.

"Shit," was all I had to say.

Normally, I would give Jon a little ribbing for getting a hard-on about a shipyard, but that was just fucking impressive. Another person who normally would be giving him a hard time was Monica, but she was staying silent, a habit she'd slipped into over the last few months.

"So Monica, how's your week going?" I asked.

She gave me a dirty look for the briefest of moments, then her expression softened. Monica and I's relationship had changed after I'd come home from Pike Prime. Not in a bad way. We hadn't gotten into an argument, nor had one of us confessed a lifelong love we'd held for the other. Just that she'd always seen herself as the tough one of the group, the protector, but I'd almost died in combat, and there was nothing she could have done to stop it. Months before, she'd learned that I could wipe the floor with her; I was pretty sure that fact wasn't lost on her when I'd gotten hurt. She wasn't the protector anymore.

"It's fine," she said after a moment.

"Fine?" Liz asked.

She huffed. "It's just... it's not what I thought it would be, you know?"

"What, like the recruiter lied to you?" Jon asked.

"No," she admitted, "It's just like she said it would be. But do you remember as kids when we'd watch crime shows? The cops were always doing stuff, ya know, catching bad guys and saving lives. I break up domestic disputes and track down people dumb enough to steal. With CCPUs, it's not even like we have to work at it," she said, dejected.

"Last night, I got a call, right? This couple is going at it. No one's being abused or anything like that. These people just really hate each other and won't break up for some unknown reason. Sorry, anyway. I get out there, and both of them are all but shoving CCPU data on me, totally giving up their privacy rights as if we'd accused them of murder. And do you know what it was all for?" she asked.

"I don't know," Jon said.

"Nothing. Seriously, nothing! One of them thought they heard the other one make a comment. So the other one got pissed and sent over CCPU data showing that they just didn't hear what the other said. So that made the other one say that the other was turning their hearing down. It was that stupid.

"So one of them starts throwing dishes at the other one, as responsible adults do, so the other starts throwing shit too. The thing is, CCPU data showed that neither was actually trying to hit the other. They just wanted the other person to stop yelling so they could hear them as they yelled. So my partner and I get them calmed down. We ask if anyone wants to file charges. Spoiler alert: nobody did, because what are you going to do? Have yourself hauled off for breaking your own shit?" She sighed.

"And?" I asked.

"That's it. That's the end of the story. Oh, and the part where they made sarcastic comments about us being out there even though they BOTH called the cops," she tossed her hands up. "This isn't the shit I thought I'd be doing. I thought I'd have made some big bust by now. But I won't. What is there to bust? Humans don't suffer from chemical addiction anymore, and if they did manage to get an addiction, their CCPU would wean them off it. So no doing dumb drug-related stuff. What about assault? People are hard to kill, and they have a computer in their fucking heads that allows them to call for help while gathering information about an assault before they are even hurt. Thinking about stealing something? Yeah, those are kids who don't understand yet that it takes us no effort to find them. Get wrongly accused of something? Just share your CCPU data, and you're free and clear. I have nothing of import to do," she said.

"The only cops who do are on Earth, but half that shit is terrorist and wack-job groups that the HFDF has to be called in on. You guys are all happy with what you do, and I'm... not. What if I made a mistake?" She crossed her arms. Then she took a drink and said, "My tantrum is done now."

Liz looked sorry for Monica, and Jon looked at his drink.

"You keep pushing on, and you make the best of it. Find meaning in what you do. Gather skills and contacts for after your term. You have years left to figure it out, and you can do it," I said.

"Do you regret your choice?" she asked me.

"No," I said right away. "But I do wish I hadn't been in some of the situations I've been in. Trust me, I know things can be hard and not what you expected."

She perked up. "Yeah, what didn't you expect?"

I saw Liz tense. I knew what she hadn't expected.

I thought for a moment. I didn't really like talking about Pike Prime. No one in the group did. Sure, we'd talk about some of the funny stuff that had happened, but rarely deeper than that.

I breathed out in a puff and thought for a moment. "Here's one. We had this recurring assignment where we had to go into the Venom bunkers. We sent in drones first, but sometimes they didn't get everything. The Venom would come at us, and we'd take them out. It was mostly boring work when you were sending the drones down. But sometimes, after you'd engaged some Venom down there, it was freaky. I mean, I was meters underground in the hardened bunker of some seriously nasty creatures. It was dark, so it was all density views and headlamps. Everything was black and white to me. No sky, no smells. Just tunnels with other tunnels that might have something in them. It made you afraid, but you had to fight your fear, you know? If you don't, your CCPU takes over, which is something I hadn't had before training. It feels odd, to say the least, like you're a human one second, and then that's turned off."

I was looking at my drink. "I didn't expect that. Or anything on Pike Prime, for that matter. Fuck, as we pushed further in, I could actually see the planet dying. A whole planet. The Pikes gutted cities freaked me out. At the beginning of our campaign, our team dropped in while the Pike were evacuating, so I saw a normal city that was all lit up. Then later, I saw the ones that had been held for a while. They were like big skeletons rising from the ground. Creepy shit, for sure," I said, a little far off.

Monica looked like she regretted asking me the question.

"Sorry, guys," I said.

Monica and Jon clearly didn't know what to think.

"The death," Liz said. "I didn't expect that. I'd never seen a dead person before," she laughed without humor. "I guess I didn't see all of a dead body then, either. The closest I saw to a whole body was headshots. Man, you know, before that I really thought humans were invincible? But seeing people all messed up? It's one thing to know what we can fix, but another to see it. You know?"

"Yeah," I said.

"We had a head come in. How the hell the BIs got that head in a med-drone with stasis before brain death, I'll never know," she started.

"BI?" Jon asked.

"Basic Infantry drone," I supplied.

"Yep, those," Liz said. "We had to re-grow his whole body. It was amazing in a way, but if I go my whole life without seeing that again I'll be happy."

Liz looked over at me, breathed out, and said, "Sorry to be a downer."

"It's fine," Jon said.

"Yeah," Monica said.

Liz looked at me again, and I could see it in her eyes. She wasn't the same person either. The others left after a while, leaving Liz and I to ourselves. We'd both been a little quiet for the rest of the time.

She was looking at her virtual beer. Her face showed no emotion, as if she were somewhere else.

"Do you still keep up with the medical people on Pike Prime?" I asked her.

She looked away from her drink, coming back to the moment. It took her a second to answer, "Yeah, a few. They are much less busy now. Mostly drones are going in the colonies. It's back to monitoring planetside medical drones and MHDs."

"That's a good thing," I said.

She nodded, sitting back in her chair. "Yes, it is." She looked around the pub and back at me. "This isn't what it used to be."

"It's us," I said, matter-of-factly.

She looked back at the beer. "Yeah, I know." Then she looked back at me. "But it's getting better."

I nodded. "It's getting better."

"I feel guilty sometimes. I'm a little jealous of the others," Liz shook her head. "I don't want them to know the things we did, but god, what I wouldn't give to have my least favorite memory of the last year be a couple yelling at each other." She sighed. "I know it would grind on you and all…"

I placed my hand on hers. "I hear ya," I said. "Would you take it back?"

She shook her head quickly. "Never. I wouldn't want someone else to do it." She breathed out. "Pike Prime was horrible, but I know that during my time there, I was part of not only helping protect all of humanity and the Pike but everything else in the galaxy. The Venom would have spread and killed everything. If helping to prevent that means I have some baggage and nightmares, that's a good price."

THREE

I sat in the briefing room with the rest of the platoon. Before us, Middleton was giving us the briefing for the day. The Arbiter was taking part in a ship-to-ship exercise. This wasn't the first ship-to-ship exercise we'd done, but it would be the last. I was looking forward to it being over. The ship-to-ship exercises were stressful, even in a training environment.

In the exercise, the Arbiter would be in the situation of having to fight another ship, in this case, a Juggernaut-class destroyer. The chances of this actually happening were pretty low. The Arbiter did not engage with other ships aside from the occasional lobbing of long-range missiles when acting within a fleet.

If the Arbiter were to find herself alone with an enemy ship, several things would happen very quickly. The first would be a threat assessment. The Arbiter was not designed for ship-to-ship combat; she's a transport. That said, she's not defenseless. If the Arbiter outclassed an enemy by a wide margin, she'd call for help, and if help wasn't coming soon, she'd engage and take out the enemy. If she faced a fair fight or was outclassed, her best options would be to turn tail and escape in one of two ways. First, she could do an emergency jump. This would mess up the jump drives if she was too close to a large gravity well but would get the ship out of dodge. If that somehow wasn't an option, or if the enemy was far enough away, then the ship would run until help could arrive. Lastly, if she was outclassed, help was not coming soon, and running wasn't an option, then she'd have no choice but to engage the enemy.

The Arbiter had extensive point-defense systems, which made attacking her from long-range difficult. She couldn't do a lot of fighting back offensively but could keep from taking a beating in long-range engagements. At close range, that was different. The ship's armor was less than stellar compared to other military vessels, and while the ship had a handful of close-quarters railguns, they weren't that powerful. But boarding parties were easy for her to put together.

On the other side of the ticket, you had the destroyer, a Juggernaut-class. That meant that long-range wasn't its thing. Getting up close and taking hits while dishing them out was.

In a real fight, the Arbiter's best chance for survival was holding off long enough for boarding parties to take over an enemy ship or push the enemy to the point where they scuttled their own ship. It wasn't a winning situation for sure. For the destroyer, boarding parties were a bit of a pain in the ass. They didn't have huge numbers of crew to fend off people aboard the ship. Also, the ship would still be in active combat, which limited the number of crew members that could deal with boarding parties.

In a way, this was a good matchup. The crew of the Arbiter would be reminded why they would run, and the destroyer might actually have to deal with something like this at some point in time. My team got a lesson in going into a fight you know you're likely to die in. Fun stuff.

"First squad, you are the first in. Bravo team, you take and hold the interior. Alpha, you will take out point defense and main turrets," the Lt. was saying.

That was the stressful part. Ships move around a lot in combat.

They are always pulling a ton of g's. On the inside of a ship, this isn't an issue, as the ship's gravity system keeps you from feeling it, but the outside? Sure, a gravity system could and would be used to keep friendlies from being killed by a ship moving around while they were on the hull. But we weren't friendlies. We were the opposite, and we'd be wandering around the outside of a ship trying to damage it. No gravity assist for us. Yes, this was training, and if we were about to get hurt, our CCPU would tell the destroyer, which would kill any maneuvers and extend its gravity field, keeping us safe in theory. Or if we were dislodged from the ship, it would also stop. But that was only a little comforting. Both of these situations had come up during training early on, and I was pretty sure that was on purpose, so we knew that the safety measures really worked. The comfort wasn't just for us but also to help the ship's crew know that the maneuvers they told the ship to do weren't going to kill people. It was like when you learned to jump from a ship. You knew that you'd be okay, but you didn't believe it until you'd done it several times.

We filed out of the briefing room. Everyone headed to the armory to get ready. In the armory, I went over all of my gear. Our suits had a bit of extra equipment. On our packs were four telescopic arms with gripping pads on the ends. They would help us move around in null g, sticking to the hull of a ship or inside the ship, for that matter. It would keep our hands free and keep us moving. We were loading up with more rockets than we normally had. They were all fake, of course; we weren't going to actually damage our own stuff. We each had a pod of eight BIs. No BBALLs. They were good in null g, but being stuck to the side of something bucking around had some benefits. The BBALLs would get messed up the first time the destroyer fired a maneuvering thruster that moved the ship toward the drone.

We did have one extra drone, a Small Gravity Drone. I know, I love how creative we are with names. It was a box with spider-like legs. That box would create gravity wells that would keep us from being flung from the destroyer by its gravity systems or from getting smashed or thrashed to pieces by high g movement. So that was cool. That said, that took a lot of energy, so the drone only did its thing when it thought we couldn't handle what was going on, and it could only do that so many times before it ran out of juice. We had to complete our mission and get into the ship or shuttle before the drone died, and we died. For the drill's sake, if the drone ran out of juice, we'd be marked KIA, and we'd lay on the hull of the destroyer with its gravity field protecting us for the rest of the exercise. It was one of the few times when you were 'killed' in training that you weren't frozen in place. Your head could move around and see. I wasn't sure why this type of mission was the exception to the rule, but it was odd watching your still-living teammates get bounced around and struggle to move while you felt no movement at all. And maybe that was the point. You could see and appreciate what it was like for people on the outside of a ship in combat.

We walked to the shuttle bay of the ship. Every fireteam had its own shuttle. Today a guaranteed number of shuttles would make it to the destroyer. In real life, that wasn't a luxury we would have. If we lost sixty percent of our shuttles, we might still take the destroyer in a real fight. More than that, though, and we'd just be hoping those that made it to the enemy would at least give the Arbiter time to get out of the area.

In the back of the shuttle was a large gravity unit. They weren't normally a necessity. It would keep us alive on our trip. Not comfortable, but alive. Once attached to the destroyer, the shuttle's core would go full bore in keeping the shuttle in place and in one piece. For the shuttles, staying against the enemy was the best call. Most, if not all, of the ship's point-defense systems would be unable to hit a shuttle that was attached, but if they moved away, they'd be easy targets.

We walked onto the shuttle, my team behind me. The doors closed, and cords came from the ceiling, connecting me to the ship.

"Alpha team is go for the mission," I said.

"Roger that, Alpha," Captain Goldberg said over the shuttle's comms.

The other teams reported in, and we waited for what felt like an eternity before the Arbiter's commander's voice came over the comms. "We will start the exercise in T minus two minutes. I expect the same level of performance everyone has shown up to this point. We might not be the favorite to win, but that won't stop us from trying."

I turned on a feed from the nose of the shuttle.

ARBITER: EXERCISE START.
ARBITER: ALL HANDS REPORT TO BATTLE STATIONS.
ARBITER: PREPARE FOR SHUTTLE LAUNCH.

I didn't feel the shuttle accelerate in the launch tube, but as it left the ship's gravity field, I felt myself slam back against my rigid suit. The shuttle banked hard, making it feel like a giant had slapped me. The visual representation of rounds and ordnance from the ship's defense systems swam in my vision. The ship lit up as missiles fired, streaking in the direction we were heading. We would use the missiles as cover. At the moment they were a bigger threat than us. Ergo, the destroyer would prioritize them. I felt myself pressed back harder as the shuttle moved forward. Around us, three small fighter drones moved. They'd try to keep anything off of us or take a missile if need be.

I could see the destroyer ahead of us as a glowing ball of incoming threats. The missiles moved much faster than we did. Some had their own defense networks built on them. Flashing filled my view as missiles met. The Arbiter was falling far behind us now. Missiles whizzed past us, and I moved my display to the Arbiter. Her point-defense system came alive, shredding them. I looked at the destroyer. It was spinning and jerking around in space, its hull seeming to spit out ordnance.

The giant hit me again as the shuttle started to dip and dodge around threats. It felt like being in a can that was being shaken.

"Braking burn," Goldberg said, with flint in her voice. I didn't want to know how stressful this was for the pilots. They didn't have the same margin of error as the rest of us did. Any one of the people on the boarding parties or the ship's fire controls could completely mess up, and nothing bad would happen. The missiles and rounds were all fake, but the shuttles hurling themselves at breakneck speeds at another ship were entirely real. If Goldberg screwed up and the shuttle's computers didn't catch it in time, we'd smack against the side of the destroyer, or the shuttle could lose control, and it would be the end for us.

The shuttle flipped, and in a moment, the whole universe moved with it. We were facing the Arbiter, and then the engines fired. I was sure that pre-Ageless humans wouldn't be uninjured in this if they even could live through it. The shuttle jolted more. There was an alert that the destroyer's main batteries were opening up. My CCPU showed the path of rounds that no point-defense system could neutralize. I didn't see explosions. That meant penetrators. Rounds that would just keep going until they were stopped. The Arbiter's interior would be in vacuum, so there would be no violent decompression, but people and systems in the way of the rounds would be gone.

My CCPU popped a message. We were closing on the destroyer. We were entering its defense system's primary kill zone. On cue, friendly shuttles began to disappear. I looked over to the shuttle with Bravo team as it flew into pieces. In real life, half my squad would have died just now. As it was, they had to land for the exercise. Dead, but not dead.

"Ten seconds," Goldberg said.

"Get ready!" I yelled to my team.

The shuttle flipped again, its anchor firing. I felt an uncomfortable sensation of being stretched a bit as the gravity system behind us kicked in. Had it failed, I would have just turned into goo. The door of the shuttle opened, and I was in null-g. The cord connecting me released, and my boots stuck to the floor. My drones ran forward, and I followed. Before I got to the skin of the hull, I felt like I was hanging upside down, jolting my perception. The destroyer knew we were here and was trying to push us off.

"Move quick. We don't have time," I ordered.

My boots clung to the hull, the arms on my pack attaching as I started to scuttle along the hull to a defense system in front of us. The ship's skin was the deepest black, the light coming from the batteries seeming to disappear on it. I glanced up, and though I was in space, I could not see the stars. Around me was a maelstrom of rounds, debris, and engine plumes. I tried to move as the ship tried to push me away and then tried to slam me back into it. I stumbled, my hands hitting the hull. My knees stuck to it, as did my hands. I crawled quickly with my POD, trying to stay in a tight group. I could see a large turret ahead flash with each round it fired. In the distance, they were exploding inside the Arbiter.

The ship bucked again, and my heart began to pound in my chest. I was going to die on this ship; I knew it! My CCPU soothed my fear just a bit. I tried to control my emotions. If they pushed too far, my CCPU would flatline me, and I didn't want that. I breathed as I moved, forcing myself to calm down.

"Move to the turret but get defense systems as you go," I ordered.

My CCPU showed that Monroe was KIA. The VR Pod he commanded us from had been destroyed.

One of my BIs approached a defense system. It moved against the battery and placed a charge. Before it was far enough away, the ship bucked, and the charge detonated, taking out the BI. Another one was lost to the Arbiter's own defense rounds. The rounds from the beginning of the fight had made it here. Rounds that were designed to protect the ship and her crew were now raining down on us. The destroyer could have diverted them with gravity fields but was letting us deal with them. They bounced off the hull, scattering everywhere.

A railgun round hit where Sweeting and his POD were digging into the hull. The status indicator for him on my HUD switched to KIA. We moved faster. Betts made it to a turret, his BIs planting charges and taking it out of commission. The other teams were on the comms; they were taking the inside of the ship meter by meter, taking heavy losses. The ship's movement slowed for a moment, and I fired a rocket at a defense system, hitting it. With each one we took out, we gave the Arbiter an advantage.

My suit pulled me down to the hull of the ship all of a sudden, making it impossible to move. My CCPU informed me that I had been hit by a piece of shrapnel and was dead. I watched as my team worked, unable to talk to them. I took the moment to shift my views to that of my team's perspective and their drones. After this was all done, we'd have things to work on as a team, and terrified as I was, I couldn't fight the urge to see how we were performing. They took out another turret before Krista bought it. Then the flashing of the battle stopped. My CCPU read a message.

ARBITER: TRAINING EXERCISE COMPLETE. ENEMY SHIP SCUTTLED BY CREW. ARBITER CREW CASUALTIES AT SEVENTY-TWO PERCENT. BOARDING TEAM CASU-ALTIES ONE HUNDRED PERCENT. MISSION END.

My suit let me move, and I stood up. The stars were visible again, no longer obscured by the violence that had just ended. My BIs, along with all the other ones marked as destroyed in the battle, began moving around. I jumped lightly, floating away from the ship.

"Heading to scoop you guys up," Goldberg said, sounding tired.

"Roger that," I said.

I turned slowly in the void of space, my heart slowing down.

"Well, I guess we won," Sweeting said over the team comms.

"Yeah, at least a few people from the ship would have made it out of here," Clay said.

"Yeah, if more than twenty percent of our shuttles had made it," Betts said.

"Wow, way to be a buzzkill, man. Way to make our deaths mean nothing!" Sweeting said with mock rage.

I laughed. Betts started bantering with him, and I ignored the conversation. Instead, I just floated slowly, turning around. The destroyer had gone to search-and-rescue day-glo orange, as had the Arbiter. But when I was turned away from the ships, the vastness of space lay before me in a way that it never could on a planet. I used my space anchor to stop my turn. I was facing the center of the Milky Way; it bloomed before me as a dense, glittering cloud of stars. More worlds than even the Human Federation knew about.

My father had always said that he liked to think this was what connected us all. He said he didn't think there was a race out there that could look at the center of a galaxy and not be struck by how big everything was. Well, nothing with emotions like those of humans, anyway. I wasn't really sure what emotions were like for the races that didn't emote in a way similar to humans. Krista and I would talk about it sometimes. What other races felt, if they felt at all. Aliens fascinated her.

"What are you thinking about?" Krista asked me on a private line.

"Just how small we are."

"Space does that," she said.

"I know it's pretty cliché," I said.

"Yeah, but I don't think that's a bad thing. How was getting killed?"

"You first," I jabbed.

"I really hope we don't end up doing this for real someday. Not even against a weak race," she said soberly.

"God, I hope not too."

In every other instance, you felt like you could come out of it alive, but stepping into a shuttle on a mission like we had today was a death sentence. It was one that I would take if I had to. I wasn't about to die doing nothing on a ship. I thought back to a few weeks ago talking with my old friends. Monica had talked about what she hadn't expected. This was one of those things for me. Having to face death, even in training, hadn't been like I'd thought. I'd felt real fear. It wasn't like a game. I knew the fear was for a reason, to teach us how to overcome it. I knew that the fear and lessons from the past few days would stay with everyone on the Arbiter. If any one of us were ever in command and in the position of having to face an enemy and send out boarding parties, we'd know what we were getting ourselves and our people into.

My CCPU pinged. The shuttle was coming to pick me up. I used my anchor to turn. I could see the shuttle gently coming my way, its door open like a giant whale eating krill. BIs waited on the inside, ready to help me if I needed it. In the center of them, Sweeting was bent over with his ass waggling at me. So much for the moment of deep thought and introspection.

Monroe's voice came over the team line, "Taylor, your safeties have been removed, fire at will."

I laughed with the team.

"That's just cold, sir," Sweeting said, standing up.

I felt the tension drain as I floated. Deep inside, I thanked Sweeting. He always knew how to break the tension of a situation. It was never appropriate, but it was one of the links in the chain that held our family together.

The shuttle picked me up, and we started heading towards the Arbiter. Not at the speed we had before, mind you. Just a gentle pace. The ship looked comical, being bright orange, but I was sure you could see it from kilometers away, which was the point. We boarded and walked into the airlock. It cycled, and my helmet came off.

"That was cute, Sweeting," I commented.

"Everyone says that about my ass," he said.

We started down the halls to the rest of the ship. We headed to the briefing room, where our stats, along with everyone else's, were gone over in detail. Our platoon had done well. We weren't the reason the enemy ship's commander decided to scuttle, but we played a role in it. Everyone's scores showed that they'd fought hard and took the exercise seriously. When that was done, I had a meeting with just Monroe, Royle, and me. We sat in his office with trays of food.

His eyes were far off, "Good work today. Both of your teams did well," he said.

"When I blow up, I do it with grace, sir," Royle said.

Monroe chuckled, "Don't kid yourself, Royle. That was your pilot who did that; all you did was litter space."

She laughed.

He looked at us, "Thoughts?"

"Never get in that situation," Royle said, "but I think if we do, our teams will know how important their jobs are."

"And that there's a difference between a station and a ship," I said, "honestly, before this, I wouldn't have thought that. Before, I thought I'd much rather take a ship than a station."

Those feelings had changed. Stations didn't move around, for one, which made it simpler, but they also didn't have as tightly packed defense systems. Today the goal was only to lose sixty percent of our shuttles. If we were hitting a station, that would be closer to five or ten percent. Plus, stations were loath to scuttle unless it was an all-military station, as scuttling would mean killing a lot of civilians.

"That's part of the point of this," he said. "It gives all of us perspective." He nodded like he'd just checked something off in his head. "You both are showing a lot of confidence with your teams. Our squad has started to outperform the other Special Teams squads."

"Thank you, sir. And the rest of the platoon?" Royle asked.

He shrugged. "With us, they are slightly above average. Not that the platoon is doing poorly, just not doing as well as we are compared to other platoons in the company."

I frowned. "Any way we can help?" I asked.

"Thank you for offering. I've asked the Lt. the same. She's working out some issues with some of the squads. Some of the people aren't recovering as well as we'd have hoped. So it's not so much a training issue. Your teams are doing well enough with it," Monroe said.

"Well enough?" Royle asked.

Monroe nodded. "Yes. Your training and personalities are different. Right now, everything is still easy for you. If you are suffering from any uncertainty, we may not know until you are in a real-world situation again."

"Any people we need to be concerned about?" I asked.

He shook his head. "None that we are seeing. Try not to worry about it."

I made a note to talk to my team later to let them know to cut the rest of the platoon some slack and build their confidence a bit. I wasn't sure if it would help, but I doubted it would hurt.

FOUR

While I had hoped we were done with our part of the exercises, it turned out we had one mission left. But I was okay with this one. The normal crew of the Arbiter was playing the role of the bad guys who'd taken parts of a station, while the garrison troops tried to take it back.

The teams trying to take it back happened to be ones who'd been staying aboard the Arbiter. I liked most of them. Even the Service Term people were fine. That said, I was looking forward to messing with them. In other exercises, we'd been limited in some way, shape, or form. This was so the people who the training was for could see what it would be like fighting different types of enemies. That's cool and all, but it also meant that my team lost a lot of the time. That was the point, really. Today we didn't have any disadvantages. Other Spaceborne teams were holding various parts of the station, and my Fireteam had engineering.

There were rules, of course. Though we had engineering, we couldn't blow the station up right away. Not only was that not what you generally wanted when taking a station, but also, logistically, it wasn't as easy as you'd think. That wasn't to say that we couldn't do it.

We could after a certain amount of time. It wasn't a short amount of time, but if that time passed, I could blow the station. If enough time passed, I could set up a dead man's switch. This was how my team won. Well, that or kill everyone trying to take the station back.

Over the comms, I heard the various Fireteams and squads lose to garrison troops. Royle's team was roving around trying to reinforce teams as they lost. Currently, she and hers were heading towards a housing sector to back up Third Squad, which was down to six people. Thus far, the garrison troops were doing well, but they hadn't really faced our squad yet. The handful of people who'd encountered Royle's team had gotten their asses handed to them.

I had my team spread around engineering. It was way too big to hold with one team, but I didn't really need to hold all of it. The main reactor would do just fine. I was hunkered down in the environmental control area. We each had likely breach points. I'd had my BIs place charges around the room behind consoles and the like. I wanted a lot of shrapnel. There wasn't a snowball's chance in hell I could hold off any real force for too long, so I needed the attackers to be wary.

A whisker pinged a notification. Some customers were approaching. I watched as a group of about twenty-five came by. I suspected there were at least three human operators in the group. They were moving slowly with their SIRs raised. They didn't check the body for a whisker. They should have. Well, they did kind of check it; they appeared to have a BI check it for explosives. That was so old school. They saw the whisker and even picked it up to move it out of the way while checking for bombs.

It was an easy mistake to make. The Whiskers, by design, were hard to detect and harder still to see if they were active. A closer inspection would have told them that I knew their numbers and the direction they were moving. They should have destroyed it. That's what I would have done, but it wasn't something I would have been religious about before Pike Prime. Anyone with combat experience would be. This told me something. It was likely that I was facing

Service Term troops. I wouldn't count on it, but hopefully, I was right. They'd be over-eager and press a perceived advantage.

"Hostiles heading my way," I said to the squad.

"Roger that, Alpha. We will assist when we can," Royle said.

"Take your time. They haven't engaged yet."

"Will do."

The troops were past my whisker. With luck, they'd have phoned in that they cleared the area, so the whisker could keep getting me intel. I was behind a console in the center of the room—not a great place to be if you were trying to blend in as a useless member of your POD. I should have been over on the side of the room. And that's what I would have done if I was fighting aliens who didn't know human operators were hiding in plain sight. These people would know I was in the room. They'd probably assume I wasn't dense enough to be in the center of the kill zone, so they'd focus their attention on the sides of the room.

A hand flashed around the door opening, and a small grenade came in. I ducked down, and there was a bang, followed by feet rushing into the room. Yep, it was the Service Term troops.

Had we not been in suits, this would have totally stunned or taken out people in the room. As it was, all of my units were hiding behind shit on either side of the room, and my helmet prevented me from being affected by the grenade. No one would walk into a kill zone, right? A wide-open space in the middle of a room? Not even these guys would. Thankfully, there'd been some debris we'd piled in the room that their grenades hit. They made the blank spot, so obviously, it wouldn't be a trap. Units started rushing into the room.

The BIs on the side of the room opened up, dropping four units. There were still about six standing in the room. They turned toward the walls, and I popped up, drilling two units in the head in the center of the group. I dropped back down and then ducked around the side of the console, buzzing in full auto and taking out legs. Two BIs ducked in the room, pulling one of the units out. I hit them both. So that was one human down.

That was twelve units down. They'd lost almost half of what they'd come with. They'll wait for backup, right? Nope! Several more grenades came bouncing into the room. They were frags, and as they exploded, I felt a couple of stings on my arms. Again they'd focused on the walls and not the center. Barrels came around the doors, firing in. My BIs began to move back. One went down. I had the other drop like it was damaged. A few units entered the room. I kneeled in front of the console I was behind and turned my SIR's velocity all the way up, firing through the console. I damaged a BI, and they scattered.

My BI got up and ran through the door. I covered it. It took a hit in the leg, and I grabbed it, taking it from the room like it was the operator. It took a few gut shots, but the enemy ignored me.

"They think they took out or injured an operator," I told the team.

I checked to see what they were doing. All were engaged in some way. Good, we only would get one chance to fool as many people as possible.

"Pull back," I ordered.

The rest of my team did so. Betts was doing the best job of looking like he was being forced out. Sweeting really was being forced to fall back, so that worked. I closed the door I was by, moving down a hallway. The drone that was down in the room had taken a lot of hits, and I couldn't access any of it. I could access its sidearm and its sights. I stayed behind a corner in the hall, letting two other BIs peek out to shoot at the units starting to make it through the door.

The rest of the group was slowly filtering into the room they'd just taken, again checking that the drone was out but not thinking about its sidearm. My whisker informed me that more troops were coming to assist the group in the room. *Nice.*

They got to the door to the hall I was in and again tossed down some frags. My BIs took cover and then popped around the corner, firing. We were nicely pinned down. The other room was filling with units ready to rush down into engineering and save the day.

I did a quick check on the battle. The garrison units had taken the rest of the station. Royle's team was trying to hold up in the residential area but was losing ground. On paper, it looked like we were about to lose. I checked on my team's positions.

"Blow them," I ordered.

I detonated the charges, conveniently covered in piles of debris in the room. The door into the hall I was in flashed, and debris flew into the hallway. My BIs rushed forward into the room we had once occupied, shooting at every head they could find, and then we ran down the hall to the reactor room.

The reactor room was a cathedral of a space, with the reactor taking up the center. We closed off heavy doors that were meant to keep the rest of the station safe from the reactor. They'd work for our purposes.

"Report?" I asked.

"Two drones down," Krista said.

"Three," Sweeting said.

"Two," Betts said.

"One," Clay said.

"Show-off," Sweeting said.

"Cut the chatter. It looks like we dropped over fifty with that. It should pull heat from any other units out there. Prep for company," I said.

The team moved quickly, taking up positions. I checked to see if I had a timer on blowing the station. I did. We had to hold out for twenty minutes. Teams were starting to head our way. They were moving slowly now, and someone found my whisker. The people coming now were clearly better than before. They were starting to work on the doors. We'd ripped out parts of the frames on the tops of the door—small ones that could have maybe happened when someone took the station. BIs put the muzzles of their SIRs in the holes and fired.

Garrison troops fell back and began to fire at the door. A small rocket came down the hall. It hit the door, blowing it out of the way. *Damn, didn't see that coming.* I'd have thought they'd be way more careful with the reactor room. They probably would have been in a real situation.

"Any help would be nice," I said to Royle.

"Thanks for pulling the heat from us. We are inbound," she said.

"Bravo is coming to hit them from the rear," I said to the team.

They acknowledged.

The garrison troops didn't flood in like some unstoppable wave of destruction. They'd learned not to do that. Instead, they were shooting down the hall, forcing my drones to either side of the door. We went from having relative control to not. We still held the advantage for now, though. The garrison team couldn't fire another rocket without running the risk of critically damaging their own station, so that was a pro for us. They had a lot more numbers than we did, and not losing drones wouldn't be high on their to-do list. It was for me.

A whisker streaked into the room. Small, yes, but not hard-wearing. A BI with its SIR set to shotgun blasted it from the air. I ordered my BIs to change positions, but the enemy already had two BBALLs fly into the room. They turned and shot at where one BI was. One of the BBALLs was destroyed, but the other managed to get a headshot in on the BI before it, too, was taken out.

Shit.

I took cover under a desk. I lost some speed if I needed to get out and shoot, but I didn't think the garrison troops were planning on rushing me just yet. My HUD was showing statuses on all of my Fireteam. Betts lost a BI. I ordered all but one BI to take better cover.

Another whisker came into the room. Again, a BI shot it but then ducked down. This time, when the BBALLs came in, that BI didn't show itself. Another did and took care of the BBALLs before they could do any damage. My team was doing likewise, but this strategy wouldn't last forever. Thankfully, it didn't need to. My CCPU told me that we now had the ability to blow the reactor and kill the station. Still, no dead man's switch.

"We can blow," I said over the squad line.

Another whisker came in. Again, a BI shot it. This time, though, it wasn't a BBALL that came into the room; it was a BI with a small frag grenade that it tossed to the position of my BI that had shot the whisker. The frag went off, damaging the BI but not rendering it unusable. There was that whole "don't use anything too big" thing the garrison people had to think about. They repeated this pattern, and I had two more drones damaged.

This could work well for them. I could kind of keep my units safe, and then they could rush us, or eventually, I wouldn't have enough BIs to hold the area, and they would come in. Some of the garrison troops were choosing option one with Clay and Sweeting's positions. My people were going to lose.

My CCPU informed me that my dead man's switch was now active. Cool. I didn't want to give the garrison troops the satisfaction of having bested any of us.

"It's time," I ordered.

My team and all of our drones stood up and casually walked from behind our cover. We'd won once we had the ability to blow the station; we'd double-won with the dead man's switch. Standing up was having our cake and eating it too. The moment I stood with my team, the training staff monitoring the exercise terminated the simulation. My team had taken zero casualties. We'd only lost half our drones and managed to take out over seventy enemy drones, along with killing eight operators.

The garrison troops came into the room, some with their helmets off. I'd started to learn some of their faces. The older troops seemed frustrated at a thorough ass-kicking but were taking it well. They shook my hand and told me I was a prick, good-naturedly. The Service Term troops did everything they could not to make eye contact with us.

For the Service Term troops, it had been one thing knowing that during the training, we'd been pulling our punches so they could learn, but a completely different thing to *know* that we had been doing it.

Back in the briefing room, we were joined by the company's commanding officer, Major Steve Breeze. He almost never came to the briefings. With him were Middleton and Monroe. The whole platoon was in the room. The Lt had been going over the report of the exercise, and it was finishing with my team standing up.

The Major had Middleton play the last bit over a few times. He was looking at the footage almost sternly. As I watched, it was pretty clear that by doing what we had done, we'd all but flipped the garrison troops off.

"That was quite the ending, Corporal," the Major said, looking over at me. "You made them look like assholes the whole engagement and then tossed it in their faces at the end."

"Um... yes, sir," I said uncomfortably.

"In so doing, you also made their commanders look like assholes too."

"I suppose so, sir."

Shit, this was not going to be good.

"No suppose, you did. You look like you regret your decision. Are you sorry for what you have done?"

"Y-Yes, sir. I apologize for making the other team look like... assholes. Sir," I said, feeling like shit. The rest of the platoon tried not to chortle.

"Why?" he asked, surprised. "I'm not. They are assholes. Well, sometimes anyways." He smiled. "Their commander. She's insufferable after these kinds of things, told me I hoped I was over losses in birthday cards before." He turned to the screen. "But I think this year will be different. In the official report, your team lost points for not holding out until the end. There was an almost nonexistent chance that you could have won and maybe then had an even lower chance of taking the station back. These are the games we play, but I know that everyone in this room knows the difference between the real world and the game. Well done, second platoon, on keeping the garrison troops from taking back the station." He looked at me. "And thank you for the video for my next dinner party, Corporal."

He left the room, chuckling. "Ha! Seventy drones and eight operators—happy birthday, Jessica!"

I felt a huge weight lift off my chest.

After the Major left, Middleton went over some of the other stats from our time on the station, a bounce in her voice and body language.

"Now for our next assignment," she said.

There were a handful of soft groans, but none from my people.

"We are going to be helping out the Exploration Corps. We will be assisting them on Lepus 328rb. There, the Arbiter troops will be assisting them with ground operations as the Arbiter helps them from space," she explained.

This shouldn't have been a surprise to anyone in the room. We'd only ever seen the rest of society helping out the HFDF, but it wasn't always that way. As I'd told the people leaving the resort last month, the Hunter Armada was too engaged to be deployed for anything major and would be for some time. But we weren't going to spend our time cooling our heels or doing exercises. We were a well-trained and organized group of people who could legally control higher numbers of drones than anyone else in society.

Further, we were on a ship that, aside from being able to carry enough supplies not to need to be resupplied for months on end, was designed to assist ground-based units. A lot of that was the Arbiter's space-to-surface sensor suite. She could track hundreds of targets and gather just about any information that was possible to get from orbit. She had a medical staff and rapid manufacturing and mining units that were standard. Her troops were able to rough it on any planet and were good with scanning, mapping, and otherwise recording their surroundings. Service Term troop transports were all but designed for work like what was needed to explore planets.

The other squads were not looking forward to being bored, but my team was jazzed for it. The last alien planet I'd camped on was full of hostiles that killed everything alive around them. Fuck that shit.

The Lt was going over the planet's specs. Also nice. We could breathe the atmosphere there, and it was around a g. All nice. We wouldn't need our helmets most of the time. On the interesting side was that Lepus 328rb once had a race that had died out well over a hundred years ago. They had about the same tech humans did pre-World War II but had died off. That was a little creepy, for sure.

"The Human Federation Exploration Corps is working in conjunction with exploration teams from the Quiver," she said.

This got all of our attention. The Quiver were our closest allies, but that didn't mean anyone outside the Diplomatic Corps and, apparently, the Exploration Corps interacted with them. Middleton paused to let this sink in. Then she looked at my team. I could almost feel Krista vibrating with excitement.

"First Squad. You have had several pleasant encounters with an alien race prior to this. You spoke with some of the Pike at the beginning of the conflict on Pike Prime and were recognized by their government after we left. This is why the Arbiter was selected for Lepus 328rb. First Squad, you will be working closely with the Quiver planetside. Each of your Fireteams will be working with Exploration Corps groups that are near and work with the Quiver. We know you will continue to represent the HFDF well," she said.

So don't fuck this up. That was the message.

"One of the things that we will be looking at on the planet is the disappearance and destruction of several of the Exploration Corps drones." A data file pinged in my CCPU for download. From my peripheral vision, I saw Krista's posture change. Excited as she was about the Quiver, we were now in the part of the meeting we needed to be dialed in for. "We do not know what has been attacking the drones. We have no reason to suspect that it is an intelligent race and is likely local animals. That said, these attacks have only occurred around former cities, and exploration teams have no clue what is doing it."

Betts raised his hand, and Middleton nodded at him. "Any chance they could be squatters from another race? They may not want us poking around," he said.

"That is a possibility. What's odd is that this is happening in several cities that aren't close together. Normally, we'd expect to see squatters in one place. Also, exploration hasn't seen anything that suggests there's been a ship there recently, along with no suspicious EM traffic or disturbance of the local environment." She looked at the rest of the room. "After Pike Prime, we aren't taking any chances. Be alert. If it turns out the locals aren't all gone after all, we will scrub the mission. If you find anything technologically advanced, report it in. There will be more information to come. That will be all," she said in dismissal.

We filed out of the room, and I headed to our squad's VR training room. Inside were rows of VR pods packed close together, their tops opening like clamshells. I laid down in mine, and the lid closed. For a moment, I was in darkness and then in a room with a door. I walked forward and grabbed the handle, the metal of it cool and hard in my hands. I turned the knob, and the door opened. The room I was in was just there as a waiting area as my pod connected to the space my friends had created. I opened the door and walked into a room with large windows and a pool table in the center. There was a fridge off to the side of the room by several soft armchairs. The door disappeared as it closed.

Jon and Liz were playing pool at the table and waved at me. Monica was sitting in one of the chairs with a drink in her hand. I walked up to the fridge and opened it. There was a soda waiting inside for me. I took it and drank. My mind knew that nothing in the room was real. How could it be? One, we were all either several AU or light-years apart, and the room didn't have any entrances. But the drink in my hand felt cold, and I could taste it. My mind knew it was in a fake place, but for the moment, it could forget that.

I sat in the chair next to Monica.

"You're late. Everything okay?" she asked.

I took another drink. "Yeah, the Major was in the briefing, and we got our new assignment. Sorry I'm late. How are things?"

She looked at Liz and Jon, then shrugged. "Fine."

Monica didn't look that fine, but I didn't want to push it with her.

"Anything new?" I asked.

She shrugged again. "Not a lot," she sighed, glancing at me, a concerned look crossing her face for a moment. "So, your new assignment?"

"Not combat," I said. "We are going to be helping out with Charles Corps. Should be a lot of drone babysitting along with long boring walks around an alien planet."

"You look happy about that," she said, a little surprised.

"Nice, Alex, that's awesome," Liz said, looking away from the game. "I'm all settled on the Helios," she said, smiling.

"She's a beaut," Jon said. "I saw her come out of the shipyards."

I paused for a moment and looked up the ship, then whistled. "Dang, a supercarrier? How'd you land that? I thought they wouldn't make you do an HFDF rotation," I said.

Liz smiled. "My time on the Healers Touch was not part of that rotation, *but* because of the experience I have, I get to serve on a supercarrier."

"Is that dangerous?" Monica asked.

I shook my head. "Not at all. She's brand new, like actually brand new and not refurbed. She won't see action for a while. For one, the Hunter Armada is out of the rotation right now. Too many boots still on the ground. Two, that ship's crew will need to be broken in, which will mean no major deployments. And lastly, it's a supercarrier! They are the biggest things in the fleet. We haven't lost one in like a hundred years," I said.

Liz nodded, looking back at the pool table. "I'm in my pod in the sickbay right now," she said and sunk a couple of balls. "I have almost as much experience as my boss. Also, thanks to my experience, I have completed more certifications than I should have by this point. The Helios is like a break. We are burning out to some coasting orbit around Hunter. The crew said we will just be waiting around for a call. In the meantime, the crew trains, and I am wonderfully bored. The most exciting part of my day is doing regular scans on people," she said.

Monica looked a little pacified. Liz noticed her look and gave me one and then one to Jon.

"Tell us about her, Jon," Liz asked.

For once, Jon looked sheepish. "Um, I don't actually have that much information about those ships… they're HFDF."

I put down my drink. "They are for long-range attacks. Heavy armor belt with tons of small fighter drones. They can send out planet-side landing parties but rarely do. That's what ships like the Arbiter are for. They can deploy long-range bombers and have a defense system that is amazing. There's a reason we haven't lost one in a hundred years. They are as true of a capital ship as you can get. No place safer in the galaxy, to be honest," I said and glanced at Monica out of the corner of my eye.

"Whatever, sounds like a drag," she said but relaxed some.

I got Jon talking about his job and Monica making fun of Jon about his job. Liz and I stayed out of the conversations. She and I stood on one side of the pool table, watching the other two.

"I wish Charles could join us more," Liz said.

"Yeah. He told me he's on the opposite schedule as us," I said.

"We need to do this more," Liz said. "We didn't do this that often in our first year."

"Yeah, with three of us all dealing with insane time demands and me not having access to VR pods for a while didn't help," I said. "But you're right." I looked at her. "We'll do this more. Well, I will try. Not sure what my data and VR situation will be when we ship out."

"Fair enough. How are you and Krista?" she asked, changing the subject.

"Great."

"Not getting tired of her?" Liz asked knowingly.

I chuckled. "Honestly, no. She grounds me in a lot of ways. I don't think I would want to live in a world without her."

"That's good."

"So, how about you? Any prospects?" I asked, eyeing Jon.

Liz glared at me, but a smirk tugged at the corner of her lips. "None at all."

FIVE

I woke up on my own, Krista's sleeping form pressed against me. I didn't have an alarm set for the day. We had a briefing at 1000 but nothing before that. The Arbiter had been burning out to jump distance for the last three days, and we had several jumps planned. The first was one to rendezvous with the Quiver ship that was going to be stationed at Lepus 328rb along with the Arbiter. We'd meet with them and get introduced. From there, we were jumping to an anchorage for supplies. I was looking forward to it—not getting supplies at the station, but being underway. We'd been involved in one training-related task after another for months. I was looking forward to the prospect of having something steady to do. I was also looking forward to doing something that felt more productive. It wasn't that training wasn't productive, but that it didn't always feel like it.

Krista shifted in my arms. I kissed her shoulder, moving up to her neck. She sighed.

"Good morning," I said.

"Good morning," she replied, waking up.

She rolled over, facing me, her blue eyes glassy. She seemed to be looking through me, then back into my eyes.

"We have a few hours until we have anything... breakfast?" she asked.

"We can do that if you like," I said, running my hand up her thigh and side.

It moved its way down her back and then back to her side.

She smiled. "Unless you're not hungry yet."

I smiled back, placing my hand on her hip and guiding it down against the mattress. I rolled on top of her. We'd gotten good at this— fooling around in tight places. Honestly, when we weren't in a bunk, I felt a little exposed. I kissed her lips and then her neck, moving up to her ear.

"I am hungry," I whispered into her ear.

My mouth found hers again, and I kissed her, enjoying the feel of her soft tongue as it danced with mine.

"Me too," she said.

I felt her hands slide down to my hips and push down just a bit. I kissed her again and followed her lead. I kissed down her neck, enjoying the way it made her breathing hitch and pick up. As I kissed down to her collarbone, I slowly moved down in the bunk as she moved up just a bit. My hands moved over her body, and I kissed and nipped her neck, making her gasp softly.

"Such a tease," she breathed.

I grinned and chuckled darkly.

"You're one to talk," I replied, then moved further down her body. I heard her chuckle seductively. I kissed between her breasts, loving the feel of them against my cheeks.

"I don't know what you mean," she said, then moaned as my lips found her nipple. "Mmmm... I'd never... mmm... never be a tease," she tried to say.

Her nipple hardened, and my tongue swirled over it, eliciting more soft sounds of enjoyment from her.

"Liar," I accused, then sucked on her nipple. I felt her writhe under me, and I kissed down the side of her breast to the other one. I felt a

56

sense of satisfaction when the only response I got from her was a mumble.

I kissed down her body, enjoying the feel of her skin. I took my time as my lips moved across the planes of her belly down to her hips and the tops of her thighs. I wanted to just go for it, but I resisted the urge. Instead, I caressed her body as I kissed along her inner thigh, feeling goosebumps under my touch. I saw them cover her body, and I smirked.

I kissed along her bikini line, loving how it made her squirm.

"Please..." she breathed.

I grinned and kissed around her slit, then my tongue ran up it, making her back arch. The taste of her coated my tongue as I found her clit, and my tongue swirled and danced around it, making her legs squirm and writhe. I heard her breathing pick up and felt her fingers in my hair.

I kept going, enjoying every second of it. My hand moved up her body to tease her nipple as my mouth worked. Her thighs rubbed against my cheeks, and her hand pressed my face into her. I let her sounds of pleasure guide me as I brought her closer to release until I felt her body tense and then shudder as I took her over the edge.

"Mmmm, fuck yes, don't stop!" she cried out.

I felt my heart race with excitement as her hips ground slightly against my mouth while she rode her orgasm until she was panting and her body calmed. I kissed up her belly and chest and then up her neck to her lips. The taste of the salt of her sweat sent a shiver of desire coursing through me, and I sucked on her lip for a moment before I plunged into her.

Her back arched again, and I groaned in ecstasy as I thrust forward, sinking deep into her warm tightness. I pushed in all the way and then drew back before thrusting back into her. I felt pleasure surge inside me, and my hips began to pump steadily in and out of her.

"Fuck, you feel good," I moaned, pushing in again.

I looked down at her, loving the sight of her moving below me. I kept going in and out of her, feeling pleasure and tension building inside of me until it finally came out in a rush. I groaned deeply, feeling myself throb deep inside of her. Her walls quivered and clamped around me, driving me out of my mind in the most wonderful way. I felt myself calm as my orgasm faded, my whole body relaxed, and I kissed her.

I laid on top of her, feeling myself relax. Being with Krista hadn't gotten old for either of us. Comfortable and a little routine, yes. But comfort was a good thing, and routine? Well, bunks and all. The inside of her leg ran up mine, and I didn't want to go anywhere.

I looked down at her.

"What are you thinking about?" I asked.

She smiled and looked around the bunk. "How many times we've done it in a bunk." She laughed. "Every time we finish, I think about how great it will be to not be in a bunk, but then every time we've had the chance—and we have all the space we want to do whatever we want—I feel like a dog that finally caught a rabbit. I don't know what to do with it."

"Oh, you know what to do with it," I said suggestively.

She grinned, her hand moving down, "Do I?" she asked wickedly.

I kissed her. "Yes, you do."

We got distracted for a while, but eventually, we remembered what we were talking about.

"Yeah, and sometimes it seems strange to think that our squadmates aren't that far away. Only a screen between us and them. I know they can't see or hear us…" I said.

"Right!" she said. "And Royle is literally right above us. You know, in training, I kind of thought the two of you would be an item."

I thought for a moment. "I can see that, but I'm glad it worked out differently," I said.

I sighed; it was time to get ready for the day. Our suits slid over our bodies, and I felt a great deal of regret as Krista's suit covered her soft skin, taking her away from me. Once in place, the screen to the bunk opened, and we rolled out. Bravo team wasn't there, but Betts and Sweeting were sitting at the table in the center of the room. They were playing chess. Sweeting was annoyingly good at it. Betts nodded at us but looked back to the board, clearly losing.

Sweeting winked at us. "How are you two doing this morning? A bit of a late start, huh?" he asked.

Krista blushed a bit.

Sweeting looked shocked. "Oh wait! You two weren't fucking, were you? And before marriage? Tsk tsk." Betts moved, and Sweeting groaned as he moved. "Check. Come on, man, I need you to try! I'm not done giving Taylor and McLeod shit. Can you do that for me? Try? I can explain how the pieces move again if you like."

"You can shoot him," I said to Betts.

"Nah, the safeties won't let me. I tried," Betts said flatly.

Sweeting laughed. From her bunk, Clay snorted.

"We're getting breakfast," Krista said. "Clay, you hungry?"

"You're still hungry?" Sweeting asked.

Clay jumped down from her bunk. "Yeah, I could eat."

As she walked to us, she hit Sweeting on the shoulder.

"Thanks," Krista said in the hall. She was smiling. "I like having you on the team."

"I like being part of it," Clay said warmly.

I agreed, and that made me feel guilty.

The three of us started down the halls that would lead to the mess. One of the things the recent training had done was to make me look at our ships and structures differently. We'd done a lot of close-quarters fighting, along with fighting in the open with the Venom and Erie, but our training had never taken place in purely HFDF surroundings. It was something I hadn't done a lot of before. As we walked, I thought about the ship, and things started to stick out to me. The first was the lights in the halls. They were in the corners connecting the walls, floor, and ceiling. It made the ship bright and gave it a slightly cold feel. Everything looked the same; without my

CCPU, I wasn't sure how easy it would be to find my way around the ship.

In case shit. That was the unofficial slogan of design and thinking in the HFDF. The walls and floor were designed in case some shit happened, and we didn't have gravity, or the walls became floors. The halls were modular, with doors that could snap shut at the ends. The doors were in case we lost pressure or to slow down an enemy that had boarded us. At the midpoint of the halls were seams where turrets could pop out. They held about as much ammo as a sphere did and had their own power cells and targeting systems. You know, in case the ship was crippled and we needed to fight off boarding parties.

Those turrets were no small issue, either. Looking at where they were in the walls made me think about the training when it had been my team's turn to board the destroyer. The fear I'd felt on the outside of the ship hadn't been present when I was on the inside, but the sense of futility had. Every inch of the ship had made us pay for what we took. I knew the Arbiter would be no different. Boarding her would be a nightmare.

We talked about in case shit all the time. But I hadn't really thought about it on the ship until now. Our bunk screen could make our bunk a pressure vessel in case we lost pressure. We wore our suits aboard the ship, again, in case we needed them for anything at all. The HFDF didn't lose so few people just because we were more advanced than our enemies but because we were more prepared. We made room for another group walking in the other direction.

We turned a few corners and were in the mess hall. We queued up and got our meals. Nothing fancy, just eggs, toast, and hash browns. Oh, and coffee. Despite our CCPUs keeping humans in perfect working order without the need for stimulants, we still were addicted to the stuff. It didn't even do anything to me, thanks to my CCPU, but if I didn't get a cup in the morning when on a ship or station? Caffeine wasn't like alcohol. I could tell my CCPU to let me get a buzz; if anything bad happened, it would kill it so I could think, and I couldn't get blackout drunk. Hell, for that matter, it wouldn't allow anyone to get a chemical dependency on anything. Likewise, our energy was so easy to regulate that there was no need for caffeine. So long as the chemicals needed were in our system, we were good. Drinking booze was for a good time and had always been that way, but why bother with a pick-me-up?

Still, I drank the coffee like it was somehow part of my life in a way that I couldn't live without. Just because there wasn't a chemical addiction didn't mean there weren't mental ones. Thankfully, liking a cup of joe in the morning wasn't anything that would impair my life in some way, so my CCPU let it slide.

We ate quickly, not talking. It was a bad habit we'd all picked up. During training, mess halls were busy, and you needed to get in and get out. It was the same on hostile worlds; if you had a mess hall, you didn't hog it.

After breakfast, we made our way to the briefing room. *I know that's a surprise.* Middleton and Monroe were there, but not the rest of the platoon. We already knew how the meeting would go down. We would go over the information about the Quiver we'd been provided until our heads wanted to explode. Then we'd go over it again. We'd talk about the day's itinerary. It was simple. We'd jump to the designated meeting spot, which happened to be at jump distance.

It was like meeting in neutral territory. We were allies with the Quiver, but that didn't mean we were going to share all of our secrets with them, and they weren't going to do the same with us. Jump tech fell into the category of things we didn't share, so meeting at a nice flat bit of space was ideal. Once the ships were in the same area, the Quiver would send a shuttle to the Arbiter. We'd meet the Quiver that we'd be working with and spend a little time in the hangar talking to build rapport. After our team was done, Royle's team would go in the hangar and wait for the Quiver they'd be working with. Then they'd go back to their ship and jump to wherever they were going next. Maybe it was Lepus 328rb, or maybe it wasn't. We'd then jump to an anchorage to take on supplies that the Exploration teams needed and be on our merry way.

Two hours later, we left the room. I was pretty sure the HFDF had just violated every law we had about psychological torture. The only one not completely tanked was Krista.

"So what do we do today?" Sweeting asked in the hall.

"Do you want the short version or the two-hour version?" Clay said.

"Ooo, I'm not sure. I feel like we didn't really cover much of the day's events back there," he said.

"I can hear you, Sweeting, and you too, Clay," Monroe said from the briefing room's open door.

Sweeting decided not to complain anymore. Clay's face flushed with embarrassment. It was a testament to the meeting that anyone on my team bitched.

We went to the hangar to wait for the ship to jump. My helmet came on in the airlock as it cycled. The hangar was almost always kept in vacuum. It was a little odd going into it. Without sound, our suit's proximity sensors were always something we had to check. Not that it was likely that anything was going to run us over, but it always took a while to adjust. We sat on some crates as we waited. The hangars were relatively empty. All of the shuttles were locked down and out of sight. There wasn't much in the way of cargo anywhere, either. I got the impression that the crate we were on was there for when the deck crew wanted to sit.

The ship started its countdown until the jump. I pulled up the exterior feeds for the side of the ship that should see the Quiver Destroyer when it jumped in. The space outside was as calm as ever. Then the stars changed, and there was still calm. I pulled up the ship's sensor feed. We were as alone as you could be.

"The Quiver aren't here yet," I said to the team, "in case you aren't watching any feeds."

"I wasn't, but I am now," Betts said.

We were to arrive first. When we did, the Arbiter transmitted its location to the Quiver. A few minutes later, there was a flash about five kilometers away as a ship jumped into the area. At once, the Arbiter's threat alarms went off as it found a ship jumping that instantly turned into a seeming void in space. A moment later, the alarm stopped as the ship identified the other ship as the Quiver. But god, it was creepy.

The destroyer had jumped in five kilometers away, well within visual range. I'd seen the flash, and now it was like it was gone. I had to toggle to the sensor feed to see the ship. There are two ways that you can find something in space: with the EM spectrum or with gravity. Or I guess if you ran into something, that would work too, but it wasn't ever really the plan. HFDF ships did their damnedest not to be seen in the EM range, barring when under thrust. Likewise, we tried to hide our gravity signature. Like when we'd been on the HFDF destroyer, its gravity field fell off quickly. That wasn't easy to do but useful on so many levels—one of them making a ship harder to find.

The Quiver ship wasn't using any gravity. It would have to when under thrust just to keep its passengers alive, but the Quiver liked being in null g. Our sensors were such that we could make out the ship, but it was eerie how hard it was for me to see. I knew that to the Quiver, the Arbiter was likewise hidden. Then the Quiver ship was bright green—not due to anything the Arbiter was doing, but because its hull was green. Ours turned orange. A giant pumpkin and a lime. It was a lime with flat-faced surfaces for deflecting sensors and ordnance coming its way. Otherwise, its outline was lumpy, like two large ovals had been stuffed into one another. Turd-shaped. It was one badass turd for sure, but a turd.

Despite its appearance, as soon as the destroyer came into view, my CCPU showed that there was information I could view. I pulled it up. The name of the vessel was the Vinur. At least, that was the name my CCPU showed me. The HF's real name for the Vinur was a giant alphanumeric string, but for our sanity, the HFDF would go down a list of "friends" from human languages and assign that name to the

Quiver ship for our time working with it. The specs we knew of the Vinur started to pop up. She had four main railgun batteries, along with several smaller ones around the hull. The bow sported four large missile tubes. We didn't have a lot of information on the defense system, other than it was advanced. Apparently, the Quiver had a habit of altering ship configurations and watering down ships that were meeting with allies, so the configuration the Arbiter was seeing may not have been normal. From the specs, it appeared that the ship was best suited for longer-range engagements—something that our intel said the Quiver preferred. They used stealth and range to fight the enemy.

An opening on the side of the ship appeared, and a shuttle detached. I rose along with my team as the Arbiter's hangar doors opened. The Quiver shuttle wasn't like ours. It was generally the same size but had a lozenge shape to it. It approached the Arbiter quickly and then flipped, burning its engines for a moment before letting its anchors slow it down to enter the Arbiter's hangar. Our squad stood in a straight line, waiting for the shuttle to come to rest in the center of the hangar. The back opened as it stopped.

Five Quiver came out of the back of the shuttle. We'd gone over them a lot over the last few days. They were about half as tall as a human. Their body could be broken down into two main areas: an upper and lower half. The lower half had four legs, each ending in four long and powerful toes that could wrap around objects like tree branches. The hind legs were larger and more powerful. The Quiver evolved in trees, and with the way their legs were set up, they were just as comfortable right-side up or upside down; they could hang just as easily as stand. Their toes ensured a good grip anywhere, but made them shit for running on flat terrain.

The lower half was connected to the upper with a thin torso. At the top of the torso were shoulders with two arms that ended in six-digit hands. Atop the shoulders was the Quiver's large head. It was oval-ish and ran parallel with the lower part of the body. The mouth was at the front, with two small arms with three fingers on them. The arms only served to assist in eating with the digits, lacking the dexterity for more complex tasks. Still, that would be handy; you could eat while doing anything else, including breathing, as the respiratory system wasn't connected to the digestive system. On the top of the head toward the back was a blowhole that went right to the vocal cords and lungs. Their eyes were on the front of the head above their mouths. I knew the Quiver were purple, but right now, all I could see was their suits.

They came off the shuttle, their thin limbs moving in a gait that was smooth but somehow unnerving. Their bodies were covered up with black suits that appeared to be nano-material. The suits had flat faces on them to deflect damage. While well-suited for null-G and trees, the Quiver were not as physically robust as humans. We were used to taking damage, with our suits' main defense being to spread impacts over the largest area possible. Our bodies worked well for this. The Quivers did not, so they deflected as much as they could. That said, being small with thin limbs, they couldn't have been easy targets. Along with their desire to engage from a distance, I doubted the Quiver got hit as often as we did.

They had packs on top of their lower bodies with a rifle that looked similar enough to ours; they did have similar shoulder, arm, and hand layouts as we did, so the gun made sense. The group approached us. My CCPU pinged me. The group was two squads of five each. One would work with my team; the other with Royle's.

It took three Quiver to breed, with each having the same reproductive organs. When they mated, all three Quiver walked away pregnant. So there weren't males and females, just its—its whose names I couldn't say because my vocal cords lacked the ability to. Likewise, they couldn't say our names. Thankfully, the HF was there to fix the problem. Why use another species' language when you can just have your CCPU translate perfectly and do it for you? They don't have gender, and therefore, gender-specific names don't work. No problem;

the HF has a solution for that, too. Do you know what else doesn't have mostly gender-specific names? Cities. Yup, why not?

The five Quiver in front of me were a tour of small North American cities. Their leader was Clovis; then, there was Canton, Ely, Pampa, and Roswell. The last name could have had some humor to it, but knowing the HF, it was probably just a coincidence that one of the aliens shared a name riddled with old alien conspiracies.

I stepped forward to our guests and spoke.

"Hello, my name is Corporal Alex Taylor. We are from the HFDF Arbiter's F Company, Second Platoon, First Squad. It is an honor to meet you," I said.

Clovis ambled forward. "My name is Clovis. We are of the Quiver ship Vinur." It waved its hand behind it. "This is my team. We are honored to meet you as well."

The two governments had scripts for us to follow. I had a set of questions that I would ask Clovis, and vice versa. I had answers prepared for each question I received, but the HFDF hadn't given me the exact wording for my answers. I had to come up with that on my own. Clovis was in the same boat. This made our conversation feel scripted—which was the point—but it also gave each of us the opportunity to show who we and our team were with the way we answered. The conversation started awkwardly but turned into a dialogue over time. By the time we'd run out of scripted questions, we were having a genuine conversation.

We talked for about an hour, with our teams speaking to each other. During this time, I was able to start getting a feel for how the Quivers' dynamic worked. Clovis and I went over some communication protocols with each other and went through the steps of setting up a direct line of communication. The last part might have been the strangest of all.

Clovis and I weren't talking directly to each other, even if it felt that way. For one, we were in a vacuum, so at least it would have been an AltComms conversation. But Clovis was from another species. What I said was routed through my CCPU to the Arbiter, and from the ship, it was routed to the diplomatic corps, who in turn sent it to the Quiver embassy, which then followed a similar route down to Clovis. With AltComms, it happened in milliseconds, but everything we said crossed literal light-years.

When we were done, the Quiver boarded their shuttle and left. We waited until they were clear of the Arbiter before heading back to the briefing room to wait for Bravo team to have their meeting.

SIX

I was finishing up my shower when I got the notification from the ship that we were about to jump. I thanked the gods that the Orion Anchorage General operated on Orion City time. So we wouldn't be jumping into the anchorage at some ungodly hour like we had before at other anchorages. Instead, we'd be rolling in around 0700. That's some livable shit right there. I walked into the post-shower room, brushed my teeth, and ran a comb through my hair.

I was still thinking about our meeting with the Quiver from the previous day. It was strange how something could seem so relatable and yet completely alien at the same time. I liked Clovis and wasn't worried about working with it. Likewise, my team was comfortable with them, too. By design, we would not be working with them directly in the field unless their Exploration Teams and ours were in the same area, but shit can happen, and it was nice to have an open channel of communication in case we needed it.

I engaged my suit, which slid over my body like a second skin. I walked out of the post-shower room and down to Monroe's office. Royle met me there. We walked in to find Monroe with a blank look on his face. He motioned for us to sit. We each took a chair in front of his desk and waited. After a moment, his gaze moved to us.

"Good morning," he said. "Sorry about that."

"Good morning, sir," we said.

"I just received a report from the anchorage. Our inspection will be right after we dock. Your teams will need to be there at 1000. We are going to be docked for a few hours," he said.

My CCPU pinged with a data packet. It contained instructions on how to get to the loading area our cargo would be in.

"That's nice they're letting us in so early," Royle said.

Monroe smirked. "They didn't want to. The rest of the platoon isn't inspecting their cargo. Of course, the other platoon's Special Teams squads, along with ours, are. I tried to tell the logistics lady at the anchorage that it wasn't anything personal, but that we are a little different."

"Makes you appreciate HFDF Anchorage staff more, doesn't it?" Royle said.

"That it does," Monroe replied.

The people at an HFDF anchorage would know that there was no way Special Teams wasn't going to inspect their dedicated cargo before going planetside. On Erie Prime and Pike Prime, our squad had been using spaces and equipment shared with all troops. On this op, we'd have dedicated drones and housing. Yes, we could live on the planet without the housing, and yes, the chances of the logistics crews fucking up were zero, but I still wanted to look at the gear that could be keeping me alive. Always planning for the shit to hit the fan and for things to go wrong had been instilled in me since joining the HFDF. My team was the same. Drop us on a planet with hostiles? Sure, go for it. Don't let us check to make sure our mostly unnecessary shelter has the food we want? That, we might lose some sleep over.

"Do we need to report back to the ship when the inspection is complete?" I asked.

"No, there are commercial and entertainment areas aboard the station. Your teams are free to enjoy themselves. Just be back before we are underway. Our time working with the Exploration team isn't going to be like living in foxholes on Pike Prime, but there won't be any bars or theaters there either," Monroe explained.

"Works for me," I said.

We left after doing a quick rundown of all the equipment we were going to be inspecting. Normally, the Arbiter wouldn't have gone to a non-HFDF anchorage if she needed to refit, but this mission was unique in that we were supporting another branch of the government. We were not only picking up everything we would need for an extended mission but also bringing supplies for the Exploration crews on the ground.

Every month, jump containers arrived for them, but this time we'd bring them. It made sense; the Arbiter was going to the planet, and it didn't exactly have issues with moving cargo. I also suspected that was why we got time station-side. Had we gone to an HFDF location, the ship would have been supplied quickly, as everything would have been on hand in the station. In this case, I suspected that they had to pull from one of the thousands of floating warehouses that formed a sphere around the Anchorage and its stations. When I left Monroe's office, the ship was moving through those warehouses.

The anchorage was like a big ball of stuff. On the outside of the ball where we'd jumped in were warehouse units that were larger than the Arbiter by a good margin. Along with them was part of the defense grid. The warehouses were spread out so that ships could pass, but they weren't too spread out. When jumping into a location, you needed clearance, or the drives wouldn't work. Part of the clearance needed was the size of the ship, but it was more based on how advanced the drive system was. There was a margin of error. For the Arbiter, that margin was 300 meters, like most HFDF ships. Add an extra 300 meters in a bubble around the ship, and that was what she could jump into. It was insanely tight. Most ships needed kilometers of clearance.

The need for tight clearance was only necessary if you needed to jump to a precise location that required a low margin of error. Like, say, a fleet of ships jumping into combat. The warehouse units acted like a wall to incoming ships, be they friendly or hostile. I watched the feeds as the Arbiter floated through. She had plenty of clearance on all sides, but it was still a little unnerving seeing objects larger than the ship so close.

As the ship docked, we took our time getting to the hatches. We didn't have far to go to inspect our cargo, and we weren't in a hurry to stand around in the way of station crew members while we waited for our stuff. The ship's hatches all had lines forming at them, and everyone who could leave was keen to do so. I didn't blame them. For most of the crew, they'd be aboard the ship the whole time we were deployed to Lepus 328rb. *God, I hated that name.* We'd be there for months, and while me and mine were happy to spend a few hours at a local lounge, it wasn't the end-all for us. After all, we would be planet-side, wandering around while the crew was stuck on the ship.

When it was our turn to leave, Krista and I walked into the station hand in hand. The terminal was large, allowing for hundreds of people to flow in and out of ships. Windows looked out to the Arbiter, which had enclosed gangways attached to her, feeding cargo on board. The flow of people in the terminal was in one direction, away from the ships. Krista and I moved along with the crowd of crew members. We followed instructions from our CCPUs to one of the station's airlocks. It opened to a cavernous room.

Along the floor were square tiles that moved cargo containers around like they were floating. Gantries moved along above us, carrying containers, and drones worked busily. We were in a sorting room, lining up containers and loading them onto the Arbiter. Off to the right and away from the main floor, as much as possible, were containers that our CCPUs told us belonged to us and other Special Teams squads. Some of the logistics crew members turned their heads in our direction, but I couldn't see the looks on their faces due to their helmets. I'm sure they weren't friendly.

We made our way to the cargo containers that were marked for our fireteam. There were three of them. One was our mobile housing unit. Another was a workshop with ammo and a small RMU. The last was just a container that held other supplies like defense towers to place around the Exploration base and extra parts.

"Alright, let's get this done quickly. Everyone inspect your personal elements. After that, we can split up the rest of the equipment. Be fast about it before the logistics crews in here throw us outside," I ordered.

The team moved to the housing unit. On the planet, the sides of the unit would open up and slide out, extending the space on the inside. Presently, the outside wall was opened, allowing logistics drones and us to load or inspect anything inside, but the unit wasn't expanded. The area we were most concerned with was the personal food storage. Each of us had a month's worth of pre-packaged food along with another month's worth of nutrient packs. There was also water, juice, and other drinks.

I looked over my stuff carefully. I didn't want to end up with the same meal for months on end. You know, like when I was on Pike Prime eating God knew how many nutrient packs. I stopped my CCPU from telling me how many I'd eaten. My food was there, along with ammo and spare nano-material. I felt better having seen it all. After I finished with that, I walked over to the container that had all of the defense equipment. It was packed way too tight for me to look at everything, but I was able to integrate with everything I was supposed to be able to. The same was true for the shop container.

We waited for Royle's team to complete their work. As we waited, I watched the logistics crews and drones work. It was all soundless, of course, as we were in vacuum. The containers moved along the floor in a perfectly timed dance. In the path, lights on the floor lit up so you knew where a container was headed. Eventually, they made it to a queue of containers working their way onto the loading mechanism, where they were moved out of the station by conveyors that loaded them into the Arbiter. Seeing the speed at which everything was moving made me wonder just how much cargo the ship could hold. It also made me wonder how much faster things would have been if some of the supplies didn't need to come from the warehouse units outside.

"We're done," Royle said over a general comm.

"Alpha, let's move out," I said to my team.

We left the way we came in. Our cargo was already moving into line with others. We stepped into the airlock, which was large enough to hold our whole squad comfortably. It cycled, and our helmets disengaged. I walked out into the wide hall that connected to the airlock and others like it. It was bland gray, interrupted with bright orange and yellow sections around the airlocks. We took an elevator back up to the main terminal.

The terminal wasn't a giant cavernous room, as the cargo area had been, but it was wide, allowing for a lot of traffic. It had connecting hallways and escalators that led to various parts of the station. There were tram tubes that ran through the sections. My team gathered together off to the side of the traffic.

"What is there to do?" Sweeting said to himself, his eyes out of focus.

"Looks like there's a lounge not far from here. We could grab a few drinks and kill some time there," Betts said.

I looked at Krista questioningly.

She shrugged. "Works for me."

"Me too," Sweeting and Clay said.

Our CCPUs plotted us a course, and we started to walk. All around us were restaurants and shops, along with every type of entertainment you could think of, from casinos and brothels to spas. These stations catered to people who spent most of their time aboard a ship. When they got to port, they wanted to unwind. I could understand that. As such, there was any type of pastime you could ever want. The one thing in common they all had, though, was that none of them seemed like the types of places that you would want to spend days on end at, like the resort Krista and I had visited. Other than residents, no one would be here that long. They didn't want permanent but rather quick fixes. I wondered what the areas of the station the residents lived in were like. At a guess, I would say nothing like the section we were in.

"Is that another brothel?" Clay asked.

I looked. And it was. We'd seen several, each with its own feel. This one had bone drones dressed in various uniforms waving at people out front. Some dressed like cops, or school teachers, and even a few had suits that looked like ours.

"Role play, huh?" Betts said.

"Not your cup of tea?" Krista asked.

"Nah," he said honestly. "There was one that didn't look too bad back aways. I might have to hit that up before we go."

"Yeah, I might have to get together with Janet before we head out," Sweeting mused.

"I thought you two were on a break?" Clay asked, referring to his relationship with Janet Kwasny from Royle's team.

"Yeah, well, she's about to go on a long deployment like us, isn't she? Taylor and McLeod are the only two I see getting lucky on this trip," Sweeting said.

Krista blushed, and I chuckled.

Clay looked like she was thinking about that. I suspected our team wouldn't be spending our entire time at the station together. My suspicions were strengthened as Clay took her hair out of its holder and ran her fingers through it.

"You're welcome," Sweeting said to her.

She hit his arm.

I leaned in near Krista's ear. "Our relationship proves to be convenient yet again."

She looked at me. "Seriously."

We found the lounge. From the outside, it had flashing lights and the softest of beats coming from the door. When we walked in, the beats weren't so soft. I could feel the music pounding in my chest. I toggled on my comms with the team. I would still move my lips and try to talk, but wouldn't have to raise my voice this way. To them, it would sound like we were talking in a quiet room. We didn't need to move our lips for this to work, but it was really odd hearing someone's voice but not seeing their mouth move. For anyone watching, you looked odd too, just staring at one another, not talking, but your body reacting like you were in a conversation.

The lounge didn't seem that lounge-ish to me with the music. There was a bar where people were crowded, getting drinks and talking to one another. Some of the patrons were in government-issued suits of some form, but most were in normal attire. We were the only HFDF in the place. Krista and I shuffled our way up to the bar and ordered drinks. We had spent part of the day in vacuum and always worked under the assumption that we would spend the bulk of our day either in a VR POD or with our helmets on. Clay and Krista didn't have on makeup or have their hair done up. Heck, Krista still had her hair up in a tight bun. For the guys, we hadn't done more than kind of run a comb through our hair.

There was another group like us. They were in orange suits. Logistics crew. They'd also spend the bulk of their time with a helmet engaged. I felt for Clay. She was sizing up the people around her and seeing that she wasn't going to be in the running. Most of the people in the lounge were from ships where they'd been cooped up for days or weeks. They were here to mix and mingle and get laid.

Betts didn't seem to notice anyone else. He walked up to the bar, people parting for him magically, and ordered a beer. He walked over to us, taking a long pull.

"What did you get?" he asked us.

"Mudslide," Krista said.

"Whiskey. You?" I asked.

"IPA," he said.

Krista made a face. "Animal."

He grinned and took another long pull on the drink.

We found a curved couch with a table that we could all sit around. Sweeting, Betts, Krista, and I got comfortable and watched the saddest contest there was: Clay trying to pick someone up.

"Any bets?" Sweeting asked.

"That's fucked up, man," I said. Then I watched her strike out with some chick who looked like she was in the medical corps. "We are all gonna place the same bet anyway."

"Not true," Sweeting said. "How long until she gives up?"

"Really?" Krista said reproachfully.

Betts shrugged. "Three more. Twenty credits."

Krista scowled at him.

"Two more," Sweeting said.

"Nah, she's got a lot of fight in her. Five more strikeouts," I countered.

Krista gave me a look, then looked at Clay.

"You guys are assholes. But… six," Krista said.

Clay looked to be laying it on thick with the medical chick. She also had no clue we were watching her. The medical lady turned around pretty obviously and struck up a conversation with someone else. Clay didn't look happy but didn't look like she was going to give up.

She found another target.

"Come on, honey," Sweeting said.

"Here it comes," Betts said. "That girl isn't even giving her the time of day."

The girl wandered off. Clay took a long drink and then moved on.

"Damnit!" Sweeting said, gaining a few surprised looks from people around us.

Betts laughed. "That's right!"

It was a sick pastime, but we all got into it. Krista seemed to be willing Clay on in some way.

"Are you helping her?" I asked.

Krista blushed. "No… I mean, I did say that blonde looked lonely."

I laughed. "Are you feeding her bad leads?"

"No!" Krista said insistently. "I only half want to win the bet; I do feel for her, though."

"You know you could…" Sweeting started.

"If you say it, Sweeting, I will find a way to shoot you," Krista said, glaring at him.

He laughed.

I sat back, confident. I knew my people. After the fifth shutdown, a dejected Clay found us and sat heavily. My CCPU pinged me with the credits the others owed me. Clay looked at us.

"Am I missing something?" she asked. "You all seem… weird."

Betts took a drink. "We placed a bet on how many times you'd strike out."

"Dude!" I said.

Clay's look of confusion vanished. "Seriously?"

"It was Sweeting's idea," Krista said.

"You too!" Clay exclaimed.

Krista looked down.

Clay looked at us. "Who won?"

"I did," I admitted.

She glared at me intensely. Weakling that I am, I said, "I'll give you thirty percent of the take."

She considered. "Thirty-five."

I transferred the credits.

"You guys are assholes," she said, chuckling.

"This is why I'm just going to get a bone drone," Betts said conversationally. "The only thing the HFDF is better at than killing aliens is our game."

"Seriously. Yeah, I guess I am hitting the drones up too," Clay said pathetically.

Betts shrugged. "Nah, it's easier, can be cheaper, and you get what you want. No one in here is getting into a relationship. They just have awkward one-night stands to look forward to."

We stayed for a few hours before Betts and Clay left, and Sweeting met up with Kwasny as he'd predicted.

"I'm glad we aren't like them," Krista said, talking about Sweeting and Kwasny.

We were walking in a quieter part of the station now.

"Me too," I said, squeezing her hand.

We couldn't have been like Sweeting and Kwasny. The HFDF would have assigned us to different fireteams. I liked both Sweeting and Kwasny, but I wondered if it would be a pain for them if their on-again, off-again relationship continued over the next few years. We found a coffee shop where we got some coffee and pastries. We sat down in the back.

The shop was quiet on the inside, with oversized chairs to sit in. As I sat, I felt myself sink in. I took a sip of the coffee.

"This is my kind of lounge," I said.

"Mine too. Funny how that changes. When I was in high school, I thought I'd love loud bars," she said.

"I did used to like them. Liz, Jon, Charles, Monica, and I used to take the train to Orion City all the time. It was never really Charles's speed, though."

"I don't see Liz liking the party scene," Krista said.

I shook my head. "Oh, she does. It's surprising, but she likes it. She and Jon both. Not every night or weekend, mind you, but when they want to, they know how to have a good time."

I thought back fondly to those days. They hadn't been long ago, but I could still see my friends all together, jumping around on the dance floor like morons. Charles pretending like he didn't mind being in the middle of a bunch of strangers. Monica, with her 'touch me and I'll kill you' look. Jon and Liz loving it, both as carefree as you could be. I was sure Jon would still be like that, but not Liz.

"What are you thinking about?" Krista asked, interrupting my thoughts.

"Just how life was. About all my friends pre-Service," I said with a shrug.

She looked thoughtful. "You've been saying stuff like that a lot lately. Is something bothering you?"

I sighed. "No. Not really... Just that things changed so much faster than I thought they would, ya know?"

"I guess. When I moved from home, I knew my life would never be anything like it was. But I also lived on a dead world in the smallest of small towns. So I wasn't surprised," she said.

"What's that been like?" I asked.

She took a sip of coffee. "Different in some ways but what I thought in others. I talk to friends, but we aren't the same people anymore. It feels like it's been years since we lived in the same place and had the same routines and experiences."

My CCPU pinged me. It was time to head back to the ship. We left the shop and walked back to the Arbiter. It wasn't due to leave for an hour, but I didn't want to be the reason it didn't leave or have to explain why I wasn't aboard when it did leave. The passageways weren't busy on the ship as we arrived; Krista and I were the first back to our room. The others came aboard shortly after us. We found our way to our bunks or the table in the middle of the room to talk or otherwise pass the time as the ship finished up and undocked.

There wasn't the excitement that I had felt on my first jump. On that one, not only would I be seeing an alien world, but I'd be fighting on it. Lepus 328rb was an alien world, but now my third, and thankfully, there was nothing I was supposed to be fighting on it. I suppose I was a little excited to go to it, but not like before. I was just looking forward to seeing a new world and exploring it. It'd be my team and the small Exploration Team. That was it unless we ran into the Quiver.

We pretty much had the whole planet to ourselves, and that sounded good to me.

I watched one of the exterior feeds as the ship jumped. Below us was a blue ocean and white clouds. The land was green and brown. By this time tomorrow, I would be on the surface, for what was looking to be a long and hopefully uneventful deployment.

SEVEN

Unlike the station, the base on Lepus 328rb operated on a different time from ours. In combat, that wouldn't have affected us much; we could fight in the dark just as well as in light. But the exploration team kept local hours, so that meant we would too. We'd jumped from the anchorage in the evening, but the exploration base's local time was 0600 on a twenty-five-hour day. That meant we were going to have to stay up until the base's evening. Our CCPUs could keep us awake without feeling it for over two days. Only on day three of being awake did you start to feel anything, but that was livable. We'd gone a week during training, and the results hadn't been pretty. After four days, our CCPUs started to lose the battle against our brains, and their ability to reduce or resolve sleep deprivation effects diminished. Sleep, the instructors said, was the only thing they could really push our bodies with that would provide a meaningful lesson. The lesson was clear: you needed sleep, or you couldn't function. The impacts of missing sleep were measured in lost lives. I couldn't help but sigh internally. I didn't want to start a mission at the end of the day. Especially on a day when I'd been in a station drinking and relaxing with my team; but sometimes, that's how it goes.

I pinged Royle.

"Squad room," she responded.

"Oh, fuck off. You always get that room," I said.

"So."

"So... my team scored higher on the last training exercise we were a part of. I remember a little deal about that," I countered.

"I don't," she said.

I played CCPU footage of the deal. It was clear. On the ship, we had a squad room to prep in and then a platoon briefing room for the whole platoon. When each team had its own mission, one would take the squad room, which was smaller and had a table in the center with a video display perfect for huddling around. The other team would take the briefing room. It had a big vid wall, but no one liked having to go over a mission there. It required that fireteam leaders act like responsible adults when dividing up time for the rooms. Unfortunately, Royle and I were not adults about it, so instead of coming up with reasonable compromises or scheduling around each other's teams, we tried to stick the other one with the briefing room.

She was silent for a moment. "Shit. Fine, you have it. How long did I agree for?"

"Next ten missions THAT start aboard the ship," I said.

She swore.

"Maybe don't suck so much next time, cupcake," I said, ending the connection.

I opened a line to my team. "In the squad room in ten."

I was on my way there, lest Royle renege on our deal and try to stake the room out. She didn't. Sometimes even children can control themselves. The room was pretty simple. The wall was made up of lockers, each holding extra supplies and ammo. Benches were on the outskirts of the room, and at the far end were two shower units and a john. In the center of the room was a table with a video display atop it that a squad could easily fit around. Despite all the tech we had and the ability to port images right into our mind's eye, people still liked to stand together, looking at the same map. There was something about it that made you feel like you were preparing for a mission as a team and not on your own.

My team filed in, most looking smug. I wondered how much ribbing they'd given Bravo team. I doubted it was more than they'd given us when we'd been the losers. I integrated with the table. Lepus 328rb spun on it. Everyone gathered around. The planet stopped spinning and zoomed in on the center of one of the continents. It stopped zooming when the display showed a fifty by fifty kilometer section of the ground.

"Here is the exploration base," I said.

A green dot lit up on the map. I drew a line with my finger.

"Twenty kilometers away is an old city from the species that used to dominate this planet."

The city turned orange. It wasn't large— or I should say, it hadn't been large when it had occupants, however long ago that had been. When I zoomed in on the city, almost none of the buildings had roofs anymore. Most weren't above five stories, and all were made with masonry. The materials we'd been provided about the former race indicated they were very humanoid, and seeing the buildings, I could really get a feel for that.

Evolution worked that way. Some body plans just worked and would show up again and again under the right conditions. Lepus 328rb was a dead ringer for Earth: similar climate and gravity, about the same amount of land, and light from its host star. The fact that a species had come along that was bipedal and had two arms wasn't shocking. The real mystery wasn't that they had been like us, but what had happened to them? It had been a long time ago—over a hundred years; somehow, they'd all kicked the bucket. We knew they hadn't nuked themselves, as they hadn't developed nukes by that point, from what we had gathered. There were no obvious signs that another race had come in and taken up shop, or if they did, they left a perfectly good planet behind.

I suspected that was part of the reason both us and the Quiver were here. Not us in the military; we were here for grunt labor and, in our case, to try and figure out what had been taking out exploration drones. But the governments, in general. We explored a lot of planets, but finding long-dead civilizations that, by all accounts, shouldn't be dead always interested us. The answer would be mundane in the end: a plague, or war, or something else like that. Still, we looked.

Dots in the city appeared. "Here are where drones have been lost," I said.

Betts looked thoughtful.

"What's on your mind?" I asked.

"They have only lost drones in former urban environments. Three bases have lost drones, right? All in former cities," he said.

That had crossed my mind. It was the only supporting evidence that some of the locals were still kicking.

"Yeah, that's the part that seems fishy to me too," I said.

Exploration drones were lost on a regular basis. It wasn't that they were low quality or not well maintained but that they were largely in the open, in places where things just happened. Losing them wasn't the issue, but that all of the ones that had been lost to things that couldn't be attributed to the elements had happened in cities. It was probable that a local species had taken up residence in the cities after the fall of society. The buildings would make for good shelter and, as such, would attract plenty of prey species. But if there was something that would attack a drone, it would probably not hesitate to attack a person too. The exploration team's suits were built with this in mind. It wasn't reasonable to explore alien worlds for a living and not expect to run afoul of local wildlife. The suits weren't as hard-wearing as the HFDF ones, but they were tough enough.

"We need to keep an eye out in the cities. If it's an animal or locals that aren't dead, we need to know about it before someone gets hurt," I said.

I knew the exploration teams were not even a little worried about this. Charles had told me so. This shit happened, and as he'd pointed out, the military had made me paranoid. I was fine with paranoia. I panned the map to the exploration base. Its layout was simple. There were six exploration ships all lined up—one for each member of their team. Those ships provided all the power needed for the base's operations. Our mobile housing unit had enough power to last for a couple of months, but it would still be plugged into the base network. One of the exploration ships could have easily powered the whole base, plus our stuff. Next to the ships, also in a line, was the base shop, lab, and shared space for recreation. To the north was a storage area, then to the northwest was a landing pad where the base's ferry booster resided.

When we'd jumped into the area, I'd seen the ferry boosters from the bases making their way to us. The boosters were drones that shuttled cargo containers to and from the ground. They clamped onto the outside of cargo containers and brought them to the surface, then, when it was time to send something up the well, they would put it in a stable orbit and return home.

Our housing unit and shop would be located on the south side of the base, closest to the city. Not for any security reasons, but just because it was the best place for us to go to be out of the way of the exploration folks.

I zoomed out, and dots appeared around the base. "When we get on site, I want to get unpacked and get the perimeter up quickly. It doesn't matter that there isn't a threat; we won't drag ass." I pointed at the dots. "Defense turrets in these locations." And then more dots. "Foxholes here."

Everyone nodded. No one would bitch about having to do their jobs, and I knew that no one would ever drag ass in my team. Outside of duty, we were all just as dysfunctional as anyone else, but when it was time to work, we all did it without complaint.

I displayed a list of drones. "We have standard PODs for this mission. Each person with eight BIs and two BBALLs. Two of those BIs will carry HIRs. As a team, we have three Heavies, two mortar drones, and two mules. In our reserves, we have four Spheres and another ten BBALLs, along with five replacement BIs.

"When in the field, there will always be one person back at base. Their POD, along with at least one of the Heavies, will be on site," I said. "I'm sure the exploration team is going to think this is overkill, but it's what we have, and paranoid is what we do. They don't run night operations here, so working out watch schedules should be a breeze. Does anyone have any questions?"

"What's the rotation for hanging at the base?" Sweeting asked.

"We'll all do it, but if someone wants to be at home more, I'm open to having them do it more often than not," I said.

"I'll do it," Sweeting said.

"I figured. You're on point for it, then. Plan on that being your gig unless I say otherwise."

At first glance, this would make Sweeting look lazy. But Sweeting wasn't lazy. Outside of duty, he didn't take a thing seriously, but he was dead serious about his job. In the field, I'd used him as a switch hitter, but I'd learned that when it came to basic base work, Sweeting was where it was at. After Pike Prime, we'd all learned to look at a stable place to sleep as a luxury in the field. But for Sweeting, he was never all the way comfortable unless he was the one running security. And he was good at it. He could check and re-check stuff all day long without getting bored or letting something lapse by mistake. From experience, I knew he would have supplies prepped before I asked for them and would have everything in the base running at optimum levels. That worked. None of the rest of us cared about it or really wanted to do it.

"How are we working in the field?" Clay asked.

"In teams of two. Exploration already works that way. Two teams of two with people back at home. It's standard safety. They might be hoping to count each one of us as that field buddy, but we aren't going for it. I don't mind if there is space between teams in the field, but I don't want to thin our lines that much," I said. "The head of the exploration base is Maria Guzman; she is calling the shots unless myself or command sees a threat, in which case we take command."

"How do they feel about that?" Betts asked.

I shrugged. "Not sure, really. They know the protocols, but they also know that we only take command if the shit hits the fan; if that happens, I'm sure they'll be all too happy to follow our lead. Otherwise, they have people to help them out."

Betts nodded.

I looked at everyone on my team. These people were my family now, and I knew each of them like they were family. "I know what we are all thinking. This should be cake. And I know I don't need to tell you this. Plan on it not being cake. In case shit," I said.

They all echoed that. The best way to keep bored was to stay prepared. I planned on being extremely bored. We stood from the table, and all of us started getting our gear ready for the drop. Royle's team joined us. Everyone worked efficiently, and none of us talked much. This was as close as I got to ritual. Every one of us would be going over the drop in our heads. You did this on the training ones too. Repetition makes habit, and good habits keep you alive in combat. I'd only made a handful of combat drops, but the ingrained ritual of prepping for a mission had made the real ones go by easier. When I'd prepped for our drop on Erie Prime, I hadn't even noticed that I was ready. I didn't remember checking any of my gear, but I had. In my head, I could almost hear our training instructor, Major Cortez, chuckle.

When we were prepped, we made our way to the drop tubes. We passed other troopers, all looking like they couldn't decide if they wanted to look smug because they weren't going planetside yet or looking forlorn about the prospect of a couple of weeks aboard the ship while we wandered around an alien world. The latter outweighed the former.

I took my normal spot at the front of the tube. My helmet engaged, and the air was purged from the tube. The door opened, and I could see Lepus 328rb below. It was nice to look at another world without having to think about what I was going to be killing on it. I could just take it in. And that's what I did. The ship told me that it would be a bit longer until we jumped. So I had time. Lepus 328rb didn't look all that amazing. I'd seen worlds like it before. Orion and Earth looked the same from space. Well, not land masses and oceans, but they had the same feel. The difference was there were under two hundred humans on this world. That population was about to skyrocket, comparably speaking, as we and other troops arrived to assist the exploration teams. But even then, it would be about as sparse as a planet could be.

Briefly, I wondered what would become of it someday. Both us and the Quiver were here, and I wasn't sure whose rock it was—or if it was no one's. That happened. We would explore a planet very much like our home world but not colonize it. We didn't need the space, and frankly, we had plenty of Earth-like planets, not counting those that were being terraformed. I suspected that the HF looked more at things like system resources when picking what systems to inhabit, along with long-term investment. The Lepus system didn't have a lot of large rocky bodies in it. That would mean having almost the same amount of defense and infrastructure without the real estate and resources. The Lepus system was not a good long-term investment, I decided.

We weren't stationary above the surface. The ship was moving along a path that allowed it to deposit troops and cargo conveniently. We were moving inland from the west coast of a large continent. As we moved, my countdown timer started. We were approaching our stop.

"Out in five," I told my team.

I stopped paying attention to the planet and did a last check of my team and gear. The lights on the floor turned green, and I ran. As I jumped, I felt gravity shift as the ship created a custom well for me and my team. It was stronger than normal, though, and I was slightly disoriented as my weight increased greatly as I fell away from the ship. Royle's team was out thirty seconds after ours. Her team was given a slightly different course. They'd be in a neighboring city from ours. But the bases weren't too far away—maybe one hundred kilometers.

All of a sudden, I was weightless outside of the ship's gravity well. I corrected myself, so I was feet down and curled into a ball. My suit locked me in that position. After a few minutes, my entry pack activated, extending the heat shield below me. My anchor kicked on, and I felt myself start to slow. It wasn't slowing me to make my impact on the planet's atmosphere any better but rather correcting my course and ensuring the heat shield hit the way it needed to in order to keep me from becoming a shooting star to those below.

I started to feel the chop of the atmosphere. This still sent a thrill through my body, and I doubted there would be a time when it wouldn't. Hitting atmosphere isn't fun even when you are in a shuttle, but when you are sitting on something that looks a lot like a sled you had as a kid? Oddly, I'd rather enter this way. Shuttles were rough, and you had even less perceived control. On jumps that weren't into combat, they were almost more worrying. Mostly because on a combat jump, I was looking at feeds of data, and there was the fear of combat distracting me.

Maybe you didn't know that was a thing. You see, you can be afraid of something out of your control, and then have another fear that's out of your control try to compete with it. It can distract you from one, and you pay attention to the other, going back and forth. In combat, I had the worry—no matter how unfounded—that my pack would fail and I would die. But I also had the much more founded concern of something on the ground shooting me. See, I had so many things that were out of my control to pay attention to: a war, burning up in the sky, and getting shot out of it. Jumping in non-combat, all you had was the second one.

I slowed down rapidly, and soon, my shield folded up, and I was free-falling in the atmosphere. I spread out my arms and legs, getting my bearings. I was right on target. I pointed myself down and fell. As I did, my units—both humans and drones—sent status updates.

Everyone was falling nicely. Below us was fairly mixed terrain. The city that the exploration team was studying was in fields, as was their base. But to the north and south, there were forests. I couldn't make out individual plants, so they were just a sea of deep green. I flipped, and I could see the exploration base.

"Exploration base, this is Alpha. We are touching down," I said on a general comm line that was to be used for joint communication.

"Thanks for the heads up… um, Corporal Taylor," a familiar voice said.

"Charles, are you the welcome party?" I asked.

"Yes, I am. Where are… WHOA!" he called out.

My anchor fired, and I slowed down rapidly, hitting the ground feet first, my legs and suit stopping me. I rose up to see Charles standing two meters away. He was wearing a green exploration suit and a look of total surprise. Presently, it started raining HFDF troops and drones. Normally, we didn't land in a tight group. Our suits were pretty stealthy, but they couldn't keep us completely hidden from an enemy when we were literally falling from the sky. That would be doubly so if there were a large group of us.

So we spread out in a drop to make it so you don't lose an entire team along with drones with one well-placed artillery round. I wasn't that worried that the exploration people were going to shell us, so we came down in a tight pack—the troops on the inside of the clump and the BIs on the outside. As I landed, my Whiskers detached, as did every one of my BIs. They spiraled out around us, looking for threats. The drones only knew one setting. That was to look for threats and take them out unless ordered otherwise. They'd see Charles and his crew as civilians and protect them just as well—if not better—than they did my people. Otherwise, the drones were in a state of constant war.

My situational awareness grew as the Whiskers gathered more and more data. They built a detailed map of the area. As they did, they began to catalog all of the other drones in the area along with local life.

92

My CCPU pulled the names of everything in the area along with everything known about all the species of plants and animals. All of this was flowing into the computers on the Arbiter, updating what the BIs and other drones saw as threats.

I walked forward and grabbed Charles's hand. His helmet was off, and his smile broad.

"You know you can breathe here, don't you?" he said to me.

"Not yet," I said. "Sorry, man. Protocol."

I turned to my team and spoke over the suit speaker system to keep Charles in the loop.

"Perimeter up, the crates are hitting atmo in three. Sweeting, Betts, and Clay, you have waypoints Alpha through Charlie. McLeod, hold this position. I will guide in the crates!" I ordered.

My team sprang to action, each of them going to the waypoints I set for them. Krista only spared a noncommittal wave at Charles as she began ordering her drones about. I deployed mine to where the housing units and other cargo would drop. Charles just watched us, his mouth open a bit.

"You gonna be like this the whole time?" he asked.

"God, I hope not," I said.

On cue, our luggage told me that it was in the atmosphere. Like us, the cargo had space anchors and the ability to turn the heat of entry into power for those anchors. They landed fairly softly and then had enough juice in the anchor to give us three minutes where they were effectively weightless. In that time, our BIs, under my direction, would place the cargo in its final resting spots.

I slapped Charles's shoulder. "Jog with me, will ya?"

I started at a trot to where the cargo was headed. He followed a moment later, catching up. We made it to the south side of the base and stopped.

"Walking wasn't an option?" he asked.

"Nope. We hurry up for shit, and then we wait for it. Tale as old as time, man; don't worry, you'll catch on. How are things?" I asked.

"Fine, got some crazy new neighbors in today," he said.

"Careful, I heard they're armed," I commented.

I hadn't looked at anything around the base as of yet, but now I did. The small skyline was dominated by the six exploration ships. Each stood upright like an old-fashioned rocket that stood twenty-five meters tall. The noses were tapered, but that was where the similarities with the old tech ended. They were boxy with flat sides, like a rectangle. On the top, right before the nose started, there was glass that appeared to be windows. They were pretty ugly, honestly, and some of the most utilitarian-looking things I'd seen. The Exploration Corps had gone for all function and no form on them. Probably a smart idea when you are light-years away from help.

Our stuff came into view. Charles looked up. I just patted his shoulder.

"Sorry, man. Soon I'll be normal, I promise," I told him.

"I'm not sure that's possible anymore, Alex," he said.

All three containers finished decelerating and stopped half a meter from the ground. I got my BIs to work.

EIGHT

I told the BIs how I wanted our cargo organized. They moved into place, and the containers lifted as the BIs moved them. They were fast and efficient. They had to be. The containers only had enough juice to make themselves weightless for three minutes. I was sure we could pull power from the Exploration Base if we had to, but I didn't want to go that route.

As the BIs worked, Charles waited, and my team reported in. Once they all confirmed no issues, I told them to come and meet me and Charles but to leave their PODs. I looked over at my buddy, who looked a little bored and put out. Then I did something that was extremely uncomfortable. I disengaged my helmet. That part wasn't what was really uncomfortable, but rather doing it on an alien world, out in the open. It was like a calling card, saying, "Hey, shoot me, or gas me, or whatever." But this wasn't a war zone, so... I technically didn't need it on.

I breathed in deeply, smelling Lepus 328rb's air. It smelled faintly of Earth. I knew that it should have had an almost sour smell, but my CCPU had adjusted my sense of smell to make the atmosphere smell natural to me. My CCPU had been doing a lot of recalibration since I'd left the ship. Humans weren't meant for this world. I had to be altered for it—mostly my immune system. There were a lot of microbes on this world that I hadn't encountered. Our body's natural immune system had been all but replaced centuries ago with an enhanced one. My CCPU had to calibrate that system with the local conditions and also keep me from infecting the local ecology as much as possible.

I looked at Charles and smiled. He smiled back and stuck out his hand. I took it.

"Welcome to Lepus 328rb," he said excitedly. "Man, this is gonna be great! How have you been?" he asked.

"Good and I'm looking forward to it too," I said.

My team was approaching, all of them hesitantly disengaging their helmets. Krista hugged Charles.

"How are you?" she asked.

He squeezed her back. "I'm good. You all a little nervous down here or something?"

She raised an eyebrow.

"Your helmets," he said.

"We don't take them off when we are on alien worlds unless indoors, as a rule. It's a good way to die," she explained.

That sobered him just a bit. "Oh yeah... didn't think about that."

"Charles, this is the rest of my team," I said, introducing each person in turn.

"It's wonderful to meet you all. Our base commander is Maria Guzman; she'd have come out and met you, but we have two team members in the field who are on their way back, so she won't leave control. I've been instructed to show you around the base and let you set up. When you're done, everyone should be back from the field," Charles said. Then he added, "Um, where are your drones? The ones you came with?"

"They are guarding the base," Betts said matter-of-factly.

Charles looked a little uncomfortable. "They won't..."

"They won't attack anyone coming back to the base. If they see something they think is a threat, they will notify their operator, who will decide what to do. Human Federation citizens will show as assets to be protected and not as threats," I explained.

"Assets?" Charles asked.

I shrugged. "To a drone, there's no difference between a rock and a person other than its priority and status."

"I suppose that's fair enough. Well, let me show you around," Charles said, a little unsure. Technically, the BIs did do a threat assessment on citizens and a background check, but I didn't think Charles wanted to know that.

We were on the south side of the base, and Charles started walking north. There was a small dirt road that had been worn into the ground, separating the base in half. On the right side of the road were base components like the lab and shared space. On the other side were the exploration ships. Cables ran from them to the other buildings, with guards over them in the road making mini speed bumps. The ships dominated the scene. We slowed, getting a good look at them.

"That's a large engineering section," Clay said.

She was right; it looked like it took up over a third of the ship.

"I bet it has a lot of acceleration," she said.

"Not really," Charles replied. "It governs pretty low. We use the ships to power and support wherever we are. They have to run life support and make any equipment work. We also use them to haul anything we need. Other than monthly supply drops, everything you see in this base was lugged out here in a container attached to the outside of ships like this. They won't accelerate too fast because whatever is attached to the outside might not be able to handle it."

He pointed out the building that contained the shared space, explaining that there was a small gym and living room with a kitchen. We were welcome to use whatever we liked. We didn't enter the lab, but he did take us into the shop. There were a couple of RMUs along with supplies. I looked at the various drones in stages of assembly and repair. After that, he showed us the storage area and the LZ where the ferry booster landed.

I looked out over the base from the LZ and was reminded of how much like Earth this place was. I was the only member of my team who had been to our home world and, further, to an area like this one. There were small hills here and there, but mostly just fields. Lepus 328 shone down on us, warming me. The air was dry and a little dusty.

"Thinking about Earth?" Charles asked, as if he could read my mind.

My team looked at him, curious. Charles had been to Earth. He'd come with my parents and me a few years ago.

"It's like where my parents grew up," I said.

Charles looked out at the base and the surrounding area. "It is."

That made me think of another soldier I'd met when we were fighting the Venom. He was from Earth. I made a mental note to drop him a line.

"Where are your folks from again?" Sweeting asked.

"Denver. It's in the center of North America," I answered. We were in the middle of nowhere—truly nowhere—but in a way, I felt like I was somewhere. I was on Earth, just in a field away from anyone else. But I wasn't. I was on an alien world that had once been home to a race not too much unlike my own. And they were dead. And we didn't know why.

"Is there anything else?" I asked, my tone taking on a business edge.

"That's it. Our people should be back in an hour or so," Charles said. I nodded.

"Fireteam Alpha," I said.

Everyone's calm and lax expressions focused on me. Their body language shifted from relaxation to readiness.

"Sweeting, Betts, Clay, get the grid unpacked and inventoried. McLeod, get the shop expanded and confirm that it is ready for operation. I will take care of the housing unit," I said.

Everyone acknowledged and jogged to their assigned posts.

"Thanks for the tour, man, we'll have to catch up later," I said to Charles.

I jogged down to the housing unit, leaving a confused Charles behind. Like everything else, it just looked like a cargo container. I integrated with it to run a diagnostic. Everything came back clean. I gave it the order to unfold. The sides started to move out, tripling its footprint. At the front was an airlock. The lights on it turned green. I stepped to the door, and it opened. The lock cycled, and I entered the housing unit. To my right were our sleeping and personal storage units. Unlike the all-metal bunks we'd slept in on previous deployments, these were far more comfortable but only slept one.

There were five personal units, one for each of us. They ran floor to ceiling, broken into three sections. The one closest to the ground held ammo and extra nano-material for your suit. It had a slot to hold your pack and SIR. It slid out like a giant drawer. Above that, with a square door that opened straight up, was the sleeping unit. It had a pillow inside of it and a thin mattress. We'd be sleeping in our suits, so this was the luxury part. Above that was another drawer, like the first, but holding all of our food and drinks. Well, other than water—though, there were bottles of that too. At the end of those was the head. In the far left-hand corner was a small kitchen for heating up said food. Folded against the personal units was a table and a few odds and ends. I had my BIs unpack and set them up.

When I was done, I left the unit and caught up with my team. Sweeting, Clay, and Betts had everything out of the cargo container laid out and organized. Krista was done with the shop. Krista and I approached the defense supplies. I pulled up a map with my CCPU and the perimeter that I had already laid out. Each of us would only have a couple of towers to deal with. I assigned locations to every troop and then had my BIs start the process of hauling boxes out to where they belonged.

We were not expecting any sort of attack, and if we thought one was imminent, I would have the Exploration team scrub before anything got close to us. But the HFDF lived by *in case shit,* so we had some stuff to set up. I jogged with my BIs out a ways from the base. The BIs started unpacking the boxes. Inside was our Standard Tower Defense—or STD. No shit, that's their acronym. Venereal diseases had been gone for literally centuries, but I grew up in a first-gen home, and no matter how old he got, my dad still appreciated a good STD joke. I chuckled as the BIs started to erect the tower.

"Something funny?" Monroe asked over a comm line, sounding genuinely curious.

"Just thinking of my dad," I said.

"But everything is alright?" Monroe confirmed. I suspected I was the only one who found the towers amusing.

I explained it to him.

"I'm glad to see that no matter how old we get, we won't make it past sixteen mentally," Monroe commented before dropping the connection.

The towers were thin with bumps along the outside. They went up twenty meters, ending with a sphere packed with different sensors. Each tower had four turrets riding on two carriages that could move up or down the tower; likewise, they could rotate around the tower, giving them any angle of fire they needed. Each turret had a single barrel that was capable of small or large caliber rounds. It could also spin and rotate as needed. Each turret had several small rockets. They had a small profile, making them hard to hit from a distance, and were tough. In short, they would be a bitch for any enemy, and every one of them around the base could support any other tower that was in line of sight.

I'd seen these things in action before. Once, at a temporary base on Pike Prime, I'd watched them light up a small group of Venom that had made it past the front. The Venom lost despite putting in a good effort. So long as the towers didn't face masses of enemies and were able to keep their ammo from running out, they would make it impossible for anything to pass them. There was ammo storage at the base, and the power cells lasted for weeks. We'd have to check on them every now and then, but otherwise, I figured the data they collected would help the Exploration people out a whole lot more than it would my team.

As my BIs worked, I looked around. The base was in a flat area of fields. I had a whisker pop up high in the air, running its feed as my primary vision. I knelt down and engaged my helmet. No danger or not, I didn't fancy standing around, not seeing my surroundings without my helmet on.

As the whisker got higher, I could see more and more around me. I stopped it at one hundred meters. I could see forever. A few kilometers away ran a road that led into an old city. I could make out fragments of the city's broken skyline. I thought I had a pretty good idea of why Exploration chose this location. It was close to the city, so you could study the old inhabitants—well, not them, as they were dead and all—but you could look at all the stuff they left behind. The base was also in an area where the team could study local flora and fauna, not to mention there was nothing obstructing flight paths for the ships or boosters.

The whisker looked around, and other than ours, I couldn't make out any structures. We weren't too far from a city, so maybe this had been farmland? Probably. Even if the locals had only eaten meat, you'd need a place for livestock, and they weren't advanced enough to have developed factory food production. That meant hectares of farmland, no matter how you split it. Well, unless you wanted to have a small community that could truly live off the land. But that wasn't cities.

I tried to picture what the area might have been like when the dead race was still around. It was sad that all I could come up with were pictures and videos I'd seen of North American farmland before agelessness. Maybe that would have been a decent analog for this place, but I kind of doubted it. In my limited experience, we had common ground with aliens, but they were never completely like us.

I checked in on my team, seeing the progress they'd made. All of them had their towers complete and were working on foxholes. I started my BIs working on digging and opened a line to Monroe.

"We are almost dug in, sir," I said.

"That's good. How is it down there?" he asked.

I looked at the feed from the whisker.

"Pretty calm and peaceful," the feed passed the skyline of the city. "And I guess a little creepy."

"Good. Bravo team is almost set up. The ships are going to be alternating what part of the planet they are covering in a few days. I'll give you a schedule and communication protocols if you need to contact the Quiver ship directly," he said.

"Are they on close fire support?" I asked.

"When overhead they are. The Exploration teams don't work at night, so once you meet with their people, you should be good to go for the night."

"Sounds good."

Monroe dropped the connection.

I sent Royle a ping wishing her team boredom and then reached out to Clovis.

"We are planetside and almost done with setup," I said.

"Thank you for the update. We came into the base already being ready for us. Do you have mission plans for the evening?" it asked.

"Negative. Our teams are running daytime-only missions currently. You?"

"Drone work only. We have meetings tonight for everyone to integrate with new team members. Our schedule shows that the Arbiter will be handling fire support for the next three local days," Clovis said.

"How do you feel about that?" I asked.

It chuckled. Well, my CCPU told me it did, "You tell me in three days when an alien ship is covering you."

I laughed, "Yeah, I kind of figured that." I paused. "May I ask a personal question?"

"Sure."

"Have you ever needed orbital support before?"

There was a pause. "I've been on missions where that was part of the plan. But always at a distance and never as backup." It didn't sound uncomfortable—like it wasn't supposed to talk about past battles. We'd been encouraged to build a rapport with each other, but I suspected there were some cultural boundaries that were being felt out. "Have you?"

"Yeah. On my first op, the ship used its laser to flame an area so we could get out, and then it dropped a bunker buster. We knew we were going to be surrounded and that needing orbital assistance was a possibility and all, but I won't forget it! We needed it a few other times, too. Shit, I watched the fleet pound a Venom colony with kinetics," I said. Thankfully, my CCPU would just not send anything that it wasn't allowed to. So long as we didn't talk about the technical details of what our ships and equipment could do, we should be safe.

"Your people are much more... forward with fighting than ours," Clovis said. "You seem to like getting into the action. We stay back from the fight if we can."

"Yeah, we were told that was a difference. Honestly, I like being up on the line. I get worried sitting back and controlling drones," I admitted.

"It is our hesitation to join the fight with our drones that makes our ground troops less effective than yours, I think," it said.

I was surprised. It was one thing to be talking with buddies and say that another force might have an advantage over yours in a particular area; it was another thing altogether to tell that force that. I thought about it. It was right. We were better on the ground, but there was a flip side.

"I suppose we are, but your fleet is better and larger than ours," I said.

"But stretched out over many more systems—and with fewer capitals than you have. But our defense grids are second to none," it said.

"We'd sure do a good job of crippling each other, wouldn't we?" I said.

"Well said. To me, this mission is not so much about helping our scientists on the ground but strengthening our relationship with the Human Federation. That was why we requested this mission," Clovis said.

"I respect that. Honestly, we were picked because on Pike Prime, I'd talked to some Pike, and then my team helped an injured Pike. They thought we'd be the best outfit to work with another race," I said.

"How does your team feel about this mission, if I may ask?" Clovis asked.

I thought for a moment. "I'm looking forward to it. This isn't something that you get to do all the time. And one of my people, Private McLeod, is…" How did I describe how Krista felt? "Well, the term that we'd use is she's over the moon."

It paused, and I wondered how that would translate.

"Sorry, that may not translate," I said.

"My translation came back with that she is very happy and excited about it."

"Good enough," I said.

"Perhaps she could be allowed to talk with my team on occasion, then? I would need to get permission from my command, and if you need it from yours, I understand," Clovis said.

I smiled. "She'd like that."

NINE

aria Guzman wasn't HFDF, but I think she could have
been. What she was, was the head of the Exploration
team. She was of average height with bronze skin and
long black hair. Thus far, her dark eyes had never looked anything
other than serious. I was alone with her in the base's common space.
The common space was an open room that featured a kitchen, a
seating area, and a counter. The walls were blue-gray. Everything
almost had a hotel feel about it but somehow felt homey at the same
time.

Maria was giving me an overview of the base and all of her staff. I
had documentation on this that I'd gone over exhaustively, as had
every member of my team, but it was always good to get it from the
horse's mouth, so to speak. Maria had insights into her team that no
report ever could convey. Even if she read the reports line for line, her
opinions would seep into the details through her tone and body
language. It was like when career troops talked to Service Term troops.

From Guzman, I was getting that she thought highly of her people,
and while she had no fear for her team from anything taking out

drones, she was happy to have extra help on-site and was likewise pleased to be working with the Quiver.

"Did Charles explain how we came to work with the Quiver to you?" she asked.

I nodded. "Yes, ma'am. My team would be working with them regardless of the Exploration team that was on the ground, but since I have a relationship with Charles, your team was selected."

She smiled tightly. "That's about right. The corps had a base here before, but we relieved the team that was here. We're lucky that Charles knows you. And I'd say we're lucky that you've interacted with other species before."

"Thank you, ma'am. Charles is a good friend," I said.

She looked at me for a moment, probably noting that I didn't say anything about being lucky to know other races. She moved on with the conversation, going over her expectations for me, all of which confirmed everything we'd been told. I was surprised that there wasn't a lecture about how she ran this base or 'don't you apes get in the way,' or any of the other shit you see in entertainment. She was here to do a job and respected that we were too. I liked her.

"I think we will do just fine together," I said.

Her smile reached her eyes. "I do too. I'll admit I've worked with a lot of Service Term troops over the years. You all make great helping hands, and you're rated to use more drones than anyone else in society. But I've never worked with Special Teams before."

"I hope to ruin you for all other teams," I said genuinely.

I called in my team, and Maria said hers would join us shortly. We were doing a group meet and greet. Everyone could ask any questions that they wanted, and everyone would get to know each other. My team entered the room and lined up beside me. Over the next few minutes, the Exploration team trickled in. As they came in, I ran a mental list of names and everything I'd been given about them. Chances were we'd be grunt labor for these people, but there was a small chance that we'd be responsible for keeping them alive. I'd never had to worry about the safety of non-HFDF people before, and I wasn't about to take it lightly.

"Thank you for coming in," Maria said. "This is my team." She pointed to each person in turn.

Shashi Knell was 170 cm tall with brown shaggy hair; he was 47, and my CCPU told me that he was in a relationship with Andy Waters, the team geologist. Shashi's job was as an Environmental Specialist, which meant that he kept all equipment on the base running along with any repair work that needed to be done. Guzman was his backup. Everyone was cross-trained, with the exception of Charles, who was still learning all the jobs. Shashi nodded at my team and stepped back.

Next was Felipe Martin, a 168 cm tall biologist. He was slender with dark hair that was combed back. Felipe apparently spent the bulk of his time not in the field but in the lab back on a planet but would go into the field every twenty years or so for experience. If shit were to hit the fan, he'd be the least of my concerns. He'd spent years in the field working with all manner of creatures; I doubted he hadn't encountered a few tight situations during that time.

Next was Charles. He was the junior person on the team and was learning.

The next person was Catherine Siwik; she was blonde, blue-eyed, and, oh my god, was she a knockout. If I hadn't been in a relationship, I'd have probably been nervous just being in the same room as Catherine. As it was, I was in a happy relationship, so I tried not to be awkward.

Last was Andy Waters; he was tall with brown hair. He didn't look like he wanted to be in the meeting. He and Catherine also highlighted the differences between the two teams. Andy's suit pants were up to his knees and his sleeves short, his neckline in a V. It was the same forest green suit that Charles had, just configured differently. Catherine's was much the same, with short sleeves and a plunging neckline that showed off just the hint of cleavage. Hers and Guzman's hair was down, and everyone had suits with short sleeves.

My people's suits came up to their chins and wrists. Both Krista and Clay had long hair, but it was up in a bun or under a nano-material cap lest they get a trim when their helmets came on. It was pretty clear, looking at the Exploration team, that they weren't planning on needing their suits to keep them alive.

In training, I'd tried to see if I could get my suit to shorten its sleeves. It didn't give me a hard no, but it was the machine equivalent of "really, cupcake?" The reality was that we always had our helmets on. In combat, duh, in the VR pods, at the shooting range, and on and on and on. I spent almost as many waking hours on the ship with my helmet on as I didn't. The people before me didn't have that life. They also stood around like normal human beings. My team was standing in a line. In our room aboard the ship, we lounged around, but we weren't there now, and it was apparent. I wondered if my team would relax at all.

Maria introduced me.

"This is Corporal Taylor. He is in charge of the HFDF Fireteam that is going to be here to work with us. I will let him introduce his team and explain his mission," Maria said, gesturing to me.

Her team looked at me with obvious curiosity.

I stepped forward. "Good afternoon, it is good to be here. My team and I are looking forward to working with each of you." I started introducing members of my team. "Every member of my team is capable and trained in every role we have. That said, you will likely see Private Sweeting the most around the base; there will always be a member of my team here, along with a defense system and their POD of drones." I explained the concept of what a POD was, assuming it would be new to them. It was. "We are here to assist your team. We are also here to help figure out what has been taking out your drones and run security if needed."

108

Andy Waters rolled his eyes at this. Maria saw it and cut in.

"Corporal Taylor and I have gone over what both of our corps have agreed on. He assures me that his team will not interfere in our day-to-day activities—something I trust him on. They will be assisting us, but they aren't grunt labor. That said, if any member of his team sees something they deem a threat, they are in control, no questions asked." She looked at each member of her team in turn, daring one of them to argue the point.

"And what all will this entail on a day-to-day basis?" Shashi asked.

"That is a great question. Maria has told me you currently work in teams of two or three. That will continue to be the case: two or three Exploration people with two or three HFDF troops. There is to always be me or a member of my team with you if you leave the defense perimeter. In the field, teams need to stay in close range of each other. This is our orders until we find out what is taking down drones," I said.

"Animals are doing that," Andy said, slightly condescending.

I nodded. "Yes, probably. But all of the incidents have happened in former urban areas. There is an extremely low chance that this hasn't been the work of local animals."

"Then what would it be the work of?" Andy asked with the same tone of condescension.

I shrugged. "Maybe all the locals didn't die, or they are squatters here, or something worse," I held up my hand, stopping him before he could speak, "and I very much doubt that it is any of those things. But we are in the middle of a war with a species that liked planets like this one, so the HFDF isn't taking any chances. Neither are the Quiver; both governments are on the lookout," I said, and the last part gave him pause. It was one thing to shit on your own government as being a pain in the ass, but when two are concerned about the same thing—and when one of those governments is the Quiver—it gives you pause.

"Like I said, there is little chance of any of these. Squatters wouldn't be likely to spread out over several cities, and they'd need AltComms to communicate. If they were a race that wasn't capable of that, you guys would have seen spikes in the electromagnetic spectrum," I said.

Felipe grimaced at that.

"Have you seen that?" I asked.

"Yes," he said, "but it's not what you think. I doubt you've had reports on the local animal life down here, have you?"

I shook my head no.

He nodded. "You see, some species down here, including a local type of predator, are able to produce and use parts of the electromagnetic spectrum, i.e., radio waves. They don't carry far, but they use them to communicate."

Catherine, their technology specialist, jumped in. "We have seen spikes around some of the drones that fit with local predators."

"So, then you have confirmed the drones' disappearance?" I asked.

Guzman spoke. "Probably, but the animals that we think have attacked the drones haven't attacked anything outside of the cities. We can't figure out why they would behave differently in the cities and not outside of them."

I filed that away. My team looked like they were making notes in their heads too. I suspected each one would be querying the Exploration database on these animals.

I smiled. "Well, hopefully, we will be able to confirm that it's those animals soon. But in the unlikely event that something goes sideways, I do need to cover a few items." I called in a BI. It came walking in and stood next to me. "This is a Basic Infantry drone or BI. It is their job to help us blend into their ranks. They look and move the way they do so that we, as operators, are less likely to be killed. You will all have limited access to the BIs. They will respond to basic commands and generally stay out of your way. If things go sideways, these will be doing the bulk of the fighting.

"If that happens, my team will be taking over; please listen and do what they tell you without question. This is for your safety and ours. If something happens, there will be two BIs sticking to each of you like glue. They will keep you safe, but they will not respond to your orders. They might direct you, though; please don't fight them." Everyone looked like they were taking note, Shashi and Charles most of all.

"Now, onto a kind of awkward part..." I paused. "If I am killed or otherwise incapacitated, Private Betts will take command. You may also hear orders from our sergeant from the ship, but field command will go to Betts," I said.

Andy rolled his eyes again. "Has that ever happened?" he asked sarcastically.

I looked at him, not really irritated but not thrilled. Meyers had prepped me for any kind of asshole.

"Yes," I said.

"To your group?" Andy asked, still sarcastic.

"Yes," I said a little coolly.

Andy was about to speak again, but Charles spoke, his voice steady. "Andy, man, trust me, you want to drop this."

Andy looked at Charles with annoyance, and then something crossed his expression. Probably a memory of something that Charles had said about me or my unit.

"Sorry about that. I want to think of your team as a bunch of kids, but from what Charles has told us, you aren't," Andy said honestly.

"It's fine. You should want to know who we are and where we've been," I said. "On that level, I have fought next to every person on my team; I would trust my life with any of them, and I have. As a team, we have seen action on Pike and Erie Prime. First waves on each. I will forward our team's service transcripts to each of you. The records will only show what is available to the public."

Andy nodded and didn't ask any more questions. Prior to the meeting, Maria had told me that Andy came off as an asshole sometimes. He didn't like new people and was pretty abrupt as a person. She said that he didn't really warm up to you but learned boundaries, and you got used to him. Fair enough. He also rarely left the base, spending the bulk of his time in the lab, so it was unlikely my team would have to deal with him a lot.

The rest of the crew seemed fine.

"What are your supply needs going to be?" Shashi asked.

"Minimal. We would like to hook into power, but if that doesn't work, we have enough power to last us over a month. We did not bring any form of transportation, however. I understand that we will be using your rovers whenever going into the field," I answered.

"Do you need them for your own missions?" he asked.

"Negative. If during our stay, command has us run exercises, we will hoof it, or a transport will come for us," I said.

With our suits, we could hoof it pretty quickly, and in my experience, the HFDF seemed to rarely use troop transports for anything that wasn't a few hours away. Catherine was the most interested in us, I thought. Aside from us being newcomers, she was the tech specialist. She had a lot of questions about our gear. I suspected that she didn't get a lot of exposure to military equipment. In many ways, her team had more advanced items than ours. Ours had to be able to withstand a lot of punishment and be reliable, which meant going with simpler tech.

"So what is an average day?" Betts asked.

Maria answered. "They vary, obviously, but we start in the morning with a staff meeting and then go about our day's assignments. We have two rovers, each one capable of holding about a dozen people on the inside if needed. One will generally be out in the field with up to two teams, and the other will be here. We only send out one rover in case the one in the field needs a pickup. I know that may sound silly, but we are all we have out here."

"Do the rovers break down a lot?" Clay asked.

"No," Shashi said, "almost never; they are well maintained. But things happen. It's normally not an issue. The rovers will drop staff in a central location, and we spread out."

That would work well for us.

"I generally don't leave the base," Andy said. "My drones will take samples or run tests and then come back here. I do go out, but not that often."

"I am also normally at the base," Maria said. "I monitor staff in the field. Right now, our main off-site team is Catherine and Charles, with Felipe going with them or with Andy."

"Do you have a lot of fieldwork?" Krista asked Felipe.

"Some, yes, but not as much as you'd think. When this planet died off, it took a lot of animal life with it. The area we are in is pretty devoid of diverse life," he said.

"But there is diverse life elsewhere?" she asked.

He shrugged. "The planet is recovering from a mass extinction. Outside of most former urban centers, it is recovering faster. Figuring out that extinction is a lot of what we are doing here."

"Any leads on that?" I asked curiously.

"War, probably," Maria said.

Her team was starting to relax now, some of them taking seats; the important part of the meeting was done.

"The thing that is so odd about it is that we cannot find who won if it was a war," she said.

"Nukes?" Sweeting asked.

She shook her head. "They hadn't gotten that advanced yet, and even if they had, there are no signs of radiation consistent with that being the cause. That and the loss of life was mostly animal, it seems. There aren't large areas of vegetation that are gone or anything that we'd expect to see from chemical or nuclear weapons." She was looking into the distance now, thinking. "We thought maybe biological, but again it doesn't really fit."

"And the bodies?" Charles said, making a point.

"Bodies?" Clay asked.

At a glance from Maria, Charles explained. "Yeah, there aren't any. If everyone just killed one another and most of the animal life here, we should be finding a ton of skeletons. There are some in graves not unlike the ones that humans used to use, but there aren't enough to account for the loss of life. And how often do you see a shooting war with no survivors?"

"The Venom were like that, but they took in all biomass and wouldn't have just up and left," I said.

"That and this happened a little over a hundred Earth years ago," Catherine said. "If there was a winning side, they should have gotten a foothold decades ago. But with it being that old and how underdeveloped this place was, we don't even have a radio bubble to try to inspect. Any print material from the time is mostly gone, and we haven't found enough for us to figure out their language. We have clues but nothing concrete."

"Is this common?" Krista asked.

Maria smiled a little. "More than you'd think. Right now, we have nothing to go on. It looks like some type of total war, but we'll find something natural that killed everyone off. Well, that normally is what happens, but the no remains thing is odd for a race that died off so recently."

We asked a handful of other questions of the team, and I got the slight impression that they were a little disappointed that we weren't creeped out at all. It was creepy for sure, but nothing was shooting at us, and even if it somehow could, it was four hundred years behind us, technologically speaking.

Lepus 328 was starting to set as we left the common building. We had watch shifts while on base spread throughout the day. The Exploration team having consistent hours, relatively speaking, made my job easier. My CCPU created a rotating schedule for the watch. Most nights, you wouldn't get a straight eight hours of sleep, but you'd still get eight hours. That wasn't bad. For most of us, if we chose to go to bed a little early, we'd get nine hours if we really wanted.

I joined Charles, walking with him from the common building to one of the ships. It was the same color of brown as the fields around the base. Up close, I could appreciate the size of the ships. Charles's stood upright with eight legs for landing gear. The engines were covered. I figured it would take a pretty strong storm to push it over. Well, that and the space anchors inside of it would make toppling it even harder.

A lift tube was at the base of the ship going up to the main hatch. I got in the lift with Charles. It was tight but fit two people. It started up.

"How is it having your own ship?" I asked.

He shrugged. "Normal. The way the corps works, we each have our own ship. It just makes things easier. It has a workspace and living area, plus storage for anything that we need to bring on an assignment. They look like we have a lot more than we actually do."

We got to the hatch. It opened for us, and we walked into a square room. There was a small amount of storage, along with a VR pod and a table. The walls were all vid walls.

"Lab?" I asked.

"That and general workspace. If we need to fly, we control the ship from the VR pod, but we don't spend the whole flight in it—just takeoff and landing normally. We can control the ship with our CCPUs. That said, when in space, you spend a lot of time in that pod," Charles explained.

The room wasn't that big, and I was reconsidering what he'd said about it appearing to be bigger than it was. In the corner was another lift, this one taking the form of a patch of floor that moved up the corner and into the room above. Charles went first, and then I joined him. I came into a room that had a head with a shower, a kitchen, and a space to work out or relax in.

I joined Charles as he grabbed a can from the kitchen. A tube came out of it, and he put it in his mouth.

"Is that food for null G?" I asked, wondering why he'd choose to eat it.

"Yeah, why? You don't have to eat it only in null." He had a knowing look on his face. "You ever had it?"

"No," I said. "The cans are more to bring, and if we are in vacuum or null, we just get nutrient packets."

"In between meals, right?" he asked.

I laughed. "No, like all the time until they can get something landed with real food."

"I see why you didn't talk about the food on deployment. Wow, that has to suck."

He walked back into the kitchen and grabbed a can. "Here, you'll like it."

The can was a two-part system. First was the canister itself, in it was whatever goo that you ate, and then the top where a nano-material tube came out. Charles had several tops. I held the canister up to my face, the tube coming out, and put it in my mouth. There was a little button that I pressed, and cool goo, the consistency of thick yogurt, filled my mouth.

"Is that apple pie?" I asked.

He smiled. "Been eating those packets so long you forgot what apple pie tastes like? Yes, man, it's apple pie. You've seriously never eaten this stuff?" he asked, amazed.

I shook my head. "No, this is great! What flavors does it come in?"

He laughed. "Everything." He pointed at where he grabbed it from. "Here is the unit; there are a couple of large canisters of the base and then some flavoring agents. I can have whatever I want. Most Exploration people eat them most of the time. They're convenient. No one in the HFDF does?"

I was about to say no but remembered that wasn't true. "Ship bound, yeah. Those people can spend days in their VR pods; the system allows for nutrient packs or this type. I know my CO eats them a lot. I figured it was just a habit from living in a pod."

"Really days?" he asked.

"Yeah, in combat, for sure. Everything you need is in them, plus they have more shielding, and if your ship gets shot up, you'll want that. I know if you crew a Centipede, you start and end voyages in the pods. But they only go into combat, no patrol routes," I said and sucked down more goo.

The living area didn't have any vid walls, and we took the lift up to the top floor. It was dominated by a bed; the walls were a transparent material you could adjust for light and privacy. You could see for kilometers. All of the other ship's tops looked opaque, and I figured Charles also always kept his one way. I looked around. The room, while not large, came with a view and enough space to stretch out. A companion drone was sitting on the bed. It smiled at us and greeted Charles.

"You have a bone drone?" I asked incredulously.

He scowled. "Companion drone. Bone drones are single-purpose; these have far more capabilities. They assist us in the field and give us something that resembles in-person human contact when running solo for long periods of time."

I looked at the drone carefully. "That makes sense. I've heard that even with VR, it can be lonely without something in the physical world to talk to. Hmmm. I swear I've seen that drone before..." God, where was it from? I knew I'd seen a drone or a person... "That's it! It looks like your ex. Oh wait, is it your ex?"

Charles looked a little put out. "One, it's a he. We look at them as people to an extent; it helps, and the system came up with the appearance; I didn't."

"So the system thinks you're hung up on someone? Wow, the HF is good at that shit, man! So it is a bone drone."

"No. It's a companion drone," he insisted. The drone echoed his statement. I ignored it.

"But do you fuck it? Sorry, him, do you fuck him?" I asked.

"Is that your business?" Charles asked.

I laughed. "Oh God, does Monica know about this? You have a bone drone of your ex, and it was provided by the government! Can today get any better?" I said to the canister of apple pie goo. I squirted the rest in my mouth lest Charles take it away.

"Says the guy banging your subordinate," he shot back, but with a smile. He liked Krista.

I laughed. "Yep. Also arranged by the government. Little creepy, isn't it?"

Charles laughed, then said, "You know, it kind of is."

I looked at the drone. "So, does it have the same kinks as your ex?"

Charles shook his head. "Fuck, this is gonna be a long assignment."

TEN

I woke to a gentle sound in my head. I was alone in my bunk, my head on a softish pillow, my suit still on. I pressed the pillow to the side of the bunk next to my head. It stuck, and the nano-material forced out any air and stretched down the wall, flush with it. The bunk was much smaller than the one I had on the ship. But it was just a bit bigger than the ones I'd used in combat, and this one had a mattress and a pillow. I wasn't overly excited about the prospect of sleeping in it for a few months, but it was better than sleeping in a metal box.

The door opened, and I slid out of the bunk. It wasn't something they trained us how to do in basic. It was surprisingly hard to get out of a hole in the wall without looking like an idiot, but with practice, I'd like to think that I'd gotten semi-graceful at it. I did a quick check on my team. Clay was outside, walking the defense perimeter; hers had been the last watch.

"Nothing exciting?" I asked her.

"Nope," she said.

I walked to the head. It had two doors: one for the john and the other for the shower unit. I walked into the shower unit, and the door slid closed. Unlike the showers on the ship, this one was a closet-sized room with a bin for my suit and cubbies that held all of our toiletries. My suit slid off, and I stepped into the cylindrical shower. The door closed behind me. I held my hands above my head, and the cycle started.

I was blasted with warm water and then soap. I scrubbed myself quickly and was rinsed off. Air jets blew on me, drying my hair and body. I stepped out, and my suit ran over my body. I took out my kit and brushed my teeth and combed my hair. The whole process took about five minutes. I left, allowing Betts in. The rest of my team was out of bed now, and I walked up to Krista, giving her a kiss.

"How'd you sleep?" I asked.

She shrugged. "Perfect, but I still missed you," she said warmly.

I smiled and kissed her again. I went back to where my bunk was and opened the cabinet above it. A large rack of packaged food slid out, cool air coming with it. I grabbed a breakfast pack and a bottle of cold-brew coffee. I slid the cabinet shut, plopped the package of food in the heating unit, and greeted Sweeting and Clay as she came back in. Betts was out of the shower, and Krista was stepping in. I took my food out of the heater and sat at the table.

I started compiling reports for the evening watches. As I did, I missed my mouth a few times and slowed down my eating. I made a note to look into switching over to the null-g goo. My team didn't comment on my now slow eating; they'd seen it a thousand times before. The reports were quick, and I sent them over to command. Monroe wasn't up yet.

I looked at summaries of other reports as they came in for the evening. One of the cities on the east side of the continent had lost another drone. I dug into the report. There wasn't much yet, but it appeared that it happened in another urban center. Fireteam Bravo of fourth platoon was going to check it out today. I bookmarked it for follow-up.

My CCPU pinged me with several updates to my biosystems to

make me more efficient on the planet. I didn't read them but told my CCPU to go buck wild. I finished with my reports and joined my team for the rest of breakfast. The mobile housing units had the effect of making you feel like you weren't on a deployment but in some kind of low-budget hotel or flat. We sat around talking and eating. When it was time, we left and made our way over to the common building.

We were the first ones there and sat on the couches and chairs, waiting for the Exploration team to come in. They filed in, greeting us, and made their way over to the kitchen and started pulling out food. I checked the time on my CCPU. We weren't early. Even Charles grabbed some food. Maria Guzman looked at us.

"You guys gonna eat?" she asked.

"We already did," I said.

She thought for a moment, and then a look of understanding crossed her face. "Sorry, I should have told you we eat during our morning meeting. It's a tradition. Your team is welcome to join us if you'd like."

"Thank you, ma'am," I said.

I made a note that tomorrow we would join them. I didn't want to be rude, and building common ground would be good for the teams. The kitchen had a high counter with stools that they pulled up to it. The team got their food and talked amongst themselves. Charles joined me.

"Morning, man. Did you have a good evening?" he asked.

"It wasn't too bad. With the time change, we'd been up for over a day by the time we got to bed last night. It was good to get some shut-eye. And my watch was pretty calm," I said conversationally.

"Watch?" Catherine asked, turning around.

I nodded, confused. "Yeah, we rotate."

"You guys have to stand watch?" she asked again.

Ah, I understood. "Yes, ma'am. Off base or off ship, we post a watch."

The rest of their team was turning to pay attention to us now. I assumed that most of them had worked with Service Term troops before, but I wasn't sure in what capacity. Our infantry companies hadn't landed yet, and now that I thought of it, I didn't think they were working directly with Exploration groups, just reporting back data to them.

"So one of you will always be awake and watching?" Andy confirmed.

"Yes, and if they see something that they deem a threat, they wake the team," I said.

"Drones can't do that for you?" he asked. His tone was flat, but after our conversation yesterday, I was sure that he wasn't trying to sound like an ass.

"They do. But we monitor them. If a drone pops an alert, one of us checks on it. We only need one team member to monitor all of the base drones and functions while the others rest. It's important to note that HFDF drones, while good at what they do, are not as good as humans are at assessment," I explained.

"Huh, I would have thought the military stuff was way more advanced," Catherine mused.

"Oh, it's advanced," Betts said. "But you have to remember its mission. Our BIs hide us from the enemy, so they have to act as human as they can. That's tanks performance. But they also have to be reliable in the extreme and be able to handle any conditions that a human can while taking a lot of abuse. All of the systems have several redundancies and are easy to repair in the field.

"Our BBALLs and Whiskers need to be compact and light. For the Whiskers, this increases their ability to hide and gather intel, and in the case of the BBALLs, it makes them a smaller target. Even the Heavies have a lot on their plate. They can track and take out multiple targets simultaneously while under heavy fire," Betts said.

"You all get shot at a whole lot, don't you?" Felipe said.

Most of my team laughed.

"Every one of us has been wounded in action," I said conversationally.

Krista beamed. "I got hit on our first drop." Her suit parted around her neck, and she pulled out a chain with a little disc on the end of it. She smiled at it.

Charles chuckled.

"You kept it?" Shashi asked incredulously.

"It'd be bad luck not to," Sweeting said, then added, "I've broken a few ribs but mostly been shot." He said like a tough guy.

"You got grazed," Clay said.

"Sorry, we all can't get hit in the leg and have a BI carry us out," Sweeting said.

She socked him in the arm. "Prick, I was moving again in less than an hour."

The Exploration team looked a little concerned. Shashi looked at Betts.

He shrugged. "Ribs and some shrapnel."

He looked at me. "Been shot a few times but lost both legs and an arm. That one was pretty bad," I admitted. Before they could say anything, I added, "We are Special Teams. Everyone has a decent chance of getting tagged at some point, but almost no one gets hurt badly enough to be pulled from the action."

"But you're different?" Maria asked.

I nodded. "Yes. We are the best the Service Troops have to offer. When something especially dangerous needs doing, we are the ones you send. When someone is in trouble, we go. We spend more time training and train twice as hard as any unit on our ship. We are the best that the Spaceborne has to offer."

They looked thoughtful.

Andy spoke, "I looked up those transcripts you told us about. You guys have been in some…"

"Shit," Sweeting said.

Andy smirked. "Yeah."

"Which is why we will listen if you tell us to," Maria said. "On the note of listening, we need to start our meeting."

My team perked up, sitting on the edge of their seats, all levity gone.

"Today, we have one team going out. Catherine and Charles are going into town. They will take the rover. They are changing out the power supplies on drones and checking on them. Corporal, who are you sending out? And what's your team going to be doing?" she asked me.

"McLeod, Betts, you have Charles. Clay, you are with me. Sweeting, you are garrison. McLeod and I have the assets; Clay and Betts out front and sweep. Spread out Whiskers and build a map. I want to know where things can hide and how stable the buildings are. Sweeting, use some of the extra Whiskers we brought to build a better picture around the base. Everyone in town look for anything hot. If you find something that's using power that's not ours, let everyone know," I said in a business-like tone.

"How deep do you want us to look?" Krista asked.

"Just the surface right now. If you spot anything that leads underground, mark it." I looked over at Catherine. "Any chance we can swing by where any of the drones got hit?"

"Um… ah yeah, we can do that." She said.

"Coloring?" Betts asked.

"Good call out," I said. "McLeod and I will have our PODs mimic the Exploration team members. Betts and Clay, match your surroundings and move silently."

"Heard, be ghosts," Clay said with a nod.

I looked back to Maria. "Perfect. When do we move out?"

"As soon as our teams are ready… let's say thirty minutes. The rest of my staff is here today," she said.

I nodded. "Ok, is there anything else?"

"Nope, that's it," she said, a little amused.

124

"Sounds good," I turned to my people. "Get prepped and ready to leave."

We all got up and left the room. Charles laughed a little openly, and the rest of his team murmured a bit. We walked to the housing units.

"I don't think they are as efficient as we are with meetings," Sweeting said.

I snorted a laugh. In the housing unit, I grabbed my pack and SIR. I loaded up with ammo and integrated with my POD. We'd take a Heavy with us but leave the other two at the base, along with the mortars. I assigned everyone two extra BBALLs.

We left the housing unit and walked over to the base storage area. There were two rovers, 1R98s. They were almost the size of a bus with eight large wheels. The front had a big windshield that curved down-ward, allowing whoever was inside to see right against the vehicle. The outside was currently light brown and could take on patterns or colors.

Shashi was excited, waiting to give us the tour.

"Have you worked with these before?" he asked.

"The military variant of it, yes," I said.

He looked disappointed that he didn't get to show off the rover.

I pulled the specs on the rover. It was alarmingly close to the HFDF version down to the model. This model lacked the turrets found on our variant, and its side doors didn't slide open for easy access by troops and drones; otherwise, it seemed spot on. The nav and sensor suite was the same.

"Why is it armored?" I asked. "I mean, I get ours being that way; these things kind of make easy targets and all."

"We may not get shot at, but we are targets," he said. "We will live in these for days when we're far away from the base. They have to be able to withstand whatever weather and whatever is tossed around in that weather. Not to mention local animal life isn't always happy to see us."

He sent me a clip from a rover he'd repaired that had a dent in the side. I wasn't sure I wanted to know what would dent one of those things. Charles and Catherine joined us. I was thankful to see that her hair was up in a bun; if she'd been planning on being in the field without wearing her helmet, I might have passed out. Both she and Charles had packs, and they greeted us warmly.

"Are you ready? And let's not do any more yes or no ma'ams, ok?" she asked.

I smiled. "Fair enough. We are ready to go. Drones on top?" I asked.

She nodded. I sent the command to my drones and those of my team to load on top. The back had a cargo lift that could lift the Heavy and secure it. The back of the rover was the one thing that was different.

"Extra power cell?" I asked Shashi.

"Mini reactor. There's an RMU inside. We have to charge power cells in the field and make or repair drones sometimes. We need the juice. It's the only thing besides the ship with its own power supply. Yours doesn't have that?" he asked.

"Nope. They get blown up too often and don't do any manufacturing. Shooting and moving only," I said.

The drones jogged up to the rover and scaled the sides, laying down on the roof, their SIRs over the edge. The Exploration people shot them a glance. My team and I would certainly have to tweak our interactions some, but they would have to learn to accept our paranoia. Catherine climbed the short ladder to the side entrance, and we all followed.

The inside wasn't as large as the outside would have you believe. There were four bunks built into the wall and a seat running in front of the massive windshield. There were lots of cabinets and a small table in the back with a small RMU. Behind the main seat were several others. We all sat as the rover started to move. Charles and Catherine insisted that Clay, Betts, Krista, and I cram into the front seat. The rover

126

hummed softly and felt like it was floating over the fields around the base.

It didn't take long for the field to give way to an old road that was cracked and broken with time. Plants grew from the cracks, covering it with almost as much life as the fields. The terrain was smoother, and the rover sped up, covering ground quickly. Whiskers zipped out into the area, flooding my HUD with data. I tried to ignore it, trusting the drones and my CCPU to find issues. Instead, I watched the landscape go by.

There weren't any rusted-out lumps of vehicles, but there was the occasional structure. Walls jutted from the ground, and I tried to picture what they had once been. Maybe filling stations? That was probably just my own limited imagination coming up with that. Still, that's what I had, and that's what I pictured. I couldn't help making the human analogy.

We were on a highway that ran between towns; people had lived here, grown up, had families, and went to county fairs. But they hadn't. There had never been *people* on this world, just aliens who might not have had counties or fairs at all.

The horizon was a bright blue, only interrupted by the shape of rolling hills and the tattered skyline of the city ahead of us. My map showed a city that spread for several kilometers. There wasn't a building that was left above ten stories, if there had ever been one. But most didn't pass six stories. What the Exploration team had gathered was that the race here was still young, technologically speaking. And while it wasn't always true, there were paths that many species followed. Some designs just worked better for different environments, body plans, and technology.

The buildings were analogs of brick and mortar; they had metal skeletons, and not all had lift systems. Some of the buildings did.

"Tell me about them?" I asked Catherine.

"Tech-wise, I assume?"

I nodded.

"Well, we can see that they were just getting a grip on large-scale infrastructure—roadways for moving material, building, and power. In some areas, we have found pipelines connecting structures that we think probably carried water," she said.

"Power?" Betts asked.

She shrugged. "Yes, some. Less than you'd think, but a lot of that could be that wiring hasn't stood up to time as well."

"Or it was mined," I commented to myself.

"Mined?" Charles asked.

"Um, yeah, well, I guess we'd say reclaimed. I haven't seen anything that looks like it was once a vehicle lying around or anything metal. If this place was in the middle of some kind of total war, maybe they needed materials, that or whoever was winning in this area did. On Erie Prime, we reclaimed or, you could say, mined the Erie Cities. Lots of resources were just sticking out of the ground in the form of buildings and vehicles," I said.

"But the large buildings and ground supplies weren't touched here," Krista said.

"That's true. Hmm, maybe they didn't have the ability?" I asked Catherine.

"Well, they would have, but you have to remember their mining technology was a far cry from what we have. Pulling up pipe and even taking out wiring and vehicles might have been more work than mining the old-fashioned way on a large scale," she said.

"And you'd make the areas you took worthless if you wanted to settle in them," I said.

The buildings that we were starting to pass looked hollow. There weren't windows, and there was scant flooring from what I could see from the rover. I started looking at the visual data from the Whiskers, using them to weave in and around buildings. There was a lot of brick and steel, but not much else. There also wasn't as much vegetation as I'd have thought there would be. There were some trees here and there, but the further we got into town, the less of those I saw. Instead, there were just plants growing from cracks and up the sides of buildings.

The streets were paved with stone, giving the plants easy access to the air. The shells of buildings loomed above us, some of them showing the long-ago touch of fire. I wondered how many of them had decayed with time or if it had been a war that ruined them. Piles of rubble were all that was left of many of the buildings. Chunks of others were taken away.

Some of them showed pockmarks that looked like where bullets had maybe once hit. It wasn't eerie so much as sad. I couldn't get the picture I'd made up in my head out of my mind.

"Looks like a lot of fighting," Betts mused.

"How can you tell that?" Charles asked.

Betts pointed. "Look at the wall. The pockmarks. They don't make patterns like you'd see in decoration. They are random or in clumps, but the patch of wall next to it is clean. The way some of the buildings are messed up or came down." He shrugged. "I've done work like this before. I can see when others have to."

The rover wasn't moving as fast now. It moved around debris with controlled ease. It came to rest in a clearing that had maybe been a park or market or whatever the hell the beings here would have used.

"We have a couple of drones to check on today," Catherine said. "Nothing too important, just power cell swaps and basic maintenance mostly."

She and Charles started going through cabinets, grabbing small power packs. They put them in their packs. We offered to carry some of them, but Charles and Catherine declined, saying they didn't really need the help. The drones jumped off the rover, spreading out. They detached Whiskers, and even more data started coming in. I set up a relay with the Exploration base, copying everything our suits and drones found into their databases. If they wanted it, great; if they didn't, then they could ignore it.

"I got your data sharing," Maria said on a private line.

"Do you want it?" I asked.

"Oh yeah. Our drones tend to be more uni-taskers—really good ones but uni-taskers. Yours, on the other hand, seem to collect a bit of everything. We'll always take the data," she said.

I engaged my helmet and jumped out of the rover. By instinct, I gripped my SIR and looked around the area with all the tools I had. My team seemed to be feeling the same way. They circled the rover, each putting their backs to it and scanning the area around us. The BIs moved around almost lazily. Each one of them tuned into the profile of their operator, making the real person harder to spot. On our side, we didn't move like normal people. But we'd learned to move just a bit more robotically. Our suits helped a bit with this, but it was also a habit now. The conditioning to blend in with our PODs was second nature at this point.

I turned when Charles and Catherine got out and did a bit of a double take.

"Your helmets have transparent fronts?" I asked. Krista and Clay turned to look.

Catherine smiled. "They have another layer that comes down with all the sensory garb on it. But we are people who like to explore. We want to see whatever new world is around us with our own eyes, even if they aren't as good."

The faceplate was wide, showing down to their chins. Part of me was a little envious that they had an option. The part of me that was always assessing a tactical situation noted that most of the face of our helmet was armor, with only the outside being sensory. A CCPU search of the specs showed their sensory capabilities were equal to my own, but the faceplate was 85% less effective than mine at stopping a bullet.

The rest of the helmet was also thinner. It wasn't weak, but it only had to worry about them hitting their heads on stuff and being vacuum rated.

We had an open line with all my team, Maria, Charles, and Catherine. This was part of the protocol; the people in the field were part of the team, so we had to keep them on the team line.

"Alpha, be advised that Exploration helmets have little to no armor," I said and attached a data packet.

"And that matters why?" Charles asked.

"Just something to keep in mind," I said.

"I just started hoping a little bit more that there isn't any Venom here," Betts said on a private line.

"You and me both," I said, then on the general, "Can you change the coloring of your suits?"

"We can," Catherine said.

As if knowing what I was thinking, she engaged the other layer on her suit, and it turned to the same gray as mine. The head was still a bit smaller, but at least they kind of blended in. Her suit went back to normal.

In a private line, she said, "Everything will be okay."

I sighed. "I'm not nervous, just ticking off checkboxes is all. Sorry the HFDF pounds some things into your head. Don't worry; you won't notice it most of the time. Once we get fully acclimated to all of you and what your gear does, it will just be in the back of our minds."

"You could try to enjoy being on a new world," she offered, not unkindly.

I laughed. "Oh, I will. We are more excited about this assignment than any other we've had." Then, on the general, I said, "Alpha, take positions and prep for movement. Charles, Catherine, this is your show."

ELEVEN

I walked around with Catherine as she checked on various drones. They weren't anything like HFDF drones. Most had a single purpose and were stationary. They had power cells that lasted for a few weeks at best and mostly had relatively tough designs.

"I'm a little surprised by how basic a lot of these drones are," I said to her as she swapped out the power cell on a geology model.

"Well, if you think about it, most don't count as drones. We are constrained by law with the number of drones we can use, so most of these are technically under the qualifications to be considered drones. We still call them drones, but if you look at the detailed information about them, you'll see they aren't. They have no more functionality than the stove you have at home or your vacuum cleaner," she explained.

I hadn't thought about that. I wasn't one of those people who had issues with the AI Involvement Laws. They were in place for very good reasons and didn't negatively impact the average person.

"I've never thought about the laws around AI that much," I admitted.

She chuckled. "HFDF wouldn't, would they? You have exceptions," she said, referring to the fact that HFDF members could use vastly more drones than anyone else in society.

"Yeah, but we need those exceptions," I started.

She held up her hands. "I know. I'm not complaining. You guys do need those exceptions, and I agree with the laws wholeheartedly. Even out here," she waved her hands around, "if we didn't have those laws, I might not be here on this planet. I just meant that HFDF uses a ton of drones, and you guys get a little spoiled with them. In part, it's why we like having you around. We can assign drones to you, and we get to collect more data."

We were in the middle of a group of low buildings but were approaching an area with some taller ones. I had my Whiskers scanning everything. I was trying to build a map of the area with the structures that were the most unsafe and those that could provide cover. As we walked, I did a check on all my team. We were pretty spread out from the rover by this point, but with four of us in the field, I was pretty confident we had enough coverage.

"How far out do you spread?" I asked Catherine.

It took her a moment to realize what I was asking. "No more than half a kilometer," she said. "We might not get attacked by aliens like you do, but we keep close enough to help out if something happens to someone. Things happen in the field, from animals to regular accidents."

We weren't at a half-kilometer yet, so I made a note of it for later. Understanding how far the exploration teams spread out could affect how my team provided cover.

"Yeah, I keep forgetting that this job isn't as danger-free as I think it is," I said.

She sounded amused. "It might not be like being in a war, but we have our risks. To be fair, with the lack of life on this planet, it's easy to forget. We're also in an open flat area with solid ground under us. This place is pretty benign."

"I take it you have been in a few tight situations?" I asked.

She shrugged. "A few, but Felipe has been in the most. Biologists seem to have this fascination with getting as close as they can to animals that want to kill them," she said with a laugh.

She was looking at the husk of a building that had once stood four stories. I followed her through a hole in the wall. My Whiskers had already confirmed the building wasn't in any danger of collapsing; we could climb around if we wanted to, and it'd be fine for the most part.

Catherine was inspecting the tattered remains of the walls, pulling off chunks of material.

"Something I can help you find?" I asked.

She broke off a large part of the wall. With her gloved hands holding a wire, she traced it along the wall. "Can you look for anything that was once electrical?" she asked.

I toggled my view to density and scanned the walls, looking for wires. "What do you want me to do when I find them?" I asked.

"Just map where they go and how big they are, if you can."

She was over at another wall inspecting the wire. I had no doubt that she could do the same thing I was going to do but wanted to see the wires with her own eyes. Experiencing exploring something seemed to be pretty key for the team here. I had my CCPU map everything I saw, along with the size of the wires. I walked around looking, the world a mess of bright lines as I scanned.

"Wouldn't be able to carry a lot of power," I pointed out.

"No, they wouldn't. This building is pretty advanced if you can believe it. Whoever these creatures were, they'd just started networking buildings," Catherine mused.

"These are data lines?" I asked.

"No," she said, "not data networking. Utilities. Power and running water. Communications would be on the horizon, and the roads we've found here suggest that they'd only been connecting cities with paved roadways for a few years. There are rail analogs crisscrossing the continents, a lot like humans were back on Earth in the 11930s."

"That's funny. Driving out here, I pictured this place like Earth from back then," I said.

"The people here were extremely similar to us. If you get Felipe talking about it, he'll talk your ear off about how rare that is. It's part of why we are so interested in this place. Where did we go right that they went wrong, ya know?" she said.

"And you're trying to figure out the tech they had?" I asked.

She stopped pulling at the walls and led me out of the building. "Yes, I guess so. I study the technology of other races. That also makes me a great backup for Shashi and even better at field maintenance. But here, most of my job is seeing just how lacking the tech was," she said, a little dejected.

"Not much to do out here?" I asked.

"For me, no. Well, I shouldn't say that. I have lots of things in the field I can do, like this, which gives me plenty of opportunities to work with new people like Charles. But most of the planets I've been on had relatively advanced civilizations that collapsed, ya know? And that gave me loads to do," she said.

"What's that like?" I asked. "Seeing the worlds that didn't make it."

She shrugged, walking over to a small open area and sitting on some large rocks. "A little eerie at first. But then you get used to it, and it's just a puzzle."

I took a seat next to her. "What kills them the most?" I asked.

"Natural disasters," she said honestly. "A lot never advance enough to truly control their surroundings and die off as environmental changes occur, just like most of life has. But some mess up their world and don't figure out how to fix it, or they blow themselves up. Some lack the natural resources to make it past certain points in development. When that happens, they plateau and are kind of screwed. Their resources dry up, and they either go back technologically or die out. Normally, it's a bit of both. Lunch?" she asked.

"Sure," I said, and then I spoke on the line with Clay, "We're breaking for lunch."

"Roger that. I'll stay in the area," she said.

On my map, I saw her units starting to circle around us. I reached back into my pack and pulled out a nutrient packet. Catherine disengaged her helmet. She looked at me, bemused.

"Come on," she said.

I checked our orders and found there was nothing against disengaging our helmets in the field for a short time if we had a proper perimeter up, which we did. I sighed and disengaged the helmet.

It was bright out, and my eyes took a moment to adjust. The area lost a little detail as I looked with my eyes instead of through the suits. The air was hot and smelled of dust.

"See, that's not too bad, is it?" Catherine jabbed.

"Yeah, yeah," I said good-naturedly.

I moved BIs into the buildings, giving us more cover. She pulled out one of the goo canisters and sucked on the end of it. I bit into my nutrient packet. The salty-sweet taste was the norm for me now. Not bad, and not good. It was just like drinking water.

"You lot seem to like those cans," I said, making conversation.

She sucked on the end of it and nodded. "They are about all I eat anymore."

"Why's that?" I asked.

"Well, I spend most of my time in the field. We resupply monthly, but if you get the pre-made food, you start to run out of options. With this stuff, you can have virtually any flavor you want." She took another pull. "And you can customize the nutrients, like if you need more energy because you are in the field, stuff like that. It's easy to bring in a pack too. How about you? Do you like those nutrient packs?"

I took a bite. "Not really. They don't have the same value that the goo you have does. The packs keep you moving, giving you just what you need. We have some other ones that are just for extra energy bursts if we need them, but the blocks do pretty well. They are all we take in combat. The cans are too big," I said as I took another bite.

She looked at the block and wrinkled her nose. "We have them in all of our packs as a backup, but I wouldn't like having to only eat them for days on end."

I chuckled dryly. "Try weeks or months. It was a month or something like that on Erie Prime before we had normal food, and during my time on Pike Prime, I had a normal meal maybe five or six times planetside."

"How long were you there?" she asked.

"About six months," I said.

"The same thing to eat for every meal for six months? No thanks!" She changed the topic. "I've studied the Venoms' tech," she said like she wasn't sure she could talk about them.

I laughed without humor. "Me too." I finished my packet, and Catherine looked a little self-conscious. "Look, don't feel bad about asking. People are curious, and I get that. Plus, war isn't like what it used to be, right? Not the human carnage of the past. That said, we don't talk about it with a lot of people who don't know what it's like."

I could see her processing that. "Look," I said, "ask questions about their tech and tactics and all that. My people will talk to you until the end of days about that, and sometimes we'll tell a story about a battle or something else. Just know that there are a few soft spots that we'll avoid. Respect those, and you're fine." I thought of what to say next. "Honestly, a part of me wants the public to know what it was like there and still is. Sometimes, news feeds aren't enough. And I get that the war shook a lot of people."

"It was freaky," Catherine said. "I mean, the HFDF is invincible, but when you guys took losses, and when we lost ships... I saw the damage on Pike Prime, and hearing about people getting killed honestly worried me. Humans don't die that much anymore, and in war? It's been hundreds of years since we've taken any serious casualties. I don't even know anyone who has died."

That was what really got people: the mortality we had forgotten. I thought back to a conversation I'd had with Monica.

"I suppose for me, I had the opportunity to do something about the Venom. Everyone else had to be bystanders. I could see where that'd mess with you," I said.

"Do they scare you?" she asked.

I thought about that for a moment. "I guess. Combat is scary, so in that regard, yeah, they scare me. That said, the losses we took on Pike Prime were nothing compared to other human wars. There was only one ship as a dedicated morgue. If you compare our losses to those of the Venom, we beat them soundly."

"I guess that's true. There was a rumor that they figured out how to find and kill human operators," she said, sounding bothered.

"Oh, they figured out how to kill us," I said. "They learned that headshots always win, but they had a hard time telling humans from machines." I read the concern on her face. "In a way, it helped us. We can repair drones in the field. For a human, a headshot is a death sentence; for a drone, it's a quick fix. Hitting a drone's chest and torso are more of a pain to deal with. And heads take up less room on the mules. I got really good at swapping heads out," I said.

She didn't look like she thought that was a plus. We were done with lunch, and I engaged my helmet again as we started to move. It was an odd feeling, being so alone. We walked through a wasteland like something out of a horror movie. But there were no monsters that we could see.

Caring for the drones that the exploration team used was kind of relaxing. As Catherine had said, they were all really simple. There was normally some type of housing, the power cell, a comms system, and whatever sensory gear they used. But as we worked, I could also see what a pain in the dick it was going to be to find whatever was hitting the drones.

Whiskers could have done the job. They had decent cell lives, a high-data comm system, and could sense everything. The problem was they were directed by that comms system; they didn't think on their own. The BIs, Heavies, and our CCPUs told them where to go and how to act. Likewise, it took a CCPU or drone to sift through that data. They rode the line of what the law would call a drone or not, but since they had to be used with another device, they were considered accessories. The exploration equipment was spread out over a large area, and as I looked at the list of gear they had, I realized I didn't have anywhere near enough Whiskers to monitor everything. And even if I did have enough of them, I didn't have enough BIs or CCPUs to control them all. The Arbiter could do it, but it could only do it for several Fireteams and not the whole planet.

"What are you thinking about?" Catherine asked me over our private line.

"How'd you know I was thinking?" I asked her.

"You're walking more like one of them," she said, pointing at a BI.

That was a little amusing.

"I can't use a brute force method with my drones to find what's destroying your equipment. And now that I know what you guys call drones don't count, I can't think of a way to fix it. I had no idea you had as many as you do. Trying to put optical sensors on all of them wouldn't be possible and would probably reclassify them as drones," I said.

"Your team can't be in control of that many?" she asked.

"No. Aside from the fact that I don't have the computing power to monitor all of that, even my people would run into limitations with the AI Involvement Laws. I don't want to say it, but I think we are going to need dumb luck," I said.

"On the bright side, at least it's always happened in the cities."

There was that. We didn't retrace our steps but took a long path back to the rover that allowed her to see a few other drones. Charles, Krista, and Betts got back before we did, with Clay bringing up the rear.

"Anything interesting?" I asked.

"Alex, look at this place, man. It's all interesting!" Charles chided.

"Sorry, I mean anything my team would find interesting in the way that soldiers find things interesting," I corrected.

"Nothing," Betts said, a smile in his voice. "Best I can tell, there isn't anything bigger than a mouse in this city."

"And no power," Krista added.

"Nothing that I found. There were a few small tunnels, but my CCPU pinged those as local predators, so maybe something bigger than a mouse," Clay said.

"Oh yeah?" I asked.

Clay sent us a picture of a small tunnel dug into the base of a building. Nothing seemed to be staring out of it.

"We call them grabbers," Charles said.

"Really? That seems really non-scientific," Krista said.

"Oh, they have one of those names, but it's long, and no one uses it. I'll send you guys a file on them; they are smaller than a human and haven't posed a threat to us. They tend to be nocturnal," he said.

I got the file request and marked it to read later. We loaded back into the rover, and it started to make its way back to the base. I read over my team's reports as they came in.

"Anything exciting at home?" I asked Sweeting.

"Negative. The towers tracked a few small animals to the south of the base, but Guzman says they are herbivores and mellow ones at that," Sweeting said.

"I'm happy you saw animal life. We didn't see anything," I said.

"Guzman told me that the animals the towers saw are super rare. There isn't much larger than a cat alive on this rock."

The rover made its way out of town and down the old road back to the base. Lepus 328 was still high in the sky when we got back to base. We unloaded and headed back to the housing unit. Betts and Clay grabbed some snacks from their storage, and I joined Krista at the table.

"Reports?" she asked.

I shrugged. "Done. Guzman said that no one is leaving for the night. She said we can join them for dinner if we want, but that people go their own way at night."

"So nothing then?" she asked with a smile.

I sat back in my chair. "Pretty much. I have to talk to Monroe, and I'll look through updates for the rest of the area, but that's it, I think."

She leaned into me. "This is gonna get boring," she said happily.

I grinned. "Yes, it is."

My conversation with Monroe was along the lines of what I thought it would be. There wasn't an efficient way to keep the exploration equipment monitored and safe. On the bright side, it was all super replaceable. I checked in with Clovis, and its team also didn't have any updates.

I started on the file that Charles sent me about the grabbers. They were ugly, with a body a lot like a centipede and four grabbing limbs at the front. They had long limbs and were powerful, with clawed ends. They would, as the name suggests, grab prey and haul it into their den. They were mostly found away from the cities where animal life wasn't so absent. But tunnels and the occasional one had been seen in the cities. It was thought that they moved around as prey migrated.

"These little shits work in packs," Sweeting said.

I knew what he was reading.

"And communicate with radio bursts," Krista said.

Clay and Betts's eyes went out of focus.

"Nasty little fuckers, aren't they?" Betts said.

"Looks like it," I said, "but they are mostly nocturnal."

"Our culprits?" Sweeting asked.

"Probably," Clay said.

She was right. That didn't mean they might not be a problem. From what information we had, they weren't able to penetrate our suits or those of the exploration team. That didn't mean they couldn't be a pain in the ass, but not one that was likely to result in someone getting hurt. Startle the hell out of you? That I was sure they could do.

When it was time for dinner, we all brought our food into the common building and ate with the exploration team. Most of them were there. Maria and Andy were playing chess. We shot the breeze with them as we ate, Catherine being a little flirty with me, and then when she saw that Krista and I were a thing, she moved on to Sweeting and Betts. Krista and I left after a while.

We walked hand in hand to the housing unit. I grabbed two blocks of nano-material and joined her on the roof. We fashioned them into cushions to lay back on and watch the sunset. As the sky turned to gold and fire, I sighed.

"This I can get used to," I said.

"Already am," she replied.

As Lepus 328 fell far below the horizon, the sky lit up with stars. All new constellations. It was a mark of how our minds worked that both of us found the constellations of our home worlds in the sky, though they were made with altogether different stars. It was just our minds finding patterns. It gave a slightly less alien feel to the planet.

Charles pinged me, and I told him where we were. He joined us on the roof.

"Mind if I sit with you?" he asked.

"Go for it," I said.

He sat next to me.

"Never thought we'd do this, did ya?" I asked.

He laughed. "Not a long shot. What do you think?"

"I love it," Krista said, "the openness and how different it is. I can see where you'd get sucked into this kind of work."

"There's a beauty to it," I said. "Not sure I could do it long term, though. Not seeing people again would wear on me."

"Nah, I have a high-data AltComms system. I can do fully immersive VR, remember?" Charles said.

"I guess there is that," I said.

"On that note, you or your team are welcome to my VR pod

anytime you want. Catherine and Maria said you can use theirs too," Charles said.

"Thanks, man, that's really nice of you guys. I'll tell my team," I said.

"Good. And when I say you can use it, Maria will probably push you guys, too. Exploration commanders are really big on making sure people don't feel too isolated. I know she isn't over you, but…"

I smiled. "Oh, I wouldn't worry about that. All of us will take advantage of that."

"Good," he said.

I gave Krista's hand a slight squeeze.

"Already used to it," I said.

TWELVE

We all sat down in the common room with the exploration team. We'd only been on site for a week, and sitting down for the morning meeting seemed natural to us. Maria Guzman was going over the plan for the day. In part, it was the one that we'd done again and again. Two exploration people and two HFDF. As was the norm, it was Catherine and Charles who were the Exploration team. For my group, it would be Betts and Sweeting with Charles, and Krista and I with Catherine. Charles would be with Sweeting, and Krista had Catherine. That put Sweeting and me out in front, scanning the area. I was trying to rotate the team through this. While the overall deployment may not have been designed to sharpen our skills, I was using the opportunity to work with the team. Scouting was something we were all good at. We had to be— it was half of Spaceborne's job. But that didn't mean we couldn't hone those skills more. Same with working on giving assets the best possible cover and all that. It hadn't taken much encouragement for people to use the time we had to try and improve.

Maria was looking out into space. "So, it looks like today we will be replacing one of the drones that was taken out a few weeks ago. We're going to place this one in a different location. We will need to retrieve the destroyed drone." She looked at me, and I spoke.

"For this, I'd request that we maintain a closer distance than normal. When it comes to inspecting the site where the last drone was, I'll approach. As per the norm, we're not expecting anything, but I'd like Sweeting to be in range for backup in case shit."

"Roger that," Sweeting said.

"McLeod and Catherine, please keep clear until I sweep the area," I said conversationally.

"Will do," Krista said.

I wasn't sure whether Catherine was happy about it or not; she looked halfway between amused and irritated. I decided I didn't really care either way. Even if I was ten thousand percent sure that nothing would hurt anyone, if I didn't take every necessary precaution, I'd hear about it later.

We'd already assigned PODs for the day, and I added the Heavy to Krista. I didn't want to deal with it, and if there was something that took out the drone, I wanted the firepower where Catherine or Charles would be. Today, Catherine would be closer to that site than Charles, so Krista got the Heavy. If something did happen, Sweeting and I would be faster without it, allowing us to contain the situation or get out of dodge. The rest of the meeting went smoothly. There was some talk about longer-range plans that they were going to start working on with Andy and Felipe, but those were over a month out. If and when that happened, I'd need to figure out who I would send into the field for a week. When the time came, I figured I'd send whoever got along best with Andy and didn't kind of want to shoot him. Sadly, I couldn't think of who was on that list.

When we broke, we left for the housing unit and then met up at the rover. Catherine was off to the side and nodded for me to join her.

"Something wrong?" I asked. "Sorry about having to slow down today. I have to clear the area first."

She shook her head. "It's fine. It's dumb, but you have your orders, and I can't get mad at you for doing your job. What I wanted to know is, why are you always assigned to me? Not that I don't like you, but I was just curious."

I smiled. "Because I'm friends with Charles. That's why we're assigned to your team, but in the field, that relationship might cause issues."

"But you're with Private McLeod..." she said.

I saw where she was going. "Krista and I have a ton of extra monitoring on our CCPUs. But also, we met in training and have always fought alongside each other. The HFDF has tested us a lot to make sure we work well in combat. If I'm about to die and tell her to save you and leave me, she'll do it. She'd hate herself, but she'd do it. They actually tested us on that. And when the shit hit the fan on Pike Prime and I got hurt, Krista continued to do her job. If she hadn't, we all might have died. Charles and I don't have that relationship, history, or frankly, government access."

"Oh, I understand," she said thoughtfully. "For the record, I wouldn't leave you," Catherine added.

I smiled. "Thank you, but I hope you'd be wrong."

She didn't seem to know what to make of that answer. She walked over to the Rover and climbed inside. No one asked what Catherine had talked to me about. Charles kind of looked like he wanted to, but my people didn't. If they needed to know, I'd tell them. Our drones climbed onto the rover, and it started up. I didn't sit up front like I had on the first day. I knew the drive, but also I wanted to be looking at my Whiskers not thinking about wherever we were heading. I sat against the inside wall and pulled up feeds. My team was doing the same. There wasn't anything new for us to see; we did this drive every day. But it was a habit for us, so we inspected the feeds as if something might be different today. It wasn't. We were patrolling a wasteland; the only thing that ever changed was the weather, which had been pretty consistent thus far.

The city came into view, and we went left where we normally went right. That's cool; that was a change. I'd asked Catherine to have the rover drop us all pretty close to where the drone had been attacked. She did so without question.

As we approached, she and Charles started puttering around with the drone's replacement. It looked like atmospheric testing. Charles started explaining how it worked, and I tried to look like I was paying attention. I'm sure it was super duper interesting. We were in a new area, and to save myself the eye rolls of telling him I needed to study the area, I just nodded and said, 'That's cool', 'nice,' and stuff like that. It'd been working for years and didn't seem likely to stop now. The rover stopped, and we unloaded. As Catherine loaded the drone onto the Mule, Sweeting and I set out. I moved quickly with my POD, keeping low, trying to see the landscape as a test. I moved efficiently, maintaining cover and using my BIs to scout ahead. The area had the holy hell blown out of it. Most of the buildings were half destroyed, with hills of debris scattered around, providing plenty of good places for cover.

I approached the area where the drone had been located. It was once a long building that was a few stories high. Thick beams of metal had brick hanging from them. Piles of debris were everywhere. Inside the building lay the wreckage of the drone. I approached it and inspected the site. The drone had been torn to shreds; bits of it were strewn all over. At a glance, there weren't any scorch marks or signs suggesting it had been burned, shot, or blown up. I pulled out my nano-material block and created a container, placing everything I could find inside it.

Once I was done, I walked around the building a bit. One of my BIs found a tunnel. It paused, and I pulled up the feed. The tunnel was going into the ground as tunnels do. The dirt around it looked like it had been disturbed. At least, that's what the BI thought, and I wasn't inclined to question it. Whatever had taken out the drone probably came from the tunnel.

I looked at it more closely, then surveyed the rest of the building. As I glanced back at the tunnel, I got an uneasy feeling.

"Alpha, hold positions," I said, trying to place the feeling.

"What are you thinking? Your heart rate is up," Monroe's voice came through on a private line.

I shook my head and felt my unease dissipate. "Sorry, sir."

"Don't apologize; what are you thinking?" he pressed.

I felt myself calm and shook it off. "Nothing, sir, just the willies is all."

"Alpha, continue to waypoints. I have the drone and will join up shortly," I said on the general line.

"You sure?" Monroe asked.

"Yeah. Just… got the creeps, I guess."

"It happens," he said but didn't push the issue.

"Do you want me in the area? Charles is close to Catherine. I could do a top-down of the area," Sweeting suggested.

"Negative," I replied. "I don't think there's anything to see here—just one of those grabber holes. It was probably one of them."

"Alright," Sweeting said, a little surprised. "Creepy little fuckers."

"Seriously," I agreed.

I moved away from the building, and my drones resumed scouting the area. Krista kept her units close to herself and Catherine, with the Heavy positioned between her and the place where the drone had been attacked. Free from having to babysit anyone directly, I meandered through the area and actually explored. I found a five-story building and walked inside. The ceiling sagged in places, and the floors were caked with dust and dirt. I found a stairwell in the center of the building.

The well was lit from above by a skylight. Maybe lit wasn't the best description, nor was skylight. The stairwell was lit from above by a hole in the ceiling. My helmet switched to low light augmentation and density overlay, showing me places that were likely not to hold my weight.

I started up the stairs. They groaned beneath my feet as I slowly moved up them. I pointed my SIR down the hallways as I reached them. At the top of the stairwell, the roof was buckling in with large holes. I found an opening I could fit through but decided not to try it. Instead, I walked down a hallway leading to a disintegrating door. I pushed against the wood, and it broke, allowing me into the room.

The space was square, with large broken windows in the walls. I walked across the floor and looked out the window. This was one of the taller buildings in the area, and I could see for blocks. I felt the temptation to disengage my helmet to look out at the dead city without the aid of my gear but resisted the urge. I would be unhappy if the floor gave way while my helmet was off.

Across the street, I noticed what appeared to be bugs flying out of one of the windows. I zoomed in and saw a large hive of some type, with winged things flying in and out. My CCPU didn't recognize them, so I had no idea what they were or what they did. That, in and of itself, was an odd feeling.

On Pike Prime, we knew everything around us. The Pike were allies and had shared scientific data about their planet. On Erie Prime, as troops moved through the area, the data they and their drones collected by just moving around was forwarded to Exploration groups. By the time I had a chance to think about the local ecology, everything had names and data associated with it. Here, they didn't.

Charles's team wasn't the first here, but they were among the first few waves. We'd only had teams on the ground for eight or nine months. My CCPU pinged me. It had been processing the images of the bugs and the hive against the Exploration database but hadn't pulled a match.

"Hey, Alex," Felipe said over a private comm, "I see you found a new life form."

"Did I?" I asked, surprised.

He laughed. "You sure did. Any chance you could send a whisker over there or something? I'd love the data on it."

I did as he requested and sent over a whisker to collect everything it could. I got another ping—this time from the Exploration system. It had processed the images of the bug I was looking at, along with a ridiculously long name that included my name. It read 'New Species,' with the person who made the discovery as Alex Michael Taylor.

"How does it feel to have credit for finding a new species?" Felipe asked.

I thought about it. "Kind of cool." I looked at the bugs again. "Really cool."

Maria came over the general comms. "Good news, everyone! One of our military grunts found a new species. It's his first."

There were pings from the Exploration teams; it felt good.

"Tonight, we celebrate," she announced.

"Isn't this common?" I asked Charles.

"Yeah, man, we find new stuff all the time, BUT you only discover a new species for the first time once. That's special, and you're now on a pretty small list of people who have found new creatures on other worlds. Congrats, man," he said with something like fatherly pride in his voice.

I exited the way I had come in and found my way back out onto the street. I continued to scour the area around Catherine and Krista but also found myself searching for anything resembling my bugs or anything else new. The area we were moving into had more of a residential feel, and again, I imagined humans in the streets. That the city was so human but wasn't was wearing on my mind. I'd never felt that way with the purple lumps of buildings the Erie had favored or the giant domes of the Pike. Those buildings had been as alien to me as the beings that built them.

Likewise, in those other places, seeing destruction hadn't had much of an effect on me. It started to on Pike Prime, but it took witnessing the wholesale death of everything for that to happen, and the emotion had less to do with the destruction and more with our view of the race that caused it. Here, that was a little different. I found myself feeling sad for whoever had been here. Their lives had been taken from them. They might have been exploring the stars by now.

I could picture the city alive and vibrant, as it changed from technology and growth. There would have been some bad that came with it, but there would have been good as well. In my imagination, the people here would have had happy outcome like humanity, not some dystopian dark future. As it was, they didn't have a future.

I peeked around a corner, scanning the area for threats. All I found was a building that had burned so hot that the metal frame had melted. There were the ever-present pockmarks on the walls, but still no bodies. No bones. We found places where clothing was either sold or distributed; the fabrics had decayed with exposure, and the colors were mostly washed out.

Andy had shared pictures with us of a place he'd found in an outlying area that had a bunch of little trinkets in it. The planet had commerce, textiles, and everything else, but it had stopped.

"Maybe someone just rounded them all up," Krista said as I shared the image of the clothing.

"Mass graves somewhere, perhaps?" I suggested.

"But who dug them?" Charles asked. "We've found graves. That's how we know what we do about the race that was here. Everything dies, and you have to get rid of it. The people here hadn't burned their dead, or at least not all of them. Their skeletons are hard and don't decompose that quickly. If everyone up and kicked the bucket, we should see the bodies."

"And maybe we will," Catherine said. "It's important to remember that we've only been on the ground for less than a year and that Lepus 328rb has almost the same land mass as Earth or Orion. It can and will probably take us years to figure out what happened to these people. We only have a handful of teams on the ground," she reminded us.

"So no horror movies, huh?" Sweeting asked.

"Probably not," she said.

"Way to be a buzzkill," Sweeting said with a huff, "nerds, am I right?"

Clay snorted on the line. "I can try to shoot him if you want?"

Catherine laughed. "Thanks. And sorry to disappoint, Sweeting. Maybe they were all killed by a blob race that absorbed their flesh and bones. Better?"

"See, there you go! Thinking outside the box. We need more of that in the exploration corps," he said.

"Catherine, the offer still stands," Clay said.

I spent the drive back to the base reviewing the data my whisker collected on the bugs. They flew, obviously, and they lived in a hive. A hive that was surprisingly dense and appeared to be made of a biological version of cement. Felipe had notes that he wanted to see what the hive was made from and how it was made. He didn't speculate on whether they were predatory or not.

We unloaded and stored our gear.

"So, are you switching corps now?" Betts asked.

"Nah, I don't want to make them look bad," I replied.

Krista laughed. I grabbed some food, and we headed to the common building. Most of their team was already there, each of them coming up to me and congratulating me for discovering my first alien. I was surprised by how happy it made me.

Charles and Catherine joined us. The latter hugged me in congratulations. I noticed Krista shoot her a dark look for a moment. I suppose I understood. Catherine was gorgeous and friendly; she was also single, and the only straight guy in the exploration base was married. Unfortunately for her, Sweeting and Kwasny were in an on-again phase, and Betts wouldn't fool around with anyone he had to spend any amount of time with.

I wanted to judge Catherine, but I remembered all too well what it had been like in training when I'd seen someone not in a full suit for the first time in a month. I could only imagine what her situation was like.

We ate, and the Exploration team seemed more comfortable with us. I hadn't noticed it before, but they'd always been a little apart. Now that one of us had found something, they saw us as part of the team. That worked for me. As the evening wore on, Krista and I left to lie on the roof of the housing unit. It had become a tradition for us.

We climbed up and lay down, looking up at the stars.

"Good day?" I asked her.

"Yeah, it was fine. I think if you want a good evening, I know someone who can take care of that," she teased.

I rolled over. "Oh yeah? You don't think anyone will be watching from the Exploration ships? I guess they are all inside the common building." I leaned down to kiss her. She kissed me back and playfully pushed me away.

"Not that," she laughed.

"Catherine?" I guessed.

"She's been laying it on pretty thick. I get it—I'm sure she's lonely."

"Yeah, I was thinking that," I admitted.

"I guess you could take care of that. I won't be mad at you, and she is really pretty," Krista said as if she was ceding some point.

I laughed. "I don't remember a head injury today." I paused. "Yeah, my CCPU said no head injuries."

She smirked. "A little test every now and then won't hurt you."

I chuckled. "Thanks. Did I pass?"

She kissed me, then looked thoughtful.

"Look, I don't want to hook up with Catherine. Yes, she is attractive, but that doesn't mean I'm dying to bang her. I don't cheat," I said seriously.

"No, I wasn't thinking about that," she looked at me, almost concerned, "what happened today? When you found the drone."

It took me a moment to think about it. I sighed. "Just got the heebie-jeebies for a bit. Don't know why. But I'm over it."

She didn't look convinced. "Why didn't you let Sweeting investigate?"

I was about to say that it wasn't a big deal, but she had me there. I thought for a moment. "I'm not sure, honestly. I guess it didn't need to be scouted that much. Do you think I made the wrong call?" Krista had never questioned an order I'd given.

She shook her head quickly. "No. It didn't need to be. But you just seemed a little off, is all. Sorry, it was nothing."

I leaned back. "I guess I saw the tunnel, and it just made me think of Pike Prime."

She considered for a moment. "I always expect to find one of them. We round a corner, and I expect to see them. I see a hole in the ground, and it's a Venom hole. I wonder how long that will take to go away?"

"I'm not sure," I said.

She rolled over, swinging her leg over mine. I kissed her for a long moment and didn't think about the Venom or Lepus 328rb. She gazed into my eyes. "So... There's something I need help with in the shop. A drone or two that needs to be worked on. Think you can help?" she asked, her eyes twinkling.

I smiled. "I think so."

We jumped off the housing unit and walked over to the shop we brought with us. We entered, and I told the system to lock the door behind us. Anyone from our team would take the hint. None of the drone parts or Whiskers in the racks were active.

I took Krista's hands, and she backed up to the work table. Her suit slid off her body, and I leaned down, kissing her lips and neck. My suit followed, and I lost myself for a time, which was something that we took. On the ship, we slept in the same bunk, always pressed together. Sex wasn't a chore, but it wasn't always the easiest. On this world, not having contact with her for hours every night made me just want my skin to be touching hers. To be in the same space as her, all alone.

I ran my hands up her sides, her skin soft and smooth, gliding over her chest, neck, and face. Her hands moved along my body, and I lifted her onto the table. We stayed crushed against each other the entire time we made love, and when our suits were back on, we still pressed close together, not wanting to be apart.

"That was different," she breathed.

"Yeah, it was. I don't know if I wanted to make love to you or just hold you," I admitted.

"Same," she said. "Odd. We've been in combat or on exercises for weeks or months, but when we... you know, for the first time, it's more of a release than anything else."

I smiled. "I like 'you knowing' with you." Then, more seriously, I added, "I wonder if it's because we have our helmets off a lot of the time, and we are social but never alone like we are on the ship."

"Yeah, that's probably it," she said. She glanced around the shop. "Still, we need to find a better place than this... hmm."

"Maybe Catherine would let us use her quarters, I mean, if she wanted to..."

"Say it, and I'll hurt you," she warned with a smirk.

I smiled. "Hey, it never hurts to test you."

She laughed. "That's a one-way street; nice try."

We kissed again, then walked out of the shop. Our team was back in the housing unit, all but Clay in their bunks. She didn't comment as we walked in. Krista kissed me goodnight and went into her bunk. I opened my food cabinet and grabbed a bottle of chocolate milk. I sat down at the table with Clay.

"How's watch?" I asked her.

"Fine. Nothing to report."

"What do you think of this place?" I asked her.

"I like it here. It's a little creepy, but the city is close enough to the training environments we've been in that it's only creepy when I think about it. Life in the base is relaxed, so that's not bad. You?" she asked.

"It works for me. I'm hoping to work with the Quiver a little more, and I have to admit, even though it was dumb luck finding those bugs today, it was pretty cool," I said.

"I bet. Normally, I don't pay attention to the little critters around us."

"Me either," I said.

My CCPU pinged me, letting me know my watch was about to start. I opened my milk and took a drink. Clay got up. "Have a good watch," she said.

"Sleep tight."

THIRTEEN

W e'd been on Lepus 328rb for almost a month, and the daily routine was starting to make time blur. We got up, had a meeting, went into the field, then ate, and Krista and I spent time watching Lepus 328 set and the stars. The days were surprisingly not boring, as there was literally an entirely new world to see. We'd found a few other species, and on one occasion, been in close proximity to the Quiver in the area. Comms had to be open for that so no one shot each other.

For my part, I spent a little while every day talking to Clovis. We'd started talking every day to build a working relationship. Over time, there wasn't much to talk about in regards to the mission, so it had moved onto personal conversations. It was odd to have an alien that I considered, if not a friend, an acquaintance.

"Any luck on your side?" I asked.

"Some," Clovis said. "They see the point that we might be forced to fight together at some point. Yours?"

"My command is fine with it. 'In case shit' is our motto," I said.

We'd been trying to put together a group exercise. From our perspective, this would be hugely valuable. We'd see how they fought, and they'd see how we did. If we found ourselves having to fight side by side, it could be handy. Our governments, however, weren't really keen on joint exercises. They'd happened on a handful of occasions, but they were rare. We didn't fight side by side with the Quiver, nor were we likely to. We had totally different battle doctrines and command structures. Further, there was the risk of somehow giving out secrets, which I found to be BS.

The Quiver had seen us fight a lot, and we had them too. That was great for command, but my team and I would have liked more. Plus, it would be cool.

"That your command has gone for it might sway mine. They have okayed us working in closer range. That won't be an exercise, but it is something," Clovis said.

"Same, and I have external raw data sharing," I said.

"Likewise. What does your Exploration team think of the idea?"

"Honestly, I haven't run much of it by them. I talked to the leader here, and she said she would like to work with your side, but other than that, she hasn't been involved. Yours?"

"They think it is wise to share data but don't care about meeting or working with anyone from the Human Federation. They are very focused on their work. They are here to study this planet and its races, not known ones," Clovis said.

That was fair. We made a note to talk later, and I dropped the connection. When I got out of my bunk, I grabbed some food and walked over to the common building. We'd debated on keeping our food in the common building, but that idea was put down when we looked at the regs and saw that, unless something happened, it needed to be stored in the housing unit as it was armored and yada yada.

I sat down at the table in the common space. Right as the meeting started, my CCPU pinged me with a notification. I stopped paying attention to Guzman and looked at the notification and smiled.

"Maria," I said when she paused.

"Yes?" she said.

"I have received a message from the Arbiter. Mind if I play it on the wall?"

"Go for it," she said.

The wall turned from gray to some footage that Fourth Platoon's first squad, Bravo Team, collected. It was from a Whisker that they had watching an Exploration drone. The drone was using ground-penetrating radar, and Fourth Platoon struck some good old-fashioned dumb luck.

The drone was pretty much a box. The Whisker was stationary, just collecting data when it noticed some spikes in radio waves and then heat. From a tunnel entrance that I hadn't noticed, a grabber poked its head out. The Exploration drone didn't pay it any attention. The grabber moved at a speed that I wouldn't have guessed possible. Its four front jaw slash arm things reached out and grabbed hold of the drone.

The grabber thrashed around, slamming the drone onto the ground. There was a squeal of metal as it bent and tore. There were more radio bursts, and then another grabber was there, and they pulled the drone apart. Its exterior was ruined; the grabbers went at the inside of it, sending bits of electronics everywhere. A third grabber joined them, contributing to the mechanical carnage. When they were done, they slinked away back into their tunnels. They'd ignored the Whisker. I doubted they could have found it.

"Jesus, that was violent," Sweeting said.

Betts looked at me. "Kind of reassessing the grabbers right now."

I nodded. "Yeah. They have a lot more power than I gave them credit for."

"I guess we know what's happening to the drones," Charles said.

"Were all the ones you lost radar-enabled?" Clay asked.

Catherine's eyes went out of focus. "Yes. Huh."

"I see," Felipe said. "The grabbers sense radio waves. I bet the drones are like banging pots and pans, saying 'come get me.'"

"Right. So, check for grabber holes when placing them," Andy said, a little annoyed. "Well, we might want to check on some of ours then."

"If you get me a list of them, we can task some Whiskers for the close ones. We have some large Whiskers on hand with decent range," I said.

"I'll get you a list," Andy said. "They are mostly mine."

It didn't take but a few moments before I got the list. There were thirty of them spread over a hundred kilometers.

"Will your Whiskers be able to cover that range?" he asked.

"Yeah, the large Whiskers have power cells that keep them going for a couple of weeks. I'll task three with the job," I said.

We had five of them on standby. They were currently in sleep mode, connected to the top of our shop. I woke them and checked their cells. Each was good to go. I had my CCPU come up with a route, and the Whiskers zipped away from the base. They'd be done in less than a day. We'd need to check every other drone to make sure it wasn't in an area that was going to get messed up, or at least, that we thought it wouldn't. That would take some time. The Exploration people had hundreds of them scattered in the area. It would take my little group of Whiskers several trips to check on them all, but it was better than having to figure out how to inspect each site for tunnels.

"Well, now that's taken care of, what's the plan for the day?" I asked.

I felt a small weight lift off my chest that I hadn't really known was there. My biggest fear wasn't that there was Venom on the planet; if they were hiding out, they would have made themselves known by this point. My biggest fear, if I was being honest, was that there were still some locals alive. That they'd been hiding underground, waiting for the world to stop ending, and then come up to find us. They'd attack us with tech that didn't stand a chance of hurting us, and we'd kill them. I'd have felt bad about that. The worst thing that could happen to a people did, and then the survivors' first encounter with aliens would be their last. Now we were just on a dead world that had some seriously crazy predators. It was still sad, but somehow better because we weren't a part of the tragedy.

"We are going to what we think was once an agricultural community. It's small. Felipe and Andy will be going. Alex, who are you sending?" Maria said.

I remembered seeing this op on the docket. Originally it had bothered me a bit. The location was about two hours away. If something happened at the base, there would be nothing the field could do to help. If something happened in the field, the same was true. Did I send four people to protect two and leave only one at the base like normal, or did I send three people into the field? Now it was easy.

"Clay, Sweeting, Betts, and myself. McLeod will be holding down the fort," I said.

Maria said she understood and continued with the meeting. When we were done, I opened a line to Clovis.

"Plans for today all set?" it asked.

"Roger that. I'm sending you a nav location. We are going to be two hours out from the base. You?" I asked.

"Staying close; we will be less than a kilometer from your base," it replied.

"I'll make sure the turrets know you're friendly. I have one team member who is going to be here. With you being so close and her being on her own, mind running backup if she needs it?" I asked.

"Of course," Clovis said.

"Thanks. Mind if she goes direct to you?"

"Yes, I think that would be best. Who is it?" Clovis asked.

"Krista McLeod," I said.

Its tone changed in a way that my CCPU indicated was 'knowing.'

"That is your mate, is it not? And the member of your team most interested in working with us?"

I smiled. "Yes, she is on both counts. What a nice coincidence this is."

There was a chuckle. "Yes, indeed. Well, to keep my people from being targeted by your towers and to ensure that our ally's base is safe when you are out, I think it's best for me to try and build a working relationship with your teammate."

"I mean, safety first, right?"

"Safety first," Clovis agreed.

I disengaged my helmet. My mouth hadn't been moving for the conversation, and I could have had it without the helmet on, but people just looked crazy when they did that. I looked over at Krista. She wouldn't ever complain about an assignment, but I knew she wanted to go out and see more of the planet.

"So about today," I said.

"I'll keep everything buttoned down here; don't worry," she replied.

"I know you were looking forward to seeing more of the planet, but I need the right people in the right position," I said.

She nodded. "I understand. It's not a big deal. We will be here for a long time."

"That's true. But as we are going to be so far away and unable to back you up in the event that anything goes wrong, I made arrangements with the Quiver to give you support if need be," I said.

"I'm sure I can handle it," she said, a little edge in her voice.

I tried not to smile.

"Be that as it may, I have to cover my bases. They are in the area today, so it works well. In light of them giving you cover, their commander and I agree that you need to have direct communication with them. I'm authorizing the connection, and Clovis would like to try and build a bit of a working relationship with you today. So that the team's function and if you need backup, it will be simpler."

Krista grabbed my hand, stopping us. Her face lit up. "Really?"

I couldn't help but smile. "Really. Their side isn't as on board with us working together all the time yet. This is a good workaround. Our commanders can say that we were just following sound judgment if either government gets its panties in a bunch."

She looked like she was going to pop, then got serious. "Wait, this is favoritism when they review our CCPUs…"

"It does not violate anything. Monroe knows about this. You, more than anyone on the team, want to work with other races. Even if we weren't together, I'd start with you. Eventually, I would like the whole team to work with the Quiver, though. But I think you're a good test," I said.

"I won't let you down," she said.

We got back to the housing unit, and I grabbed my pack and SIR. I opened my food locker and picked out a couple of drinks for the day and a snack. I figured with the drive, I'd have time. Everyone was about ready to go when the first of the Whiskers made it to one of the drones. I pulled up the data feed in the corner of my vision. The Whisker started to scan the area, first high above, then getting closer and closer to the ground. It found the drone in perfect health with no tunnels near it. The Whisker moved on to its next location.

I joined Clay, Sweeting, and Betts as we walked out toward the rover. I wasn't super excited about spending hours on end in a tight space with Andy Waters, but there wasn't much I could do about it. I did add two GPs to the list of drones we were taking. If we found any grabber holes when we were out, it might be handy to map them and see how extensive their network of tunnels was. I also changed everyone's PODs to six BIs and six BBALLs. For the team, I decided not to take the Heavy but rather a Mule, four Spheres, and a swarm of the normal small Whiskers.

"Hey, McLeod, if you get a chance today, can you break more large Whiskers and eight Spheres out of storage?" I asked over the team line.

"Yeah, will do. Do you want more BBALLs?" she asked.

I thought about it. "Sure, let's have a few more on deck. I think we need to move over to a scout POD configuration."

"Do we want to go all scout?" Betts asked.

"Not just yet. I want to wait until we have a full handle on the grabbers and where their tunnels are. I get the impression they'd rather hit ground targets instead of air. The BIs will lower the chance of that being people," I said. "Also, until we get more confirmed grabber-related drone murders, I don't want to go full scout."

"Understood," Betts said.

I didn't have my helmet on for this and was talking like a normal person. Charles had come out of the common building when I passed and waited for me to be done.

"Have big plans for the day?" I asked him.

"Lab work. What's a scout configuration?" he asked.

"A standard POD is what we've been using. A scout configuration is heavy on units like Whiskers, BBALLs, and Spheres. Light on BIs," I explained.

"And how do the BIs help you with grabbers?"

"A big part of how we work with our PODs is blending in. Our BIs act human-ish, and we move a little like a drone. It makes it hard for nonhumans to make us. In this case, the BIs are generally on the outskirts of our groups, making them better targets for a predator like the grabbers. When we know more about them, we probably won't need the BIs. But having them now may net us more data about how they hunt or if they will attack something the size of a human and if they'll do it during the day," I said.

"See, man, look at you setting up experiments like a real scientist," Charles joked.

I laughed. "Hey, we are real scientific. All the data our CCPUs and drones gather during fights gets pushed down as updates to make us all better at what we do. On Erie Prime, there were units whose PODs were configured in ways to find how the Erie set up ambushes and picked off units."

"And then you all got an update?" Charles asked.

"Yep. Down to the rounds used. But if a grabber attacks a BI, you all will get a lot out of it," I said.

We were at the rover now. Felipe and Andy were there, the latter loading equipment onto a lift on the back of the rover. He turned to me.

"You bringing the big drone?" Andy asked.

"Nope, not today," I said.

"Good," was all he said as he went back to his work.

When he was done, I gave the order for the BIs to load up on the top of the rover with the Mule. Betts asked if he could ride up top. I told him to go for it. I joined the others inside and sat down on one of the seats against the wall. Sweeting was sitting up front, looking out the window. Clay took the seat next to mine, and Felipe and Andy fiddled with stations in the rover.

"All ready?" Felipe asked.

"All ready," I replied.

The rover started to move. The two Exploration people set up workstations toward the back and began working. I turned to Clay. "Wanna sit up front?"

She shrugged. "May as well. I figured Andy and Felipe were going to, but I guess not."

We got up and moved to the front seat, Sweeting moving over to give us room. He stretched back in his seat. "Part of me wishes I would have joined Betts on the roof. Might be good laying up there," he said.

"There's a roof hatch," I pointed out. "You could go up."

"I might," he said.

The rover was heading away from the city on the same road we'd used every day. Ahead of us were just plains and rolling hills, as far as I could see. As per their norm, the Whiskers were fanning out ahead of the rover, easily keeping pace with it. I paid a little attention to the data coming in as we drove. Sweeting started to drift off, and after half an hour, he got up and went out the roof hatch, leaving Clay and me.

We sat quietly for a while as the landscape shifted from grass to trees to grass again. The rover turned off the road and went across untainted land.

"Any ideas on who you are going to send on the long mission?" she asked.

"A little. Monroe and Middleton want me to stay back at base," I sighed. "Not sure I want to send four people into the field for that long. Guzman said that she would authorize the other rover to travel in the area when the other team is out. We may not need to have someone at the base strictly speaking, but I'd like to. I'll probably send three people out for the long trip, maybe. Any thoughts?" I asked, turning to her.

She shrugged. "I guess three makes sense. It'd be nice to have someone in the field who isn't attached to an Exploration person. And that gives two back at base. If something goes down, you have the base defense system, and you can still support the people at the base if they go out."

"Yeah, that's what will probably happen," I said.

"So…"

"Not sure yet." I looked to the back of the rover. "Everyone will be in tight quarters for a couple of weeks. I want to make sure everyone gels, you know?"

She smirked. "I do. So, who's on the shortlist?"

I sighed. "Sweeting, Betts, and McLeod. Betts, either way, I'll put him in charge in the field. But the rest could change."

"Seems like a solid choice to me," she said.

"Are you itching to go on it? I know McLeod wants to go, and Sweeting doesn't give a shit one way or another. He might prefer staying back," I said.

The truth was, Clay was tactically on par with Betts and me. She also was my best switch hitter. If you wanted to hold ground, Krista was your person every day. If you wanted to take it, that was Betts. Sweeting was great at taking care of a base, but in normal combat, it was he and Clay that I shifted roles around the most. Clay was a better scout than Sweeting, and he was far better at running a base. He'd be good for keeping the camp in working order for a few weeks, and I worked better with Clay between the two.

"Nah, I don't know that I really care if I go out or not," she said.

We passed by what looked like a broken-down silo or at least something that resembled one.

"I wasn't expecting what a buzzkill this job can be, ya know?" she said, looking at the silo.

"I do. The training exercises can be fun, though," I said.

She smiled. Clay lived for the training. She was always pushing herself in whatever we did.

"I do like that part of it. And I like this assignment so far. We just aren't ever really needed where good things are or have happened so far. I mean, look at this place; the planet is pretty, but the ruins?" she said.

I laughed at that. "True. I guess it would be nicer if we were just exploring a world that hadn't seen its most advanced species die off."

"Right! Don't get me wrong, there is something on every world that tries to kill you. That's fine. The grabbers don't really bother me. They are a predator doing predator things. I may not be thrilled if the wildlife tries to eat me, but it's nature."

"One could make the argument that a species likely killing itself is nature, too," I said.

She rolled her eyes. "You know what I mean."

"That still won't stop me from being an ass."

"You are that," she said with a smirk.

"But I agree. This place is cool and all but sad, too. Maybe we'll get lucky, and this was still just a natural disaster that killed everything, and it isn't the planetary equivalent of a children's story with the moral of 'don't kill each other,'" I said.

She snorted. "And I might fly. Please, the Exploration people might think that there's some ecological reason these people died out or that it was some really bad war that started them down the path or whatever. This place, when I see the wreckage, it gives me the creeps. Something seriously sinister went down here. We just haven't figured it out yet."

I looked out of the rover. "Yeah, I know," I said softly. I couldn't say that Clay wasn't thinking straight or that I didn't agree. I did agree. Something really fucked up happened here. There were no bodies, no information, no animal life, and lots of destruction. Finally, I said, "I just hope we aren't here when the federation figures it out."

Later that night, I stood in Maria Guzman's ship by her VR pod.

"So, you have a guy's night planned with Charles and a friend you grew up with?" she asked.

"Ah yes, ma'am," I said.

She looked thoughtful. "Two hours," she said.

"Thanks, I really appreciate you letting me use your pod. I won't go past two hours," I said, a little surprised by the time limit.

"No, that's not the limit; that's the minimum. If your buddy needs to go, that's fine; you find a club or something to connect to. No going off on your own or with just Charles," she said sternly.

"Ah, um okay," I said.

"Look, I know you aren't my crew; you and I are equals, but I take isolation seriously. When we have teams put under us, they drill that concept home," she said.

"I'm sure that could be an issue. Honestly, it gets a little strange for us in combat. I have to gauge how my people are doing constantly. We don't have VR in the field and may not be out of our helmets for weeks on end," I explained.

She looked thoughtful. "I've always wondered how you guys handle that. There are long-term troops that come in, correct?"

"Yes. But when the careers start landing, we generally have an infrastructure. That said, they do have long stints in the field. We use our Fireteam and Squads to help combat the isolation," I said. "And I guess if I'm being honest, we normally don't have a lot of time to think about the fact that we haven't seen another human face for weeks."

She still looked thoughtful. "If you don't mind, I'd love to talk to you about it more sometime. It's interesting seeing how other corps handle the field. But for now, you have guy's night. Get to it!" she said as a friendly order.

I obeyed.

The man cave that Charles, Jon, and I used was designed to make fun of other young male man caves. The room had no doors, the walls were wood, and posters of scantily clad women adorned the walls. But if you looked at the ladies, they all were making strange faces, or if you looked close, hands were swapped, or eye colors didn't line up—dumb stuff. Jon and Charles were already there.

"Hey man, been a while," I said to Charles.

He chuckled. "Guzman, give you a time frame?" he asked.

"No less than two hours. Hey Jon, how's it going?"

I clapped Jon on the shoulder.

"I'm good. How's being Charles's assistant?" Jon asked.

I looked at Charles. "Did you tell him that?"

Charles chuckled. "I mean, it's kind of true… if you think about it."

I smiled and turned to Jon. "Did Charles show you his bone drone?"

"You have a bone drone?" Jon asked Charles.

Checkmate. Assist that.

FOURTEEN

Betts had been on watch in the middle of the night when the Exploration drone lost connection. The Exploration team would find the information waiting for them in their morning notifications, but my team received real-time updates if someone was on watch. At 0143 local time, the drone went offline. After five minutes, it did not report back in. This was the cue the system needed to send out a notification. Betts got the notification and deployed a large Whisker we had on standby in the area. It took the Whisker an additional six minutes to arrive at the drone's location.

Betts kept the Whisker high in the air, inspecting the site. The drone was destroyed, but there was nothing living in the area. At 0200, he woke me with the report. I looked it over.

"Do you want me to send anything else to the area?" Betts asked.

I thought about it for a bit. "Negative. We will inspect it in the morning. This looks consistent with what has happened elsewhere. Leave the Whisker on site in case they come back."

"Will do."

When I woke up in the morning, I'd almost forgotten about the conversation. I pulled up the feed from the Whisker, and it was still in the air, watching the area. The grabbers had not come back in the middle of the night. As I showered, I completed my report and sent it off. I grabbed some food, and we headed into the morning meeting. Obviously, part of the day's plan was going to be replacing the drone, but in a new location. We'd also be looking for the hole the grabber came out of.

"My people will be Catherine and Charles," Maria said.

Catherine looked a little put off by having to deal with the drone. Not that it wasn't her job, but that she didn't want to be put behind. Andy and Felipe had just come back from a two-week trip out of the base. Maria had allowed Catherine into the field on a couple of occasions, but without the aid of Charles. Clay or I would join her in the field, but we weren't the same as Charles. He knew what he was doing, and Clay and I were more of a hindrance than a help. I didn't think she was pissed that she was being told to go replace a drone, just that the drone needed replacing to begin with. That was fair.

"That sounds like a plan. Sweeting, you are here; Betts and Clay, you are with Charles," I said.

"Have your Quiver counterparts talked to you about when they would like to train together?" Maria asked.

"Clovis and I are still working on getting the details all settled. I told it that you guys had a little bit of a backlog on fieldwork to clear out, but hopefully, in the next couple of weeks," I said.

"Any plans on where or what you will be doing?" Shashi asked curiously.

I shrugged. "We'd both like to do some urban exercises. Nothing with live rounds, we don't want an incident or to mess with anything you all might be studying. When we do it, we'll keep close, but we'll probably be off base for a few days."

THE DRONE HAD BEEN TAKEN OUT IN A WAREHOUSE DISTRICT OF SOME TYPE. Catherine allowed me to send a BI into the area to see what was there. The large Whisker from the night was still there, but I wanted to be sure.

"Feels strange it just being the two of us," she said.

"McLeod is pretty close by," I said, pointing to a building where Krista had a sniping position set up.

"Not the humans. The drones; I've kind of started to see the basic infantry ones as people," she said.

She couldn't see my smile. "Yeah, the BIs do that. But there are a lot of advantages with the scouting PODs, though."

We'd changed up the POD complements since the team had come back to base. Each human operator, including the Exploration team, had to have two BIs that were assigned to them. But the PODs were now a combination of spheres and more BBALLs along with two large Whiskers apiece and ten extra regular Whiskers. The PODs could cover a lot of ground and weren't bad for coming to someone's aid. The Spheres could haul ass.

"Do you like this configuration more or less?" Catherine asked.

"I like it fine," I said honestly, "The right config for the right job, ya know? When we first came here, we were geared up more for a heavy fight, not that the Spheres can't mess some stuff up. This config gives us a lot less in the way of cover as we don't have as many BIs to hide in, but it also would give us a lot of notice."

We retrieved what was left of the drone without any issues. It was just as trashed and messed up as others had been. Catherine gathered it up, putting it in a box. I had the BIs help gather the bits that had been thrown around the area. I called the mule, and we put the box on it.

"These are handy," Catherine said, nodding at the mule.

"You don't have them?" I asked.

"We do, but they are smaller. This one also seems a little more hard-wearing," she said.

"Yeah, they can get the shit beaten out of them. They are pretty simple, though; just a floating platform."

I told my POD to start searching the area, looking for any tunnels or other parts of the drone. I found a spot inside a small building to sit in. The roof was gone, and one of the walls was too. Krista pinged me, letting me know that I was out of her line of fire. I sent an acknowledgment. I sat down and rested against the wall. Catherine dropped next to me, her helmet sliding off. Grudgingly, I disengaged mine.

"So, what are we doing?" she asked, a slight smile on her face.

"Mostly scouting the area," I said, and chuckled when I took in her confused expression. "This place has good cover. I'm not actively helping with scouting but running the drones. PODs like this mean a lot more sitting tight for us—too much going on to be active."

She nodded slowly. "So your plan is for us to sit here for the rest of the day?"

I laughed. "No. Just until they scout the area is all. If we can find tracks or something like that, it might help us figure out how the grabbers hunt and work. Could make for losing fewer drones."

"I can get behind that," she sighed and looked curious. "Can I ask a personal question?"

"Go for it," I said.

"You and Private McLeod."

"Yeah."

"What's that like?" she asked.

"What do you mean? Like how does the chain of command work?" I hedged.

"No, I understand that. But being in a relationship with someone you fight with—isn't it hard in combat? And how about times like now? Charles told me you two share one of those shoebox of bunks on the ship, but you can't here. Or when you don't even have a bunk at all."

"It's got its pros and cons, I guess," I said after thinking for a moment. "Combat is hard in some ways. I love her, and I have to order her into harm's way a lot. And even though I'm confident in her abilities, it does weigh on me. That said, it does with my whole team. We are set up almost like a family." I went down the list of questions. "Sleeping in the bunks sucks at first, but you get used to it. Almost dependent on it, in a way. Our first time staying in a place with a normal bed, it took a little getting used to.

"In the field, it's harder. We are so close but rarely have any physical contact without our suits."

"You can do it through them?" Catherine asked, amazed.

That got me laughing pretty hard, and it took me a moment to calm down. "God no, though after weeks or months, that would sound good to you. Those suits cover so much that even though you know it's a person in them, they look like a drone. Once we have our columns defined, we get mess halls on planets, and there I can see her face and touch her hand, but in the field, I can't. I can hold her hand, and with our suits, I can feel her glove, but never her skin. I can hear the tone in her voice but never see her eyes. And when I can, it's only her hands and only her face. That's the hardest part. There's an isolation to this job. And in a relationship, that makes it hard; you go from that extreme isolation to being crammed together. Don't get me wrong, when you first come off an operation, all you want to do is be closed in your bunk with that person for days on end."

She looked thoughtful. "I wondered if it would be hard."

"How about you?" I asked.

"Me? Nothing to say there. I'm single," she said, a little defeated.

"I could see finding dates hard to do on alien worlds. Does being single bother you?"

"Tell me about it. It does and it doesn't. I don't feel down about myself like I can't find someone. I just don't have the opportunity. When I am back on a station, I like to let loose and have fun. I'm pretty social. There are lots of clubs and bars, and that can be fun for a while. But nothing ever more than a fling or a one-night stand. It's that or do the long-distance thing."

"Shashi and Andy are together. You don't want to do that?" I asked.

"They have been together for a long time. That's different. If I was somewhere populated for a few years and found someone who was also in the corps, I'd love having what they do. God, it would be amazing. But if it was a new relationship or a person that didn't do good in a situation like we have…"

"Stuck on an alien world for months in a confined area with someone you hate. Yeah, that might not work."

She winked at me. "See, military types aren't dumb after all. But instead, all I have is my bone drone." She sighed.

I laughed. "Charles gets mad at me for calling it that."

She smiled. "He's new. Yes, they are indispensable for our jobs, and they keep us sane. I can talk to mine like it's a person. But I know it's not a person, so in the relationship department, it's a bone drone. It can totally scratch that itch, but the not being truly alone? Not as much."

My drones were done searching the area. There was nothing new they found. We engaged our helmets and left the building.

"You two fool around?" Krista asked me dryly.

"Did you know that our suits can part right around the crotch? And with the extra power and stability they give you… I haven't had a lay like that in ages! Honestly, I think I might have hurt myself," I said.

"Fuck you," she said, but I could hear the smile in her voice.

"We talked about our relationship mostly."

"She asked me about it before. I feel for her. She wants to not be alone, but the woman loves her job more than anything else," Krista said.

I followed Catherine around for the rest of the day. Afterward, I went to Charles's ship to use his VR POD. As it closed, I found myself in darkness that dissolved into a room with a door. I was wearing a pair of jeans and a T-shirt. The fabric felt a little odd against my skin. I walked to the door and opened it. It opened the digital pub my friends and I liked. Liz was sitting at a high-top table, her feet swinging like a kid. She saw me and waved. I walked over to her, taking a seat. A waiter came by and deposited two glasses of beer on the table.

Mine was a deep rich brown, and I took a pull on it. It tasted good, and despite how fake everything was, I felt like I was at home.

"So, how's the Helios?" I asked her.

"It's good, I really like it. Like a lot more than I thought I would. I kind of figured I'd get tired of being on a ship, but I haven't. I don't even walk around it all that much," she said.

"That's good. Are you planning on joining the HFDF then?" I jabbed.

She rolled her eyes. "No way. I'd have to do basic and all that."

"I see... but you've looked into it," I countered.

She shook her head. "Nope, but my boss has told me several times about it. If I could serve permanently on a ship like the Helios without joining the HFDF, though, I'd be game. How's Lepus 328rb?"

"It's good. We figured out what's hitting drones, so that's good. Now it will just be helping out the Exploration people."

She looked at me thoughtfully. "You seem happy about that. That's good."

"I am," I said, "there's a peace to it here."

"I bet. What you and Charles have shown me makes it look nice. Aside from the creepy dead city."

I smiled. "There's that. But nothing here shoots at me, and I get to work with the Quiver."

"Is Krista still loving that part of it?"

"Oh yeah, she thinks it's great. I like them, and I hope to stay in contact with Clovis when this is all done, if possible, but she's all in. Honestly, I think this might make her want to join the diplomatic corps someday," I said.

"Really? That's good. I hear that it's really hard to get into," Liz said.

"Normally yes, but with our experience, I would think that anyone from my team would be a shoo-in. We've actually worked with other races, and thus far, it's gone well. We're even planning a small training exercise. We've all gotten a number of certifications from our time with the Quiver. They wouldn't do us any good outside of government work, but if we wanted to stay working for the HF, we could," I said, "And before you ask, the pay is fantastic."

"So, do you think you'll go that way? You know when your term is up."

I thought about it for a while. "Honestly, I haven't thought about it. How's Monica? She doesn't talk as much as she used to."

"Yeah, after coming clean about not really liking being a cop and you and I telling her the shit we've seen, she doesn't talk to me as much. Not that I think she's mad, just a bit embarrassed," Liz said.

"Did I tell you she talked to me that night we all had dinner after our first year?"

"No, you didn't," Liz said.

"Yeah. Seeing the war scared her. I think she's having to come to terms with there being more out there than just humans, and the humans we've dealt with haven't been that bad."

"Do you still talk to that guy from Earth?" Liz asked.

"Takeo? I do," I said.

"How's he? I didn't follow up with him after he left the Healers Touch."

"He's doing well and is back on Earth now. He didn't have any other injuries after he left the ship. His platoon did lose a squad, though," I said.

"All of them?" Liz asked, bothered.

"Yeah. Shuttles got hit trying to pull them out of a hot zone," I said.

She looked down at her drink. There was a time when news like that would have made her cry, but it didn't now. The loss of a squad bothered her, but she'd seen it before. Her lack of distress was what saddened me the most. She sighed and took a drink.

"I wish this was real," she accused the glass.

"You know it's almost been a year," I said softly.

She looked at me, her face pained. She reached out and put her hand on mine. "I know."

I looked down at my drink. Fuck, why did this always come up? Would Pike Prime ever be behind me?

"How's the team?" she asked.

"Trying not to think about it. I told Maria that we were taking that day off. She understood. Not sure what we are going to do. Clay seems the most uncomfortable about it, like she's intruding on something. I don't think she likes the reminder of how she joined us," I said.

"I doubt she does. Well, I'm just glad that you guys are on Lepus 328rb."

"Thanks," I said.

She looked like she wanted to say more, her eyes glassy. "You know that was the worst day of my life?" she said.

"Um, I didn't," I admitted.

"It was for Jon, Monica, and Charles, too. But me worst of all. One of the people I'd grown up with, one of my very best friends, was dying, and here I was in orbit, unable to do anything," she said. We'd talked about Meyers dying, but I hadn't asked her about how she felt that day. I felt a little guilty now.

"They had to pull me off duty," she continued, like she was admitting something shameful. "That's why you came to the Healers Touch. It wasn't so you'd know someone when you woke up. It's so I could keep working. And then you were there and… and… and it was like I'd forgotten everything they'd taught me." The tears were running down her cheeks now. "You were so, so hurt, and I'd seen it a million times before, but I didn't know them. They weren't like a brother to me. God, the whole time you were there, I just tried to do my job, tried not to fuck it up. If I did my job, everything would be okay."

"I know," I said, my voice thick.

"But it wasn't," she admitted, "No matter how good I was, it wasn't okay. Because every time I fixed someone, I got a death toll report, or another person came in, and they were all you. Every one of them. I had to turn off my sense of nausea for the rest of my time out there. And then there was the fear. What if those things jumped a ship in? What if the Healers Touch didn't execute an emergency jump in time? We weren't armored. We weren't able to take hits. I'd think that and then think about how if that happened and we did jump, how our drives would be totaled and that there would be one less hospital ship to help the wounded."

I didn't tell her that it wouldn't have happened. She knew it hadn't, but she was right to fear it.

"I thought about that some. What if something jumped in and took out your ship or one that Jon was on? But mostly, I was thankful that it was me on the ground and not anyone I knew," I said.

She took another sip of her drink. "And we lived knowing that humans were all too mortal and that you'd already almost bought it once. I cried myself to sleep the night you had to drop onto that hellhole again. And when you jumped out of the system, I've never been so thankful for anything."

I squeezed her hand. "I'm sorry."

She looked me in the eyes. "Don't be. That was hell, but I am so proud to know you and yours. That's why I like being on the Helios. I know the kind of people I'm with, and I'm proud to count myself among them."

"They're lucky to have you," I said.

She smiled tightly.

FIFTEEN

I hefted the exploration drone onto the mule. I had no clue what the thing did. I could have asked Catherine, but then she'd have felt obligated to explain it to me, and I would have felt obligated to act like I actually cared. No one wanted that. All I knew was that it had a faulty part that was giving them bad data. I shouldn't say that's all I knew. The thing was also goddamn heavy, even with my suit. I could have had a BI move it, but this was the extent of the work I had planned for the day.

"Do you feel like you've accomplished something today, Corporal?" Catherine asked me.

"Today's work has been both meaningful and fulfilling. Honestly, my life probably just hit a plateau. Nothing will be better after today," I said sardonically.

"I'm glad I could be here for it. I feel like we've shared something deep and personal."

I sent the mule on its way to meet up with Charles. As I sent it, I did a quick check on the map of the area. Charles, Betts, and Krista were about a kilometer away from us, working their way north. We didn't have anything else for the day other than hoofing it back to the rover. I plotted some waypoints that would get us there quickly.

We'd be passing through some warehouse district dotted with what I assumed were office buildings. Most of them were piles of debris that spilled into the streets. But aside from being kind of a windy route, it was clear, and we'd make good time. We'd still been bringing one Heavy with us out in the field. We didn't need it, strictly speaking, but it wasn't doing anything at the base, and the rover wasn't weighed down by it. We'd use it for the occasional exercise when we were out and about. I plotted a course for it back to the rover as well.

I opened a line to Catherine and Clay. "I have a course plotted; we are going north. Sub-team two is to our east. Clay, stay west of Catherine and me. The Heavy will meet us back at the rover."

"Roger that, heading to waypoint," Clay said.

Catherine and I started to walk. It wasn't late in the day, and Lepus 328 was still high overhead. I looked up at it, searching for the icon that showed where the Arbiter or the Quiver ship was. I found the Quiver Destroyer pretty much right above us. My CCPU told me the Arbiter was over another part of the continent. The two ships took turns providing cover for ground units since there were more Quiver in this area than anywhere else, meaning we often had the Quiver ship directly overhead.

I pinged Clovis. "Heading back to the rover."

It pinged me back an acknowledgment. The Quiver were a couple of kilometers to the south of us. We walked without talking much. I had my suit pass through sensory information about the air around me. I felt a cool breeze run over my body and then the heat of the light from Lepus 328. It was a nice day. I wanted to take off my helmet but resisted the urge. We didn't have cover and we weren't in the base.

The biggest downfall of the helmet was the lack of a sense of smell. It had sensors to analyze the air, but for some reason, the HFDF didn't give us that sense. The planet didn't smell bad, even in the city. The death had happened decades ago; now it just smelled of plants and dirt. On the breeze at the base, we'd sometimes catch a whiff of something sweet in the air.

I adjusted my grip on my SIR, focusing. My mind was wandering. The streets were narrow with all the rubble from the buildings. Their broken walls rose around us like a brick-and-mortar forest. Twisted metal skeletons could be seen, and sheets of broken glass lay about. With every step we took, little swirls of dust filled the air. Most of the buildings had once been four or five stories, but there were warehouses, or what I assumed were warehouses, scattered about. Not large ones, mind you.

"What do you think they made here?" I asked Catherine.

She looked around as we walked. "I've wondered that. There isn't any equipment around, or at least none that we recognize. Even before everything went bad, these streets weren't wide, and the buildings were not large, so they couldn't have been making anything large around here."

"Textiles?" I offered.

She shrugged. "Maybe, but there are warehouses and what appears to be office buildings, no factories. Looks familiar, though..."

"Yeah, we were here a few days ago. That drone that was taken out. I figure if the grabbers didn't bother us then, then they won't now," I said, and pointed.

Ahead, to our right, was the warehouse where we'd found the drone remains. As we approached it, there was a heap of rubble to our left and then another building that was severely damaged.

"Now I remember," she said. "We came from a different..."

I cut her off, raising my hand. My CCPU pinged me. A Whisker had found something new.

"Hold up, a Whisker found a new hole," I said.

I pulled her off the road and behind some rubble in the building that was the most intact.

"All units, this is Sub-team One stopping. We have found a new hole. Sending in Whiskers to investigate. Felipe, you're the biologist; if this is a new hole, is there any data you want?" I asked, including the base staff.

"I'll take all the data you can give me. Can your drone go down the hole? I don't want you to lose it," he asked.

"It can. If it picks up anything and can't hide, I'll pull it out before it's spotted, though part of me is curious if the grabbers could find a Whisker," I said.

I had the Whiskers check the area to make sure there weren't any grabbers above ground and gave Clay instructions to cover us. If there was a grabber down there, I didn't want to hurt it, but if it saw us and came for us, I didn't really want to get thrashed around either. The surface was clear.

"Picking up radio waves," Clay said.

"I see them," Catherine said, sounding excited. "Are they deep?"

"Roger that," Clay said.

I opted to use a normal Whisker; they were a bit of a pain to spot, and I thought if there were active grabbers in the area, it might be good to stay stealthy. I pulled up its feed at the mouth of the tunnel. Fresh dirt was spilled around the area. The Whisker started into the hole. It ran at a slant down and then dropped.

"They run deeper than I would have thought," Felipe said.

There were more bursts of radio, but the Whisker moved on. I felt a little uneasy; the last hole I'd scanned like this was a Venom one. I reminded myself these weren't Venom. On closer inspection, the tunnel looked nothing like a Venom hole. The walls were rough, and the tunnel wasn't dug to the Venom's lowest standard. I relaxed a bit. The Whisker went deeper. It found a junction and entered. This tunnel looked older.

"Was that a cable?" Charles said. He, like everyone, was on the feed.

The Whisker backed up. "Looks like it," I said. A cable was running along the side of the tunnel. "I wonder if they are using old tunnels from the race that built this place?"

"Probably," Felipe said. "That'd explain why we don't see their movement. Well, Catherine, I guess you can add mass transit to your list of things to look at."

"Guess so," she said. She looked like she wanted to get up and go into the hole.

I toggled the feed to see if we could get a better view of the wires. First, I checked the density, seeing that there wasn't any running in the dirt, and then infrared.

"Sub-team two, haul ass back to the rover. Clay, prep for leapfrog! Exploration team, I am taking command," I barked. I hailed the Arbiter. "Arbiter, I have live wires. I repeat, I have a power source."

"Clovis, we aren't alone," I sent to it.

"Alex, what's going on?" Catherine asked, trying to stand. I put my hand on her shoulder and forced her back to kneeling. My Whisker was heading back up the hole, picking up radio waves that were closing in fast.

"Catherine, there is live power in the hole. It's not grabbers," I told her.

"Contact!" Clay said. "Contact to the east."

I pulled up her feed. From one of the older holes, a grabber slinked out. But it wasn't a grabber. It was larger and had a fairly large turret on its back. The turret scanned the area. Great, it could target.

"What the..." Catherine said, sounding afraid.

"Talk to me," Monroe said on a private comm line.

"We have contact with what looks like an armed grabber. Permission to hail the Quiver Destroyer," I said.

"Granted."

I contacted the Quiver ship. "Vinur, this is Fireteam Alpha requesting possible orbital cover."

"Affirmative, Alpha. Requesting location information for fire support," the ship's fire officer said.

I gave it to them. There were other grabbers in the area now; their turrets looked old and worn, but they swiveled with ease.

"Are those lasers on it?" Catherine asked.

Yes, I had noticed the laser targeting systems.

"I thought they weren't that advanced?" I asked.

"I guess we were wrong."

Lovely. I routed the Heavy to us. We needed to move, but doing so would mean giving up our cover and hiding spot and opening us up to their line of fire. I could be wrong, but I was pretty sure the grabbers would shoot at the aliens in their city. I checked and saw that Betts, Krista, and Charles were almost back to the rover.

"Do you want me to come back for support?" Betts asked.

I thought for a moment. "Negative. As soon as we can, we are out of here."

I opened a line to Catherine. "How are you doing?"

"I'm terrified," she said, sounding it.

Once I took command, I could see some of her vitals. My CCPU confirmed that she was indeed terrified.

"Catherine, I need you to do anything I tell you when I tell you. Can you do that for me?" I asked her calmly.

"Yeah, I guess so. I mean, yes, I can." Her voice trembled.

"Good," I said, ever calm. "Soon we are going to start moving. I want you to stay low and in front of me and your BIs; they will stay with you. If one of them tries to move you, let it. This is just like when you come on an animal. No different. Once we can, we will be out of here."

"Okay, like an animal," she said, trying to calm herself. I figured she'd had to book it from a few of those over her career.

"Clay, we might need some sort of distraction. Preferably not one that makes it look like an advanced race is on this world to challenge these things," I said.

"Roger that. A rock?"

If it ain't broke, don't fix it. My CCPU pinged me; there were now more radio waves. They were coming from a grabber that was coming up from the rubble on the building next to us. Shit.

"This is about to go sideways," I told command.

"Clay, get ready for action," I said.

The grabber crested the rubble. Its turret spun quickly, resting on a Sphere I had low to the ground. It fired on the Sphere. I grabbed Catherine, pulling her behind me, and snapped my SIR up, targeting the grabber. Its turret started to turn. I squeezed the trigger of my SIR. It vibrated in my hand. Five armor-piercing, high-powered rounds hit the grabber. They went right through it, and it thrashed, the turret having a hard time training. I put the SIR on auto-select. It went with rounds that worked well on the Venom. I fired again, and the grabber went down.

Catherine screamed, falling to the ground and pulling her hands over her head. The rubble around us flew apart with rounds from the other grabbers. I ducked down and popped over the small wall, firing small-cover rounds. The grabbers moved fast to cover, their turrets firing at me. They didn't seem to need help finding targets. The rounds went wide, though, and my CCPU told me they would have a hard time penetrating my suit at range.

"You alright?" I asked Catherine.

I didn't see any injuries. She was breathing hard. Fuck, she was panicking.

"Sweeting, I need mortars!"

"They are on the way," Sweeting said.

"We have more hostiles coming out," Clay said. "I've been spotted; moving locations."

"Do you need assistance?" Betts asked.

"No, get to the rover," I said.

I popped up again and fired. Some of the rounds hit a grabber near where the turret was. The creature dropped dead. I noted the location and pushed an update to the drones in the area.

"Update going down," I said.

"An update?" Catherine asked frantically.

"Yes, it will make the drones better killers. When we can, we are running," I said.

I checked, and the Heavy was close. But so were the grabbers. Another came over the rubble, and a BI jumped in front of Catherine, taking several shots. It stumbled. I moved in front of her. Bits of shrapnel hit my suit from the rounds fired by the grabber. The BI killed the grabber.

My CCPU said that more were inbound. The BBALLs and Spheres popped in the air, firing down, trying to press the grabbers into cover. They slunk under the rubble like it was nothing, and the drones didn't have shots. Fuck, they were rushing us. I could run and get out, but I didn't think Catherine could. She was curled on the ground. I heard Charles on the comm line screaming at me to get out. Krista was restraining him.

There was a thunk in the distance, and my CCPU pinged me that a mortar had just fired. Sweeting hadn't messed around at all. A BI by Catherine jumped on her, covering her. Twenty meters in front of me, the round exploded. With it, the air filled with dust and bits of rock and debris. I lobbed a few grenades at grabbers and shot others. My right shoulder jerked, flinging me to the ground. I rolled automatically and brought up my SIR. There was a grabber that was currently being killed by two BBALLs.

"ALEX, OH MY GOD, ARE YOU OK?" Catherine was screaming.

I didn't respond, but I moved to cover. There were more mortars, and then the roar of a Heavy opening fire. It chewed through the brick and buildings, sending the grabbers running.

"Vinur requesting close-in fire support," I said.

"Roger, Alpha. What do you need? Please note we have a more limited orbit-to-ground arsenal than your ship," the fire controller added.

I didn't need much, just for the grabbers to stay underground. And the Quiver had what I needed—railguns.

"Three kinetics as we leave should do fine. Not high power, just enough to keep them underground," I replied.

I gave the order for a BI to grab Catherine and force her to move. She was still asking if I was hurt.

"I'm fine; we need to move!" I said.

I checked my CCPU. I was fine, just a bruise. The grabbers were focusing on the Heavy, giving the Spheres and BBALLs openings. The Arbiter's computers were recommending more updates. I pushed them through. It wasn't something that I liked to do in combat, but I thought it was the best call right now. More mortars hit, and before the dust cleared, I ran to the far wall and jumped over it to cover. Catherine was on the other side, being pulled by her two BIs. I ran up to her and took her hand, pulling.

"Come on, you got this; come on," I said to her. "Clay, fall back!"

"Falling back," she said.

We darted around two buildings, spilling into a side street. The Heavy was pulling back now, the grabbers taking and holding their cover in the tunnels. Keeping Catherine in cover and not in the open was proving to be nearly impossible. She was full-on panicking at this point. My CCPU pinged.

"Incoming," I said over the line.

I pulled Catherine behind a building as three railgun rounds tore through the air and hit the area we'd just left. The ground bucked beneath my feet, and I felt Catherine cling to me hard, her suit lending her strength. I felt fleeting pain in my ribs. Her CCPU was busy dealing with her fear and not controlling her suit, and it was crushing me. I overrode it, and her grip loosened a bit.

"You have two cracked ribs," Lisa Middleton said over the comms. "What the hell is going on?"

"Nothing, ma'am. Catherine's CCPU didn't override her suit controls, but I did. I'm fine," I said.

"Catherine, we need to move. You can do this," I told her.

I had to peel her arms from around my torso. She wasn't budging. Fuck, I didn't want to do this.

"Taylor, get moving!" Monroe ordered.

With a pang of guilt, I gave her CCPU the command to flatline her emotions. I heard her gasp over the comms.

"Okay, I'll go now," she said in a monotone, like someone coming to their senses but still confused.

We moved, her movements like that of the BIs. I doubted Catherine had ever felt what it was like having your CCPU flatline you like that. Personally, I hated it. Not at the time. In your mind, you know something is very wrong, but you don't feel anything, so you don't care. You care later, feeling betrayed in a way, even when you know it's coming. We trained to keep our emotions in check so that it didn't happen in combat.

Clay joined up with us, and we moved from cover to cover, now that Catherine wasn't panicking. As we approached the rover, the Heavy made it to us. I had it, and the drones load up. Catherine jumped in the rover with Clay and I following. I gave the command for it to start moving. It lurched forward.

"I have a meandering route set," Betts said.

Charles slammed into me, his arms coming around me. I was so happy that my CCPU was dulling those ribs.

"It's okay, man, we made it. It's cool," I said.

He let go; his helmet was off, his face a mask of fear. "What was that? Are you hurt? How did the grabbers have guns?"

"I'm fine, nothing bad, and I have no idea how the grabbers got that."

Catherine was sitting against the wall, her helmet off. She was looking forward, her eyes red and her face pale. Her CCPU was allowing her to feel again. Krista knelt in front of her, but Catherine didn't respond. I let my helmet come off. I looked at Charles.

"Sorry, man," I said.

"Take care of her," he said.

I knelt down in front of Catherine. "Hey."

She looked up at me.

"You're okay now," I said.

She looked down. I sat next to her and put my arm around her shoulders. She leaned into me, her head resting on my shoulder. I checked on her CCPU. As soon as I'd said I was taking command, all the exploration teams' stats were available to me as if they were my own people. Catherine's CCPU had been doing some double duty keeping her from going into shock. It had stopped it from happening, but between that and me flatlining her emotions, she was probably still frazzled. It took her a few minutes before she seemed to start relaxing.

"I'm okay now," she said, looking at me.

I looked into her eyes as if I could see more than my CCPU was telling me. Her face had some color back to it. That was good. I checked our location. We were out of the main part of the city.

"Okay," I said, giving her a slight squeeze.

I opened a line to Guzman.

"How are my people?" she asked worriedly.

"Fine. I need you to prep for scrubbing the mission," I said.

As I did, Charles's head swiveled in my direction.

Maria wasn't as slow to respond as I thought. "Will do. Are you ordering an evacuation?" she asked, no hint of resentment in her voice.

"Negative. Not yet; I want to see what command says," I said.

I dropped the line, engaged my helmet, and asked Catherine and Charles to do the same. Clovis and its team were heading back to base, as were every Quiver and HF unit on the planet. When I got back to the base, I was sure there would be a flurry of conversations with all levels of command. But I had twenty minutes until that happened. Time to think. Time to wrap my head around what had just happened. I leaned back on the wall and started going over the data.

I looked over at Betts; he was looking in my direction. I couldn't see his eyes to know if he was actually looking at me. But I felt them—not irritated or angry but curious. Why hadn't I had him back us up?

Monroe and Middleton would have the same question. Why didn't I use Betts? He could have been an asset had things gone worse. Or Clay, for that matter? Why didn't I have her take a more aggressive role?

"Are you okay?" Krista asked in a private line.

"Yes. I think so."

"What's on your mind?" she asked.

"Not sure yet. Thank you for handling Charles," I said.

"Of course."

I brought the rest of my team on the line. "Sweeting, I left a few Whiskers behind."

"I see them. Nothing has come up after the Quiver," Sweeting said.

"Good call on that," Betts said. "I doubt they'll poke their heads up for a bit."

"That was the hope. Do you guys have any ideas about today? Any input would help; you know what my next few hours will be," I said, referring to the debriefings to come.

No one had any clues about what to make of the day.

"We are about to make it back to the base," I told Monroe.

"Roger that. We have all the ship's computers working on the data from the fight. There are a few updates that are about ready," he said professionally. "Good work today. I know no one was expecting that, but you got the civvies out of the area."

"I feel like a dick for having to control Catherine like that," I admitted.

"As well you should, but you had to do it. Better to do that than have her die. Orders are to stay in the base but not leave the planet unless you have to," he said.

"If we get attacked?" I asked.

"If that happens, scrub the exploration people and wait for EVAC. Hopefully, that doesn't happen. Are you going to be good to go?" he asked.

"Yes, sir," I said.

"Okay. You know I'm going to ask. Why didn't you use Betts or Clay more?" he asked, not sounding upset.

"Don't know, sir," I admitted. "Sorry, sir."

"You got the job done; you did things well, just not the way you normally work, and your CCPU says you're conflicted about it. We can talk about it later," he said.

"Yes, sir," I said.

SIXTEEN

As the rover pulled into the base, the atmosphere shifted palpably. The people here had gone from routine work on a largely uninhabited planet to being in the middle of a field all alone, where the locals could shoot at you. As the rover stopped in the middle of the base, I got over the base line.

"This is Corporal Taylor. Please do not leave the perimeter I have defined until further notice." And then, just to my people, "Perimeter up."

Betts, Clay, and Krista jumped out of the rover as the drones poured off the roof. They each jogged to their respective locations. Everyone knew their roles and stations by heart.

"Sweeting, give me a report on base defense," I said on the team line.

"Nothing coming in the area as of yet. Heavies are on standard patrols. I broadened the Whiskers patrol routes and have a couple of GPs checking the area, starting in the center of the base and working outward," he said.

"Good call. It would suck to have something dig under us. When I talk to command, I'll get us some more GPs so we can keep that locked down, along with some more drones," I said, and then addressed the thing we were all thinking about. "We learned today that the grabbers aren't just predators; they can use technology and have tech that is way more advanced than should be on this planet. I think it would be unwise of us to underestimate them. That said, remember we are the bad guys here; they probably see us as invaders. So long as they keep their distance for now, do not engage unless you think they will be a threat or they fire on you."

Everyone acknowledged my orders. I hated having to add that last part in, but it was true. We were the invaders, and in all fairness, we didn't mean any harm or know that there was anything advanced here, but we were still invaders. We'd placed probes around the planet without permission and now had killed a bunch of the locals, not to mention having another race drop some railgun rounds on them. Dick moves for sure, but again, we had ignorance on our side.

I followed Catherine and Charles as we headed for the common building. I needed to talk to the exploration team, or at least Guzman. I wasn't entirely sure what to say to them or how they'd react to the day. Charles wasn't talking much, which was pretty standard for him when he was stressed. Catherine seemed to be recovering, and now that she was back at the base, I figured she might be a good resource.

As we walked into the common building, everyone crowded around Charles and Catherine, hugging them and asking if they were okay. I stood off to the side and waited for Maria to give each of them a once-over. She finished with the two of them and came over to me, looking me over.

"And how are you doing? Did you get hurt?" she asked.

I smiled tightly. "I'm fine; nothing that hasn't already almost healed." At the puzzled look on her face, I added, "A little shrapnel hit me and a few cracked ribs."

"And that's fine?" she asked, concerned.

"Generally speaking, if it doesn't damage a vital organ, it's fine," I said.

She nodded. "And we aren't scrubbing?"

"Not unless you want to," I said. "Though my team will stay put until ordered otherwise."

She sighed. "Well, if it were up to me, we would leave, but as it is, we have been told to stay put unless otherwise instructed by our higher-ups or if your team deems us in danger. The order came down as you were entering the base. They said more information will follow. Do you mind telling me what is going on?"

"If I knew, I would," I said. "If I had to guess, I would say it has something to do with the grabbers having tech they shouldn't have."

We were stopped by Catherine walking over to us. She looked a little embarrassed. "Thank you for today," she said. "And I'm sorry about your ribs."

My smile wasn't tight this time. "It's fine. You were panicked; I'm sorry I had to flatline your emotions... I know it's uncomfortable."

"I understand, you needed to do it... do you do that to yourself? Is that how your team keeps it together?" she asked.

"No ma'am," I said. "We've felt it in training. That feeling you have of your brain trying to reboot right now isn't optimal. Your CCPU has to dump a lot of stuff in your system to do it, and in the process, it can get rid of useful emotions like fear. We train very hard to maintain control," I explained.

"How is fear a desirable emotion?" Andy Waters asked.

"Fear keeps you from doing dumb things," Felipe said matter-of-factly. "Evolutionarily speaking, fear is very handy."

"I guess so," Andy grunted. "So are we going to be attacked by those things?"

"Not sure. If we are, my people have a perimeter around the base. We hope to have plenty of warning before the grabbers come, if they do at all," I said honestly.

"And if they come?" he asked.

"Then we will hold them while you guys EVAC. Once you are clear, we will fall back for extraction or neutralize the threat," I said.

He didn't roll his eyes, but it looked like it took an effort not to; that said, his tone was a lot warmer than I thought it would be. "Look, I know you guys aren't kids... but I don't feel comfortable with the idea of leaving you behind..."

"They aren't kids," Catherine asserted with surprising confidence in her voice. "They're extremely good at what they do. Andy, we'd only get in the way," she said, looking at him. "Trust me. If I hadn't been there, they would have gotten out much faster."

Andy looked apologetic. "Sorry, I'm just a little stressed at the moment."

"It's fine," I said.

"That said, is there anything we can do to assist your team?" Maria asked.

"On that one, yes actually. The Arbiter's computers are processing all the data, as well as the Quiver. We've pushed down some updates already, but anything your people can do to help us understand the grabbers would be helpful," I said.

"Updates?" Maria asked.

"Yes. We send updates to the drones to make them better at their jobs. I pushed down one live update when we were fighting and another when we were on our way back. One thing that would help is to have a better idea of how advanced the grabbers are," I said.

"And how they got that way," Maria added. "They are not supposed to be the dominant life form here."

Her team looked thoughtful now. That was good. Get them doing what they were good at.

"Can you share your data with us? As soon as the first shots were fired, the only feeds we had were from Charles and Catherine," Maria said.

I granted them access. Their eyes glazed over.

"Jesus," Shashi murmured under his breath.

From the looks on their faces, I suspected that the feed from

Catherine was lacking the detail mine and the drones had. That was fair. She was taking cover and not trying to get shot.

"I missed a lot," she said, sounding worried. "They're so fast!"

The grabbers were quick little fucks, for sure. But in my limited experience, the more legs something had, the faster it appeared but the slower it was. I doubted the grabbers would be quick over long distances or would be as fast as we were. But I also didn't know that they had turrets with targeting systems on their backs, so yeah, maybe they held underground marathons on the weekends for all I knew.

"I wonder how they are attaching the guns," Felipe said almost to himself.

"I was wondering that too," Maria said. "And how they built them; they don't have anything that would act like fingers."

"Couldn't a machine put them on?" I suggested.

"Yes," Catherine replied, "but how did they develop the technology? The race that was the dominant one here was nowhere near this level. It appears that the turrets aren't as advanced as anything we have, but they're leaps and bounds ahead of where they should be."

"New tech?" Charles asked.

Catherine shrugged. "Maybe. Looks like some parts of it are… yes, some of this looks newer than other pieces."

The vid wall flashed on, and there was a really, really zoomed-in view of what I presumed was a grabber turret. I hadn't really taken the time to study the turrets when I was getting shot at. Now, though, I could see what Catherine was talking about. The main housing was solid, with a few openings for the targeting system and the gun itself. The housing looked like it had the shit beat out of it, as did parts of the gun. The barrel had a shine that spoke of newness.

"We will work on this and let you know what we come up with," Maria said. "Can we find you and your team in your housing unit?"

"Thank you, but no. They are in foxholes around the base. I will be joining them shortly. If you need to see us in person, please let me know before you come," I said.

I started to walk away.

"You're really going to sleep in a hole in the ground?" Andy asked.

I kept walking. "Ha! Since I've joined the HFDF, I'm pretty sure I've spent more nights in a hole in the ground than I haven't."

As I exited the building, I jogged over to my foxhole as I checked in with my team. There was nothing that had happened since we'd gotten back to base.

"Please thank that fire control officer for the close support today," I said as I opened a line with Clovis.

"I will do that. Did your people make it out?" it asked.

"We did, thanks. Did you run into anything?"

"We saw some of the grabbers but did not need to engage. Our science staff is worried and preparing for EVAC. They will not leave unless ordered to do so; however, is yours staying here?" it asked.

"Yes, they are. Orders from above to stay on-site. My guess is the HF wants some answers about what a race like the grabbers is doing with tech that shouldn't be here and how they are using it since they don't have the physical ability to build anything with fine parts," I said.

"Those are good questions. I will put them to the staff here. We strengthened our fortifications. Do you have any thoughts about why they would reveal themselves after this much time?"

"No, I don't. Could just be dumb luck," I said.

"That tends to be the case more often than not. I will let you know if we learn anything or encounter them," it said.

My debrief with command was just as amazing as I'd anticipated. They'd gone over all my reports and the data from the drones. They asked how the team was doing and what equipment I thought I needed. I considered requesting a Rhino just to see if I would get it but decided against it. Instead, I asked for one more Heavy and another Mortar drone, along with more BBALLs, a few Spheres, and a couple more BIs. Oh, and GPs. Lots of those. My plan was to place the GPs so we'd know if anything was in the ground within three hundred meters under the base. I also requested two re-armors. They could pick up a small amount of cargo, namely ammo, and then fly it wherever it needed to go. They weren't too big but fast and made keeping a front supplied much easier.

Command had started by saying that I was getting more ammo and parts. We weren't planning on holding the area for a long siege, but in case shit, ya know. I was going to use the BIs to load the re-armors should the shit hit the fan. With all the drones and the perimeter of STDs, we could hold off a pretty decent assault. My hope was that we were going to have to haul all that shit back up the well when this was done. A world with pallets of unspent ammo was fine with me.

I shifted in my hole to find a more comfortable position and one that gave me total cover. Lepus 328 was starting to set. My CCPU notified me that the drones I'd ordered had hit atmosphere and were inbound. We'd wait on some of them until tomorrow. The grabbers were supposed to be mostly nocturnal. If they knew where we were or were out looking for the things that had killed several of their buddies today, I didn't want to be out in the open. I didn't see much need to change the watch schedule for the evening. Not that I thought anyone would get much sleep tonight.

"Thanks for having my back today," I said to Clay late in the evening.

"Anytime. So much for boring," she said.

"Yeah, I think we don't have to worry about that. I guess we should be happy we got this long. Or bothered that it took us this long to notice something was off with the grabbers," I said.

Before she could say anything, my CCPU pinged. There was a notification from the HF. Lepus 328rb was being re-classified. There was a technologically advanced race on it. That changed things. The system was now subject to the naming system that the HF used.

"The fuck kind of name is Tooth?" Sweeting said on the general line.

Lepus 328 was now the Tooth system, making Lepus 328rb Tooth

Prime, and the grabbers, or at least the ones we'd found today, the Tooth. I also noticed that the government noted that if the Tooth we'd encountered today happened to be a different species from the grabbers, I would be noted as the first Human in contact with them, along with Catherine and Clay also being mentioned, with the latter being noted as the person who discovered the Tooth since Clay's drones had been the first to see them.

"Hey, we maybe discovered a new technologically advanced race," I announced on the main line.

"And we killed it; go us!" Sweeting said.

I laughed.

"And we might get to kill more," Betts said with an edge in his voice, "I have contact."

My levity vanished. I pulled up what Betts was looking at. They were far from the base, still near the city, but small groups of Tooth were heading out like bike spokes from the city. Probably scouting parties.

"We have contact," I reported on my command line. "Small groups. My guess is scouts."

"Roger that; keep us updated," Monroe responded.

"We have contacts, some heading your way," I said on my line to Clovis, sending the coordinates.

I sent a ping to Royle about it.

"We have a line on them," Clovis told me.

I watched with my team as the map showed updates of the Tooth moving around. As they did, there were radio bursts. I thought about waking one of the Exploration crew so they could get live data. I pinged Maria to see if she was awake.

"Is there something I can help you with?" she asked.

"Maybe. Are you awake? We have Tooth in the area; wondered if you could help us get some insight into them," I said.

"Are they close?" she asked, sounding worried.

"Negative. Looks to be scouting parties," I said. "Hopefully, they won't venture out this far. They don't appear to have any vehicles, so they aren't moving fast. If they wanted to attack us, they'd need to wait for reinforcements."

I guess they didn't really need to wait; a scouting party could attack us. It just wouldn't go well for them. I was now working under the personal theory that the Tooth were responsible for killing off the old race that ruled this world. And to do so, you couldn't be morons, nor would you send a scouting party to attack a force that had mopped the floor with you earlier that day.

"You sure?" she asked.

"Yeah, pretty sure. So, I was wondering if you might be able to help us figure out just how advanced they are. I can move some Whiskers in close enough to collect more data. I know we got a lot today, but I figure until we know everything, we can always use a bit more data," I said.

"Yes, that is true. Do you want everyone up?" she asked.

"No, I think just you is fine. Unless you're tired, in which case I can just do my thing, and you guys can look at it in the morning," I hedged.

"I'm not sleeping tonight," she stated matter-of-factly.

I moved one of the smaller Whiskers near the Tooth. I wasn't sure what all they could do yet and didn't want to give ourselves away.

"Will that drone alert them?" she asked.

"Might," I said honestly, "but the Whiskers are a bit of a bitch to find by design. The Venom had to be pretty close to them to locate them, so I think we will be fine. I'm going to bring my team on the line."

"There are only ten of them," Krista observed. "And they're spread out in groups of two. It has to be scouting parties."

"I agree," Maria said. "What we've seen of the grabbers is that they hunt in groups of two or three."

"You mean the Tooth?" Betts asked.

"No, I mean grabbers. We don't have confirmation yet. The Tooth might be related to the grabbers, but there is no way the clever but un-advanced predators we've seen have the intelligence to coordinate scouting parties and attacks," she clarified.

"So, the drones?" I asked.

"Maybe these things. Maybe not. They look different. The Tooth are bigger than any grabbers we've seen, and our AI tells us the radio bursts they are using are slightly different."

"So if these are different, why haven't they killed the grabbers?" Clay asked.

"Not sure," Maria admitted.

"You know, in the movies, the science people always have a theory or answers," Sweeting said.

Maria chuckled. "And the soldiers are just a step above apes that shoot first and don't think about the consequences."

"Sweeting, I think she's got your number," Clay teased.

"Thank you, Clay; that is exactly my point. When Taylor went all action movie on those Tooth earlier, we held up our end of shooting first. Now it's the nerds' job to hold up their end. So, Maria, I'm going to have to insist on a perfect theory that will pan out at the end of the day," Sweeting declared.

"Nerds?" Betts said. "The HFDF and Exploration Corps have similar academic requirements for entry."

I didn't stop the banter. I'd found that my team worked best that way. It kept their spirits light while keeping them on their toes. It was better than being bored and unprepared or at each other's throats with nerves.

The Tooth continued their search for several hours. They were spread thin and moving in every direction, which was good because it meant they probably didn't have a clue where we were. Maria eventually went to bed, and my team started sleeping when it wasn't their watch. Unless told otherwise, we'd be staying put for the next few days. I tried to get comfortable in my hole. I managed a few hours of sleep before my watch began.

When I woke up and took my report from Krista, the sky was pre-dawn dark, littered with stars. The Tooth had retreated back to the city. The base was silent. The air had a coolness to it that my suit toned down somewhat. It would have been beautiful had we not been lying outside in holes by necessity. But here I was, lying in a hole on an alien world where things very much wanted me dead. So, instead of being at peace, I had a little nagging voice in my head and a weight on my chest.

I scrolled through messages from my friends who weren't on the planet. Jon, Monica, and Liz were losing it. How could they not? Charles was out here. I'd signed up to be shot at; it was my job, but he was supposed to be the loner who toiled away, learning the secrets of the cosmos. Instead, he was here with me. In all fairness, I was still the only one of us who'd ever been shot at. Monica had in training, but that didn't count. I'd been shot at by three different races now. Not too bad for twenty-two years old. On the downside, I'd either been shot or hit by shrapnel from three different races.

As Tooth peeked out over the horizon, Charles pinged me.

"What's up?" I asked.

"Can I come see you?" he asked.

I checked the area. Still nothing. The Tooth, like the grabbers it appeared, didn't seem to like being out in the daytime if they had a choice.

"Yeah, that's fine," I said.

I watched as Charles trotted to me from the base, trying to keep low. It was something he really didn't need to do, but I wasn't about to discourage caution. He hopped into my foxhole. A BI moved, giving him room. He settled down.

"So this is life, huh?" he asked, trying to break the ice.

"A lot of the time, yeah. How was your evening? Thanks for handling everyone. How are they?"

"Of course. They understood that you were busy. They are worried. I'm sure they have a thread without us where they are being more honest. We met up at the pub. Monica was tense and quiet. Jon was Jon, and Liz... she seemed really well put together, but like something was just under the surface," he said.

I felt a pang of guilt about that. "She gets like that. She was like that on Pike Prime. I didn't start to understand what it was like for her until recently." I looked over at him. "You know I'm not going to let anything happen to you, right? We're really fucking good at what we do; none of you are getting hurt." I was a little more forceful than I had wanted to be.

He shook his head. "I know. Thank you for that, by the way."

I looked forward again. "No need to thank me. That said, if there's a next time, maybe don't fight Krista or whoever is trying to hold you back."

"Sorry about that, man. I won't do it again," he said, sounding guilty. "I know I shouldn't have. She's strong, or her suit is. I was a little surprised that she wasn't ahead of me," Charles admitted.

"Nah, she wouldn't do that," I said. "She knows better. She has too much discipline, and she knows it would make things worse. But I'm sure she wanted to. I won't lie; that can be hard. Doing your job when the people you care about are in danger."

"You guys were pretty impressive out there. You've sent me clips before of drops but never any combat that you were in. Is that always what it's like?"

"Not if I can help it. We try to be further away if we can. Or be in a better position. We just weren't expecting anything yesterday. It didn't help that we were discounting radio bursts. We won't do that again. But even then, yesterday went pretty well. No one got hurt. Well, Catherine cracked my ribs, I guess. I didn't know your suits could give you that much strength," I admitted.

He laughed. "Yeah, they give us a boost for sure. I don't know. I feel like we've gotten a little bit of a chance to see what the other one does for their term. You've experienced mine, and I don't think I want to see any more of yours."

"Yours is relaxing. Oddly, though, I think I still like mine better," I said, a little surprised.

"You've always been the oddest one of us," Charles mused.

"Says the guy with a bone drone that looks like his ex," I countered.

"What the hell, man! You told Jon about that shit, so he told Monica, and now she gives me shit! I told you it's not a bone drone!"

"Catherine called hers a bone drone," I smiled inside my helmet, savoring the sweetest taste there is. Victory.

SEVENTEEN

As Tooth rose above the horizon, it looked like it was going to be a beautiful day on Tooth Prime. We were buttoned up like we had been for the past week. I'd taken to having the team work in shifts, allowing people to sleep, eat, and shower in the housing unit we'd brought with us.

Barring the night the Tooth had sent out search parties, we hadn't seen them anywhere near the base. Whisker and orbital data showed that they were most active in the city during the night, early morning, and evening. There weren't any Exploration drones left in the city. They'd all been found and destroyed by Tooth. But there were a handful of Whiskers. Now that we were paying attention to the radio bursts and looking at past data, it was pretty obvious that the city had been active. Data collected prior to our encounter indicated that most of the bursts originated several meters underground. The Exploration teams had assumed these were grabbers and creatures like them in sewer lines.

At some point, the Exploration teams would have begun exploring underground. When they did, they'd have found the Tooth. We weren't sure why they'd been on the surface the day we walked by, but it didn't appear they were leaving it any time soon.

As Betts settled in for his shift, I gave him an update.

"Nothing anywhere near us last night. Just groups roaming around the city," I said.

"Drone hunting?" he asked.

"I presume so. I've kept the Whiskers away from them as ordered, but I'm not sure the Tooth could find them," I said.

"Yeah, I don't know that they could. They had a hard enough time with some of the smaller Exploration drones, and they don't have any stealth. How long until you think they send parties out of the city again?" he asked conversationally.

"Not sure. I've thought about it, but I don't know. We just don't know enough about them," I sighed. "Clearly, they didn't find anything amiss the night they left the city. If they had, I have to assume we'd have been attacked by now, or at least seen them in the area watching us. They might not come out of the city again unless provoked."

"But you don't buy that," he said.

"No, I don't. I think it's pretty obvious these things are responsible for the lack of animal life on this planet. And we haven't seen any evidence from the old dominant race. They killed them off, and then most of the rest of the animal kingdom. I don't think you kick a habit like that."

"No, you don't," Betts agreed.

The big question was what our next steps would be. Clearly, Tooth Prime was inhabited, which put it in the category of places we didn't stay on. I assumed we'd get the order to pack up shop and get ready to head into orbit sometime soon.

I left the base perimeter and made my way to Maria's ship. She normally worked out of the lab or her office in the lab, but I'd requested everyone to try to be ready to leave at a moment's notice. No one had fought me on it, which was nice. At first, most of the Exploration team seemed eager to get the hell off the planet, but they had slipped into a tunnel vision of looking at data in a way only a true nerd could.

I walked up to Maria's ship and took the little lift to the hatch. It opened, and I found her sitting at her desk. I was just a little early for our daily meeting. She looked up at me and said hello. I went and took a seat at a table and waited. Right before our meeting every day, we received a data dump of updates and orders. I arrived early enough to look them over, and then we'd talk. My CCPU pinged me about the day's dump.

"That's interesting," she said.

"Yes, it is," I said, knowing what she was talking about.

"What does yours say?"

"Today, a shuttle for an intelligence officer named Tania Koffski will be arriving. She will be giving our teams instructions and direction on further missions on Tooth Prime, along with a full briefing. What do you have?" I asked.

"Pretty much the same."

I pulled up the data I could on Tania. She was in her thirties, which put her on the young side for being an intelligence officer. She'd served her Service Term in the Exploration Corps and then moved on to the Diplomatic Corps and eventually Intelligence.

"You ever have anything like this?" I asked Maria.

"No. Never dealt with intelligence directly. Exploration does a lot of work for them; they are almost part of our corps, but we are always on the data-collecting side. I suppose we shouldn't be all that surprised that one of them is coming here. Have you worked with them?"

I thought for a moment, "Kind of. I babysat some drones on my first op. I didn't know anything about the officers, though. They weren't really conversationalists."

Maria nodded, "From what little I've talked to them, they seem to come from one of two lines. Either they were HFDF, or they came from the Exploration Corps. I haven't met one that came from another branch, or at least not from their Service Term. The HFDF ones tend to be a little more of what you'd think a spook to be. The Exploration ones are more analytical."

That fit the corps. Tania would be planetside in two hours. I opened a line to Monroe.

"Just getting the information," he said. "As your briefing came in, so did mine. Middleton is trying to figure out what is going on. This Tania is coming from Alpha. A little notice would have been nice," he finished, irritated.

"Have you talked to her yet?" I asked.

"Quickly. She seems fine. In all fairness, I think she jumped on the first ship she could get her hands on. With how little time there was before she boarded the Arbiter, she must have been stationed somewhere at jump distance," he said.

"So she's on the Arbiter then," I said.

"Yes, meeting with the skipper and all the higher-ups. She has been aboard for most of the morning. I have a meeting with her and the other squad leaders in thirty. If I can, I'll let you know what's going on," he said.

"Roger that," I said and dropped the connection.

"Monroe doesn't know what's going on. I guess we will find out," I said.

"I'm sure we will," Maria said.

I notified my team that we'd be having a visitor and told them that I didn't know much yet. It was a little on the rare side for us. Normally, we had all the information we needed and then some. I suspected that we usually had the intelligence folks to thank for that.

After Monroe's meeting, I was told that Tania was coming planetside to talk with us face to face and that we would be assisting her. After she was done with us, she was going to make personal stops at every HFDF base along with the Quiver ones. Beyond that, Monroe said that we would be briefed by Ms. Koffski.

I received a notification that a ship had left the Arbiter and was heading to the Exploration base. I joined Maria outside near the north end of the base as we waited for the ship. I pulled up its specs.

Tania Koffski was aboard an Ambassador Class Sloop. They were about the smallest ships the HF had that were capable of jumping. They only held a maximum crew of two. They were also fairly under-powered. They weren't anything you'd send an actual ambassador on. But an aide or apparently an intelligence officer?

I was a little worried about the ship being spotted by the Tooth, but thankfully it came in low to the ground and kept clear of the city. As it landed, I appreciated just how little the thing was. At least for a jump-capable ship. It was boxy and white, landing on its side and not verti-cally like the Exploration ships. A hatch on the side opened, and stairs folded down to the ground. A blond woman in a gray suit came down the steps. She walked up to us, shaking our hands.

Her grip was firm, and her gaze all business.

"Thank you for meeting with me," she said after introducing herself.

I was trying to place her suit. My CCPU started a search.

"It's HFDF; seemed to be appropriate," she said.

"Um a..." I started.

"I can see every inquiry you make about me or my mission. Come in, please," she said, beckoning me into the ship. I set my CCPU to not auto-search anything about Tania.

She walked up the little set of stairs, followed by Maria. The inside of the ship was like a closet. To my left was a head and shower. To my right were two VR PODs; in front of me was a small counter with a heating unit for food and a cabinet. I gave the space a quick glance. The door to the ship closed.

"I wanted to talk with the two of you prior to any meetings with your respective teams. I am aware that my visit may seem a little rushed. It has taken a few days for the events from last week to make their way through the intelligence departments to come to a decision to send me. I am stationed at a joint diplomatic and intelligence station at jump distance from Alpha," she explained. "Now that we have that question out of the way, I will get to the one that matters the most. Why am I here, and why are you still here instead of in orbit?"

"That was the question on my mind. I figure it must be a good reason to go against every protocol the Exploration branch of the Human Federation has," Maria said.

Whatever the rank of Tania was, it didn't seem to intimidate Maria. That said, she didn't sound hostile. Maybe she did to Tania, but I had been around her enough to know that she meant what she said. I was curious too.

"It's a good question." Tania's voice became less sure. "What do you know of the Venom?"

"The Tooth are not the Venom," I said flatly and, after a pause, "Ma'am."

"Tania, call me Tania. I'm not your commander. And you are right; they are not. But humor me. Can you think of anything the Venom and the Tooth have in common?" she said.

I sighed, thinking. "They both live underground, work in teams, or at least from what we've seen. They have weapons built right into them. And they seem to have a similar body plan. And they are both hostile; though in the case of the Tooth, I don't really blame them," I said.

"Have you wondered if you shouldn't blame the Venom either?" she asked.

"Come again?" I asked.

"The Venom. Do you blame them?" she asked.

I thought for a moment, "Yes. They killed billions. Not really the good guys."

Tania nodded, "They are extremely hostile. Do you know how long they have been on the scene, technologically speaking? And their history?"

"Not sure. I want to say they have been attacking others for about twenty years. I heard something about them taking their tech from the other planet in the Venom system," I said, though I was starting to feel unsure. I felt like I was in school.

Tania gave an understanding nod. "Maria, may I call you Maria?"

"Yes," Maria said.

"How do we gather information about aliens spanning back decades?" Tania asked.

"Radio. Most species use radio to communicate prior to discovering AltComms. It creates a bubble around the planet. Some signals are too old or too faint to find, but new ones can be recorded and interpreted with enough time," Maria said.

Tania looked at both of us for a moment. "I'm not trying to sound patronizing; just making sure that you two are on the same page. You have very different backgrounds, and I don't want confusion. We have been looking at the Venom system, trying to find a radio bubble. The Venom have AltComms, which is tech that usually gets developed around the same time as faster-than-light travel. If you look at humanity's bubble, it is hundreds of light-years away from Earth. Picking it up and recording it is difficult but possible. And we haven't been adding to that bubble for almost two hundred and fifty years.

"That's normal. But the Venom don't seem like the type to wait hundreds of years before attacking the rest of the galaxy. But like we've talked about, they probably borrowed tech from their sister planet. The Venom do not have a body plan conducive to technological development, nor do they have the social leanings for it. We are confident that the Venom have stolen or reverse-engineered all of their technology. Advancing from violent and non-advanced to advanced in a short period seems a little odd. So did taking technology from a race that didn't have a radio bubble and was likely thousands of years more advanced."

That did seem a little strange to me. Maria's face looked calm and blank. I'd seen that when she was thinking hard about a problem. She understood Tania way more than I did.

Tania went on, "So since this seemed odd, we looked at the data more. And do you know what we found?"

"A bubble," Maria said confidently.

Tania smiled darkly. "We did. About two months ago, we found it and have been trying to confirm what we thought. We did, and the bubble confirmed another theory that we had already developed. Do you want to know how far away from the Venom system we found the bubble?"

"How far?" I asked.

"Eighty light-years," she said.

"What? How is that possible? How many light-years thick was it?" Maria asked.

This rang a bell for me. I remembered Charles talking about it before. You had the forward edge of a bubble, that was when the race developed radio technology. Then you had the end of the bubble, which represented when AltComms came around and was in wide-scale use. Measuring how thick a bubble was and its makeup gave you a good idea of how fast a species advanced technologically.

"Ten," Tania said. "And it was simple. So simple we thought it was a blip. It wasn't. The signal came from Venom Major, and it was extremely new tech for that world. It lasted for ten years showing growth, and then got faint quickly and stopped. We think it stopped shortly after the Venom invaded from Venom Minor. The people on Venom Major weren't advanced enough for a space program. The Venom didn't get their technology from them. They also didn't cover hundreds of thousands of years of evolution in a decade on their own either," Tania said.

"Someone made them?" I asked, agitated.

"Yes," Tania said. "We think it was the same race that altered the Tooth. They are way too advanced, and they are too similar to the Venom."

"Wait, that could be a coincidence..." Maria started.

"Yes, it could. That they are the fourth race we've found like them makes it a pattern. On every world, we have found the native species is about where the people here were. In each case, they all died out quickly. Sometimes, the planets have no life on them. But in the case of Tooth Prime, there is life. If the Tooth are like the Venom, when we get samples, we will find heavy modifications," Tania said.

I felt my face flush. "Who made them?"

"We don't know yet. We are trying to figure it out. We think the Venom were the last iteration of whatever they were working on. Tooth Prime died out about twenty years before the Venom got started on Venom Major. Since the race here wasn't that advanced, we don't know how long the war lasted here," she said.

"You said when we get samples?" Maria asked. "Is that why we're still here? To get samples? I'm not sending my people into that situation."

"Yes, that is why you are here," Tania said.

Before she could say more, I spoke, "I'll get you samples."

Maria looked at me angrily, but something in my face calmed her.

"What do we need to do? I won't put my people in too high of risk. But if need be, I'll get you what you need," I said, meaning it.

I wasn't sure if I had been this angry before. We'd been through hell, and Meyers was dead because of someone's science project? Unbidden, I remembered talking to Clay about how we were part of a genocide. It had bothered me to think about it, and that was when I thought the Venom were just evil.

Tania looked at me thoughtfully. "We need to collect data on them. We just need clues as to who altered them."

"What are we going to do when the HF figures out who did it?" Maria asked.

"Oh, we'll wipe them out," I said. "Trust me on that. The Venom have killed billions, and some race made them…"

"Then they are the ones who have the blood of those races on their hands," Tania said. "I can't speak for the government, but I think you are probably correct. I will provide detailed reports to both of you. This information and everything on this mission going forward is classified. Corporal, I know your team has clearance, and this won't be the first classified op for you. Maria, I know that is a new concept for you, but you cannot share this with anyone outside of here. Enough people know what has happened here already. Going forward, your CCPUs will make sure you don't send anything to anyone that is classified. You may tell people that you are learning about the Tooth, but you do not tell people why you are learning about them other than trying to figure out how they came to be. There is to be no mention of the Venom. Understood?"

"Yes, ma'am," I said.

Maria said she understood, though I could see that she looked uncomfortable about the whole thing. That seemed reasonable.

———

"THIS IS FANTASTIC," ANDY WATERS GRUMBLED AS TANIA SPOKE TO BOTH teams.

She had moved from her questioning approach of explanation to a normal presentation. I wasn't sure which I preferred. I suspected that Maria got more out of having to answer her own way into an explanation. In that vein, I was sure the rest of the Exploration team would feel that way. My people? We took orders. And being how we were going to be the ones in the line of fire, I appreciated her not beating around the bush.

There was more grumbling from the Exploration team. My team sat silent, taking everything in with only the occasional flicker of emotion on their faces showing how they felt. Not thrilled was the general emotion that I was seeing. When Tania was done, she looked at my team.

"Do you have anything you'd like to ask? You lot have been quiet this whole time," she said.

The Exploration team looked at my team as if they'd forgotten we were there.

Betts looked at me. "What is the tactical plan on this?"

Tania didn't look offended that he'd talked to me instead of her.

"We don't have one yet. We will soon. As of now, until we have a plan, we will continue to hold our perimeter. Given our orders haven't changed, if things get hot, we EVAC the Exploration team and fall back to our own EVAC positions." I looked at Tania. "Are our orders going to be changing?"

"Yes, but not when it comes to the evacuation of the site. That remains the same. I will be working with your command after my visits to help them come up with a plan. We need data on the Tooth; we are looking for clues. The Quiver will do likewise. To that end, I suspect that will require time in the field," she said.

"I'm not going out there," Andy said firmly.

"No, you won't," I said. "We won't need any of you in the field. My people will handle that."

"Unless you are ordered to take us," Catherine said, sounding worried and angry.

"I won't be," I said confidently.

Tania spoke, "The Corporal is correct. Sending untrained people into a possible situation would not only risk your safety but also decrease Alpha Team's ability to do their jobs." Her tone was matter-of-fact and didn't leave any room for question.

The Exploration crew didn't say anything else. Maria Guzman looked like she was deep in thought. Though it might have been a comfort to her that her people would not be going into the field, I knew she wouldn't be happy that mine would be. I wasn't either, but it was our job. As we left, my team headed towards the housing unit. We would be talking alone. I wanted to get everyone's thoughts on the matter. It wouldn't affect our orders, but people needed to be heard.

Tania pulled me aside.

"Thank you for being direct with my people," I said.

She nodded. "Of course. They are the ones that will be in the most danger. With you and Guzman, I thought it good for her to come to the same conclusion that my people had. Do you have faith in her ability to keep her people calm and effective?"

"I do. She's good with them."

"And your team? I know this can't be good news," she said.

I shrugged, trying not to look like anything other than impassive about it. "It's what we do. We have experience with the Venom, so if the Tooth are what you think they are, that should give us an edge. My team will get the job done."

She thanked me and walked over to her ship.

"Tania," I said, "if you don't mind, please keep low to the ground when you leave. I don't want the Tooth to know where we are."

Her smile seemed genuine. "Don't worry, Corporal. I started in Exploration but have plenty of former HFDF on my team who have pounded a few things into my head. I won't give away your position."

I thanked her and walked back to the housing unit. The team was all sitting around the table, silent. Meeting with the Exploration team, they kept passive, but I could see the stress in their eyes now.

"Thoughts?" I asked.

"Not happy, sir," Clay said. "I'm conflicted about this. The Tooth are victims, and now so are the Venom. I don't like being the bad guy."

I sat, "We aren't the bad guys," I said, and before Clay could speak, "we are reacting appropriately to a threat. Whether the Venom are victims or not, we had to take them out."

She looked down. "I know that. But I don't like it."

"Will you be good?" I asked.

"I will," she said.

Sweeting looked thoughtful but not overly bothered. I suspected that in a few days, he'd have something to say, but for now, he was just waiting for whatever came next.

I could see that Krista was uncomfortable but not losing her edge at all.

"You good?" I asked.

She shrugged. "Not the news we wanted, but it makes sense. More just hoping that the Venom were the last race, whoever made them messed with. And that they were the end goal."

"You want the Venom to be the end goal?" Sweeting asked, curiously.

"Sure do," she said. "We've seen them and beat them. It was awful, but we did it. If they were the end, then we don't have something worse they've made around the corner."

Sweeting grinned. "You do find the silver lining everywhere, don't you?"

"Nothing says happy like genocidal aliens," Krista snorted.

"I didn't say it was a sane lining…"

Everyone chuckled. It broke the mood, and I could see everyone relax. This was just another op. I felt some of my own tension lessen, but only a bit.

"Betts, you aren't saying much?" I said.

"Oh, he doesn't want to go underground," Sweeting said.

"Shut it," Betts said, then sighed. "And yeah… fuck, why does it have to be tunnels again? Couldn't it be surface fighting?" He sounded exasperated.

"I don't think it will be the same. The Tooth look like they are nowhere near as advanced. Not sure what their purpose was, but if they are older than the Venom, and they haven't advanced as much as them, then I'd say their progress has stalled out. That's good for us. Also, we aren't going to wipe them out. This isn't an extermination. We are gathering data. It will be scouting and maybe some probing attacks. I don't see this going down like Pike Prime," I said. "For the rest of the day, take it easy. We can stay on base. We haven't seen extensive daytime activity from the Tooth since we first encountered them. We have a perimeter that can see well out into the field."

I dismissed them and opened a line to Monroe and Middleton. We still didn't have orders yet, but we figured there were a few givens.

We'd be in the field, and we were going to be planetside for a while in a possible hostile situation.

"What are the big issues we need to account for?" Middleton asked.

I thought. "Transportation. We are too far away to hoof it to the city all the time unless we want to camp out. We can use the rovers here, but while they are tough, they aren't configured for the work we might run into."

"I don't want you in a situation of staying in the city if we can avoid it," Monroe said.

"And the Exploration Rovers won't work." Middleton sounded thoughtful. "We have a couple on the Arbiter that are configured for Career troops. They would get the job done. We don't have enough for every team, though… could have some made or shipped. I'll look into transportation."

"Thanks. Some diggers would be good. If we find ourselves having to deal with the Tooth underground, I would like to have the ability to tunnel," I said.

"That is a good idea. Do you need more GPs?" Monroe asked.

"May as well. We have the extras around the base. Nothing is getting close to us, but in the field, that would be nice. When back at the base, we could use them to map the area around the city. Maybe a Rhino," I said light-heartedly.

Middleton laughed. "Don't tempt me. I've considered sending one. If you see vehicles, you can count on it."

I'd controlled a Rhino once in basic. I guess I didn't control it so much as I gave it orders. They were pretty autonomous, and we only got the chance because the HFDF wanted us to be able to have an appreciation for everything in the field. It was fun, in a way. I'd seen them in combat, and they were terrifyingly awesome.

"I will talk to Clovis and see what their plan is. It might behoove us to work in close coordination in the field," I said.

"It would," Monroe said. "From our understanding, the Quiver have the same mission as us. Since we are going to be in a live-fire situation, the working relationships your teams have built will be useful. How's the team?"

"Fine. Not happy about it. Not in a we don't want to work way, but in a concern about dealing with anything resembling the Venom," I said.

"That's fair. And you?" Monroe asked.

I was silent for a while. "I'm uncomfortable with it. Not sure why, sir."

"Nothing wrong with knowing that there's an issue. Want me to engage with Dr. Philips?" Monroe asked, referring to the ship's therapist.

I wanted to say no, that everything was fine. I sighed. "Yeah, may as well. Between how I feel now and not using Betts the other day, and with Meyers passing almost a year ago..."

"Will do," Monroe said.

"Do not feel bad about this," Middleton said firmly. "This is how we work. You see something that seems a little off, and you get it figured out before it's an actual issue. Jesus knows both Monroe and I have been in that situation multiple times. Shit, I'm still coming to terms with the people we lost on Pike Prime."

"As am I," Monroe said. "I meet with him once a month. As you grow in the HFDF, you'll lose reservations about it. You'll see the ship's therapist as any other doctor. If you got hurt, you'd go to a medical doctor. This is no different."

I didn't know that. But it made me feel better. If my COs found it normal and they'd been doing this for years, I needed to get on board. A thought popped into my mind.

"Betts is stressed about fighting underground again. He seems more than fine, but I'll ping Philips about that as well," I said.

"And this is how we keep the troops in top condition," Monroe said. "Fix a leak now, and you don't have a flood later."

EIGHTEEN

In the time it took for us to get our orders, Middleton and Monroe figured out transportation. It looked like the HFDF Career troop rover variants wouldn't be the best way of going. They were used primarily by Career teams who were out in the field for prolonged periods of time. Heavily armored and armed, with plenty of space, they were like deadly RVs for alien worlds. However, they weren't all that practical for day trips. The Arbiter also didn't have enough of them on board. She could make them, of course, but they required delivery to the ground via a large shuttle. Not stealthy or practical, considering there were eight teams on the ground, each of which would need at least one of the rovers.

Instead, we were getting Transport Pads. They were as basic as basic came, consisting of lift units that were connected together and covered with decking. If you wanted more lifting power, you stacked the lift units. Want a longer range? Toss some power cells between the lift units. Need more than three meters by seven meters? That's easy too; the frames allowed them to connect to other pads. You could even stack the pads to save space. Perfect, right?

Mostly. Easy, yes, and versatile they were as well. But they didn't have any armaments whatsoever. They also didn't have seats, so instead, we'd use inverted U-shaped bars that connected to the deck that we could hold on to. And they also used power—a lot more than their wheeled or tracked counterparts. Thankfully, the last one wasn't really an issue for us. Each pad would last about two days before needing to recharge the cells. They would deplete our housing unit's power supply fairly quickly. Thankfully for us, we had access to power. The base was run off the Exploration ships—ships built for that very reason. As such, the whole base could run off one of the ships. We had six.

Our three Transport Pads came down in containers dropped from the Arbiter. Tooth was starting to set as I tasked a group of BIs with unpacking and assembling them. By morning, I was sure we'd have orders.

Charles approached me as I supervised the drones. He looked at the Pads. "Kind of... simple, aren't they?" he asked.

"Oh, in the extreme. There's nothing luxurious about them, for sure. But they are faster than a rover and can cover more terrain." Anticipating his next question, I added, "We have three. There will always be one of us at the base, so in the field, we will still have sub-teams of two. One pad for each team, and then another to carry the Heavies. The bars fold down on these, and they have a low profile, so keeping them out of sight should be pretty easy."

"And if things get crazy? Can they get you out?" he asked, a hint of worry in his voice.

"Nope," I said, "if things look like they will get bad, we will leave. If things go to hell, we'll need a shuttle or a gunship. But my definition of crazy and yours are probably pretty different. What we faced the other week wasn't anything crazy. It wasn't fun, but it wasn't crazy. Just a surprise. The pads would be fine in that situation, if not better than the rover."

"Not sure I want to see crazy then," he mused.

"You really don't," I commented.

At dinner, I watched the data coming from the city. The Arbiter was parked right above it. The Tooth had a tempo to their days. When it was light, they had small patrols darting around the city. At night, those patrols pushed just past the city's borders. From their movements, we'd figured out likely tunnel entrances and routes they took. They ran a tight perimeter for how few units they had on the surface. It made me wonder what they were like a hundred years ago. There hadn't been signs of a conflict since then, so I assumed that the Tooth were a little rusty. From what we could tell, they hadn't spent much time topside in a long time either. That begged the question of when they were going to send dedicated parties out of the city in search of the creatures they'd found and fought.

After dinner, Krista and I went onto the roof to look out over the field as Tooth set. We'd all been quiet during dinner, all of us getting back into the routine of watching enemy movements. She leaned next to me, my arm wrapped around her shoulders. We were both tenser than we had been a few weeks ago. Not stressed or worried, just ready. There was always a feeling of things just about to go wrong when you were on a world with hostiles.

"It's not the same," she said sullenly.

"Not as relaxing, for sure," I confirmed.

The sky was turning from reds and oranges to deep purples and blues. Stars were winking into existence on the far horizon. The air had a hint of coolness in it. It wasn't relaxing anymore, but still pretty.

"You seem stressed," she said.

"Yeah. I talked to the ship's doc, and he agrees," I said.

"So what has you bothered?" she asked.

"The doc says that I worry about my team. It's hard to put into words, really," I sighed. "He says it's normal. This is the first engagement we've been in since Pike Prime. We really didn't have time to let that place sink in when we were there, you know? Now that we've had a break from combat, though..."

"Odd how that is. I mean, this is so much less stressful than Pike

Prime or should be. But I'd gotten used to constant combat and being in danger. I feel like I'm jumping into a pool that is way colder than I remember it being a few moments ago," she said.

"I like that analogy," I remarked.

She smiled. "I'm wise."

I chuckled. We were silent as the sky filled with stars. My CCPU overlaid the Arbiter's position. Even if we had our helmets on, we wouldn't have been able to see it. Its hull was combat black with all of its passive and active camouflage on. It would just be another black spot in the sky. Before the horizon obscured the last rays of light, my CCPU pinged. Our orders were in.

I gathered the team in the housing unit. Everyone sat expectantly.

"No surprise we are going to be starting out by scouting the Tooth in person. The goal is going to be to ascertain what they are able to find. So, for the next few days, we will keep a decent distance. Over time, we will close that gap and see how close we can get. We need to gather everything we can on their patrol styles and communication. When we are reasonably confident, we will see if we can get a whisker or two into their tunnels. Before that, we will start to map them with the GPs. The Venom were able to tell when we were using the GPs. The hope is that if we have figured out the Tooth's day-to-day routine, we will be able to see if they can also figure that out," I explained.

"And if they can't?" Clay asked.

"Then we should be able to get a clear picture of what's going on underground. It will heavily influence how we approach scouting the tunnels. If they can see the GPs, that might also influence what we can do."

Our orders were clear. We weren't to engage the Tooth unless they engaged us. If they did, we were to try and leave without having to get into a prolonged fight. After all, we were the bad guys here. Our missions would be daytime only. After figuring out if the Tooth could see the Whiskers, we would leave some behind for the evenings. Our PODs were a little on the wonky side. They were much larger than normal: five BIs, two Spheres, four BBALLs, four Large Whiskers, two GPs, and each of us had a mortar assigned to us. On the team side, I had two Mules, two Heavies, three Transport Pads, and two re-armer drones that could ferry ammo to units from the Mules or supply crates on the Transport Pads. While it was a little daunting for the team, I had fewer drones to deal with than normal, and our PODs were a far cry from career PODs.

Two of the BIs in each POD had HIRs, or Heavy Infantry Rifles— something we hadn't used much since Erie Prime. The HIRs were longer than the SIRs but packed a lot more power. They were handy for the Erie, as they were effective at long range and could disable vehicles and punch through most walls to kill something on the other side. They hadn't done well against the Venom, primarily because the Venom hid in little holes and preferred tight spaces. The Tooth seemed to have a surface presence here, so maybe we'd need the HIRs. Plus, there was a chance that the Tooth had vehicles we didn't know about.

We'd used a large number of drones in training before, and I had no doubt that my team could handle it. That said, we'd kind of taken over the Exploration base. We had to have the units that went out into the field, but also spares and parts for them. Still, we only had enough infrastructure to keep everything working. The Exploration Base might be evacuated at the drop of a hat. If we left, the HFDF didn't want a ton of equipment left on the planet. But it meant that we were leaning heavily on the Exploration equipment, primarily power.

I'd never had to think about power in the HFDF. It was easy to come by in most bases. Charging cells wasn't anything you put thought into. It still wasn't something that took time out of our day. It was just that before, we'd always been connecting to a supply that the HFDF provided. I wasn't sure why I didn't trust the abilities of the Exploration ships to keep us powered. Their equipment had to be just as reliable as ours, if not more so, but it was another corps, so I couldn't help but feel uneasy.

I felt calm about the coming day as I lay in my bunk that night.

Sleep found me quickly, and in a blink of an eye, it was my watch. I'd taken the last watch of the night. Nothing had happened overnight. The Tooth hadn't left the city like they had the first night, and their surface numbers were comparable to other evenings. I'd sent a message to Clovis telling it the orders I received, along with a map of the city and how I planned on deploying my people. By the time I woke up, I had the Quiver plans for the day as well.

We were splitting the city in two. Clovis had three units, including itself, that were going to take the northern part of the city, leaving us with the south. We were going to keep communications lines open for all units during the day. And we had as much data sharing activated as we could. Unfortunately, we hadn't gotten the opportunity to train together. It would have been nice. Instead, we were going to have to learn on the fly if anything happened.

The documentation we had on the Quiver said they were much more cautious than we were. The Quiver operators avoided direct battle as much as they could. Instead, they sent in their drones. I made a note to myself to go over the Quiver drones in the morning meeting before we went out. My team should have been familiar with them, but I wanted to make sure.

The Quiver used four main types of drones in their PODs. Whiskers were a given. Command Drones, or CDs that looked like Quiver operators and acted like them. Crabs, which were controlled by the CDs, were small four-legged drones with three arms—two for doing arm-like things with digits on the end and another that had a gun that rotated. They were quick, agile, and could target well, but had dick all for tactics and required the oversight of a CD or a Quiver. Last, they had Darts, which were bigger versions of the BBALLs.

The CDs were the key to the Quiver POD. They each had their own PODs of Crabs, Darts, and Whiskers. A single Quiver operator could command large numbers of effective PODs without losing performance. There were limits, of course, but it made the average Quiver soldier versatile. But the CDs were also the weak spot. They weren't super tough, instead leaning on processing power. As they were lost, other CDs had to take control of more and more Crabs, which again, are morons. If an enemy could find CDs or operators, they could turn the Quiver's strategy on its head—if you could find the CDs or operators, that is.

As a change, the Exploration team filed into our housing unit. We hadn't asked them to, but they wanted to help, and it somehow felt right. This wasn't the HFDF helping the Exploration Corps anymore; it was the other way around. They all looked around the housing unit. None of them had ever been in it.

Charles pointed at one of the bunks. "Is that where you guys sleep?"

Betts chuckled. "Those are luxury. Normally, in the field, they are all metal with no padding. Heck, because these have pillows, we don't even need to keep our helmets on in these to be comfortable."

Maria clasped her hands in front of her. The normal look of command on her face was gone, replaced by uncertainty.

"We have our orders to learn what we can about the Tooth as you gather information. But we would like to know how to help you when you are in the field or if there is anything we can do to make life safer and simpler for you?" she asked.

"Thank you," I said. We had already come up with a list of things we'd like. "Andy, you have detailed maps of the area. Can you tell us where would be a good place to build tunnels if I were a Tooth and in the market for a new access route to the aliens invading my planet? At some point, we'd like to get GPs in some of the areas as more of a warning if we can manage it. The mission might be to gather data, but we need to not be killed in order to do that."

"I can do that. I can tell you they haven't dug anything since we got here. A lot of the seismic equipment I had in the field was underground and still online. It wasn't looking for active tunneling, but I ran the data again, looking for anything digging. Unless they are extremely deep, they haven't dug anything more," he said.

That was good, I thought.

"Thanks," I said and passed on a list to Maria for anything else we thought we might find handy. "Do you guys want to stick around for our briefing? You don't have to if you don't want to."

None of them moved. I nodded and started my briefing.

"Today's mission is simple. We need to start figuring out how close we can get to the Tooth without them finding us. We also need to gather as much information as we can about their patrol routes. We will be remapping the whole area. It's probable that orbital assets have been unable to see everything the Tooth have been doing. We need to know if there are traps and if they have vehicles or ammunition depots on the surface now.

"Our PODs for the day will be five BIs with two carrying HIRs, two Spheres, four BBALLs, four large Whiskers, two GPs, and a mortar. Keep the mortars back but in a support position. We will be working from the outside of the city in. The Quiver have the north. We'll move slow, start with regular Whiskers, then large ones. If you can, get the GPs in the area to find any places the Tooth can hide. Keep on the outskirts of town, three BIs in."

"Engagement?" Clay asked.

"Not unless you are attacked directly; get drones out if you can. If you can't decomp them," I said.

"Decomp?" Catherine asked. "Sorry, go on, I didn't mean to interrupt."

"It's fine," I said. "Nanobots will take them down to materials. We call it decomp for decomposing. And in case you haven't looked it up, the HIRs are Heavy Infantry Rifles. They pack a lot of punch."

"Thanks," she said.

I looked at my team. "Sweeting is at home. Everyone else is going out. Krista and Betts are on Transport Pad One, Clay and I on Two. On Three will be two Heavies that will assist if things go south. They also have extra supplies. Any other questions?"

"Why are you taking those platforms instead of a rover?" Andy asked.

"The rovers don't have any defenses. They'd just turn into coffins if we were in them under attack. The pads are fast," Krista answered.

"Shit for cover but harder to find and easy to get off of," Sweeting added. "Plus, they fly and don't leave tracks that will lead back here."

"If there isn't anything else, let's get moving," I said.

My team stood, and everyone went to their bunks, opening ammo cabinets and pulling out whatever we needed. The Exploration team watched a little awkwardly. It seemed to be sinking in that we were leaving without them. We each did a check of our gear, the motions second nature to us. I integrated fully with my POD, running checks on everything.

"Alpha, prepping for departure," I said to command.

"Roger that, Alpha. The Quiver are already moving out," Monroe said.

"The Quiver are heading out," I told the team.

We all walked out of the housing unit. Our PODs were on the transports. I patted Andy on the shoulder as I passed him. He was an ass, but he cared. My helmet snapped closed, and I boarded the transport. It lifted off the ground and glided away from the base. I pulled up a feed from one of the drones and saw the look on Charles's face change as he thought I couldn't see him anymore. He'd seemed so unworried, but I could now see deep lines of concern on his brow. It made me think of what Liz had told me about how she hated it when I was on a mission. I killed the feed.

"You good?" Monroe asked.

"Yes, just saw the look on my friend's face change, is all. Just a pang of guilt," I said.

"I don't think we really know how hard it is on those we leave behind. Try not to make it worse by getting torn up," he advised.

"Awww, but I wanted to get another new limb," I joked.

Monroe laughed. "That's the first time I've heard you crack a joke about that. That's good."

"Maybe that means I'm not going to pieces," I hedged.

Monroe barked a laugh. "No, no, not until you have kids—no dad jokes from you. That's an order!"

The pad flew silently over the ground, and the horizon began to reveal the city in the distance. It kept south and away. We wouldn't be moving deep into the city today. Instead, we'd start on the outskirts and slowly see how far in we could go. If today went well, then tomorrow we'd start a little further in, and so on.

I knew that Charles was worried about me. I also knew there was no way for me to make him feel better about it. I understood that. But I wasn't worried. For the next few days, the most I'd be doing once I was on-site was lying in a hiding spot. Today, even the BIs wouldn't be in any danger—just the Whiskers, if they could be in danger. Only the Venom had targeted them, and only when the Whiskers were able to be seen and targeted, which wasn't that often. We'd learn the most tonight when the ship watched the expanded patrols. If they found any evidence of us, we'd probably see it as new activity. If they didn't notice us, we could push in over the next few days until we were in sight of the daytime patrols. It'd get a little tense then.

The pads stayed just above the ground as they flew, rocking us back and forth as they avoided obstacles and hugged the terrain. I put my hand on the BI in front of me, giving me more perceived stability. My vision dropped away, replaced with a map of the area. I updated my asset information, seeing the additions from the Quiver. I could see all of their operators and PODs. Each Quiver had four CDs along with a complement of eight Crabs and four Darts. Each of the CDs had the same PODs. There were also swarms of Whiskers. I dropped the Quiver Whiskers from my display and marked all Quiver units as friendly. In the unlikely event we were fighting in close range today, our rounds would treat the Quiver like they did us. The SIRs would make sure they were fully fragged by the point of impact. That was handy.

We were feeding operational data between the groups but not targeting. I could see the intended paths the drones would take, and they could see the paths our drones were taking. From that, the BIs could infer targets and tactics to an extent. This was where the BIs would have issues. I had the Quiver combat profile and detailed information about units loaded onto the BIs. But they also had to have that for the Tooth as well. They'd need to predict the behavior and interactions of two different types of groups and treat them accordingly.

Normally, the processing abilities of the BIs weren't something I had to worry about, but for this op, I'd need to lean heavily on the computer we had on the ship. The BIs had limited capacity; their computers weren't big or powerful, and their systems needed to be small to avoid damage, hard-wearing if they took damage, and not drain power. Most systems had several redundancies built into the drones in case one went down. They did a damn good job at everything but had their limits.

I tasked the computer on the ship to prioritize drones engaged in combat and near Quiver units. This way, those drones would be optimized and hopefully not lose effectiveness. For my own part, I'd spent the time we had on the planet studying the Quiver and their tactics—something I was sure they were doing as well. Being able to work as a homogenized group at some point seemed inevitable.

The pad dropped off Clay and her drones. I focused my map on the area I'd be dropped in. There was a small group of squat buildings that might have something. On-site, I moved low to the ground, letting the Whiskers lead the way by a large margin. I found a drainage pipe. Well, I assumed it was drainage… maybe it wasn't… whatever it had been used for, it was big enough for me. I slid in with two of my BIs staying close for coverage. From there, I watched feeds.

The BIs stayed back and waited for the Whiskers to scout the areas before I sent in the large Whiskers. The Tooth weren't going to get the drop on us. Everything was watching to see if any radio waves popped up, but they didn't. The Whiskers made detailed observations of where the ship had seen Tooth movement. If we could figure out tracks, that would help us with finding and avoiding the Tooth.

"Anything you want us to look for?" I asked the Exploration team.

"Can your Whiskers detect anything in the air? Perhaps scent?" Felipe asked.

"Yes, but not well. They can gather some raw data, but the ship or your system would need to figure out what the data means," I said.

"Wouldn't scent be useful in combat?" Charles asked.

"Only if you know what the scents are and if they give you more notice than anything visual or audio. Plus, Whiskers need to be small and hard to find," I pointed out. "The Whiskers are looking for things in the area, not those that were in the area so much. The BIs are good at figuring out patterns, so they find tracks well." After thinking for a moment, I added, "The Quiver Whiskers have a slightly different design. They may have more options. I'll ask. And the BIs can smell pretty well, though again, it isn't their primary means of observation."

I opened a channel to Clovis. "Do your Whiskers have a strong sense of smell?"

Our Whiskers were just little floating rings—hard to see and hit. They did great with sound and visual observations. The Quivers had more substance to them. They were also much easier to find, my hope was they had more capabilities.

"Yes, atmospheric sensors are part of their suite. Though I cannot provide you with their precise abilities for obvious reasons," it said.

"Totally understand. Ours have dick in the way of smell. They can detect a bit, but it's not enough to track anything with. Our BIs, on the other hand, have a lot more built into their helmets," I said.

"It's amazing the things you can do when you don't need your helmet to hold a head. If we find anything that is useful, I will pass it along for your BIs to use." It paused. "We don't have a lot of documentation about your suits. Can you smell in them?"

"Thanks. And yes, same as the BIs, but the data doesn't register as scent. Humans don't lean as heavily on the sense as much as other species from Earth. On a foreign world, it would range from uncomfortable to useless," I said.

"That is much the same for us. For us, evolution favored the ability to see well in low levels of light and to detect movement and distance with great accuracy," it explained.

The Quiver were interesting. They were herbivores, but much of their body layout was suited for what you'd think of a predator to have. I thought about asking the Exploration team about it later. For the moment, I was lying in a pipe and needed to focus on the Tooth.

I checked in with my team, and there wasn't anything going on. That was good. Today wasn't about finding something new; it was about finding a safe path into town and dipping our toes back in the water. If something hostile popped up today, we'd have to push back even further from known tunnels, along with reassessing the Tooth's capabilities.

After a few hours, Charles spoke to me on a private line. "How's it going out there?" he asked, not sounding like he was sure himself.

"Fine," I said honestly. "Right now, we aren't seeing anything. Krista had a Whisker catch a glimpse of a Tooth, but the Whisker was high along a building, and the Tooth was far on the horizon at the Whisker's max range. Tonight, we'll be able to see if the Tooth noticed where we were. If they don't, tomorrow, we will do much of the same but leave behind a few Whiskers to monitor overnight. We will slowly move into the city. If all goes well, within a couple of days, we'll be fully inside the Tooth's patrol lines, and they won't know it."

"And if they find you in those lines?" he asked.

"We'll get out. Don't worry; we're actually pretty good at this. How's your team?"

He sighed. "Yeah, I'm starting to get that. They are fine, I guess. Worried about you guys. Andy has been pacing around. He's a bit abrasive but a pretty good person. Maria and Catherine are watching the feeds and then they've been going through all of the battle data you provided for us."

I remembered that now. I'd shared a lot with them. They could see training and most of the engagements we'd been in. Everyone on the team had consented to the data share. "How's that going?"

"Their opinions about you guys are changing. Everyone has been going through the data since the shit hit the fan. You know you never shared any of the videos of you or your team getting hurt with anyone besides Liz?" Charles said a little accusingly.

I did a quick check on everything to see that we were still in the clear.

"She had access because she was in the medical teams helping us," I hedged.

"I'm not pissed, man… but I can see why you don't fear injury as much as I do. We can really take a lot, can't we?" he said.

"That we can."

It was true. Growing up, you felt pain—not enough to debilitate, but enough that you didn't risk hurting yourself. Our CCPU's slowly turned on the functionality that made us pound for pound better than anything nature could have conjured. Sure, we didn't get sick from birth and always healed fast. But by the time I joined the HFDF, my CCPU wasn't limiting anything, and while I knew what I could take and do, I didn't really appreciate it until I'd been through training and then once I'd been hit a few times in combat.

Losing limbs had reinforced that when you got torn up, you were less effective, but healing as fast as I had with no physical pain taught me not to be crippled by fear. Our bodies are machines—keep them in good order, and they will work the way you want and need them to. But if they get damaged, there is only one irreplaceable part.

Our drones were back to us long before Tooth started to set. We loaded onto the pads and headed back to base. We'd figured out how far into the city we could go and hadn't discovered any new tunnels, which confirmed what the ship had seen from space. Tonight, we'd see if the Tooth figured it out.

NINETEEN

I sat in a small office in a VR space as I waited for Dr. Philips to arrive. I met with him and Dr. Albright on a regular-ish basis. Maria had offered her VR pod for the meeting so I could meet with the doctor face-to-face.

Dr. Philips walked in through a door and approached me, extending his hand. I stood and took it. The doctor preferred the handshake over a salute. I wasn't sure if the gesture was meant to make the troops feel like we were on the same level or if it was a reminder for him. I sat down in a chair and waited for him to speak.

"How are you doing this morning?" he asked.

"Not bad. We are going to be escalating things in the field today, so I'm a little preoccupied with that," I said.

He nodded. "I saw that."

We'd been watching the Tooth for a week. We knew their habits and patrol routes. We were now able to get well inside those routes, bringing us close to the tunnels that led under the city. Thus far, the Tooth hadn't seemed to notice us. The Quiver had a few scares with their Whiskers being spotted. Ours were a little harder to see, and the Tooth hadn't noticed anything.

243

The day's mission would be to see what the Tooth would do if they found a BI inside their patrol lines. The drone would only have the aid of its Whiskers. It would not be making a concerted attempt to fight off the Tooth. When it was found, we would see if we could get it out of the area. We were planning to have it decomp once we found what we wanted.

"What do you hope to accomplish today?" Philips asked.

"To see what we can learn. If the drone gets out easily, that's almost a waste. Likewise, if it gets destroyed instantly, that's also a bit of a waste," I said.

"So you want it to do a good job before its demise?" he asked.

I smiled. "Yeah, I guess you could say that. Either way, the drone is screwed, I suppose."

"That it is. And how is your team?"

"They're doing well. Everyone is back in the mode of being in combat; we're running a tight ship," I said.

He looked thoughtful. "There have been some frustrations as of late, haven't there?"

I sighed. "Yes, I suppose there have been."

"And what are those?"

I thought back to an op from the other day when I'd pulled Sweeting back from some Tooth that were in his area. He had a path out, but I changed it and made him leave before he really needed to. I'd had things like that with everyone on my team.

"That I am... babying my team. They feel like I'm not trusting them to do their jobs. No one is mad yet, but there is some tension about it," I admitted.

"Is that true? Are you holding them back?" he asked.

I thought about it for a moment. I had known the question would be coming. I wanted to say that my command hadn't changed, but that would have been a lie.

"Yes, it is. It's not something that I'm aware of at the time, but I have been holding my team back," I admitted.

"I know we've spoken about Private Meyer's death before. Is that still impacting your decisions?" he asked.

I thought for a moment.

"Yes," I said. "It doesn't help that it's been a year. But when we are in the field, I start to get worried. I know I shouldn't let it impact my judgment."

"By and large, it has not. Your team's frustrations may weigh heavy on you, but overall, your command is still solid. You have done well for someone who has lost a team member. As we've talked about before, dealing with death in general is a learned behavior—one that our race has generally forgotten," he said warmly.

"Yeah, I know."

"Do you? You had a cat growing up. Did it die?"

I shook my head. "That cat is over two hundred years old and doing well."

He nodded sagely. "I know James was the first person you'd known who has passed, but has anyone you know had a pet that has died? Or have they known someone who has passed away in your lifetime?"

I thought about that for a while. "No."

"Did your parents talk about death growing up?" he asked.

"Yes, they did. They always said that everyone dies. It's a common statement, but it sounds different from a first-gen. We talked about relatives that had passed, the normal stuff," I said.

He nodded. "But it's not normal. You see, you hit it on the head when you said that first-gens are different. When they say something about death happening to all of us, they actually mean it. Your team has handled the death of a team member extremely well due to you and Corporal Royle's reactions. Well, that and James Myers was not a beloved member of the team. By keeping himself separate from others, it lessened the impact of his death. Returning to my main point: for your team, death wasn't anything they or their parents have ever had to legitimately think about. While you and Royle have not experienced it, you have heard about it because both of your parents have dealt with it in their lives. You've heard how to mourn, and your team took that lead from you," he said, almost proudly.

"But I'm still holding my team back," I protested.

He nodded. "Yes, you are. But not in a way that risks them. You keep them safer and still get the mission done. There will come a time when you don't hold them back anymore, but in the meantime, relax. You are doing good. Maybe talk to them and explain what's going on in your head."

"I guess I can do that," I said, not really wanting to but under-standing the need.

"And I hear you cracked a joke about your injuries."

I chuckled. "Yep."

"What changed?" he asked.

Again, I thought. "I guess I realized that there's a lot that we can live through and that things are going to happen. I can't let that hold me down. And before you say it, I know you're going to say something about how this applies to leading my team."

He raised his hands in surrender with a smirk on his face. "Never."

I laughed. "Thank you for helping me out."

He looked serious. "Of course. And maybe today or this week, talk with your team—not about things now but about James. Also, good luck on your op today."

My vision went black, and then the VR pod opened. I got out, and Maria was at the desk in her ship, looking at the screen. She turned to me.

"How was your meeting?"

"Productive," I said. "Thank you for letting me use the pod."

"Anytime. Are you worried about today?" she asked.

"No, not really. Don't get me wrong; if I were the BI that we'll be sending in, I'd totally be panicking right now," I said, trying to sound lighthearted.

"But there's no chance that your team will come in any danger?" she asked.

I didn't want to tell the Exploration people everything, but I didn't want to lie to them either. "There's always a chance that we will see action. Today, I hope we don't, but we might. At some point, though, we are going to need to see the inside of those tunnels, or intel will want more data, or something will come up. When it does, I have no doubt things will get lively."

"And if the Tooth find us after you kick the hornet's nest?" she asked, not angry, just concerned.

"Then we hold them, and your people leave. We'd have plenty of warning for you to get out of dodge," I said.

She scowled for a moment. "I wasn't worried about that. I know we will leave before the Tooth get here."

"I know what you meant," I said warmly.

Later, I gripped my SIR tightly as I hid behind some of the omnipresent rubble of the city. We were all well within the Tooth's patrols. About twenty meters away from me, a group of them moved along at a slow pace. I stayed still. I wasn't the one the Tooth were supposed to find. I had a feed from a Whisker up.

There were three Tooth moving down a street. They walked on the walls around them as much as the ground. They'd move a bit and then stay still, the turrets on top of them swirling around. When they stopped, they hugged the ground. I wasn't sure if they thought this hid them or if it was something else. Knowing that they had been fucked with by another race made us all unsure. What behaviors were from when they were just normal grabbers? What was programmed into them if their behavior was altered, and what didn't have any meaning or purpose at all?

They'd feel around with their arms and then move along and stop again. It seemed as though they didn't have a strong sense of smell in the traditional sense but rather could detect scents with their arms. Felipe said that the Grabbers did this as well, and it was a core part of their hunting technique. For their part, the Quiver Whiskers could track them by scent, but audio and visual still worked better.

As I watched the Tooth more and more, it seemed obvious they had been altered. Life came in all forms and sizes, but in the case of technologically advanced life, there were some general trends. One of them is that you had to have the ability to manipulate the world around you into delicate machinery. You could be a genius, but unless you pushed a rocket out of your ass, you needed to build the thing. Some body plans came up more often than others. The Tooth didn't really have those. The Venom had fingers, and the workers and breeders had more than enough brains to at least copy things. They just hadn't had the temperament, or if I was being fair, the working intelligence until they were altered. The Tooth had been given a few upgrades and some toys. Even I could see they were a proof of concept at best. It made me wonder if the Venom were the final product or also some prototype.

The Tooth moved along. Soon, they'd find the BI. I'd brought an extra one as it didn't seem wise to hinder myself or a teammate purposely. We had the BI surrounded, so to speak. We wanted to see how the Tooth would respond all over the city. I had the Quiver patched in, though they were keeping more distance than my people.

"Alright, the Tooth should be approaching the BI. Let the test begin," I said.

In all fairness, this was test three. We'd slowly been making the BI less stealthy, trying to see what the Tooth's threshold was. In the coming days and weeks, we'd tweak the test as the Tooth's alert was raised. The end goal was to snag one of them and see as much of their tech as we could.

The BI wasn't fully in the open, but it wasn't far away from the road. We'd found that when it didn't move at all and was camouflaged, the Tooth could get at least five meters away and not detect it. This time, the BI was going to twitch.

The Tooth were about ten meters away. One of them had just nestled down to the ground. The BI shifted ever so slightly. Our sensors picked up spikes of radio, but the Tooth didn't move. Instead, the others stopped moving and huddled down. The BI didn't budge. The Tooth's turrets swiveled around, painting the area with targeting lasers. Still, the BI did not move. One of the turrets swept the BI's area and stopped for a moment.

"They have acquired it," I said.

The other Tooth started to move around carefully. The radio bursts kept up at the same pace. They began to move almost as if they hadn't found the BI, but their turrets kept scanning the area around it, and they were moving in a way that would allow them to attack it more easily. Still, the BI didn't move.

"This is why it took us so long to find them," Betts said. "Look at how they are taking their time."

"It's different from when we first encountered them," Krista noted. "It's like they are hunting the BI."

"This falls in line with the hunting style we have seen the grabbers engage in the wild," Felipe said.

"So this behavior is natural. I wonder if what we saw the other week was one that was part of their upgrade. They are acting like different creatures," I said.

"Our team says this is different than what their patrol patterns would suggest would happen. I think this goes a long way to confirming that behavior modification was also part of their alterations," Clovis said.

"Seeing activity here," Betts said.

I pulled up what he was looking at. There were more Tooth heading toward the BI's location.

"I've got activity as well," Krista said.

I started checking in on other Whiskers and orbital assets. The Tooth's patterns had shifted. I was surprised to see how they'd all reacted.

"They are all agitated, but other than the few groups near your position, there doesn't seem to be any clear plan for what the others are doing," Middleton said.

"They know that they need to be on edge but don't know what to do with themselves," Monroe observed.

"I'm pulling the BI. If the Tooth get much closer, that turret will get a kill shot, and we won't learn anything else," I said.

I sent the order for the BI to get out of the area. It moved, and then the Tooth darted toward it like they had the exploration drones. The BI fired at them, keeping its shots wide. The Tooth scrambled, their turrets buzzing a reprisal. Their movements changed as they found cover. They rushed the BI, which was retreating.

My CCPU pinged me. Tooth all over the city were moving.

"That's a change," Betts said.

The group he was watching was leapfrogging from place to place, with one Tooth going in the lead and then hunkering down as the others passed by.

"Are they trying to find cover?" Clay asked.

"Looks like it, but they aren't doing that good of a job," Monroe said.

The BI was at a jog now, easily keeping ahead of the Tooth. I watched the map as the Tooth in the area converged. We were deep inside their patrols, all of which were collapsing in.

"Alright, let's head out," I said. "I don't want to be tripped on. Sweeting, you got this?"

"Roger that, I'll monitor the BI and keep it from crossing your path," he said.

I cut my feeds and started to move slowly out of the area. At one point, I had to stay still as a group of Tooth came within twenty meters of me. I watched them as I crouched behind a wall. Their jerky leapfrog pattern seemed purposeful to me—not like they were trying and failing at something, but doing exactly what they meant to.

The Tooth managed to surround the BI by the time I made it to the transport pad. Sweeting sent an order to it, and it jumped on top of a building, the Tooth firing on it the whole time. It found a gap in the walls and hid in it. Sweeting started the decomp process on it.

"They'll have a hard time finding it before it decomps," Sweeting said.

"Good work," Monroe said.

The pad started to move away from the city. I watched the map of the area as we left. The Tooth had gone from their well-defined patrol routes to chaos. They were moving all around the city quickly.

"It would be hard to hide from them," Krista said. "I mean, they aren't following any pattern; they're all over the place."

"It may not be an organized hunt, but it would work," I said.

By the time we made it back to the base, the Tooth had settled back into their patrols, almost as if nothing had happened. The exploration team was waiting for us when we arrived. They all looked tense and worried. We unloaded, and the drones went over to their storage area.

"A little close, wasn't it?" Catherine asked.

I thought for a moment. "No. Sweeting put the BI in a safe place to decomp. The Tooth didn't find it. We could have probably left it overnight and gotten it back in the morning. Oh well." I was a little irritated we hadn't thought of that. Shit, with how the Tooth were now, the BI could have gotten out of the city and hoofed its way back to base. I needed to be better with asset management.

She looked confused and a little irritated. "Not the drone. I don't care about that. You! Those things came within a few meters of you."

"Oh yeah... I guess they did. Well, it was twenty meters, so not thaaat close," I said, and then, reading her expression, I added, "I would have been fine had they found me. I had BIs close by, and the area was zeroed with the mortars. At worst, Clay was in the area for backup, and there was a lot less than when we met the Tooth the first time."

She looked a little like she wanted to say something else but didn't. I appreciated the concern, and I could see how Catherine, out of everyone, would be the most concerned since she'd actually been shot at by the Tooth. After dismissing my team, I headed out to my favorite foxhole. We'd kind of poked at the hornet's nest, and while I didn't need to spend my watch in the field, I wanted to anyway.

Time in the HFDF was an odd combination of being way too close to people and way too isolated at the same time. I loved Krista, but on the ship, we were together constantly—not even really having space to sleep comfortably unless we wanted to be in different sealed bunks. On Tooth Prime, I saw her every day, but I was never alone. My only time alone had been in the field when I was connected to everyone or when I was in my bunk.

My team wasn't going to bother me on my watch. It was an unspoken rule. On your watch, you were on your own. You only had the drones to keep you company. I'd assigned myself a two-hour watch with an hour perimeter inspection after that. Everyone on the team did these. The watch was normally silent, leaving you to your thoughts but not in a little box. And frankly, the perimeter check could be done by the person on watch or in your bunk, but most of us walked around the base to each tower.

So long as the person on watch didn't sound an alert, you could go helmet-free if you wanted. That gave me two hours to just be alone and then another hour to walk on my own. I relished it. I sat in the hole and disengaged my helmet. The late afternoon air felt wonderful. We'd come to this place at the perfect time as far as the seasons went. In two months, it would start to get cold, with rain falling most of the winter with some snow. We'd caught the tail end of the hot season.

I breathed in deeply, closing my eyes. After a few moments, I checked the map to see that the city was normal and that there was nothing anywhere near the perimeter, which dipped below the horizon. I'd get a notification if anything left a one-kilometer perimeter around the city or came within seven of the base.

My CCPU told me that Catherine was approaching. That was fine. I liked my alone time, but what I really wanted tonight was to be outside without my helmet. If Catherine wanted to hang for a bit, that was fine. She stopped a ways away. I poked my head over the edge of the hole and saw her with her helmet on, lying on the ground. I resisted the urge to smile. At least they'd learned to be wary, even if it wasn't warranted right now.

"You're fine; come on in," I said.

She got up and crawled into the hole, her helmet sliding off.

"I didn't know I didn't need to be careful out here," she commented.

I shrugged. "Being careful is generally a good idea. What's up?"

"Sorry if I came off rude this evening when you got back," she said, sounding honest.

"Nothing to be sorry about."

"You don't seem to be all that threatened by the Tooth," she said.

I thought for a moment. "I am," I said slowly, "but my idea of a threat might be a bit different." I thought about how to explain it to her. "Today, did you see how they reacted to the BI? Not at first, but when they went after it?"

"Yes, I was watching the whole thing, trying not to wring my hands too much," she admitted.

"Did you see how the Tooth in the area acted? And how hard it was for them to find the BI even after they were alerted?" I asked, leading her a bit.

"Everything in the area converged on it, but I guess I can see where you are coming from. They had a hard time finding it. But the ones close to you were looking for danger," she countered.

"I don't think they were," I said. "I think they were looking for threats along the way, but they were moving too fast to do a good job. The BI had to move twice to be targeted. Don't get me wrong; those turrets would have figured it out given enough time, but the ones near me were moving fast and loud."

"So what? They were trying to scare you out? They didn't know you were there."

"But I might have been. They didn't know about the BI until they found it. I think they were kind of looking for prey but also hoping to startle anything out. What I saw that concerned me was the way they converged. A couple of Tooth would be easy. Their weapons aren't that accurate or powerful at any range. But get a bunch of them on you? And the way they zip around, finding little nooks and crannies to move through? You could get yourself in a real shit show that way," I said seriously. "We got lucky when we found them. Had we been in the position that BI was in today, we'd have been in a lot closer fight."

"So don't lose your cool, and if you get spotted, run like hell because they suck at range and aren't fast," she said.

I liked that she was thinking about how to avoid them; that was a good thing. "That should do you. Humans are quick in comparison. Zip around a little bit and try to stay low and hard to hit until you have about three hundred meters of space, and then book it. Keep ahead of where they will converge, and you'd be fine," I said with just a hint of worry.

"And you're on edge because?" she said.

"That works for Humans, not the Quiver," I said with a sigh. "They are quick in short bursts, but they are made for climbing. Even with their suits on, a nonsuited human could outrun them in the open."

"So if they get into a situation, there isn't the option of outrunning them as easily. But the Quiver are much better at stealth than we are," she pointed out.

"That's true." I chuckled. "They could probably step on a Quiver and not know it. Still, I want to see how they plan on avoiding them. Sooner or later, we are going to have to throw in together, and I don't like not knowing my partner's tactics like they're second nature to me."

She nodded, understanding. "You aren't worried about them getting caught on their own. You're thinking about a team engagement and how it will play out. Yeah, I can see where you aren't a fan of uncertainty like that."

"No, I'm really not. It's one thing to figure out your enemy; it's another to do that and think about your ally at the same time and how that works with your people, who have altogether different types of drones, body plans, tactics, and strategies. There's a reason we don't often fight in combined groups," I said.

"Maybe you should," she said warmly.

"I'll be sure to bring that up with the Human Federation the next time they ask for my direction," I said sardonically.

We were silent for a short time.

"I know you and your team haven't been thrilled with the turn of events, but are you still finding this mission interesting?" I asked.

"Well, it hasn't been dull, that's for sure," she said with sarcastic joy, "and yes, it has been. We provide data for the HFDF from time to time. Mostly, it's from lightyears away. For me, the few times I've had to do work for the HFDF outside of my Service Term, it was on data that had been collected by radio observatories or by field reports from troops. I've never been in a position to see a technologically advanced race on its home turf, let alone see how dangerous they can be."

"So you're going to join the HFDF after this, then?" I asked.

She laughed. "Jesus, no. Honestly, I see some time away from the field in my future," she admitted.

I felt a twang at that. "Why? Are you worried about what's happened here happening again?"

She shook her head. "I'm not worried. This is rare in the extreme. Finding an intelligent race on a world while we are on-site is rare. Finding one that is technologically advanced? That doesn't happen. My specialty is in studying alien technology, right?"

"Yeah."

"Well, the only time I get fieldwork is if I'm on a world like this one. We don't go to worlds with active tech because that would imply there's a race living there using that tech. So that means if I'm in the field, it's on a world where there was a race with some sort of tech that's not there anymore. I've been to a lot of worlds that have died off.

Sometimes it was the home species' fault, and for others, it was nature. In all the cases, it's a little depressing," she sighed. "I've been doing it for years now. I was thinking that I would go for a change of pace at the end of this gig anyway. I'm sure after a few years, I'll rotate back into fieldwork again. How about you? Do you think you'll stay in the HFDF after your term is up?"

"Probably. Right now, Krista and I have a large chance of staying together according to our trainers, and the HFDF thinks that is going to increase the chances that we stay on after our term. I'm sure I will sign on longer when it's all said and done. Not sure what I'd do, though," I said.

"It's limited when you enter a Service Term, isn't it?" she clarified.

I nodded. "Yep. There aren't a ton of jobs that we can do in our first term. I get it. Every job is a foundation for the future and is in a field that works well with new people. The longer you are in and the more you learn, there are a lot of directions you can go in. So I'm sure the HFDF will be right, and I'll stick around."

She left after a while, and I was left to my thoughts again. I composed a few messages to my friends. Monica still seemed a little standoffish. In time, she'd come back around. We'd started posting daily recaps for family and friends. It was like having a journal but only with the stuff you wanted other people to know. I hadn't paid much attention to them. Mine auto-generated every day, and I gave it a once-over before I went to sleep. It was dry and vague. I hadn't been good about looking at my friends'.

When I looked at the board, I was surprised to see that most of my friends were reading it every night. I felt guilty for not looking at theirs. Then, on a hunch, I had my CCPU do a quick scan and found that everyone read mine when I was on an alien world. I still felt a little guilty. They were looking because they were worried. I tried to push it from my mind by reading about Jon's life. He was, as always, still amazed and in love with the fact that Humans made shit. His posts conveyed the sense of wonder he felt. I decided to try and make mine a little better.

I walked the base, checking and re-checking everything we had. I checked the reports from the other teams and checked on the city again. Everything was calm and as it should be. God, how I wished it would stay that way.

TWENTY

My CCPU pinged in my head, giving me a fifteen-minute warning. I left the housing unit and walked over to one of the transport pads. Today's op was like so many of the ones we'd been doing. We were in the process of gathering information for what I was sure would be an eventual mission into the Tooth tunnels. We needed to get as much information about the tunnels before we went in, though.

In a perfect world, we wouldn't have to blow anything up. That wasn't just the polite thing to do, but it would also help us gather the intelligence we needed.

The tunnel we would be looking at today was on the south side of the city. It was the closest we'd found to the edge of town, which made it a good candidate for getting the hell out if things went to shit.

I loaded up on the transport, standing in the center of a bunch of BIs. I instantly stopped paying attention to my surroundings. I brought up a map of the area and started going over Tooth troop movements. They were virtually unchanged from when they'd first made themselves known to us. They also ran like clockwork. In all fairness to the Tooth, the pattern of their routes wasn't easy for a person to figure out.

The ship's computer, on the other hand, had a knack for it. The Arbiter could give you a path to move along and a speed at which to do so where you could walk in the open without crossing paths with the Tooth. It was something that we used. Not that we would be dumb enough to wander around in the open, but that we could move without worry of being spotted. We had the least patrolled spots figured out and the best vantage points.

The exploration base was below the horizon now. The pad was moving quickly, keeping in the low spots between hills when it could. Eventually, the skyline came into view. As it did, I pulled my attention back to my surroundings.

"Two teams, Alpha is McLeod and I, Bravo is Betts and Clay," I said, with just a hint of boredom to my team. "We are five out," I said to the command channel.

"Roger that. Be advised that the Arbiter is dropping supply shuttles to fourth platoon. Orbital assets are forty-five out, as are the shuttles," Monroe said.

I relayed the information to my team. I checked with the Quiver to see if their ship was in fire support range. It was right above the city. The Arbiter and the Vinur had been doing a good job balancing coverage, as they both supplied ground units from orbit. I always had mixed feelings about having the Quiver ship as my cover. On the one hand, it had the ability to send a lot of firepower to the planet, but it felt slightly uncomfortable having to be covered by aliens. That, and I couldn't get assets on a target as fast as I could with the Arbiter.

We got off the pads in twos. Krista and I started to make our way into the city. We followed the directions our CCPUs gave us to a tee while still keeping every stealth protocol we had. Slipping into town wasn't hard. On the comms lines, the exploration crew chatted among themselves, noting everything we passed. For them, these trips had turned into a sit-in-the-common-space-and-watch type event as they analyzed everything around us. In a way, it was a little distracting, but not so much that I couldn't do my job well. They also understood that if the shit ever hit the fan, I would cut comms, and they would only be able to hear us but we would not hear them.

I crept along against a wall, trying to keep low and out of sight. More than that, I tried not to make any sound. The city was dead quiet, making sound our number one enemy.

I looked at my team's waypoints and the estimated time they would arrive at them.

"No sign of the Tooth. We are about fifteen out from being in position," I said to Clovis.

"We are on-site, sharing drone placement now," it said.

My CCPU pinged with new information. I overlaid it on my map of the area. The Quiver were keeping themselves back from the tunnel that we would be trying to get close to. Each had several control drones, along with a bunch of crabs.

The locations showed the Quiver and the CDs were hiding in any structure they could find. I suspected that they'd be hard to find inside. The Crabs were on walls and the ground, set up like turrets. The Darts were keeping to the lips of buildings.

I found a tucked-away spot to hide and started checking on the Tooth's movements. The exploration team seemed to quiet down as if their chatter on the comms would somehow alert the Tooth.

"We are in position," I said to Clovis.

"Roger, sending waypoints."

The map updated with each of the Quiver team's waypoints.

"Updating the map," I said to my team, "plot support paths. If things get out of hand, I want to be able to cover our retreat and theirs."

Krista and I were closest to Pampa, with Betts and Clay covering Clovis and Roswell. The tunnel they were investigating was shielded by some broken walls. The Quiver would need to send a Whisker high to get a view of it and then start trying to find a way inside if it was heavily guarded.

"Looks like three Tooth," Krista said.

"No way a Whisker gets too close to them," Sweeting noted.

"Agreed," I said. "They will either have to see if they can lure the Tooth away or hope they leave on their own."

"I don't think the chances of them leaving their post are high," Clay said.

She was right, of course. Every time we'd done something to make the Tooth react, they didn't leave tunnel entrances. It was inconvenient. Not that I blamed them; who is going to leave the entrance to their home unguarded when hostile aliens were attacking, right? But it was going to pose a problem for the Quiver and us. Our Whiskers were harder to spot, but not so hard that they could fly right by a Tooth without the Tooth figuring it out.

"Maybe a night op would be best," Betts said.

"The Tooth live underground. They do well in the dark," Krista said.

Betts sighed, "They do live underground, BUT we haven't seen anything to suggest that they have outstanding sight. Think about it. They use the turrets on their heads or backs, or whatever part of the body the exploration team is calling it. They use those to sense a lot around them. They might have shit for vision. The local grabbers have shit vision. Why would these be any different?"

Felipe chimed in, "Betts has a point. There is nothing to suggest that the Tooth have any outstanding night vision. Many species that live in dark places don't rely on visible light."

"Okay, right, but the turrets seem to do just fine finding things, plus the Tooth are out at night, right? Is that because they are at a disadvantage in the dark?" I countered.

"What if the turrets are primarily infrared?" Catherine said.

"Okay, that should be just as useful in the day. Why go out at night?" Clay asked.

"Give me a moment," Catherine said. "The Tooth are like the grabbers, right? So, they would be nocturnal, but they can still see during the day. Felipe, back me up here, the grabbers use scent and sound to hunt mostly."

"Yep, from what we can tell," he said.

They were trying to help, which was nice. And I thought I knew where they were going, but I was going to let it play out.

Catherine continued, "So you only need to get past the turrets at night. The Tooth's vision will be hindered."

"It might work," I allowed, "Our Whiskers don't put out dick as far as heat goes, but those turrets are going to still see them if they get too close. And at night, there's a lot more Tooth out and about."

"Yeah," Catherine said, dejected.

"It's all good," I said. "Today, it's the Quivers's turn to figure it out with their equipment. They are better at stealth than we are."

"Do you have any idea how you are going to get past the guard without pissing it off?" I asked Clovis.

"We are working on several strategies," it said.

"Right, so you have squat."

"If my translation of what you said is correct, yes, we have squat," Clovis said.

It was cool; we were in the same boat after all. In the distance, a Tooth came into my line of sight. I held still and had my display zoom in on it. The Tooth was lazily checking out a patch of grass. Its turret was swiveling around, pausing here and there. As was my habit now, I had my CCPU record everything it could. The Tooth huddled down for a moment and then went on its way. I pulled up the video from it and zoomed further in on the turret. I froze the frame. It was so odd to see the range of age on the pieces. Some of the parts looked like they were new, without tarnish, while others looked like they had been installed years ago.

It wasn't a design choice we'd realized. Every turret had different parts that showed signs of age. Catherine said that it spoke to the level of technology and the amount of technology the Tooth had or their relationship with it. The Human Federation had mastered rapid reclamation and manufacturing. Everything my team had was made the day before it was given to us. But it wasn't made cheaply or flimsy. Short though our gear's planned life was, it was built to last for years and years. Everything was kept in good condition in all parts of our society.

The Tooth might be lacking the tech needed to keep themselves in perfect condition. This would be something we would want to know, as it would influence our strategy. Likewise, if the Tooth just didn't care, that too would have an impact.

"We have an idea," Clovis said.

"What is it?" I asked.

"We do not think that we can sneak by the Tooth without a distraction. We have been trying to think of ways to sneak a Whisker into the tunnel on one of the Tooth, but that seems unlikely," it said. "We also would like to avoid killing the Tooth at the tunnel and going in, if possible. What we would like to do is disable the turrets on the Tooth at the tunnel. When they are down, we will have two Whiskers fly in the opening and find a hiding spot. The Tooth will surge in the area but will calm eventually. At that point, we can guide the Whiskers further into the complex."

"Roger that," I said. "What assistance do you need?" I asked.

"I thought you didn't want to get into a fight?" Charles said on the comm, not sounding happy.

"I don't. If we are in the right positions, the Tooth will head to the tunnel and pass us by," I said.

"And if you aren't in the right positions?" he asked.

I tried not to sigh, "Then we do our thing," I said, then to my team, "When the Quiver send us what they need and how they want to do it, prep to move to retreat positions. When the hornet's nest gets kicked, I want us to be able to support with drones but get out of the area."

My team acknowledged.

"We are going to rearrange crabs for the attack. There are three

Tooth; we will have three crabs with synchronized fire. We will not need backup. Would you like to send in Whiskers?" Clovis asked.

"Roger that, Clovis. I will keep my people out of the way. And I'd love to send in a Whisker. If this works, it will save us having to do the same exercise," I said. On the command line, I said, "We are going to send in a Whisker with the Quiver distraction. My team will be out of the way."

Monroe acknowledged.

I looked at the map and set new waypoints for my team. Clovis sent over their attack and exit vectors, and I took those into account. The map then updated with where the Quiver ship thought it might need to fire to cover possible retreats. I updated my team's retreat routes to avoid those areas. I sent Clovis my team's plans. The Quiver would wait until everyone was in position and the Tooth's patrols were in the best place.

"We are in position," Clovis said.

"We are too," I said back.

"Waiting for a window," it said.

"How are you guys holding up?" I asked the exploration team.

Maria laughed, "Based on how calm all of you sound, I would say we are not as good as your team. You aren't worried at all?"

That made me smile, "There is always a little apprehension, but this isn't that much different than when we were provoking the Tooth to see what they could do. The only real difference is that this time, we have an objective other than evasion and learning their tactics. The Quiver will strike, and everything will start moving quickly. Things will change. An exit plan, or maybe the initial attack. Something will not go how we want it to. We'll assess and change what we need to do."

"And if things go completely bad?" Andy asked.

"Well, to a big extent, that's out of our control. But we will do like we always do. We will assess and do our best, which is saying something. We'll control what we can and leave the rest up to the universe."

I snorted, "Don't have a choice on the last one. If you try and change what you can't control, you only fuck up the things you do have control of," I said.

"Yeah, well, I can still worry," Andy said, but I wasn't really paying attention.

"What's up?" Monroe asked me on our private line.

"When we try to control the uncontrollable, we mess up what we can control," I said.

"I know, you already said something to that effect. What has your emotions spiking? Though they seem to be settling into calm," he asked, concerned.

I was taken back to when Meyers bought it. I could see the world blowing up around me and saw him go down. Then back further to seeing the Venom surrounding us. We had no clue and couldn't have. A moment of pause on mine, Monroe's, or Royle's part would have meant that we all bought it. We controlled what we could.

I sighed, "It was just bad luck. But Andy is right too, and we can feel what we want."

"Taylor, come again," Monroe said.

"Sorry," I said, shaking myself, "Meyers. It was bad luck, shit luck really, but we did what we could and had we thought about how shitty our luck was, everyone would be dead. That was the best outcome, and I don't have to like it."

Monroe was silent for a moment, "It really was. You seemed worried, so I added Philips on the feed, but I'm not sure I needed to."

"I'm glad you did," Philips said. "Are you clear now, Corporal?" he asked me.

I fought the urge to nod, "I am, I think."

"Good, I believe you. This won't be the last time you have this conversation with yourself, but it is a start. Best of luck today," Philips said in a sign-off.

I looked at my waypoints for my people. They were all in the safest places they could be, but not in the optimal position. I looked at the proposed plans they'd sent when the Quiver told us what they were going to do. I'd changed all of them, and put each person in the spot I thought they'd be safest, not where they would be the most effective. That was fine to a large extent, but if I continued to micromanage when things got dynamic, that would cost time, and time cost lives.

I resigned myself to trusting my people.

Our window would take a while. All of the Tooth at the tunnel and in the area needed to be in the right position. Also, there needed not to be any patrols that were too close to the Quiver drones that would be firing. The Crabs were made to be expendable, but I didn't blame Clovis for not wanting to waste them. So we waited. And then waited some more.

The chit-chat from the exploration team told me it had been sufficiently long for them to forget their worries. The universe has perfect patience. For me and mine, our stress levels wouldn't be changing for the day. Until we were back in base, we were on. That meant that the universe would need to find other marks for its fun. As soon as the exploration team all laughed at a joke, Clovis spoke.

"We are going. Fire," it said.

In my feed of the tunnel, the Tooth jerked as their turrets were hit. Both sets of Whiskers darted for the tunnel and then for cover. As that happened, there was a flurry of radio bursts, as we'd expected. The map in my HUD became the chaos of moving hostiles.

"Contact," Krista said calmly.

"Roger that, sit tight," I said, looking at the map.

The exploration team seemed confused.

"We are retreating," Clovis said.

"The Quiver are pulling out, prep to leave," I said to my team.

"What's going on?" Andy said.

"We are in motion, is all. Everything is fine; this is the plan," I said.

Then there was an explosion. Damnit, why did I say things were fine?

The map lit up.

"Explosion by the Quiver," Clay said.

I set new waypoints for my team. "Fall back, fall back! Where did the explosion come from?"

There was another, and this time, the Quiver part of the map showed downed drones.

"They have set charges in the area," Roswell said.

"What is going on?" Maria demanded.

"Pampa, you have incoming," Betts said.

The map showed Pampa's position with lots of Tooth. The icons that represented Quiver drones showed that Crabs were engaging, as they did more Tooth diverted to the area. *Shit.* I cut the exploration team's incoming audio feed.

"Exploration's incoming feed is cut. They can only listen," I said to my team, "Clay and Betts, go north and attack Tooth lines; we need to pull pressure away from Pampa so it can retreat."

"Pampa, you have help on the way," I said to the Quiver team.

The map was getting more out of hand, but nothing by me yet.

"Might need EVAC," I said on the command line.

"Shuttle is away," Monroe said.

More explosions started to rock the area. A few buildings caved in. That answered a question about how the Tooth fought. They'd wired parts of the city. My CCPU pinged me. One of the Quiver CDs was reporting that it was under attack. I watched on the map as the Quiver lost CDs. As they went down, the Crabs started getting thinned out. There was another explosion in a different part of the city. I looked at that part of the map. Tooth were heading towards more Quiver drones.

"You seeing this?" I asked Sweeting and Krista.

"How are they finding them?" Sweeting asked, "The Quiver are all hiding in buildings."

There was an emergency ping from Maria.

"Everything alright?" I asked her, worried that I'd missed something.

"We are; you aren't! They are using sound," she said. "We've seen the Tooth lower themselves to the ground; they aren't trying to get cover. They are listening to the ground."

"Right, they make an explosion, which makes the drones seek cover, which makes sound. Then, as the Tooth go to the area, the CD has to move, which means it now makes more sound, which in turn attracts the Tooth to the CDs, which the Quiver strategy depends on, and so on and so on."

As soon as Clay and Betts started moving, Tooth in the area started heading in their direction. Krista and I were only safe because we hadn't moved yet, but that would change as more Tooth flooded in from different parts of the city. I directed the Heavies to leave their cover on the outskirts of town and start heading inward. I gave the order, and the mortars started opening fire. I had my CCPU plot a firing solution that would hopefully keep the Tooth on paths we wanted.

"Mortars will open up paths. Heavies inbound. Bravo team, keep moving. Don't let them overwhelm you. Once you have their attention, move to waypoint echo before heading to the extraction point," I said. "McLeod, we will start distracting on my mark and head to waypoint foxtrot before we move to extraction."

Bravo's drones showed that they were engaged. Clovis and Pampa were moving southeast, with Roswell giving them cover and moving back slowly. The Heavies had found the Tooth and were opening fire. The map was a mix of confused-looking icons as Tooth, HFDF, and Quiver units moved around.

I got a proximity warning that the Tooth were going to be crossing my path.

"McLeod, as they come into view, light them up and then move back once a group of them heads our way," I said.

I poked my head out, resting my SIR on some bricks. The Tooth would cross my line of fire. I set up three fire zones, with mine in the center and a BI on either side of me. I told the drones to hold until I gave the order to fire.

The Tooth scuttled into view, filling one drone's zone and then mine. As they started to enter the last drone's zone, I gave the order to fire. My SIR gently nudged my shoulder as I fired. My first burst hit one of the Tooth's turrets, sending it rolling with the force. Before the others could train on us, we took them out. The map updated, showing Tooth starting to head in our direction. Hopefully, they would be spread too thin to mount a threat.

I started to move out of the area. There were more explosions from the Tooth. Some in my area now, but they were localized to buildings. My CCPU pinged. Pampa had lost a CD. I didn't watch as the crabs and darts shifted to their new CDs orders. What I did watch was a pile of rubble blow in my path. A chunk of something slammed into me, knocking me on my ass. I rolled, moving for cover, my side going numb from what my CCPU thought was just going to be a bruise. But hey, kudos to me for not breaking more ribs, right? As I took cover, I did a check of drones. I hadn't lost any to the explosion.

The walls in the area sparked with the fire from Tooth. I sent up a Whisker to target them. There were two. I popped up and fired, hitting one. I ducked down, moved, and repeated, hitting the other in the leg. It flailed away.

I set up zones to give Krista and her drones cover as they moved through the area. As soon as I was done with that, Krista and her drones moved into my field of view, keeping down and away from enemy fire. The Tooth were backing off from us a bit, something that was doubly true for the Heavies, which were slowly working their way across town, dividing north from south. The Tooth's weapons sucked at range against the Heavies' armor, and getting close to Heavies tended to be bad for one's health. For their part, the Heavies were using primarily high-caliber armor-piercing rounds that were cutting through the walls of buildings. The Tooth had no cover or ability to move in the tight spaces they preferred. When they'd pop out of hiding to book it, the BBALLs supporting the Heavies had easy pickings.

I made a quick note of that and attached it to my performance report for later. I got up and moved quickly, keeping low and avoiding the Tooth. Bits of debris filled the air as they shot at me, but my CCPU told me that the rounds causing the debris wouldn't have pierced my suit. I told the BIs just to keep the Tooth at bay using covering fire, and not go for kill or injury shots. No reason to be bigger dicks than we already were.

As I took cover again, I looked at the map and did a double-take.

"Clovis, do you need assistance?" I asked.

There had been several more explosions since I'd engaged the Tooth. In some of those, the Quiver had lost more CDs.

"We are heading for extraction. A shuttle is on the way," Clovis said.

"The Quiver are taking some pretty heavy drone losses here; what do we think will happen?" I said on the command channel.

"We see that they have already started to lose combat effectiveness," Middleton said. "If they lose many more CDs, their side of the fight will collapse."

When that happened, the Quiver might take losses, but on top of that, there would be a flood of hostiles coming our way, and we weren't in a position to deal with half our front falling apart. I hunkered down, trying to come up with options. I could see that Middleton was right; the Quiver were losing a ton of crabs as they lost CDs. Most of the Quiver themselves were getting hindered and pinned down. I opened a line to the Vinur.

"This is Alpha Team requesting assistance," I said on the comms.

"Roger, Alpha, what do you need?" the Vinur replied.

"I need small kinetics in the areas I'm sending. Trying to get the enemy to take cover so all friendlies can get out," I said.

There was no response for a moment. "Roger, commencing bombardment."

"Kinetics inbound. As they hit, move like hell," I said to my team.

"Clovis," I said.

"I saw the order; good thinking. We will move when the rounds hit," it said.

I felt the rounds hit before I heard the sound of the atmosphere ripping. Then, there was dust north of my position.

"Go, go, go!" I ordered.

Bravo team started to move on the map quickly. Feeds showed the Tooth scrambling for cover like terrified animals. It looked like whoever made them didn't give them the same determination they had the Venom. Krista and I fell back as the Quiver did the same. Their formations had completely fallen apart, the remaining CDs and operators unable to handle all of the crabs and darts. I hated myself for thinking it, but I made a mental note of the weakness in case I ever needed it.

Not that we were unscathed. We'd lost a handful of BIs, but no Spheres or BBALLs, and the Tooth were avoiding the Heavies like their lives depended on it. Which, in fairness, their lives did depend on avoiding the Heavies.

"We are heading to the waypoint," I said on the comms.

Krista and I started to head toward the first point that would lead us out of the Tooth's main area so we could swing around to the shuttle. Clovis and Pampa were clear of the area, and Roswell was almost out.

The ground shook again, but not from our railgun shots. I crouched down as dust and debris filled the air. My helmet toggled over to a different view, and the dust disappeared, replaced with a mostly monochrome view of the world.

"Stay clear of the buildings," I told Krista.

We did so, working our way slowly through town, trying not to engage the Tooth, who didn't seem to want to get too close. There was the occasional shudder, and a building would go down.

"Roswell is down," Pampa said on a general comm.

I stopped Krista and me.

"Come again, Pampa," I said.

272

Clovis answered, clearly concerned, "Roswell was caught in an explosion. It's alive but pinned down. The crabs are unable to free it," Clovis said with forced calm.

I looked at the map. We were near its location. I did a quick check on supplies.

"Roger that, heading that way," I said on the general. "McLeod, head to waypoint X-ray, set a perimeter, and I will extract."

"Negative, Alpha, the area is too hot; it is too dangerous," Clovis said without any emotion in the transmission.

I looked at the map again. It was pretty hot. I stayed put for a moment, checking the map for everything in the area. I delegated control of the mortars and Heavies to Sweeting.

"Sweeting, keep them pinned down with the mortars and get the Heavies over there ASAP," I said.

"Positioning for covering fire; Heavies inbound," Sweeting replied.

"McLeod, proceed to X-ray," I said.

"Proceeding," she said.

I saw a series of emergency pings from the exploration team. I looked, and Clay was almost at the shuttle. I routed the message to her.

"Deal with them, please. If it's important, let me know," I told her.

"Clovis, we are proceeding. Please give me an EVAC waypoint," I said.

After a moment, a waypoint appeared on the map. Krista and I moved as quickly as we could to a heap of a building. I could see a leg popping out. Krista took her position and started firing on the Tooth, who were still keeping a distance from us. The sound of mortars filled the air. I disabled the feature in two of my BIs that made them act human. They started working on extracting Roswell as quickly as they could. I laid on some dirt and rubble with my SIR. Zones popped up in my field of view. I could see the Tooth in the distance. They would fire at us but were generally avoiding us.

I zoomed in on one and set my SIR to high velocity. I plinked the turret, sending the Tooth tumbling. Others scattered.

"They aren't behaving like they have in the past," Krista said.

"I think they are scared. They aren't the Venom," I said.

"I feel like an ass."

"I know."

Clay spoke, "All of the messages were just panic and questions about your sanity," she said.

"Thanks, Clay, what did you say?" I asked as I sent another Tooth rolling.

"That everything would be fine and that we know you're crazy," she said.

"Come on, Clay, you can't say that. Taylor had to do it! Saving hurt aliens is kind of our thing," Sweeting said.

I barked a laugh. "It's not a thing," I said.

"It's a thing," Betts said.

I was about to retort when the BIs finished digging out Roswell. It was pretty fucked up with several broken bones, and its suit had removed a leg that was under a support beam. The Heavies reached the area.

"Use the Heavies as cover," I told Krista.

I ran over to the unconscious Quiver and picked it up. The Tooth fled as the Heavies did their thing. I booked it for the Quiver transport. Crabs were all over the buildings in the area, keeping everything at bay. A medical drone met us, taking Roswell.

"What is your escape route?" Clovis asked.

I looked at the map. Dammit.

"South past the city and then around," I said.

"Get on; we are taking Roswell to the ship and then can take you to your base," Clovis said.

"Boss?" I asked Monroe.

"You're fine to leave with the Quiver. Each take two BIs. I will guide the others out of the city. Good work," he said.

I told Krista what we were doing and ran up to the shuttle.

TWENTY-ONE

The inside of the Quiver shuttle was dominated by open space with hand—or, I should say, foot—holds on the floors, walls, and ceiling. The med drone moved to the front as Krista and I gripped onto a couple of the holds, our BIs behind us. The Quiver packed around, leaving their drones outside as defense. My CCPU pinged me, letting me know that the Tooth's stance of keeping away from us had changed. They were converging on the area but still leaving the Heavies plenty of breathing room.

The shuttle's doors closed, and as the engines roared to life, a low hum vibrated through it. I ordered the Heavies to start leaving the area. The shuttle pitched, and for a moment, I was worried something was wrong. The nose flipped up, and I gripped my handholds tightly as the shuttle lifted into the air.

Behind me, Clovis moved, climbing up the shuttle with ease.

"Thank you for saving Roswell," it said.

"Of course, we weren't going to leave it behind," I said, instantly feeling bad. The Quiver were going to leave Roswell behind, and it was one of their own. Given that they didn't have a choice, there was no way that Pampa or Clovis could have gotten Roswell out. "We were in the area and had the drones; it wasn't an issue."

The shuttle pitched more, and the acceleration increased. I gripped tighter on the hold and felt myself begin to come off the wall. My boots' magnets activated, holding my feet against the wall. It wasn't a comfortable feeling. I noticed the Quiver all hugging the wall, little lines of nano-material extending from their bellies, connecting them. I tried to get closer to the wall and set my suit to be rigid. My body froze in place, but I was able to relax my muscles. After relaxing for a minute, I had the suit loosen some, so that I was mostly held fast. I had to work a little, but it was more comfortable.

I wanted to look around the Quiver shuttle, but I still had people to worry about. I pulled up the map of the city, seeing that Clay and Betts were on the shuttle and leaving. For their part, the Tooth were keeping to cover. I assumed that the orbital bombardment had shaken them.

"Do you think the race that used to live here had aircraft?" I asked Catherine.

"You cut the line after getting into a fight with aliens and then jump on an alien ship, and the first thing you ask is if a dead race had planes?" she asked, sounding perturbed.

"Ah, yeah. Do you think they did?" I asked again.

She sighed. "Not likely, and if they did, they were rudimentary. Why?"

"The Tooth don't like being bombed," I said conversationally.

"And there are people who do?" she asked testily.

"No, I guess not. But the Tooth do fine in ground fighting; it's something they have knowledge of, but they don't do well with orbital bombardment; it makes them turn into scared animals. Plus, I've never once seen anything they had take off. They don't have anything mechanized. So either they don't have that kind of equipment, or it's not in the area. If they had it, there's no way it wouldn't have been employed by now," I said.

I opened the line up to the rest of mine and the exploration team. I hoped that people would be calmer if they came in partway through a conversation.

Sweeting spoke, "They don't have the equipment, no way. We've been here for a while, and the Tooth haven't sent for reinforcements. We haven't seen any nonmilitary vehicles, either. They don't have them because they didn't need them."

"Why wouldn't they need them?" Charles asked.

"Because vehicles and aircraft either weren't necessary to defeat whatever race was here before, or because the Tooth didn't need those things for the race that made them to complete their objective," I said. "Which, honestly, I bet it's the latter. There are roads here, so the old race had to use vehicles regularly, but the Tooth didn't take any of that tech."

I felt the shuttle pitch again, more gently this time. We must have been reaching space. I compiled all of the data we'd gathered, along with my thoughts, and sent them to Tania. I left the comm line and opened one with Krista.

"You good?" I asked.

"I am," she said honestly. "I know today is a bad day for the Quiver, but I'm excited to go on a Quiver ship, even if we can't leave the shuttle."

I smiled. "That is kind of neat, isn't it? I'm going to check on Roswell."

"How is Roswell?" I asked Clovis.

"It will be fine. It sustained many broken bones and internal damage, plus the leg that needs to be grown back. We are keeping it unconscious for the time being," Clovis said. "I apologize, but in all this chaos, I haven't taken the time to look at how you and your team are doing. Did everyone make it out okay?"

"I have a few bruises, and so does Clay, but that's about it. We lost a few drones. My Heavies are moving out of the area, but the Tooth are not following. How is the rest of your team?" I asked.

"Shaken. We were going to have to leave one of our own to die. It's not something we experience often. I think Pampa may feel slightly ashamed. I do. My teammate was saved by another race that was willing to put themselves in harm's way when we weren't."

"That's not fair. We had more drones and were in a spot to help," I countered. It was a fair argument. My team wasn't struggling in the least bit in the engagement. We'd have had to come up with an excuse not to help.

"And had you been in a bad spot, would you have still helped?" Clovis asked.

I thought for a moment. I thought back to Pike Prime when we'd helped Pike flee on our last drop. We'd been willing to get hurt, and if I were being honest, we'd have been willing to die. There was no doubt in my mind that today wouldn't have been any different. "Yes," I said, almost in defeat, "we don't leave people behind."

Next to me, Clovis bobbed a bit, and my CCPU told me this was like a nod.

"We do," it said, "rarely, yes, but that is due to the fact that we take as little risk as possible. Our intelligence says that you will take more losses in a war than we would and that you would take much greater risks. But you also do not take your losses as hard as we do. Not that you do not care for your comrades, but that the HFDF can always say that it did everything it could to have saved someone. We always have the question left of what we could have done. Today we also saw that the HFDF is better prepared than we are when it came to this particular situation. This is something we knew; just as you know there would be situations where the tables would be turned and it would have been us saving you. But knowing that those situations exist and being in one are different."

"Sorry," was all I said.

"Do not be. You saved my teammate and friend," Clovis paused. "We are approaching the ship. Normally, you would not be allowed past the hangar unless you were unarmed and in clothing provided to you, as your suits, like ours, are weapons."

CHAPTER TWENTY-ONE

"Hold up clothing?" I interrupted.

"Yes. Our ships are in a state of null G, and magnetic boots and gloves make movement simpler for your kind. We could make these items, of course, but as you just saved one of our own, the commander has waived the rule. You may wear your suits without the weapons inside the ship. Your drones will be fine inside the hangar."

I sent a ping to Monroe asking if we could ditch the drones.

"I'll have to find out if we can ditch the drones. We might have to stay in the hangar," I said.

"I understand. We need that shuttle for the next few hours, so you would be in hard vacuum for periods. I know your suits can handle this without issue."

"They can," I said.

"You are good to leave your BIs; their safeguards are deactivated," Middleton said.

"Roger that, thank you, ma'am," I said.

It was an odd feeling being inside the shuttle. Normally, I could access any feed I wanted on a ship that I was in. Not in this one. All I could see was the dimly lit interior of the cargo area. Across from me, Krista was just looking ahead, like me, unable to see anything outside. I felt the ship start to slow, and Clovis told us we were about to dock. I shifted, waiting. The shuttle shook a bit, and then the door to the cargo bay opened. The Quiver med unit floated by, and then, one by one, the Quiver pushed off, floating out of the hold. Krista and I followed with our drones bringing up the rear. As I passed through the door, I put my foot down, the magnets in the boot turning on and latching me to the floor. Krista and my BIs did the same. We walked away from the shuttle, standing off to the side.

The inside of the hangar wasn't large; I reminded myself this was a destroyer, not a troop transport. The shuttle we'd come up on was the only one the ship had. The hangar had enough space for Quiver to move around and maybe do a little work on the shuttle, but it was otherwise small and simple. The walls, floor, and ceiling were flat metal, interrupted by seams for doors and storage. The hangar door was open to space. I looked out and saw Tooth Prime.

My CCPU received a message from the Quiver ship asking for an interface. I allowed it. Unlike integrating with something, the interface only allowed me a small portion of what I could do through a nonintuitive app. Like other interfaces, I could also see all of the security protocols and measures that were in place. I was notified that I could not access the wide array of information I was used to. Even though it was supposed to be all but impossible to hack a CCPU, the HFDF didn't take chances.

We followed the Quiver team to the far wall of the hangar. Clovis told us the BIs could stand in the corner to be out of the way and hold all of our gear. I handed them my SIR, pistol, and vambraces. Lastly, I handed them my pack. My suit was good for a while without the pack. It still felt strange. The door opened to an airlock, and we all got in. My head almost hit the ceiling, and I was reminded that I was on a ship for creatures much smaller than I was.

The airlock hissed, and my helmet informed me I was in a pressurized area with breathable air. The Quiver disengaged their helmets as the door to the inside of the ship opened. Krista and I did likewise, both trying not to hold our breath. On the other side of the door was a short hallway that was a hexagon. It connected to another passage that, like it, was also a hexagon. But I didn't need to worry about hitting my head. All the surfaces were covered in nano-material that was a silvery gray. Lights were scattered along the walls, bathing everything in light. I knew the Quiver evolved in dense trees with low light, and for some reason, I'd assumed the Quiver ship would be darker on the inside than it was. As it was, the passage was brighter than being inside an HFDF ship.

As we entered the larger passage, I could see up the length of the ship, or it appeared that way. The passage was wide, with the walls covered in circular handholds, just like the inside of the shuttle had been. The Quiver flowed up them, their four-toed feet grabbing with ease. Though I guessed 'flow' wasn't quite right. They glided from hold to hold, their movements graceful and smooth. The passage was wide enough for Quiver to be on the walls and floating down the center.

Other hexagonal passages connected to the one we were in. Clovis gave us a moment to orient ourselves.

"The commander would like to meet you," Clovis said.

"Do you need to tend to Roswell?" I asked.

Clovis's head was a deep purple like all the other Quiver around us. Its eyes were like large black stones set into its head. I could see the blowhole widen and contract as it breathed and spoke. My CCPU was keeping my ear from registering the sounds around me, but I could still see the hole move as Clovis spoke. I couldn't read a Quiver face, so I had no idea what expression it wore, but it said, "No, I am not a medic. Roswell will be fine. Now come." Clovis said and gently pushed off from the wall.

It floated down the center of the passage, its legs curled up under it. Krista and I followed, moving from hold to hold. Pampa brought up the rear, not floating but staying to the holds. We'd been in null G plenty of times; we had to train in it, but it wasn't natural for a human. People had learned to embrace it, with some preferring the lack of gravity, but that didn't change the fact that our bodies were made not just for gravity but also for spending the bulk of their time in a particular orientation. The Quiver's home world obviously had gravity, but they spent most of their time in the trees. Being upright for them didn't mean as much as it did for humans.

Clovis made it to another passage and waited for us to join it. I could almost feel Pampa wanting to guide us along. As Clovis floated, waiting for us, I saw its position change. Even though Clovis didn't move a body part, the Quiver would shift.

"My system tells me that your facial expression is one of confusion," Clovis said as we approached.

"How many space anchors do you have?" I asked.

"You don't know?" Clovis asked, then bobbed. "Right, your government is restricting your access, no automatic search. Our suits have five, though none of them are as strong as the one you have. Why?"

I felt like I'd solved a puzzle. "That's how you move in null G."

"That makes sense!" Krista said. "I got the handholds you all have, but I was wondering how you were moving so perfectly."

Pampa spoke for the first time. "We have one main anchor at the center of our mass and four others. I know the term we use is translated to anchor in your language, but it's not appropriate. Ours are extremely efficient and smaller. We can use them to stop from falling, yes, but more often, we use them to adjust position in space. They are not anchors as much as thrusters. We just need short bursts of power."

Pampa separated from the wall, setting itself rotating. It slowed and then rotated a different way without moving anything. It stopped moving and floated.

"How's it work planetside?" I asked.

The Quiver's back legs were powerful, and they were known for being able to jump great distances without the aid of a suit. Some of the information I'd read about the Quiver popped back into my mind. Our anchors were larger than theirs for a few reasons. One was that we only had one of them, so it had to do all the work that theirs did. Ours were also less efficient but leaned on stopping things. It took a toll if we used an anchor to jump. I remembered that the Quivers were a lot like what kept the BBALLs and Whiskers in the air. I hadn't given it thought before now.

"They allow us many more options when moving. We can jump and avoid an object or change trajectory, or orientation for that matter," Pampa explained.

I could picture that. Being in a forest-type setting with the Quiver having a full range of movement while my team and I were stuck on the forest floor or trying to climb objects. It wouldn't go well. But I could also see where the Quiver would struggle in flatlands or even more in urban environments. There was a reason the Tooth were easy for us, but not for the Quiver.

As we moved through the ship, Quiver floated past us. I noticed they didn't all have the same types of suits. There were some similarities. They were all made of nano-material, but they had different thicknesses and colors. Clovis told me that there wasn't a standard issue suit that all wore like the HFDF. It also said that the suits were the common clothing for the Quiver.

They floated through the ship as if they were born in null G. Some held whitish chunks of food up to their mouths as they went by. I tried not to look around too much like I was some kid who was at an amusement park for the first time. When I glanced at Krista, she wasn't trying to hide her fascination at all. She was looking around wide-eyed at everything we passed, an open smile on her face. Seeing her that happy made me smile.

Quiver would pass by us in the passages, none moving as if they were irritated with the slow apes bumbling around. But I also had no clue what irritation on a Quiver would look like.

"I'm sorry we are so slow," I said to Clovis, "I hope we aren't bothering your crew too much."

"Not irritated. Many are interested to see humans, and all of us feel grateful that you saved Roswell. We also know that humans aren't suited for null G. Your anatomy is all wrong for it," Clovis replied.

We'd come to a split in the passage with a door on it. Clovis turned to us. "This is the ship's bridge. I know that you will try to be formal and professional, but I would ask that you not use the magnets on your boots on the bridge."

I nodded, reminded that we were acting as ambassadors for the Human Federation. Next to me, Krista's face was serious and focused. The door opened, and we followed Clovis. The request to not stick to any surface was made clear instantly.

For humans in the old days, a ship's bridge was full of different equipment with crew manning stations. CCPUs and VR Pods changed that. The bridge on the Arbiter was a plain rectangular room with nothing on the walls. From the floor and ceiling, VR Pods were arranged like the petals of flowers around base stations. Each Pod had room and gimbals on it in case the ship moved in a way that the graviton system could not dampen. Further, each base station had the ability to produce quick gravity fields to keep occupants safe. The ship could be getting the holy hell beaten out of it, and the people in the pods would not be jostled.

The Vinur's bridge was a sphere with mushroom-shaped pods connected to every wall. The central space in the room was only big enough for a few Quiver. From briefings, I knew the pods were VR pods. Had one of us activated our boots, we'd have been standing on top of someone's pod or possibly on top of an occupied pod. I could see where Clovis did not want us to do that. In the center of the room was a Quiver floating, looking at us. My CCPU said that it was named Vail. Vail was the commander of the Vinur. I attempted to stay upright and saluted the creature. I kind of managed it, but not very well. It's sad to say that I felt semi-happy to see that Krista had issues with hers. It was better to be unified morons than to be alone.

"Thank you for saving Roswell," Vail said.

"You are welcome," I said, trying not to repeat my mistake from earlier.

"I know you see it as just doing your job, but to the Quiver, you have done much more than that. I wanted to bring you here to talk to you for that reason. I want to impress upon you the service you have done." It waved a hand slowly. "One of the things that our races have in common is how we value the lives of our own kind. We both put high value on the individual. We are slow to sacrifice our own. We are also ageless, which compounds this. We further the compounding by continuing to breed much longer than nature planned. Do you know the impact this has had on your society?"

"A bit," I said. "Now that all generations continue to breed, the oldest of us are still invested in the youngest. The older generations control our society, but by having young, they are invested in us. Our lives are not something to be wasted. Understanding the loss and suffering of loved ones is what shapes many of our values and laws. Sorrow does not age," I explained.

Vail was silent for a moment. "This is something that you seem to feel strongly about."

"My parents are first generation," I admitted, slightly embarrassed, then added, "They have hammered that into me my whole life." I sighed and looked away for a moment. "And I have started to learn those lessons for myself. I have lost people under my command. That experience has made death… a much more real thing for me."

"Ah, and now you see the seeds of our gratitude. Our kind has been ageless much longer than yours. The sorrow you speak of is strong within us. Not overwhelming, but it is there.

"But even before we were ageless, we placed a much stronger value on the individual than your kind. I do not mean this as a slight but as a fact. We have not had an internal war in thousands of years. Our society is structured differently than yours. Not better or worse, just different. Even our interpersonal relationships."

Vail looked at each of us in turn. "You are mates, correct?"

I was a little taken aback that it knew anything about my team on a personal level.

"Yes, we are," Krista said.

"You generally pair off. You breed in that pair and raise offspring. We do not. Our family groups are made up of five. It takes three of us to mate. We do this with two other family groups. Each group comes away with a child born of all three. In that way, those families are connected, and that connection spreads with each generation."

"I don't think we could do that," Krista said.

"Of course, you couldn't. For you, the act of reproduction comes with not only physical pleasure but heavy emotional impacts. Only one of you can carry a child, and only one of you fertilizes. For us, we all have all three sexes but cannot breed with ourselves or just one other Quiver. But for us, reproduction does not feel good or bad; it just is. There are no emotions connected to the act. Our connections with others extend to more than one other Quiver.

"For countless generations, we have lived like this. My neighbor is raising my offspring. My offspring has a sibling with my other neighbor. If I hurt another, I hurt my own family. When one of our own is hurt or dies…"

"They are family," Krista said, understanding.

"Yes," Vail confirmed.

In that moment, I began to understand the Quiver: how they viewed the universe, how they operated, and their aversion to risk. I also saw their commitment to relationships with other races. They weren't going to risk anything. And I started to understand what we'd done. By having to leave Roswell, they were abandoning a member of their family—a family member that we had risked ourselves to save.

I suspected that the Quiver felt the way about us as I would if the tables were changed and it was Krista or Charles instead of Roswell.

"We won't hesitate to do it again," I said honestly.

"We know that. And we love you for it. Now, on to business. Our shuttle is busy for a few hours. You are a guest on this ship. I apologize that we do not have any food that you would find appealing. But if we can provide anything, we will try."

"Thank you, and we don't need anything. We might need to grab some nutrient packs from our drones if we get peckish," I said.

The Quiver put Krista and me in a small room to wait for the shuttle. We'd hoped to see the ship but hadn't really expected to and hadn't asked. As it was, we were two of only a handful of humans who'd been on a Quiver warship, let alone past the dock. It was an uncomfortable sensation not having access to everything my CCPU could offer. Thankfully, we still had comms. I opened one to Maria back at the base.

"Sorry for the delay in getting back to you," I said.

"It's not your fault, but I'm not happy." She sighed. "The order came down to begin disassembly of the base. We will leave in a few days."

"I kind of thought it was going to go that way. Sorry you have to leave. Those Heavies will be back to the base soon; Betts tells me they are a little dinged up, but my team will get them fixed. Your people will have plenty of cover until you leave," I assured her.

"We should leave. We should have left as soon as the Tooth were discovered. I get why we didn't, but we don't belong here." She paused. "How are you doing?" she asked, sounding concerned.

I smiled. "Still not a shitty day," I said honestly. "None of my people were hurt. Well, maybe a few bruises. We didn't lose a lot of drones, and we accomplished our mission. Now, the Quiver? They had a shitty day. Clovis told me that their bases are leaving the surface, and in the meantime, there will be no missions outside of those bases. We'll be the only ones in the field until the Quiver figure out how they want to crack this nut."

"Wait, your team isn't leaving after us?" she asked.

"Well, yeah, I mean eventually, but we don't have orders to EVAC. Unless I'm mistaken, we will need follow-up missions once we look at what the Whiskers are gathering. The Arbiter has supplies for months. We could be here for some time," I said.

"That's bullshit!" she said. "It's not safe."

"That's our job," I countered.

"Also bullshit," she said coldly.

I thought for a moment. "Look. I don't want to stay on this planet any more than you do. Well, you might want to be here less than I do. But I don't want myself or my people to be hurt. That said, it is our job, and we are good at it. We have a clear advantage over the Tooth. But even if we didn't, we would still be here." I thought for a moment, "You've seen data on the war with the Venom. I know you have also looked at many of my team's logs. The Venom are planet killers, plain and simple. Someone made them, and that same group could have others out there, maybe even ones that are worse. Whoever made the

Tooth and the Venom killed this world too. Probably others. We need information."

"Why? So we can go kill whoever made the Tooth?" she asked, sounding a little defeated.

"Yes," I said. "Yes, so we can kill them. And so we can find whatever else they made. We stop this now, and it will save billions of lives, and who knows how much suffering. So my team will stay on this planet as long as the HFDF tells us to, and we'll do it without complaint."

TWENTY-TWO

Life is all about discovering new things about yourself. I was discovering that I didn't like entering a planet's atmosphere in an alien ship. Normally, entry wasn't really that fun. Not so much frightening as uncomfortable. Or so I'd thought. It turned out that my CCPU had been controlling my sense of unease this whole time. It wasn't directly messing with my emotions, but I was always fully integrated with whatever I was on, so my CCPU just answered questions as they popped up. A typical me-to-CCPU conversation might go like this:

> Me: What's that sound?

> CCPU: Just the shuttle heating up from friction.

> Me: I'm not gonna die, right?

> CCPU: Nope, you're totally fine.

However, my CCPU wasn't fully integrated with the Quiver shuttle. So the conversation was more like this:

Me: What's that sound?

CCPU: How the hell should I know?

Me: Am I gonna die?

CCPU: Digital shrug. Maybe?

Okay, it wasn't really like that, but it kind of felt that way at the moment. The shuttle was decelerating hard, and I could hear the roar of air against the hull. My back was to the floor of the shuttle, and my whole body was being pressed hard against the floor. It made me feel for people in early spaceflight. When those astronauts came back home, they had to deal with this. And, like me, they had no control over it. All they had was the knowledge that if the heat shield gave out, they were screwed. In all fairness, the ship I was on had a lot more control than those early spacecraft.

The deceleration eased, and the flight smoothed out.

"How are you holding up?" Clovis asked.

"Fine. I like entry a lot more when I have a full connection to the ship. This is worse than normal, I won't lie," I said.

"I'd have thought jumping onto a planet from a ship like your team normally does would be worse."

"Yeah, I don't have a good answer for that. I'm not sure why it feels worse on a ship," I said.

Our descent got smoother as the shuttle slowed down. We'd come down far away from the city, with the Quiver keeping close to the ground as they approached the base. Krista and I got off the shuttle, followed by our BIs. It was late at night, but the base was bustling as the exploration team's drones worked, taking structures apart. The exploration ships themselves stood tall and silent. As I walked, I pulled up reports from the base defenses and anything I'd missed while on the Quiver's ship. I could see that my team had positioned themselves out in the field behind the towers closest to the city.

"Report?" I asked them.

CHAPTER TWENTY-TWO

"All clear," Betts said. "I'm sure Guzman will want to talk to you."

"I figured," I said as Maria Guzman emerged from a building and walked quickly toward me.

Krista jogged off to resupply and join the team. I walked toward Guzman. In the dark, it was hard to read her expression.

"Good evening," I said.

I could hope that she was in a good mood, right? She'd sounded uncharacteristically calm when we'd talked while I was on the Quiver ship. I wondered if that had just been controlled anger.

"You cut off our comms," she stated flatly.

Yep, it had been controlled anger.

"Sorry, Maria, I had to. I couldn't have my team distracted," I said.

"You know you have been wrong time and time again on this whole thing," she said. "You keep telling us that you guys have things under control and that everything is fine, but a Quiver almost died today, Corporal! Would have died if you and your girlfriend hadn't risked your necks for it."

My gut reaction was to get pissed, but I tried to fight the urge. Maria was scared. And she had every reason to be. She had no control over the situation and was responsible for her team. In my head, a thousand reasons why we had things under control went through my mind, along with other reasons for why Roswell was injured.

"I'm sorry, Maria. You're right; this isn't how we saw this op going at all. Today, things went sideways, and we had to adapt to that situation. And while I wish I could say that you are wrong about the risks we take, I won't. We do take risks. Sometimes, they pan out, and sometimes, they don't. One thing I'll promise you, though, is that we don't take those risks lightly and not without thinking."

"So, are you worried about the base getting attacked?" she asked.

"Honestly, I am a little. That's why my team is in the field," I said.

"So we can run and leave you all here." It was a statement.

"If that's what needs to happen, yes. That's our job. If it's needed, you will have to leave us," I said calmly.

She shook her head, pissed. "No, that's not how this works. This isn't you, and yours risk your lives and die. I know you're legally adults, but you're still kids. This isn't right."

"So we just leave?" I asked.

"Yes, Alex, we all just leave! No one has to die here."

"Where do they die then?" I asked.

"What? Nowhere. Why would you think that?"

"Because that's what happens. Normally, you'd be right. We'd pack up and leave; as your ships took off, we'd be loading birds to head out. But this isn't normal. We have to figure out who did this. We can't afford too many more Venoms. Believe me on that. It took a lot of resources and lives to take them down, and they still aren't wiped out yet. I've seen what's coming if we stand by," I said.

The whole exploration team had seen some of the action my team had been in on Pike Prime. I sent Maria footage from the last fight I'd been in. The one in the city where the Pike had been caught off guard along with my first day there, seeing the lines of Pike fleeing their homes. Showed them dying on the side of the road. I watched her expression fall as she watched.

"That's where this goes," I said.

She looked at me and sighed, her expression a little dejected. "There just doesn't seem to be a good option," she finally said. "The team is still up. I know they are up to date, but you should talk to them."

"Fair enough," I said.

I followed her to the common room. The kitchen and most of the furniture had been disassembled. The exploration team was milling around the vid wall, looking at orbital images of the planet. Charles and Catherine were quietly talking off to the side. Andy noticed me first.

"How was the Quiver ship?" he asked, catching me a bit off guard.

"It was good. Interesting, to say the least."

"Andy has decided that he isn't going to worry about you anymore," Catherine said acidly.

"I didn't say that I wasn't going to worry, just that I have been wrong not to completely accept that our HFDF friends are more than capable of doing their jobs," he said in a tone that said this was not the first time the subject had come up.

"Am I missing something?" I asked.

"The Quiver are pretty good at what they do, aren't they?" Andy asked.

"Yes," I said and then headed off what was going to come next, "but this is not the ideal conditions for how they work."

"But it's ours?" Andy asked.

I shrugged. "It's more like fighting on Earth than Quiver Prime. You could say we have an evolutionary advantage. Plus, our style is to be much more involved with combat than the Quiver. Our ground forces are more capable."

Andy looked satisfied. "And you saved them. And we didn't have anyone get hurt or lose a bunch of drones?"

"No," I said, "maybe a bruise or two."

He pointed at me triumphantly, "They are badasses! They are good at what they do. We were told that these people were elite, and they are. They have risked their safety for us. They have all bled for the Human Federation. We haven't. What I saw today and the footage I've finally taken the time to watch have convinced me that I have been out of line, not taking them at their word. If Corporal Taylor says they will be fine, they will be. They've earned that, I think."

"I'm not saying that they don't..." Catherine paused and almost seemed to growl.

"Thank you," I said.

"Betts said you guys aren't leaving," Charles said, concerned and changing the subject.

"We are not. Still got some work to do," I said. "But your part of this mission is wrapping up. That's a good thing."

My CCPU pinged me. I'd given Tania Koffski control of the Whisker we'd dropped in the Tooth hole the moment I could. I was insanely curious about what was down the hole, but at the time, I had been a lot more interested in not dying.

I pulled up a comm line with her. "Yes, ma'am?"

"I'm sending you and the exploration crew footage. Please review it and give me your thoughts. Congrats on your visit with the Quiver. Their ambassador has already reached out to us. You and Private McLeod made good impressions, as did the rest of your team."

"Thank you, and we will look at it," I said, then to my team, "Bring it in. We have data from the Whisker to look at."

I looked at the expectant exploration team. "Want to review data on the Tooth's tunnels?"

They perked up a bit. It was obvious that everyone was tired from a long and tense day, but no one was going to turn down the chance to look at an alien's home. We waited as my team filed in, everyone standing around the vid wall.

When the Whisker zipped into the tunnel, it had found a nice place to hide and lay low until the Tooth had calmed down. Koffski had waited several hours before deciding that the Whisker wasn't going to be spotted. Data flashed as the feed came up, showing the Whisker's status.

"It's only been out of hibernation for two hours," Betts commented.

"Why was it hibernating?" Catherine asked.

"They're harder to find. In that mode, it just waits for a wake-up command. It won't record any data, and its color scheme is the same as when it went into hibernation. It would have been almost impossible for the Tooth to find if it were in a tight place unless they knew it was there. The downside is that it could be destroyed, and we wouldn't know about it," Betts said.

"I'm sure she wasn't happy to do that, but it was a good call," Clay mused.

The feed was just black as the Whisker came online. Then, it started to scan the area, looking for radio waves. It found lots, but nothing close to it. I found myself tense. I knew for a fact that the Whisker was currently online, and losing them wasn't a big deal, but I felt worried somehow.

It started doing other scans. The screen split, showing a map as it was made. The Whisker passed data up to the ship, which was trying to use its single point of data collection to build the underground environment.

TWENTY-THREE

I watched as the exploration ships slowly lifted from the ground. As they rose, they moved away from each other and from the base. A few hundred meters off the ground, the engines on the upper parts of the ships began to fire, allowing them to use more than just the anchors to ascend. They moved faster in the air, my helmet having to magnify them by the time the covers on the main engines opened and the mains fired up.

I kept watching their progress until I received notification that the ships were in orbit. Over the next few days, they would meet up and secure all of the cargo that was already above Tooth Prime.

"Alright, the team is in orbit. We have one week to finish this," I told my team.

A week was the timeline to grab some Tooth, get them to a shuttle, clean up our base, and get off-world. For all the waiting and watching that had been this deployment, it felt good to have a timeline that didn't end with "TBD." We weren't going to be doing it all on our own, thankfully. Intel was working on a way to capture a Tooth and hold it so we could deliver samples back to them. Bravo team would be joining us for backup, and the rest of the platoon would take care of the base.

It was a lot of assets to have on the ground, but it made me feel better. We'd killed the Tooth before and otherwise harassed them, but we'd never taken bodies or tech. Now we'd be doing both, which had a lot of shit hit the fan potential.

As soon as the exploration ships were out of sight, I walked to the housing unit for my last meal. There was no point in dropping housing units for the whole platoon for a few days, nor did it make sense for my team to stay in the housing unit while everyone else slept in holes in the ground. After lunch, a shuttle from the Arbiter would be depositing Bravo team and picking up the housing unit. We'd keep the shop and add transport pads.

With the exploration ships gone, the feel of the base had shifted. In one way, it felt calmer, as we didn't have any non-military types to protect, but it also felt more real. It was like we'd been guests at someone else's house, and now we were home. Things were different, even down to the way we sat around the table eating lunch.

When Bravo team arrived, I trotted up to Royle and her team. "Good to see you," I said as I approached them.

Her helmet slid off her face. "Tell me about it. Shit, it feels like we've been half a team this whole time."

When she put it that way, I could sense it. Part of the feeling of coming home was Bravo team. We worked together more often than not. Being away from them did feel odd.

She ordered her people to leave their gear near the shop, leaving her and me alone to walk the base.

"Tour?" I asked.

She nodded.

She knew every piece of equipment we had in place, its condition, and history, but she still walked around with me. She and I had done this in every camp we'd ever set that the other one joined and every base our teams had been at. It was a habit that I doubted either one of us would ever be able to break.

"How do you think this is going to go down?" she asked. "My people are green when it comes to the Tooth. We scouted a few abandoned tunnels, but there was no combat or even sightings."

I thought for a moment. "It could go either way. They have surprised us on a few occasions, but it hasn't ever been anything that we couldn't handle or that pushed us."

"The Quiver can't say that," she said.

I shook my head. "Didn't see that coming. Neither did they, I guess."

"It's good to know that we really are on more even ground than I ever thought. Growing up, I thought that they could wipe the floor with us whenever they wanted," she said.

I'd had a similar view. "I told Clovis that once. That I always thought that the Quiver could kick our asses. The funny thing is, it told me it felt the same about us. That said, their navy isn't anything to fuck with," I said.

"Or ground armies in forests." She stopped and looked around at the fields surrounding the base. "You know this is going to go to hell, right? Not this planet. This place has already gone to shit, but when it hits the fan with whoever did this," she said, gesturing around her, "fuck, these sons of bitches have now killed entire worlds without having to pull the trigger themselves."

"They better hope they can hold their own when we find them," I said.

She nodded. "Yeah, it won't matter, I guess. The HF and the Allies are going to erase them from the history books."

"I suppose we will," I said, then changed the topic. "Getting close to the Tooth isn't going to be the problem. It's going to be keeping every one of them in the city from coming down on us."

"Retz thought we could use the Whiskers to ping the area with radio bursts. Maybe confuse them and buy us some time to snatch some samples and get out," she said.

"That could work. I think it could keep some of them off us if they think there are attacks coming from multiple angles," I sighed. "On that front, we could have drones pick fights in other parts of town. The Quiver could distract as well."

"Are they willing to do that?" she asked.

"They will. They want the data from a sample almost as bad as we do," I said.

"But they aren't going to collect their own?"

"Nope. Not right now. They aren't as interested in the biological data as we are. Clovis said their Whisker has gotten most of what their government wants. Honestly, I think they would snag a sample if we weren't here. As is, I don't think they want to risk another joint mission, or at least not without more boots on the ground."

"That's fair, I suppose," she said.

The rest of the platoon dropped in far away from the city and hoofed it to our location. They seemed kind of happy about it. I suppose being stuck on the ship had made them restless. Monroe and Middleton were also on the ground. They had a meeting with Royle and me in the shop. I wasn't all that surprised to see Koffski with them. If I had to put money on it, Koffski wanted to meet with Royle and me, and Monroe and the lieutenant wanted to watch over it.

Royle and I snapped salutes as we entered. We greeted Monroe and Middleton with both seeming genuinely pleased to be there.

"Good evening," Koffski said to us.

"We have been working on a plan, but I assume that's going to change?" Royle said.

Koffski's lips twitched with the hint of a smile. "Not that much. How you get to the Tooth and get away is in your court. I'm just here with the toys," she said.

My CCPU pinged with new data.

"We have units that are coming down shortly," she explained.

"Catch at least two of the Tooth along with working tech and place them in the provided containers. Shuttles will take the Tooth. The shuttles will move in the opposite direction from where the base is in case the Tooth have some way of tracking their troops."

I looked at what was sent and tried not to shrug. It always amazed me how low-tech, high-tech things could be. The containers were pretty much boxes that would theoretically keep the Tooth out cold and then nets to capture them with.

"Nets, huh?" I said without being able to help myself.

"They are a bit more than that. They will keep the Tooth contained while you move them and constrict around the turrets," she explained, then added, "But yeah, mostly just nets. If you kill a Tooth without damaging the turret, that will work for the technology sample we require."

"That could make it easier," I said. "I'd rather not kill one of them just to make my life better, but that could be the best option."

"That was our thought," Monroe said. "On the living samples, take out the turrets and then take a turret from a dead Tooth."

"We will have to kill some. They move in groups of three to five more often than not. I doubt we would get the drop on five of them without killing some or losing a ton of drones," I said, thinking to myself.

"When are you planning to move?" Koffski asked.

"Tomorrow works for me," I said. "Royle?"

She shrugged. "Let's get it done."

Koffski looked a little surprised, and I caught a glimpse of smugness on Middleton's face. Monroe, for his part, smirked.

"Take away your little hotel, and you get stuff done, huh?" he said.

I stretched. "I have become accustomed to a certain lifestyle."

He chuckled. "I'm sure. After you take the Tooth, hold up here. We will wait to make sure the intel team has what they need before we dust off."

"We will know shortly after the samples are back on the Arbiter," Koffski said.

"Third and fourth squads will be your backup in the field," Middleton said. "They will keep well out of your way, but if things go sideways, they will cover your retreat. Unless you think you will need closer support."

"Thank you, but we should be good. We know the Tooth and their movements. I don't want to throw a new element into the mix. The Quiver team will be on the other side of town if we need a distraction. The Tooth seem to be extremely reactive. We've used minor threats to move them around before. We'll get it done."

Koffski, Monroe, and Middleton left a few hours later on Koffski's shuttle. It was starting to get dark, and I walked over to the area around the stacks of supplies that my team had claimed. Betts and Retz were sitting around a crate with cards that had been fashioned from nano-material.

"Our digs took a hit, boss," he said as I approached.

"Seriously. At least we will only be roughing it for a bit," I said.

"I'll take it," a girl from third squad said. "We've been stuck on the ship for weeks."

"What did they have you guys doing before?" I asked, feeling a little bad that I hadn't looked at what the rest of the platoon had been up to.

"Exploring," she said. "Nothing around any towns or cities. We were setting up and maintaining drones for the exploration teams that were too far for them to go out to. It was nice."

"Busy?" Betts asked.

She snorted. "Shit, no. Don't get me wrong, we had a full day planned every day, but it was checking drones out in the wilderness. I've spent my time planetside hiking. Once you get past how creepy the lack of animal life is here, this place is pretty. But once you lot found the Tooth, we were back ship side in case we were needed for support."

"Which we didn't need," Retz said with a smile.

"Of course, you didn't," she said sardonically.

I wondered if every Service Term ship had the dynamics we did between special teams and regular Spaceborne. I suspected they did. The Spaceborne troops were in a different spot. Most of the troops on the ship were infantry, which Spaceborne thought they were better than, because, well, we were. But then you had special teams, which were really only in the platoon in name. The regular Spaceborne personnel got a little twitchy around us. We had almost no interaction with the regular infantry troops, but when we did, they treated us more like career troops than equals.

I tried not to get into the politics of it.

I looked at the map of the area. The STDs were coming down, and the other troops had taken up positions around the perimeter. While I was looking forward to not having to care for the perimeter, I tried not to get miffed they had a few less-than-ideal positions. Whatever, I was not going to cause issues. In the end, it was unlikely the Tooth would attack us, and if they did, there was more than enough HFDF here to probably clear out the city.

What I did was check on the map of the city and overlay Tooth patrol routes. Someone tapped my shoulder. I looked over at Betts, Retz, and the girl from the other squad, who'd been joined by others.

"Sorry, checking on the city. What's up?" I asked.

"They just want to know what it's like fighting the Tooth," Betts said. "I gave them my take on it."

I nodded. Reports with video and stats were great; they were really all you needed to learn about an enemy, but emotionally, everyone wanted to talk to someone who'd been in the thick of it, no matter how much better a report was.

"They are pretty quick, but not fast. They zip in and out of tight places, but if you were in the open, you could outrun one at a light jog. The turrets built into them are effective at close range but lose power fast. I don't think they were meant to take out armored personnel.

They move in groups; when you attack one, every Tooth in the area swarms you. That's what you have to watch for. If you get too many of them, you'll be in trouble. Also, avoid buildings. They like to blow them up," I said.

The others seemed satisfied that my account lined up with the reports they'd seen. I went back to looking at the map. I had my target. The Tooth had one patrol that was consistently in the same spot, and it consistently had a group of five Tooth. I shared the info with Royle.

"So we hit at the right time, and they will have a hard time getting backup there fast," she said. "I'll come up with a plan for diverting the Tooth around them."

"Thanks. I think if we hit them at the same time, it will keep my group of Tooth exposed longer for us to grab a few of them."

"How do you think that is going to go?" she asked.

"I'm not sure. Right now, my plan is to kill three of the Tooth and disable the turrets on two of them. I'll take the two living and unarmed Tooth as samples and the turrets from the dead ones. It should take maybe five. We can do it tomorrow afternoon," I said.

I notified all the appropriate parties that we would be going into town tomorrow. The ship said that shuttles would be on-site at whatever pickup point I designated. From there, we would head back to base and wait for Koffski to confirm that we had what we needed. I was within two days of being off Tooth Prime for good. Not that it had been a bad planet to be on, but once we'd become the proverbial bad guys, I had been looking forward to leaving.

Later that night, I lay near some crates and looked up at the sky. My CCPU pinged.

"Hey man, how's orbit?" I asked Charles.

"Fine. Just getting everything prepped for when we leave the system," he said.

"Is that a pain in the ass?"

"Nah, it's fine. All the cargo pods connect to the outside of the exploration ships. It just takes a while. How's the ground? Are you happy all of your other buddies are there?"

"I'm happy that the rest of my squad is here. It's been strange not working closely with them. The rest of the platoon is here, so at least I don't have to watch the perimeter anymore. They've been cooped up on the ship for a while and are all too happy to be planetside, even if it's just guard duty for a few days," I said.

"So you think you'll be done soon?" he asked.

"Yeah. Tomorrow, we will try to grab the Tooth, and if that goes well, then by the next morning, we will be heading out. I'm not sure where we will go after this, though. The Arbiter was slated to be here for six months; there's no point in keeping us in orbit after this is done," I said.

"Maybe training exercises?" he asked.

I shrugged, which he couldn't see since he wasn't even on the planet. "We'll be planetside, would be my guess. Maybe on Arrow or, if we are lucky, Orion. How about you?"

"Orion. We still have a lot of data to sift through about the planet, as well as a few probes in orbit. My timeline won't really change, just the place I'm working from," he said.

"That's nice. Do you think you will stay with this team?" I asked.
"Is that an option?"

"I won't. After my Service Term, I could apply to be on it if it's still around. Maria's team has been pretty transient as far as these things go. Planetside teams can be like that. People are rotating in and out. The crews tend to be customized for the planet they're going to. Catherine, Andy, and Shashi have been working together for a while. But I think Catherine wants to get out of the field for a bit. Nothing to do with this assignment, just that she's been in the field for a while," he said.

When we were done talking, I checked on the Tooth one more time before falling asleep. When I woke, the sky was cloudy and the ground a little damp. If there was a benefit to sleeping in the open with our suits, it was that you didn't notice getting rained on in your sleep.

"We are supposed to get more rain today. Is that going to be a problem?" the squad leader from second squad asked.

"We'll be fine. Unless the weather is horrible, the Tooth won't alter their patrols. But if it gets too muddy, that will slow them down," I said.

Our squad ate breakfast together in silence as we all went over the plans that Royle and I had come up with. The rest of the platoon was chatting with one another. Some were over the platoon comms, and others were on breaks around the crate we were by. None of them paid attention to us. We all had our ways before a mission. We tended to be silent, going over the day's plans, and checking and rechecking equipment. By the time we left the base, every one of us had gone over the op a dozen times and thought of every contingency we could.

Our squad split into groups. My team stayed on a couple of transport pads, but Bravo was far more spread out. Royle had two of her team attacking the other side of town as we hit our area. The Arbiter would be on standby for orbital support, but our primary orbital asset would be the Vinur. They'd asked to be orbital support on this op. I figured it was a good way for them to stay engaged, and I suspected they also wanted to make a point of having my team's backs. On the other pads were third and fourth squad, who would be away from the city but close enough to help.

The chatter stopped as we approached the city.

"All teams, this is Middleton. Everyone call out when you are in position," Middleton said over the platoon com.

The other teams would make it into position before we did. I got off the pad with my team and started to move into the city as the other squads confirmed their positions.

"First Squad, all squads in position. Please give a timeline," Middleton said.

"This is Bravo; we are getting into position," Royle said.

"Alpha, same," I said.

Monroe got on. "Be advised, Alpha, the Tooth patrol is en route; sending ETA."

I took a position on the second story of a broken-down building. I'd move to a fallback position as soon as the action started. We were covering a street where the Tooth should move. If our timing was right, each of Royle's and my units would have a shot on a Tooth.

"Alpha in position; I see the Tooth," I said on the comms.

"All units hold position until Taylor gives the command to fire," Middleton said.

All the teams gave their acknowledgment.

"HFDF Team, this is Vinur fire command. Railguns are targeted, transferring fire command to you," the Quiver destroyer said.

That felt a little heady. I didn't have actual command of the Quiver ship. Rather, like all our ground troops with active targets, we'd be synchronizing fire. When I pulled the trigger on my SIR, my CCPU would send the command to all units to fire simultaneously. It would also ping the Quiver destroyer, which would fire several rounds that would hit shortly after we'd all fired. When I fired, a whole lot of death would occur automatically. I wasn't pulling all the triggers, but in a way, I was.

"Roger that," I said to the ship.

The Tooth came closer to me. As they did, I targeted one and saw my team targeting the others. There were only four today. My CCPU notified me that all of Royle's team had targets and Whiskers in the area and were ready to start transmitting radio waves on my command.

I let the Tooth amble closer, scuttling along and stopping, hunched on the ground to listen. I felt like an ass, but not enough to hesitate. When they were all in range, I squeezed the trigger. My SIR nudged my shoulder as a burst rattled out. The Tooth dropped instantly. Another went down, and two others rolled as their turrets were hit. At once, the Whiskers hit the whole city with radio waves. Royle's team engaged, and the map showed the Tooth's patterns stop and seem utterly confused. Then, the railgun rounds hit, shaking the ground and filling the air with dirt.

The BIs were in motion, shooting nets at the two living Tooth and jumping on top of them, trying to immobilize them before they could get hurt. Two others ran up to the dead Tooth and started hauling them away.

"We have the samples and are loading," I said.

I jumped off the roof and waited for the explosions to start. The sample containers were on site now, and the BIs were wrestling the Tooth into them. I gave the order to fall back when all four containers were loaded. Still, there were no explosions.

"Fall back to the extraction point. Command, we have the samples," I said.

We all started to fall back. I watched on the map, seeing the Tooth scramble for cover. They'd learned to avoid death from the sky.

"Vinur fire control, the rounds seem to have a strong effect," I said to the Quiver.

"Would you like another volley?"

"Yes," I said. "There's no need to target units; just keep them looking for cover."

"Roger, firing now."

As we moved to the extraction point, I heard the air tear and rip as the rounds streaked through it. There were more ground-shaking thuds and dust in the air, but the Tooth stayed hidden. As we left town, we picked up speed until we reached two shuttles waiting for us. The BIs loaded up the sample containers, and the shuttle jerked in the air, leaving the area. Their engines glowed brightly as they left.

"Samples are in the air," I said.

"Good work, everyone," Middleton said. "Head back to base and await instruction."

"What went wrong?" Maria asked in a line with just my team.

Sweeting laughed. "Nothing. It went better than we hoped. I guess you lot were bad luck."

"What Sweeting is trying to say is that even though our motto is 'in case shit,' sometimes shit doesn't happen," Krista said.

"And he's an ass," Clay said.

"So, nothing bad?" Maria confirmed.

"Just for the Tooth, ma'am," Betts said.

"Thank god. You people wear me out. And we aren't bad luck, private," Maria said, and dropped the connection.

TWENTY-FOUR

After getting back to base, we waited for word from command. As we did, I watched the city. There was nothing at first, just dust settling, but then gradually, a few Tooth scurried from cover and beelined for tunnels. They weren't coming back out. I watched for hours with nothing major happening. Occasionally, a Tooth would pop out of a tunnel, check the area around it, and then head back underground.

"You seeing the city?" Clay asked me.

"Yeah, pretty quiet," I said.

"I think the Tooth figured out that they are outclassed here."

"Maybe. I hope our samples work out. I don't know if we will get as easy a chance again," I said.

"We came in a lot harder than in the past. I bet the radio waves freaked them out. Could you imagine what it would be like if you were standing around and then all of a sudden heard thousands of voices shouting at you, and then the ground started exploding?" she asked.

I thought about that. "Making me feel real good, Clay."

She chuckled, "Sorry."

"Don't be," I said. "It would terrify me. It would be even worse if I'd just learned I wasn't the only thing in the universe." I sighed. "Still, we killed fewer Tooth today than we thought. Royle's team targeted turrets mostly. Only one kill."

"Same with our people," she said. "I guess only five or six dead is good for us."

"You counting the samples?"

"You know it," she said. "It needed to be done. But I'm not happy that this whole mission has been around hurting victims to find whatever caused all this."

"How long do you think it will take us to find them?" I asked, referring to whoever had caused all this shit.

"I don't know. But I hope it's during our term," she said bitterly—a tone that was rare for her.

"They won't be easy to take. It will also mean totally annihilating them," I said.

"So you don't want to be part of the first wave?"

"I didn't say that," I said. "Just saying it will be hard."

"More training?" she asked.

"More purpose to it," I said.

My CCPU pinged with a message. After I read it, I opened a channel to the squad.

"Intel is in. They got what they needed," I said.

Moments later, Monroe said, "We have what we need. Pack up and get ready to dust off first thing in the morning."

The rest of the night wasn't all that busy. We didn't have much that needed to be taken down. All we had was the shop, which folded up as quickly as it had been unfolded. It was going to take us more time to load onto shuttles than anything else.

In the morning, the first shuttle arrived along with three large cargo shuttles—the type the ship used to ferry Rhinos to the ground. They had enough room for all the cargo we had, troops, and drones. I watched as the BIs grouped up and took cargo on board the shuttles.

They moved quickly, packing cargo and then themselves, leaving room at the head of the shuttle for humans. Everyone but my team loaded up. We were going up with the normal shuttle. If something got these, we'd be back up.

The cargo shuttles lifted off and roared into the air, not trying to be stealthy in the least bit.

"One last sweep," I said to my team.

We all ran in different directions to check the base perimeter one last time. I also pinged every piece of equipment anyone in the platoon had used to make sure it was accounted for. It all was and showed as either with my people or heading into orbit. On the map of the city, the Tooth were still keeping to their tunnels. That worked for me.

"Load up!" I ordered, joining my team in the shuttle. Before I got in, I checked to make sure I still had a little chunk of brick I'd taken in town one day. I wished I had been able to get a small bit of the hive of the bugs I'd found, but I didn't want to disturb them. The chunk of brick was in my pack.

"Everyone got something?" I asked.

"Rock," Sweeting said.

"Brick," Clay said.

"Same," Krista and I said.

"Rock for me," Betts said.

The doors closed, and I felt myself lift into the air as the shuttle took off. The floor vibrated as it sped up until the sound from outside stopped as we reached the vacuum of space. I wish I could say that as the shuttle docked, I pulled up a feed of Tooth Prime and watched it grow small as we flew away. As it was, there were still a handful of teams on the ground waiting for other Exploration teams to pack up and leave. They had a two-day schedule, which for us meant we had two days in tubes waiting on standby. It was boring but normal. It gave me time to talk with the Exploration team and catch up with my friends. We'd planned another dinner. The Arbiter would be heading back to Orion Station. We'd spend a few months there training and working with different groups. We'd spend a lot of time filling in for different garrison troops so they could schedule training. But we got weekends off along with a week's leave when we got to the station. It wasn't too bad.

After we started to head to jump distance, Tania Koffski scheduled a meeting with me, Monroe, and Middleton. We met in Middleton's office—something I hadn't seen much of. Koffski wasn't unpleasant in any way or even secretive. I'd always assumed that the intel people would be a little dickish. My only experience with them had been on Erie Prime on my first mission. But when I thought about it, they probably weren't really chatty because they had a lot of work to do and a lot riding on that work.

"How is everyone doing today?" Middleton asked as we sat down.

"Good, thank you, ma'am," I said.

She looked over at Koffski. "Well, Tania, this is your show."

"Thank you, Lisa, and thank you, Corporal, for you and your team's work on Tooth Prime," Tania said.

"Thank you, ma'am," I said.

She smiled. "Not your commander. Tania is fine."

"Er, thanks, Tania?"

Her smile warmed. "Based on your history with the Tooth and the Venom, I thought you might want to be in the loop about what's going on."

I perked up. "Yes, I would. Can my team be in the loop as well?" I asked.

"Yes, they can." She looked serious. "But no one else. In the past, your activities have largely not been classified, and as such, what you know about enemies also doesn't need to be classified. This is different. Do you understand?"

"Yes, I do," I said.

She nodded slightly. "As you and the Exploration team know, the Tooth and the Venom were altered to make them this way."

"Yes."

"We have samples of three other races that have been altered as well," she said.

"I haven't heard this," Middleton said, surprised. "I knew we had suspicions but not confirmation."

"Hence part of the reason this is classified. Two of the races were defeated by their home worlds. We have samples of technology that are of the same origin as what you found here and some of the Venom's tech. The other race died out. We think they might have been the first. The planet is a nuclear wasteland. We don't know if it was the test race that did that or the group that created them trying to clean up after themselves. We suspect the prior."

"Does that mean the Tooth could have been a failure or could still pose a problem?" Monroe asked.

"No, they will not. Their biology has been altered in a way that is not sustainable. They have decades left before they go extinct. We suspect this was built into them. As your teams saw, it was clear there was no plan to keep their equipment going for very long.

"We are dealing with a race that has killed planets in an attempt to create something, and then when they made the Venom, the Venom killed whole systems. The samples we have now will help us find those who did this. We don't know how long, but we or one of our allies will track them down."

"Then what?" I asked.

Tania smiled tightly. "I'm not the one who will make that call, but what do you think will happen?"

"Yeah, I figured," I said.

"Would you like to be kept in the loop? I can't update you on everything, and you won't be able to tell those outside of your squad," Tania said.

"Yes, ma'am, I mean Tania, yes I would," I said.

The smile returned. "I thought so." She breathed out. "That was all I had. Well, and also to say well done with the Quiver. Their embassy contacted the Human Federation and would like to present you and your team with their version of a medal for your service to them. The details of that need to be worked out, but it's safe to say that you made your government very proud and that many will watch your career with interest."

"Don't try to poach my people when they are still in their Service Term," Middleton said with mock outrage.

Tania chuckled. "Not poaching, planting seeds." She winked at me and walked out.

"What was that about, ma'am?" I asked Middleton.

Monroe barked a laugh. "You and yours have managed to land in it with alien races several times, and in each of those instances, you've acted in a way that makes the HFDF look good and have impressed those races. You have received a commendation from two races and have been on a Quiver CIC."

"Before you search that, the answer is fifteen," Middleton said, then reading my confusion. "That's the number of Humans who have been on a Quiver CIC—fifteen, including you and Private McLeod. And you and your team will be five of fifty humans the Quiver have ever given commendations to. Keep making us proud."

"Will do," I said, and then was dismissed.

The rest of the trip to jump distance was going over reports and watching the Exploration ships from the Arbiter's external feeds.

"You guys are so slow!" Sweeting said in a VR room with our team and the Exploration team.

"We are carrying a lot of crap," Catherine said.

"Not as much as the Arbiter," Sweeting said. "Is there a reason your ships are so damn slow? Don't tell me they are underpowered. I've seen the drives on them."

"There is a reason," Andy said. "Our gravity system has a governor to keep us from accelerating faster than the cargo containers can take—5g max, which you know."

"The system itself can only handle 7g," Catherine said.

"That sucks," Betts said. "The Arbiter can sustain way more than that with 50g bursts. Or so I've been told."

"Shit, when would you need that?" Andy asked.

"Combat," I said. "At flank speed, we can reach jump distance in a day. It seriously cuts down the lifespan of the drives at that speed, but we can do it in a pinch."

"And you can jump sooner and better than us, too," Charles said. "Jon has been telling me about it. You guys can jump right on top of a gravity well with several meters of precision. We can't. We need two kilometers of room coming in close to a planet."

"I know they try to keep the jump accuracy pretty tight. But on speed, we are slowish for the fleet," I said.

The VR setting was nice. It made it seem like we weren't flying through space in six different ships. But my team also had limited VR time for personal use. So after an hour or so, it was back to either training in the VR Pod or back to our quarters. It was a nice, boring trip to jump distance, and then we were over Orion.

Krista and I met Monica at the station. Jon had taken leave and would be joining us later that day. I hugged Monica when I saw her.

"Hey, how's it having everyone plan their leave around you?" she asked, hugging me back.

"The way it should be," I said. "Sorry though, the HFDF doesn't have the same flexibility. Too bad Liz can't join us," I said.

Monica shrugged. "She'll be done with her rotation on that carrier soon. Charles will be on Orion for a while, and Jon and I get time off. Do you know your posting yet?" she asked, a little nervous.

I smiled. "Yep. Orion City and the surrounding area. The local garrison teams are due for updates, and because my team worked so closely with the Quiver, they wanted us close by for debriefings. I get to spend weekends at home if I want."

Monica grinned. "Man, look at you. You better be careful, or you'll turn into a boring normal person."

"He's plenty boring," Krista said, hugging Monica. "How's your job?"

Monica's smile faded a bit. "Meh. Not what I thought."

"Sorry," I said.

"Don't be. It's fine, just not what I expected."

"Is that a bad thing?" Krista asked.

We started walking. "I don't know," Monica said honestly. "Is yours what you thought it would be?" she asked us.

We both said no.

"But you're cool with it?" she asked.

"Most of the time," I said.

We took the Lift down to Orion City and then the train out of town. We had lunch with my parents, who said we could stay at the house if we wanted. It was going to be nice being home. It was odd having my girlfriend stay with me, but that was getting older, I guess.

Dinner consisted of Charles, Monica, Jon, Krista, and me sitting on a blanket on one of the docks on the sound. In the distance, Orion City was tinged gold with the setting sun.

"Can you talk about what intel found?" Charles asked, "assuming they told you."

"They did, and I can't," I said, looking over at him and Monica. "Sorry about that."

"Would we want to know?" he asked.

I just shook my head.

"No," Krista said. "You know enough to know that you don't want to know more."

"You're kind of freaking me out, guys," Monica said. "Is everything going to be okay?"

She hadn't been privy to most of the mission. She knew enough, but not all the details.

Krista turned to look out over the water. Her face lacked the normal happiness I'd gotten used to. It was replaced by a calm concern. "It's not okay now, but we'll make it okay," she said. "It will just be a question of lives."

ABOUT THE AUTHOR

Nicholas Taylor is a fantasy and science fiction author. He was born in 1981 in Denver, Colorado, where he lives with his wife and family. Nicholas was an imaginative child who enjoyed writing stories and daydreaming about new worlds and places from a young age.

In his twenties, Nicholas rekindled a love for reading and consuming fantasy and science fiction. The culmination was his decision to write a novel in the winter of 2007. That first novel was Legon Awakening, which ran as a weekly podcast and was later released in print, digital, and audio editions that thousands have enjoyed.

Nicholas enjoys writing fiction that pulls readers into immersive worlds with likable and relatable characters. He strives to draw the reader into the scene with the characters, allowing them to explore magical realms or distant planets.

For more about Nicholas Taylor
Visit:
www.NicholasTaylor.co